"Just how much do you know about ranching?" he asked.

She stared at him, confused. "Not much. Why?"

"Well, because that's the job I'm here about. Graham wanted someone to run the ranch. Someone who was good with horses," he finally said.

"Run the ranch?" Chloe repeated. "You're here about ranching?"

"Funny, I thought I just said that," Chance answered. "What are you here about?"

"Why, counseling, of course," Chloe replied.

"You mean the boys?"

Her smile was natural. "Horses don't listen to me."

He laughed. Now it all made sense. They were here about two different positions. "I could teach you how to make them listen to you."

"You're talking about the horses, right?" she asked, a hint of mischief dancing in her eyes.

He found himself being pulled in by those deep pools of blue. "Right," he finally replied. "I've got no trouble getting horses to listen to me. Most people, though, just ignore me like I wasn't there."

"I don't believe that for a minute," she said with feeling.

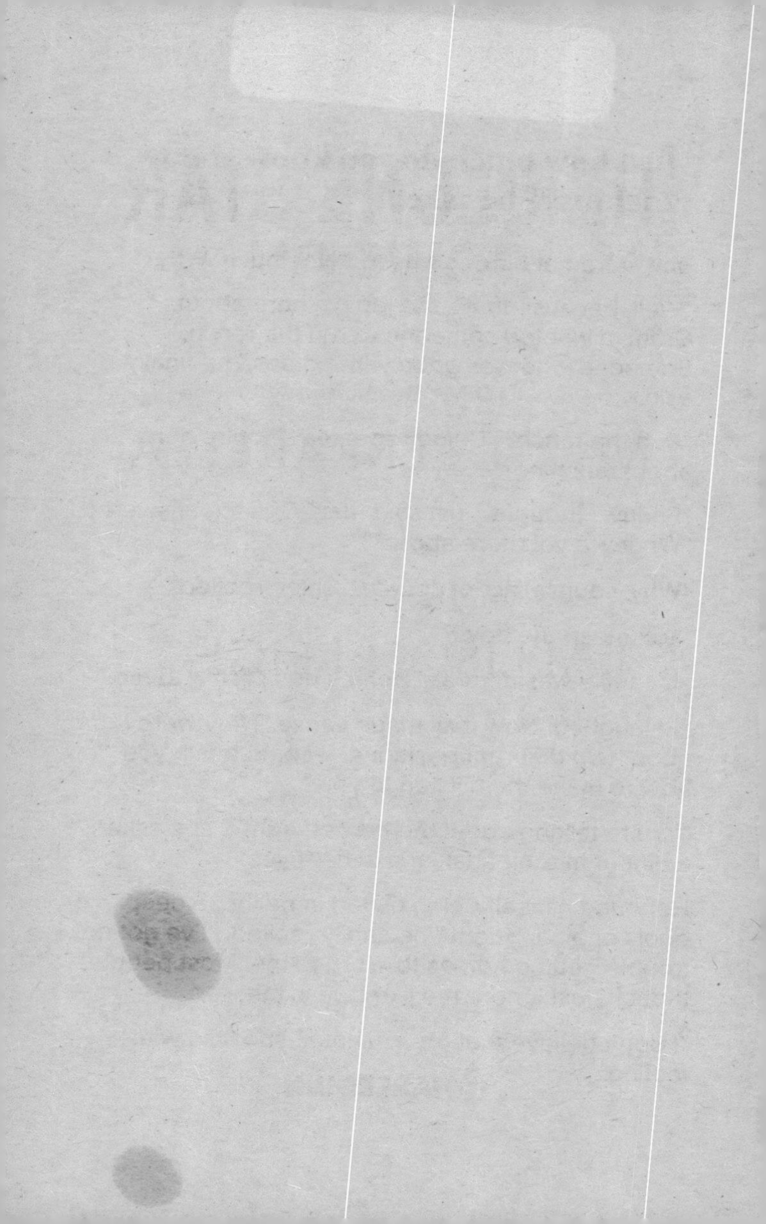

HER LONE STAR COWBOY

USA TODAY Bestselling Author

MARIE FERRARELLA

&

New York Times Bestselling Author

ALLISON LEIGH

2 Heartfelt Stories

Fortune's Second-Chance Cowboy
and *Wild West Fortune*

Special thanks and acknowledgment are given to Marie Ferrarella and Allison Leigh for their contributions to the Fortunes of Texas: The Secret Fortunes continuity.

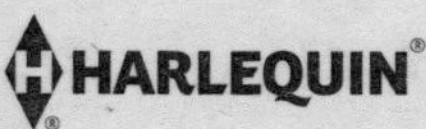

ISBN-13: 978-1-335-42736-6

Her Lone Star Cowboy

Fortune's Second-Chance Cowboy
First published in 2017. This edition published in 2022.

Wild West Fortune
First published in 2017. This edition published in 2022.

Harlequin Enterprises ULC
22 Adelaide St. West, 41st Floor
Toronto, Ontario M5H 4E3, Canada
www.Harlequin.com

Printed in U.S.A.

CONTENTS

FORTUNE'S SECOND-CHANCE COWBOY 7
Marie Ferrarella

WILD WEST FORTUNE 213
Allison Leigh

USA TODAY bestselling and RITA® Award–winning author **Marie Ferrarella** has written more than two hundred and fifty books for Harlequin, some under the name Marie Nicole. Her romances are beloved by fans worldwide. Visit her website, marieferrarella.com.

Books by Marie Ferrarella

Harlequin Special Edition

Matchmaking Mamas

Coming Home for Christmas
Dr. Forget-Me-Not
Twice a Hero, Always Her Man
Meant to Be Mine
A Second Chance for the Single Dad
Christmastime Courtship
An Engagement for Two
Adding Up to Family
Bridesmaid for Hire
Coming to a Crossroads
The Late Bloomer's Road to Love

Visit the Author Profile page at Harlequin.com for more titles.

FORTUNE'S SECOND-CHANCE COWBOY

Marie Ferrarella

To
Tiffany Khauo
who is about to have her own population explosion.
Tiffany, this one's for you.

Prologue

"Hello, Chloe, are you still there?"

Chloe Elliott's hand tightened around her landline's receiver as she heard the caller's deep male voice asking her the same question again.

Was she still there?

Part of Chloe felt like answering the question by simply hanging up. She'd had enough disappointments in her twenty-six years to last a lifetime, why would she set herself up for yet another one?

But there was this other part of Chloe, the part that *needed* to believe that good things could happen, that they still *did* happen. That was the part that had been instrumental in making her get out of bed every morning even after Donnie, the husband she'd adored, had been killed while serving in Afghanistan after they had been married for only an incredibly short two years.

That was also the part that had decided to make her gather her courage together and to try to get to know her father's family.

The father who had, up until just recently, been a complete mystery in her life.

Ever since she could remember—until she'd gotten married—it had been just her mother and her. There had *been* no other family members to speak of, and that had been just fine with her. Filling in the blanks for herself, Chloe assumed that her father had been her mother's high school sweetheart who'd been killed in a car accident before he could marry her nineteen-year-old mother.

Because that had been her belief since forever, Chloe hadn't been prepared to learn that her father was actually tech giant Gerald Robinson. And even more, that for years now he'd been living under an assumed name. Gerald Robinson was in fact Jerome Fortune, one of the famous Texas Fortunes, no less. Neither had she been prepared for the eight legitimate Robinson offspring, giving her half siblings she'd never known she had.

And that didn't even begin to take into account the various illegitimate offspring the man had left scattered in his wake, as well.

All in all, it had been a great deal for her to take in and process.

Realizing that the man on the other end of the line, Graham Fortune Robinson, the third of Gerald's eight children, was still waiting for a response, Chloe answered quietly, "Yes, I'm still here."

Chloe could almost hear the pleased smile in her half brother's voice as he continued. "You might not remember me, but we met at that big family dinner at Kate Fortune's ranch."

How could she not remember? Chloe thought. She remembered everything about that evening, which had come about when Keaton Fortune Whitfield had contacted her out of the blue to tell her that he was her half sibling and invited her to come. And just like that, she'd gone from having no living relatives, now that her mother was gone, to having so many of them that she needed a scorecard just to keep track of them all.

She remembered how frightened and excited she'd been, walking into that huge mansion that evening. She'd harbored such great hopes.

Hopes that had been completely dashed when she'd met Sophie Fortune Robinson, her father's youngest daughter. At least his youngest *legitimate* daughter, Chloe silently amended. Everything had gone downhill from there when she'd introduced herself to Sophie. The latter had looked utterly appalled to meet her, and if looks could've killed, Chloe definitely wouldn't be alive to take this phone call right now.

Not that she could really blame Sophie, Chloe thought. It had to be quite a shock to find out that the man she had thought of as her father all those years had a completely other identity that she knew nothing about.

"Yes, I remember you," Chloe finally responded to Graham's comment.

She recalled that Graham had been the handsome, energetic young rancher and businessman whom Kate Fortune had tapped to run Fortune Cosmetics for her. It was obvious that the reserved woman had been quite proud of him.

"I know this must seem strange, my calling you out of the blue like this," Graham said.

"No stranger than finding out after all these years that my father was Gerald Robinson," Chloe replied, wondering where all this was going.

After that family dinner, she would have bet that that was the last time she would ever see any of those people again. And, to be quite honest, the run-in with Sophie had left a bad taste in her mouth. She'd decided to keep her distance from the Fortunes, especially since her mother had never had an interest in reuniting with her father.

"If I remember correctly, you have a degree in counseling, don't you?" Graham was saying.

She was surprised that anyone even noticed her that night—other than thinking of her as an interloper. After all, how else would anyone regard their father's bastard child? Chloe thought ruefully.

"Yes, I do," she said uncertainly, waiting for Graham to get to the point—and wondering if, once he did, she was going to regret it.

"I know this might seem unusual to you," Graham continued.

Unusual doesn't begin to cover the half of it, Chloe thought.

"—but I'm calling with a job offer."

"A job offer?" Chloe echoed, stunned. "But you run Fortune Cosmetics. And I don't know anything about cosmetics, other than what I have in my medicine cabinet."

She heard Graham laugh. "You won't have to. Have you ever heard of Peter's Place?"

"Of course I've heard of it. That's a therapeutic ranch for troubled teenaged boys."

"Right." He sounded pleased with her answer. "Currently, my wife, Sasha, is the only counselor there. Because of a recent, rather generous donation from the Fortune Foundation, we're going to be expanding Peter's Place. I've been doing double duty running the ranch as well as helming Fortune Cosmetics. Frankly, between that and taking care of a baby plus our eight-year-old daughter, I'm spread pretty thin. I—we," he amended, including his wife, "could definitely use a bigger staff. Now, I realize that you're just starting out, but I've got a good feeling about you, Chloe. I'd like you to come down to Peter's Place for an interview—it'll pretty much just be a formality. And while you're here, you can take a look around the ranch—that is, if you're interested," he tagged on. It was clear from the way he spoke that he really hoped she was.

Life had robbed her of some of her optimism, making her suspicious of things that seemed to be too good to be true—which was why Chloe didn't immediately jump at the offer, the way she might have only a few years ago.

"Like you said, I'm just starting out. Why would you be offering this to me?" she wanted to know. "It sounds like you could hire anyone you wanted to."

"I know. And that's what I thought I was doing," he told her. "I've made inquiries about you, Chloe. According to my sources, you're talented and you have a way with people. And," he added most significantly, "because you're family."

You're family.

Chloe felt a funny little sensation in the pit of her

stomach. For most of her young life, it had been only her mother and her against the world. And then she'd married Donnie, only to have him taken from her all too soon two years ago. There was a part of her that was *starving* to be part of a family, even as part of her distrusted that feeling and the invitation she was being tendered.

Still, because there was that hunger to be part of something greater than just herself, to be accepted into a family, Chloe heard herself asking, "When would you like me to come down?"

Chapter 1

Dear Lord, what am I doing?

The question echoed in her brain as Chloe pulled up before the main ranch house of Peter's Place.

Yes, she really wanted to be part of a family, part of this family, but did she really *want* to leave herself wide open like this? To get this close to the Fortunes? After all, she sternly reminded herself, her encounter last month with the clan was less than successful to say the least.

It all came vividly rushing back to her now as she turned off the ignition and sat quietly in the car for a moment.

She never should have agreed to this interview. She was too intimidated by Kate Fortune, the family matriarch, who Chloe figured would be at this meeting. And why not? She seemed to run everything associated with the Fortune family.

Kate Fortune might well be ninety-one years old, but she looked decades younger and was sharp as the proverbial tack. The woman was not exactly the warm, cuddly grandmotherly type.

Was it too late to change her mind? Chloe thought not for the first time.

Then again, it wasn't as if she was exactly hip-deep in job offers, able to pick and choose which position she was willing to accept. Given that, this job that Graham was offering her was at least worth a look. Heaven knew she wasn't getting anywhere looking for work so far and she knew that Donnie wouldn't have wanted her to give up on life just because he was gone. And who knew? Maybe she'd actually get it and things would work out for the best.

There was always a first time, Chloe told herself philosophically, doing her best to bolster up her flagging courage.

"Well, here goes nothing," Chloe murmured under her breath as she unbuckled her seat belt and opened the door.

Glancing up into the rearview mirror before she exited the vehicle, she made one futile attempt to smooth down her wayward curly blond hair. Not that it did all that much good, she thought ruefully. Her hair seemed to have a mind of its own.

"Just like me," Chloe murmured, thinking of what her mother had often said.

You just keep dancing to your own drummer, Chloe. The world'll come around eventually to join you.

Satisfied that she looked as good as she was going to look on this crisp March day—the wind had seemed determined to restyle her hair the moment she'd stepped outside—Chloe got out of her sedan and closed the door.

She didn't bother locking the vehicle because it wasn't the kind of car that anyone would think to steal. It had already gone through several owners before she'd bought it a year ago. Close to ten years old, it ran mostly on faith and used parts.

Warning herself not to expect too much, Chloe went up the three steps to the ranch house front door. Mentally counting to ten as she took a deep breath and centered herself, she knocked on the door.

The second her knuckles made contact, the door seemed to fly open. As a matter of fact, she could have sworn that the door opened a second *before* she actually knocked on it.

But that had to be her imagination—right?

"Oh, Chloe, you're here," Graham said, looking startled to see her.

He wasn't in the doorway alone. Chloe recognized the pretty blue-eyed blonde right behind her half brother. It was his wife, Sasha. The petite woman looked even more frazzled than Graham did.

"I'm sorry. Did I get the dates mixed up?" Chloe asked, looking from Graham to his wife. It was the only conclusion she could draw, given the expressions on their faces and their almost breathless manner.

"No, no, you've got the right date," Graham assured her. "But something's just come up. There's been a sudden family emergency. I just got a call from our babysitter that Maddie—that's our eight-year-old," he explained quickly, "decided that she'd give flying off the swing a try." He frowned, shaking his head. "It didn't turn out quite the way our fearless daughter had hoped. From all the screaming and crying, the sitter thinks that Maddie broke her arm. We're just on our way out to meet them at the hospital."

"Oh, I'm sorry," Chloe cried, genuinely concerned. She could just imagine what was going through their minds. But at least they had each other to lean on. "Is there anything I can do?"

It took him only a second to answer Chloe. "As a matter of fact, there is."

"What do you need?" she asked, ready to pitch in and help.

Chloe thought he was going to ask her to accompany him and his wife to whatever hospital their little girl had been taken. Maybe they were too rattled to drive safely. But that wasn't what he needed her to do.

"Would you mind sticking around for a while?" Graham asked her. "I've got someone else coming in for an interview and I couldn't reach him on the phone. I was going to call you as soon as we were on the road," Graham quickly explained. "When he gets here, tell him that as soon as I make sure that Maddie's all right, I'll be back. I know this is a huge imposition on you and I wouldn't ask if—"

"That's okay," Chloe said, cutting him off. She could tell just by his tone of voice that if he remained, the man's mind wouldn't be on the interview. "Go. See to your daughter." She all but shooed the couple out. "I'll stay."

"We won't forget this," Sasha promised, tossing the words over her shoulder as she and her husband rushed out of the house.

Chloe offered the couple an encouraging smile. "Glad to help," she called after them.

After all, it wasn't as if she was exactly pressed for time, Chloe thought, watching the duo get into their car and drive quickly away.

Besides, Chloe reasoned, walking back into the ranch house and closing the door behind her, this way she could get a look at whoever it was that she would be competing against for this job.

Chloe looked around. She liked the looks of the ranch from what she'd seen of it, driving up here. Maybe she was reading things into it, she thought, but it had a good feel about it.

Chloe sat down on the sofa, prepared to wait. She remained sitting for all of five minutes before she began to feel restless. On her feet again, she started to prowl around the large living room with its comfortable masculine furnishings.

Definitely a good feel to the place, she thought as she moved about, touching things and envisioning herself working here.

She looked at an old-fashioned clock with gold numbers on the fireplace mantel, and she could almost feel the minute hand dragging itself in slow motion, going from one number to the next.

How long was she expected to wait? If she'd had some sort of a handle on that, then she could put things into perspective—or at least know when it would be all right for her to leave.

The sound of a back door slamming made her jump. As did the sound of a wailing baby.

The next second, a rather beleaguered-looking older man came in, holding the crying baby in his arms and looking as if he was at his wit's end.

Without bothering to ask her who she was or to introduce himself, the man complained, "I can't get her to stop crying. I've tried everything and she just keeps right on bawling. Do you know how to make her stop?" he asked pathetically, holding the baby out to her like an offering. "Please?"

Chloe stared at the stranger, stunned. She didn't know the first thing about babies, and for all this man knew, she could have been some random thief who had just broken in to the house.

But he looked so distraught, she decided to skip pointing that out. Feeling sorry for the man, she said, "Give her to me," although, for the life of her, she had no idea what she was going to do.

"Thank you, thank you," the man cried. "This is Sydney. I'm Sasha's uncle Roger, by the way," he said as he placed the baby into her arms. "Graham and Sasha had an emergency and asked me to watch the baby while they were gone." He flushed, embarrassed. "I said yes before I knew what I was getting myself into. I thought the kid would stay asleep. But the second they were gone, she started crying." And then Roger stared at the infant, relieved and awestruck at the same time. "Hey, will you look at that," he marveled, looking from Sydney to the woman holding her. "She's really taken to you."

To Chloe's absolute amazement, the baby had stopped crying. She would have said there was some sort of magic involved, except it was obvious that Sydney appeared to be fascinated with the way the light was hitting the sterling silver pendant she was wearing around her neck.

The pendant that Donnie had given her just before he'd shipped out, she thought sadly.

Even now, you're still finding ways to help me out, Donnie.

"More like she's taken with my necklace," Chloe told Sasha's uncle.

To prove her point, she grasped the pendant and moved it around ever so slowly. Sunlight gleamed and shimmied along its surface. Sydney followed the sunbeam with her eyes, mesmerized.

"Hey, whatever it takes." Roger laughed. "I'm just really relieved that Sydney's finally stopped crying. I was afraid she was going to rip something loose inside that little body…or that I was going to start to lose my hearing. For a little thing, she's sure got a mighty big set of lungs on her."

For the first time, Roger turned his attention to Chloe. Apparently realizing that he didn't know who she was, he asked, "You a friend of Graham's and Sasha's?"

"Not exactly," Chloe replied.

She wasn't really sure how to introduce herself. Yes, she was Graham's half sister, but she was still getting used to that title herself. She didn't know if she was comfortable enough to spring it on anyone else yet, not to mention that Graham might not welcome their connection becoming public knowledge.

Sitting down on the sofa as she continued to cradle and entertain the baby, Chloe evasively explained, "I'm here to interview for a job that's opened up at Peter's Place."

"Ah."

Roger nodded his head as he sat down, too. "Great place," he told her. "Sasha and Graham do a lot of good here. And they could certainly do with a few more willing hands to help them out with the work. You got a job in mind?" he asked.

"I'm applying for the counseling job," Chloe explained. Now that he was no longer distraught because he couldn't get the baby to stop crying, the older man seemed very easy to talk to.

"Counseling, huh? Like my niece."

She nodded. "Do you work at Peter's Place, too?" she wanted to know.

Roger's face registered surprise. "Me?" he cried, obviously stunned that she would think that. "No, I actually own the spread that Peter's Place sits on. The Galloping G Ranch," he told her proudly. "My house is down aways. I just came by when Graham and Sasha called, saying that they needed someone to watch Sydney here for a while. They forgot to tell me that I needed to bring my earplugs," he added with a laugh. "You don't mind my asking, how many kids have you got?"

"None," she replied, sincerely hoping that the pang she felt making that admission wasn't evident on her face.

She and Donnie had really wanted to start a family, but they had held off because Donnie was going overseas. He'd said that he wanted to be around while she was carrying his baby. Besides, he had told her, they had time. They had their whole lives in front of them.

Until they didn't, she thought sadly. She really wished he had gotten her pregnant before he left. At least she would have had a part of him to help her ease the pain of loss.

"I'm sorry. Did I say something to upset you?" Roger asked, clearly concerned.

Chloe shook her head. “No, I was just thinking of something.”

“Oh, well, good. I wouldn’t have wanted to upset you, especially since you’ve been such a help with Sydney here and all.” He glanced at his watch, then looked up at her almost sheepishly. “Um, listen, I really need to make a phone call. Since Sydney here seems to really like you, would you mind holding her a bit longer while I make my call? Shouldn’t be too long,” he added.

The man was already edging his way toward the back of the house as he spoke. It was obvious that he was hoping she’d agree.

Chloe really wanted to hand the baby back to this man, but she couldn’t very well turn down his request. Besides, she *had* promised Graham to wait until whoever he hadn’t been able to reach on the phone turned up for his interview, so what was one more thing added to that?

“Sure, I can watch her,” she told Roger.

The heavyset man beamed at her. “Thanks,” he cried. “You’re going to love working here. They’re both really great people,” Roger told her, giving her a quick fatherly pat on the shoulder just before he turned on his heel and quickly disappeared, leaving the same way he had entered.

“Looks like it’s just you and me now, Sydney. I’m Chloe, by the way,” she told the baby, who was staring up at her with enormous blue eyes, looking as if she was hanging on every word. “Your dad’s half sister,” she explained. “What’s that?” Chloe pretended to lean in toward the baby to hear the “question” that Sydney had “asked.”

“You didn’t know he had a half sibling? Well, he

does. Several of them from what I hear," she added with a laugh.

"Your grandfather really took that 'Be fruitful and multiply' passage in the Bible to heart, I guess. I've got a feeling that there's going to be lots of us popping up around here from now on. I hope when you start talking, Sydney, you're going to be good with names," she told the baby.

And then she smiled down at the sweet, innocent face that seemed to be listening to every word she said.

"You don't have a clue what I'm saying, do you?" Chloe asked and then laughed. "Know what? Maybe it's better that way. Maybe it'll all sort itself out by the time you're old enough to know what's going on. Until then—"

Chloe stopped talking abruptly when she heard someone knocking on the door.

Knowing it wouldn't be Graham and his wife, she figured it was the other candidate. *The one who's after my job.* She set her shoulders to do battle. "Let's go see if we can scare him off or talk him out of it, okay?"

Sydney made a little noise, and then the next moment Chloe saw that there were bubbles being formed around the infant's rosebud lips.

Chloe laughed, delighted. She shifted the baby, holding Sydney a little closer to her as she rose and began to head for the door.

"I'll take that as a yes," Chloe told the baby.

Sydney responded by making even more bubbles.

Chloe opened the door, but whatever greeting she had come up with to offer the person on the other side temporarily vanished.

This was *not* the type of person she had expected to

see when she opened the door. Given the position that she assumed they were both competing for, Chloe had unconsciously thought that he'd be a rather scholarly-looking man. The kind who seemed to fade into the woodwork without anyone taking notice of him.

Instead, what she found herself looking at was a cowboy, most definitely an adrenaline-stirring cowboy. The kind whom women were given to fantasizing about whenever the word *cowboy* came up.

The man standing before her had to be about six foot three with shoulders wide enough to give him trouble getting through narrow doorways. He had somewhat unruly, dirty-blond hair and eyes so blue they looked as if they'd been cut right out of the sky. He was wearing tight jeans, a long-sleeved denim shirt, boots and a Stetson—set at what could only be described as a sexy angle. In summation, he looked picture-perfect.

If she had to guess, she would have said that the cowboy was somewhere in his late twenties.

What she didn't have to guess at was that the man was utterly gorgeous.

The second the thought occurred to her, it hit her with the force of a thunderbolt.

Gorgeous?

She hadn't even so much as *noticed* another man since Donnie had died, much less labeled that man as "gorgeous." What was happening here? she upbraided herself. Had she just lost her mind?

Chapter 2

Chance Howell realized that he wasn't just looking at the petite blonde holding the baby, he was actually staring at her. That couldn't be viewed as exactly getting off to a good start with who he assumed was the potential boss's wife. He'd gathered some background on Graham Fortune Robinson and knew the man had two kids, one of whom was an infant. Hence the logical leap.

"Um, excuse me," he began, feeling rather tongue-tied as he took off his hat and held it in his hands. "I'm Chance Howell. I've got an appointment with Graham."

"He's not here right now," the woman told him. "He was called away because of an emergency, but he wanted me to tell you that he'll be back soon."

"You must be Sasha. His wife," Chance added when the woman who was looking at him with large cornflower-blue eyes gave no indication that he had guessed her name correctly.

"What? Oh, no, no, I'm not. I'm Graham's half sister."

"Well, it's nice to meet you, 'Graham's half sister,'" Chance acknowledged, putting his hand out to her.

The woman shifted the baby to her other side so that she could shake hands with him.

"Chloe," she told him. "My name is Chloe. Chloe Elliott. And I guess we'll be interviewing for the same job once Graham gets back."

Chance could only stare at her. What was she, five-one, five-two? Did she say they were going to be competing for the same job? She didn't look like a rancher, and she certainly didn't look like any former military person he'd ever met. The ad he was answering was for a rancher, and it had said that preference would be given to any veterans who applied.

But then, what did he know? The world had been doing a lot of changing in these last few years. Black was white and white was black, and he'd heard that with proper drilling, tiny little ladies like her could mop the floor with guys like him.

That might even turn out to be an interesting experience, Chance caught himself thinking. The one thing he was certain of was that he was glad that the petite blonde wasn't married to the man who he hoped would be hiring him.

He glanced down at her hand, which she had tucked around the baby. It was still clearly visible for his purposes.

There was no wedding ring.

Maybe things were looking up, Chance mused. He could use a little good luck right about now.

"What branch of the service were you in?" he asked her, curious.

Chloe looked at him quizzically. "Service?" she repeated.

"Yeah, you know, navy, army, marines, air force. Service," he repeated. Had she been in some sort of secret branch? he wondered. Was that why she looked so reluctant to say anything?

"I wasn't in any branch," Chloe told him, looking bewildered. "What makes you think I was in the service?"

Aware he might have made a mistake, Chance backtracked. He didn't want to get off on the wrong foot by insulting the woman.

"Well, the ad said that preference would be given to veterans," he began, feeling as if he was on really shaky ground here.

"I didn't see the ad," she told Chance. "Graham just called to tell me about the position and he asked me to come out to the ranch to interview for it. And then he got called away because of that emergency."

He nodded. "Right. The emergency," he repeated. "So you said. Um, do you have any idea when he might be coming back?" He wasn't much for small talk, but this had to be a new low, even for him.

Chloe shrugged. "Not a clue. He just said he'd be back as soon as he could." She paused for a moment, as if searching for something to say in order to fill the stillness. "So, you served?" she asked.

Chance nodded. "Special Forces in Afghanistan—until that IED sent me straight to the hospital, and eventually, stateside."

"Recently?" she asked, trying but failing to covertly scan his appearance.

The cowboy looked perfect, but she knew that there were some injuries and scars that weren't visible.

But in her opinion, the worst ones were the ones that didn't allow you to come home at all, other than in a coffin.

"No, I've been home for a few years now," Chance told her.

"Where's home?"

"Here and there," he answered vaguely. "I go wherever the work is." He didn't want it to sound as if the reason for his nomadic existence was because he didn't do a good job and was let go. "I don't stick around long in any one place," he confessed.

"Why? Are you looking for something?" Chloe asked.

"Not particularly."

It wasn't that Chance felt he was actually searching for something specific, he just stayed in one place until he began feeling restless. It was as if something inside him would suddenly tell him that it was time to go.

"I already know that the only place I ever feel like I'm at peace is on the back of a horse. I guess you could say that's my haven, my church," he explained.

She smiled at him, and it seemed to make its way to her eyes. "Lucky for you, you can keep your church close by so it's there whenever you need it."

He smiled back at her. "Something like that."

It wasn't really like that, but he wasn't about to correct the blonde right off the bat. They hadn't even known each other for a total of five minutes yet. Correcting her wasn't exactly the way to get to know her any better.

He did, however, appreciate the fact that she wasn't grilling him, trying to make him explain his thinking. Some of the women he'd encountered would try to do just that—especially the ones who made it clear that they wanted him to stay with them.

Just as Chance was searching his mind for something to say, an older man burst into the living room.

Chloe looked at the older man in surprise. She'd completely forgotten he was in the house, making a call. "Did you finish making your call?"

He looked at her a little sheepishly. "It took longer than I thought," he apologized.

Obviously realizing that Chance had no idea who this man was, Chloe made the necessary introductions.

"Chance, this is Sasha's uncle Roger. Roger, this is Chance Howell. He's the other person Graham was going to interview today."

"The one he couldn't reach," Roger acknowledged, nodding his head as he shook hands with Chance. "Matter of fact, that's why I came back. Graham just called me to say that he and Sasha will be home soon. Looks like Maddie just broke her wrist, not her whole arm, but she's still got a big cast and from what I could tell, that is one unhappy eight-year-old," he added sympathetically.

"Anyway," Roger continued, addressing Chance, "Graham told me to tell you that you can reschedule your interview if you don't want to wait around until he gets in." He turned to Chloe. "Same goes for you if you're getting a mite antsy, waiting for him. Course, since you're so good with the baby and all, I'm hoping you'll stay."

"Sure, that's okay," Chloe told Sasha's uncle. "I'll stay until he gets here. No point in my going back and forth."

"Same here," Chance chimed in. His eyes met Chloe's and just for a moment, the job he had come out to apply for slipped into the background for him. "I'll be happy to stay."

What he really meant was that he was happy spending a little more time talking to the petite blonde with the sunbeam smile—even if talking didn't exactly come easy for him.

Chloe felt a quickening in the pit of her stomach. It was identical to the one she'd experienced when she'd first opened the door and caught sight of the tall, rangy-looking cowboy.

Careful, Chloe. Remember, been there, done that. You really don't want to go down that road again, do you? You know exactly where that road leads.

Donnie had been her first love. She'd fallen really hard for Donnie and had felt like jumping out of an airplane without strapping a parachute to her back. The feeling was nothing short of exhilarating, but in the end, leaping out of an airplane without a parachute was just asking for trouble, and that was the very last thing she wanted in her life: the kind of trouble that led directly to heartache.

But on the other hand, Chloe reasoned, she didn't want to come across as rude, either, and being nice—cautiously nice—to Chance didn't hurt anything, she silently insisted.

The trick was that she had to remember not to get carried away.

Before she could say anything to him, Sasha's uncle stepped up.

"While you're waiting for Graham to get back," Roger offered, "I could give you two a tour of the place if you're interested."

"You mean of the house?" Chloe asked, looking down at the baby in her arms.

Sydney, to her surprise, had fallen asleep. Chloe had been so taken with the handsome cowboy, she hadn't even realized. Nor did she realize the pain in her shoulder till now. She didn't want to take a chance on waking the baby up, but on the other hand, she would really welcome the opportunity to set Sydney down in her crib.

"Well, the house to start with," Roger said, answering her question. "And then the rest of the ranch. I could take you two on a quick tour in my truck," he added in case they were worried about missing Graham when he and his wife returned.

Chloe looked down at the baby. "I don't want to risk waking Sydney up."

Roger looked as if he suddenly realized the position that Chloe was in.

"I guess I completely forgot about making you hold that little one," he confessed, embarrassed. He looked at Chance.

"It's up to you, Chloe," he said. "If you don't feel comfortable about waking that little baby, we can stay right here and wait for Graham and his missus. I don't need special entertaining," he went on to tell her as he smiled. "I'm just fine the way I am."

You certainly are, Chloe thought.

The next minute, ashamed of herself, feeling guilty at being so flippant about Donnie's memory, she admonished herself for thinking that way. She really had to get hold of herself. What was wrong with her? This wasn't like her at all.

"I don't want to keep you from seeing the ranch," she protested, ready to wave Chance and Roger off on their way.

"If I get the job, I'll be seeing it soon enough," Chance told her. "And if I don't get the job, well then, there's really no point in taking a tour around the place, now is there?"

Roger looked a little perplexed as he listened to the exchange between the two younger people. Lifting his somewhat sloping shoulders, he shrugged and then let them fall again.

"Suit yourselves," he told them. "But meanwhile, I can show you where Sydney's room is so you can at least put her down in her crib. That way you can see if you can still move your arms." Turning, Roger beckoned for her to follow. "It's this way, Chloe."

She saw no reason not to do that, as long as she could hear the baby if she started crying again. She was fairly confident that there had to be a baby monitor in Sydney's room.

Feeling a sense of relief that she'd at least be away from Chance for a minute or two—enough time to break whatever spell he'd seemed to cast over her—Chloe happily fell into step behind Sasha's uncle.

"Guess I might as well come, too," Chance said to them. "No sense in standing around, talking to myself."

Oh, joy. Just what she needed. More of the handsome cowboy.

Chapter 3

Chloe eased the baby ever so slowly into the crib. She held her breath the entire time until she was able to successfully withdraw her hands from around the baby's little body.

Sydney made a little noise, then sighed before settling back to sleep.

Success! Chloe silently congratulated herself.

She took a step back and almost gasped as she bumped up right against Chance.

"Oh, sorry," he whispered, immediately moving aside. He wasn't sure if he was apologizing for being in her way or for feeling that sudden zip of electricity surging through his body when it made contact with hers. Granted the contact wasn't of the intimate variety that he was normally accustomed to, but there was still just enough to get him going.

Chloe instantly turned around and nearly caused another, far more dead-on collision between them. At the very last minute, because Chance had moved back so quickly, the one-on-one collision between their two bodies was avoided.

She wasn't really sure if she was relieved—or perhaps just a little disappointed.

Again? What is the matter with you? she silently demanded.

Yes, the man was attractive, she acknowledged, but lots of men were attractive and she hadn't been drawn to them. So why was this man, this *cowboy*, different from the others?

He's not. Get a grip, Chloe, she ordered herself angrily.

"Um, that's okay." She flushed, absolving him of any guilt in what had just transpired. "I shouldn't have moved so suddenly." She looked down at the sleeping infant. "I just didn't want to take a chance on saying something too loud and waking up the baby."

Since the room was relatively small, Roger had kept back, standing almost out in the hallway. He peered in now at the sleeping infant.

"She sure is a pretty little thing, ain't she?" The whispered rhetorical question was steeped in complete admiration. And then he looked from Chance to Chloe. "You got any kids?" he asked Chance.

The cowboy looked surprised by the question. "No."

"You already told me that you don't have any," Roger said to Chloe. And then he laughed to himself, as if he knew something they weren't privy to yet. "Well, you two are young yet. You've got time."

Time—that was what Donnie had thought. They had

time. Time to be together, time to enjoy one another before they took that step to become parents. Again she wished with all her heart she had insisted on getting pregnant before he had left for overseas. At least she would have had Donnie's child to hold in her arms instead of all that emptiness that he left behind.

"But once you've got 'em," Roger was saying, "there's just nothing like it in the world. Makes you realize just what you were put down here on earth for, what makes everything else all worthwhile." Rousing himself, he beckoned them out into the hallway. "C'mon, we'd better slip out before I forget myself and start talking loud again."

Roger put a hand on each of their shoulders—he had to stretch in order to reach Chance's—and he guided them both out ahead of him.

The hallway was too narrow to accommodate all three of them. Roger fell behind them again.

As she and Chance fell in step beside each other, he glanced her way. "You want kids?" he asked her out of the blue as they made their way back down the stairs ahead of their unofficial escort.

"Right now, I just want a job," she told him honestly. The next second, she realized that he might think she was trying to guilt him out of competing for the position he was here for. "I mean, if I turn out to be more qualified for it. But if it turns out that you are, well then, I'll just have to keep on looking for something," she concluded.

Chance caught himself studying her. Something just wasn't adding up for him.

"Just how much do you know about ranching?" he finally asked her.

Reaching the bottom of the stairs, she stared at him, confused. Why would he ask her such a strange question? “Not much. Why?”

Something’s really *not adding up*, Chance told himself. “Well, because that’s the job I’m here about. The one I’m interviewing for. Graham wanted someone to run the ranch. Someone who was good with horses,” he finally said when she just kept looking at him.

“Run the ranch?” Chloe repeated, confused. She’d gotten the impression from Graham that she and Chance were here about the same job. She looked at him now. “You’re here about ranching?”

“Funny, I thought I just said that,” Chance answered. Judging by the expression on her face, she *wasn’t* here to apply for that job the way she’d made it sound earlier. “What are you here about?”

“Why, counseling, of course,” Chloe replied in no uncertain terms.

“Counseling what?” Chance asked, clearly surprised by her answer. And then it suddenly occurred to him what the sexy-looking blonde was saying. He had to admit that what he’d just asked made him feel like an idiot. “You mean the boys?”

Her smile was a natural reflex. “I kind of have to. Horses don’t listen to me.”

Chloe’s sense of humor tickled him and he laughed. Now it all made sense. They were here about two different positions. “I could teach you how to make them listen to you.”

“You’re talking about the horses, right?” she asked, a hint of mischief dancing in her eyes.

He found himself being pulled in and mesmerized by those deep pools of blue. It took effort to tear his gaze away. "Right," he finally replied. "I've got no trouble getting horses to listen to me. Most people, though, just ignore me like I wasn't there."

"I don't believe that for a minute," she told him with feeling. How could *anyone*, male or female—especially female—not notice this man? His presence seemed to just fill up the very space around him. Heaven knew he certainly did that for her.

The way he was looking at her right now made her feel like nervously shifting from foot to foot. The butterflies in her stomach were multiplying at a phenomenal rate. It was hard to gather her thoughts together to answer him.

"For one thing, you're really tall." She knew that wasn't much of an answer, so she searched for a better one. "And you have this commanding air about you. If you *were* a counselor, I'm sure that the boys here would listen to whatever you had to say."

"Good thing we won't have to put that to the test," Chance answered, then confessed, "I'm not much when it comes to giving orders. I had enough of that when I was over in Afghanistan."

The mention of the place that had seen Donnie die had her quietly saying, "At least you got to come back."

The words slipped out before she could think to stop them. Any hope that Chance might not have heard her died the second she looked up into his eyes. He'd heard. There was curiosity mingled with a touch of pity in his blue orbs.

The moment grew more uncomfortable for her.

"Did you lose someone?" Chance asked kindly.

Her first impulse was to deny his assumption. But

that would be like denying Donnie had ever existed, and she couldn't bring herself to do that.

So after a couple of beats had gone by, she answered him. "Yes."

"Brother? Father? Husband?" Chance kept guessing when she made no acknowledgment that he had guessed correctly. By the time he'd reached the word *husband*, with no visible response from her, Chance shook his head. "No, never mind. Don't tell me. It's none of my business. Sorry I asked," he apologized. "It's just that sometimes it feels like some kind of exclusive veterans club—the kind you really don't want membership to," he added ruefully.

"Does that mean you wish you hadn't gone?" she asked, curious.

How many times had she lain awake at night, wondering if Donnie ever regretted enlisting before the war had taken him from her. Even now, after all this time, she hadn't really come to any sort of a satisfactory conclusion.

"No," he told her honestly. "I went to fight for my country, and I'm proud of that part. I just wish I hadn't seen what I'd seen. Nobody should see that kind of thing," he said quietly. "Nobody should have to live through it, either."

Then, as if he replayed his own words in his head, Chance blew out a breath, mystified. "How'd I get started on that?" he asked. The question was meant more for him than for her. Clearing his throat, he abruptly changed the subject. "Anyway, at least now we know that we're not out for the same job."

Roger, who had been hanging back quietly this whole time, finally spoke up.

"Well, glad that's been cleared up—and just in time, too." His attention was immediately redirected to the sound of the front door being opened. "Looks like your future bosses are back," he told Chloe and Chance with a broad wink.

They turned toward the front door in time to see Graham and Sasha walking in, along with a little girl. With her straight blond hair and her delicate features, she looked like a miniature version of her mother. All except for the arm that was in a cast and held by a sling around her neck.

Chloe winced in sympathy. That had to be Maddie, she thought, her heart immediately going out to the little girl. She hoped that Maddie wasn't in too much pain.

"Well, we made it back," Sasha announced. "Sorry for the wait." She looked around. "Uncle Roger, where's the baby?"

Roger pointed to Chloe. "This one got her to go to sleep just like that." He snapped his fingers to illustrate just how fast Chloe had performed what was clearly a magic trick to him.

Sasha smiled warmly at Chloe.

"Well, I'm won over. You've got the job," Sasha quipped.

"You're not serious, are you?" Chloe asked uncertainly.

"No, she's not," Graham agreed. "But almost," he told Chloe. "Sasha goes on gut instincts, same as me," he told her.

"Hey, kiddo, you want to go upstairs and lie down?" Roger asked his grandniece, who had momentarily gotten lost in this verbal exchange between the adults.

"No," Maddie cried, protesting the very idea. "They

had me lying down forever when I was in the hospital, getting all those pictures took of my arm." She looked at her cast. "What I want is you to sign my cast," she declared, pointing to the newly applied cast with her other hand. Barely an hour old, the cast already had a handful of autographs and well-wishes written on it. "I got these from the nurses. And that's from that doctor who put it on," she told her granduncle, pointing out the different signatures. "Isn't it neat?"

"It sure is," Roger agreed with the kind of enthusiasm that appealed to young children. "Neatest thing I've ever seen. What do you say you and me go get us a sandwich in the kitchen and I'll see if I can come up with something real good to put on that cast?"

Maddie perked up visibly. "Can I have anything I want to eat?" she asked eagerly.

"You can have anything that's in the refrigerator," Roger qualified with a wink.

Maddie's grin all but split her face. "Cool!"

Roger pretended to misunderstand her declaration. "Cool or hot. Whatever's there, is yours."

Sasha exchanged looks with her amused husband. "I think maybe I should go supervise," Sasha said, following her uncle.

Wanting to be as accommodating as possible, Chloe called out after Sasha's departing back, "I'll just sit right here until you get back."

"You can if you want to, but feel free to move around if you like. You've already got the job," Sasha called back over her shoulder, accompanying her injured daughter to the kitchen.

Chloe looked at Graham. Sasha hadn't asked her a single question that had to do with the job she was applying for. Just what had gotten the woman to decide in her favor?

"I'm confused," Chloe confessed.

He laughed. "Sasha'll do that to you," he said in a completely understanding voice. "I feel like my head's been spinning ever since I first met her. But since she's a better judge than I am when it comes to this position, I've made up my mind. You do have the job." And then he grew more serious. "Do you mind being left alone for a few minutes?" he asked. "I'd like to ask Chance some questions in private."

Then, before she could answer him, he made a suggestion. "Feel free to look around the house, or to join Sasha, Maddie and Uncle Roger in the kitchen."

Chloe shook her head, declining both offers. Right now, she just wanted to sit exactly where she was and absorb what had just happened.

And, in her opinion, what had just happened amounted to being given a job, a rather important job in her estimation, practically sight unseen.

Well, she'd been seen, Chloe amended, but obviously a great deal had just been read into whatever Sasha Fortune Robinson *thought* she saw in her.

"I'm good, thank you," she told Graham, turning down his offer.

In response, her half brother smiled at her and nodded. "I won't be long," he promised.

Her half brother.

It was still hard to think of him that way, Chloe thought as she watched him take Chance into what appeared to be a den that was directly off the living room.

Hard to think of herself as being anyone's half sister.

Or a half sister to what amounted to practically a

legion of other half siblings, she added silently. She'd grown up thinking she had no family at all beyond her mother and now she had more family than she could shake that proverbial stick at.

And one of those half siblings had just given her a job.

Not just *any* job but the kind of job she had set her heart on before she'd ever sent in her application to college. So far, she'd been stitching together a living taking anything she could get—even working at a local coffee shop on weekends to help pay her rent. She felt as if she'd finally crossed a threshold into her field.

Talk about luck.

Glancing around to make sure no one could see her, Chloe pinched herself. And then, just to make certain, she pinched herself again because she had to admit this all seemed like some sort of dream. A dream that she was going to wake up from at any minute now.

Except for the part about Donnie, she thought grimly. If this *was* a dream, he'd be right here beside her.

But he wasn't.

She was sitting in this big old living room all by herself, waiting for her half brother to come back in and tell her all the details she needed to know about this job she was going to be starting. She was convinced that she'd gotten this position strictly because she was "family" despite all of Graham's talk about instincts and gut feelings.

No matter, she was determined to prove to them that they hadn't made a mistake in hiring her. She was going to work really, really hard and be the best counselor they could have possibly hoped for. She owed it to them.

Most of all, she owed it to herself—and to the memory of her husband, who had always encouraged her and told her she could be absolutely anything she wanted to be once she set her mind to it.

She glanced toward the door that Graham had closed behind him and Chance. She wondered how the interview was going.

She really hoped that Chance was going to get the job. She'd gotten the impression that although Chance wasn't down on his luck, landing this position at Peter's Place was really important to him.

Without realizing it, Chloe crossed her fingers for him, wishing that she was one of those people who actually believed in sending good vibes. Because if she was, she'd be sending them right now.

She watched the door intently.

And when it finally opened, only a few minutes later, she popped to her feet like a newly refurbished jack-in-the-box. Fingers still crossed, her eyes immediately went to the taller of the two men emerging from the room.

Chance was smiling.

She was confident that she knew the results before he said a word.

Chapter 4

Chance's smile was as broad as his shoulders as he crossed to her.

"Looks like you turned out to be my good-luck charm," he told Chloe. "'Cause I got the job."

"Luck has nothing to do with it," Graham told him, reaching up just a little to put his hand on his newest ranch hand's shoulder. "The people you worked for all spoke very highly of you. As a matter of fact, Kyle McMasters said to tell you that if it doesn't work out for you here, he'd be more than happy to have you come back to work for him at the Double M."

Chance made no comment regarding his former boss's remark. Instead, he looked at his new boss and asked, "When can I start?"

"Bright and early tomorrow morning'll be fine." As a rule, ranch hands were usually up around sunrise, if not before, so Graham made a suggestion. "How does seven o'clock suit you?"

The early hour didn't faze him in the slightest. He was accustomed to being up earlier, even when he wasn't working. It was just the way his inner clock worked. "I can be here earlier if you need me to be," Chance told him.

"No, seven'll do fine. You can bring your gear then and move in to the bunkhouse," Graham told him. "We've got two on the premises. One just for the ranch hands and the other one's where the boys stay."

"Sounds good to me," Chance replied. "All I really require is enough space to stretch out at the end of the day, nothing more."

Graham nodded. "We're going to get along just fine," he predicted. "Just to let you know, I've got plans for you. You're not just going to be a ranch hand. After you get the lay of the land around here, and things look like they're going well, I want to make you the coordinator for Peter's Place."

Graham smiled. "I think your being ex-military might just come in handy. The boys who are here now need a firm hand and they need to be made to respect authority. That's not to say I want you coming down hard on them. Just make sure they don't take advantage of you or anyone else here," Graham added. He looked deliberately at Chloe as he said the last part.

Chloe appreciated the thought, but she had been looking after herself for a long time now.

"You don't have to worry about me," Chloe told her half brother. "I might not be as tall as you two, but I'm not a pushover, either. And I can definitely take care of myself."

Graham held up a hand. "I never meant to imply that I thought of you as a pushover. But knowing someone has your back certainly doesn't hurt in this kind of a situation," Graham assured her.

Then he launched into a rundown of the current residents staying at Peter's Place. "Right now, we've got four boys staying here. They're all decent kids, but for one reason or another, they've lost their way and all of them feel like they've been dealt a pretty bad hand." He spared a glance at Chloe. "Sasha can do a better job filling you in," he said to Chloe.

As if on cue, his wife came in from the kitchen. "Did I just hear my name being mentioned?" she asked, a bright smile on her face. Before Graham had an opportunity to respond to her question, Sasha told her husband, "You'll be happy to know that breaking her wrist did not affect our daughter's appetite. She's eating up a storm in there. Uncle Roger's whipping up his 'famous' corn dogs wrapped in bacon for her. I set the limit at two but I've got a feeling he's not going to stick to that. Maybe you can make him understand the wisdom of not letting Maddie stuff herself to the gills."

"I'm on it," Graham said, beginning to leave the living room.

Sasha looked at Chance and Chloe. "So, I take it that they both said yes."

"That they did," Graham said, tossing the words over his shoulder.

"Well then, welcome to Peter's Place," Sasha told the duo warmly. "I hope you like it here," she added. "We try to keep it homey. For some of these boys, this is the first actual 'home' they've had in quite a while."

The sound of a baby crying was heard coming over

the monitor that Chloe had positioned on the wide coffee table.

Sasha sighed wearily as she looked at the monitor. "Looks like I'm being summoned," she told Chloe as she started to get up.

"Why don't you stay here and get Chloe up to speed on the boys who are currently here?" Graham suggested. Sasha began to point out the obvious, but never got very far. "I'll go see to Sydney," Graham told her. "I'm sure Uncle Roger knows enough not to overfeed Maddie. If he doesn't, Maddie's got enough sense to stop." Pausing for just a moment before he went up the stairs, he turned toward Chance. "And I'll see you in the morning."

"Count on it," Chance told him. Putting his Stetson on, he tipped it ever so slightly to the right, unaware that he was creating a rakish image as he did so. Chance nodded first at Graham's wife and then at Chloe. "Ladies, I'll see you tomorrow," he promised just before he headed for the door.

Chloe just stared at his retreating form. A very sexy form, she had to admit.

"He's a tall one, don't you agree?"

The comment snapped Chloe to attention. She hadn't even realized she was still staring at the closed door. "What? Oh, you mean Chance. Yes, I guess he is at that," she murmured.

When she looked at Sasha, she thought she saw a hint of a grin on her lips. She hoped that Sasha didn't think that there was anything between her and Chance—or that there would be in the future. She'd come here strictly because she wanted work as a counselor and nothing more, she silently insisted.

"So tell me about the boys at Peter's Place," Chloe urged. She thought it best to change the subject immediately.

Sasha sat down beside her on the sofa, and then a sudden thought occurred to her. "Oh, where are my manners? Having your daughter break her wrist kind of knocks everything else out of your head," she apologized, then asked, "Can I get you anything? Something to drink perhaps?"

Chloe shook her head. She didn't want anything to distract her. Right now, all she wanted to do was focus on any information that Sasha could give her. She wanted to be as fully prepared as possible when she finally met the boys who had been sent here to atone for their misdeeds and to ultimately become better people.

"No, I'm fine. Really," she stressed when Sasha looked at her somewhat skeptically. "Just tell me about the boys I'm going to be working with. I want to learn all I can about them."

Sasha seemed to ponder her reply for a moment, no doubt wanting to cite the boys in the proper order.

Then she began. "The first teen we took in here at Peter's Place is Jonah Wright. A basically good boy, Jonah kind of hit a rough patch when his father ran off, deserting the family. Consequently, to make ends meet, his mother had to hold down two jobs. Because she wasn't home very much, she expected Jonah to look after his three younger siblings. I don't have to tell you that that's a lot of responsibility to heap on such young shoulders. Jonah loved playing baseball after school and he had to give that up in order to be there for his siblings.

"After a while, life felt as if it was crashing in on

him and Jonah just kept getting angrier and angrier. He started ditching school, vandalizing property and getting into fights almost all the time. He started shoplifting and got away with it the first couple of times.

"And then he got arrested. They were going to send him to jail, then at the last minute, the authorities decided to send him here instead. It was kind of touch and go with Jonah for a while, but he turned things around and it looks like he's on the road to getting his life back." Sasha smiled, clearly pleased to be able to relate this to Chloe. "Things look pretty promising and he's even going to be playing baseball soon, just like he always wanted to."

Sasha stopped for a moment, seeming to gather her thoughts.

"The second teen who was sent here was Ryan Maxwell. He was a lot less hostile than Jonah was when he came here, but he was also a great deal more depressed and withdrawn."

"Do you know why he was depressed?" Chloe wanted to know.

Sasha nodded. "Both of his parents died and social services sent him to live with his uncle. Family isn't always the best way to go," Sasha told her. "In Ryan's case, his uncle turned out to be a lowlife. He stole and spent all of the money that Ryan's parents had set aside to pay for his college education. Personally, I suspect that Ryan got into trouble and vandalized private property just to get away from the man."

"You're probably right," Chloe agree. "He probably felt he had nothing to lose and just maybe something to gain if he got away from his uncle."

Sasha smiled. "Since he came here, he's been doing

a lot better. He's now in both a math club *and* a science club in school. If he keeps things up this way, he's on track to get a college scholarship," Sasha told her proudly. "And if that happens, he can write his own ticket. His future is a great deal more promising than his past."

"And the other boys?" Chloe asked, wondering if their stories would wind up ending this well.

"Well, the last two are newer and I'm afraid they haven't really adjusted to living here—yet," Sasha emphasized, obviously holding out a great deal of hope for the fates of both of these newer residents at Peter's Place. "Brandon Baker lost his older brother in Afghanistan, and I get the distinct feeling that he's just mad at the whole world right now."

Chloe could certainly identify with the way Brandon felt. When Donnie had been killed, there was a point when she'd been convinced that her anger was going to suffocate her. It had been touch and go for a while.

"And the last boy?" Chloe prompted.

"That would be Will Sherman. His mother is a single parent, and she has her own share of problems. The woman is an alcoholic," Sasha confided. "The Dr. Jekyll/Mr. Hyde kind who takes all of her frustrations out on Will. A social worker found him wandering the streets one night, so battered she didn't know how he was able to even stand up, much less walk." Tears shone in Sasha's eyes as she told Chloe, "When the social worker questioned him, he denied that his mother had beaten him. It was heartbreaking how protective he was of that woman. But it was obvious to everyone who came in contact with this boy that he couldn't be allowed to go back home. It was just as obvious that it would be just a matter of time before Will turned to less than acceptable ways, trying to support himself on the street.

"He's been here for a while, and I think he still feels that life has abandoned him, just like his mother has. He needs to learn how to relate to people and how to trust again."

Finished with her brief summation, Sasha paused and looked at Chloe. "Well, have I managed to scare you off yet?"

Chloe didn't have to hunt for words in order to answer her. As far as she was concerned, what Sasha had just outlined was her mission in life. Helping boys like the ones she spoke of.

"No, of course not. It's obvious that all these boys need help, and that's what I'm here for. What kind of a counselor would I be if I turned tail and ran at the first sign of a problem?"

"Possibly one who slept better at night?" Sasha suggested, a hint of a smile playing on her lips.

"The exact opposite," Chloe contradicted with feeling. "I wouldn't be able to sleep, knowing I didn't even try to help these boys. That I'd failed to reach out to them. Nobody deserves to have their dreams shattered the way these boys have, or to have their mothers beat them every time they descend into an alcoholic stupor."

Chloe knew the sort of first impression she made and the image that she projected when people first met her. She made people think of a sweet Girl Scout selling cookies door-to-door. But she wasn't interested in selling cookies.

"Believe me," she said, "I know life isn't all milk and cookies, but it shouldn't be all pain and sorrow, either."

As she spoke, Chloe could feel that she was really getting into the spirit of this new job she was about to undertake. She also felt she had a lot to offer.

"I know what it's like to grow up without a father and be raised by a single mother. I know what it's like to have to do without things other kids have, and I *definitely* know what it's like to lose someone and how that can cut right into your very soul." Her eyes met Sasha's, determination shining in them. "I think I can really help these boys," Chloe told her sister-in-law with fierce feeling.

Sasha beamed at her as she took the woman's hands in hers.

"I think you can, too," she said. "And I'm really glad Graham suggested that we hire you." She let go of Chloe, then tilted her head as if in thought for a moment. Then she said, "You know, we have an extra bedroom right here in the house. It might be easier for all of us if you lived here, on the premises."

Chloe hesitated, which prompted Sasha to quickly make another suggestion.

"We also have a small guest cottage on the property right behind the house. Now that I think of it, that might be more to your liking. You'd still be on the premises, but there wouldn't be that feeling of having Graham and me breathing down your neck," she added with an understanding smile.

"Oh, no, I wouldn't feel that," Chloe protested.

She didn't want to insult either Sasha or her half brother. They had gone out of their way to reach out to her while the others hadn't. That meant a great deal to her. She doubted that either one of them could begin to understand how much this new connection—being part of the family—meant to her. She was thrilled and excited about it and didn't want to do anything that would make them regret bringing her into the fold.

"Well, I'd feel that way in your place," Sasha said quite honestly. Her eyes met and held Chloe's. "Chloe, I have just one real hard-and-fast rule," she told the younger woman. "Always tell me the truth. No matter how you think hearing it might affect me, *always* tell me the truth. This way I won't have to wonder if you're being honest with me, or if you're just trying to spare my feelings."

Chloe took a breath. "Okay, this is me being honest. Yes, I can see how having me live here would be more beneficial so I could be on call anytime for the boys, and yes, I would rather have my own small space than live in the main house with you. That way, I won't be underfoot," she added.

Sasha laughed, looking pleased at the progress they seemed to be making. "There now, was that so hard?"

"Actually, yes," Chloe admitted. When Sasha raised her eyebrow quizzically, she explained, "I don't like worrying that I might be hurting people's feelings."

"Well, I for one would rather have my feelings hurt than find out I have been lied to—even if it involves just a little white lie," Sasha added with a wink. "All right, it's settled," she announced, rising to her feet. "You'll be moving in to the guest cottage," she told the other woman. "It hasn't been used for a while, so if there's anything you find that you need—or that needs fixing—please don't hesitate to tell either Graham or me.

"While I have to admit that we aren't exactly the handiest people in the world, we do have the connections to always find someone who is." Again, she took

Chloe's hands in hers. "We want you to be happy here," she told Chloe.

"Just being given the opportunity to try to help those boys you told me about will make me happy," Chloe responded.

"Good, I'm glad." Sasha released her hands. "But don't expect miracles," she warned. "This isn't some TV drama where everything's tied up neatly with a big red bow and fixed in sixty minutes—not counting commercials," Sasha added flippantly.

"I know that," Chloe assured her. "I have a degree in counseling, not fantasy."

"As long as we're on the same page," Sasha said agreeably.

Just as Chloe rose to leave, Graham came in carrying Sydney. The baby was crying just the same way she had when Chloe had first encountered her.

"What's wrong, little one?" Sasha asked her daughter.

"I'm not sure. I changed her and I don't think she's hungry. Uncle Roger said that she was screaming her lungs out earlier, until Chloe—" he nodded at his half sister "—got her to stop."

"Chloe?" Sasha asked, looking at the other woman with interest.

"All I did was just hold her when he handed her to me," Chloe said, not about to take credit for any sort of "miracle."

The next thing she knew, Graham was handing the baby over to her.

Startled, she took the baby and after a few seconds of rocking, Sydney stopped crying again.

Sasha looked on, clearly surprised and very pleased.

"Maybe we should offer you two jobs here at Peter's Place," she quipped.

Graham exchanged looks with his wife. "Works for me," he chimed in.

In response to their words, Chloe felt a warm feeling spreading out all through her. A feeling of acceptance.

She blinked several times to keep the tears back.

Chapter 5

"Looks like today's moving day for both of us," Chance observed the next day, peering into the guesthouse through the door that Chloe had left opened.

Startled, Chloe swung around, her hand pressed against her pounding heart, to find the tall cowboy standing just outside the doorway. Naturally assuming that she was alone, she had just begun arranging the furnishings in her new quarters to her liking.

The guesthouse was actually more of a large studio apartment with a small bathroom attached to it than an actual house in the traditional sense. But located about a hundred yards behind the main house, it felt like her own private little space, which was all that really mattered to Chloe right now. It made her part of the whole organization, yet just separate enough to satisfy her need to be alone at times.

Except that right now, she wasn't alone.

"Hey, I didn't mean to scare you," Chance apologized, crossing the threshold. "I guess I should make more noise when I come up behind someone."

Embarrassed at her reaction—he was probably going to think she was afraid of her own shadow—Chloe waved away the cowboy's apology.

"No, I was just really focused on trying to figure out where to put my things." She glanced around again. Somehow, with Chance inside, the space looked smaller to her than it had a few minutes ago. "I think I brought too much with me. I just wasn't sure what I was going to need."

He'd seen a sedan parked by the guesthouse. There were a number of boxes and a couple of suitcases in the backseat.

"You have a place of your own apart from here?" he asked. Sometimes he forgot that most people did. He'd moved around so much since he'd been discharged from the army that when he was in between jobs, he just lived out of his truck. It was simpler that way.

Chloe nodded. "An apartment in town." It wasn't all that big—but it was bigger than the guesthouse, she thought.

Usually one to keep to himself, Chance realized he was asking too many questions, but curiosity was spurring him on. "If you've already got a place, why aren't you staying there? Can't be that far away from the ranch," he guessed.

"Sasha thought it might be easier if I was on the premises to begin with. You know, just in case there was some kind of an emergency with one of the boys, they wouldn't have to wait for me to drive in." Replaying her words in her head, Chloe laughed. "I guess that sounds kind of dramatic, doesn't it?" She supposed she could have just told Sasha that she could make the run from her apartment to the ranch quickly enough if the need arose. "It's just that this is my first real counseling job and I don't want anything to go wrong."

She saw a look akin to sympathy enter Chance's piercing blue eyes. "Oh, it'll go wrong," he said with certainty.

This wasn't the sort of pep talk she'd expected, Chloe thought. As a matter of fact, it sounded more like some kind of prediction of doom.

She stared at him. "What?"

Maybe he should have explained what he meant when he said that, Chance thought. "No matter how perfect things are, something is always bound to go wrong. It doesn't have to be some kind of a major disaster—and it usually isn't," he said with certainty. "But it's a fact of life that things do go wrong, usually when you least expect them to. Once you make your peace with that, you can relax and get the job done," he told her. "Just remember, do the best you can. Nobody expects perfection."

Easy for you to say, she thought. *Just look at yourself.*

"Do things go wrong for you?"

What he'd just said made her curious. She imagined that Chance was quite good at what he did. Practice alone probably made him perfect, and from what she'd gathered from Sasha, Chance had worked on ranches both before and after his stint in the military.

He laughed, tickled by the fact that she actually thought he might say no.

"Do you want that alphabetically, chronologically or listed in order of importance? And if it's the last one, would you like that in descending order or ascending order?"

Realizing that maybe she'd made a mistake, Chloe put her hands up as if to ward off any further questions.

"Point taken," she told Chance.

Looking at him more closely, she decided that he looked pretty relaxed. Since he'd mentioned something about it being "moving day" for both of them, she assumed that Chance had finished moving in to the bunkhouse. Men always had less baggage than women, she thought enviously. "I guess you're all settled in."

Chance moved his shoulders in a careless shrug. "A couple of changes of clothing, an extra pair of boots, razor, shaving cream and toothbrush. Not exactly much to 'settle,'" he told her, going through everything he'd brought with him.

Chance looked around the guesthouse. There was a combination stove, refrigerator and sink unit against one wall with a table for two right in front of it. Next to that was a sofa that he suspected pulled out into a bed. It was facing a small flat-screen on the wall that looked as if it was the latest piece of technology. Near the flat-screen was a chest of drawers.

It seemed like almost too much space for him, he thought.

"Need help with anything?" he asked her.

She'd already gotten started. "I just need to bring in a couple of suitcases and three boxes from my car. Oh, and I picked up two bags of groceries on my way here. But now that I see the size of the refrigerator, I'm not sure if it'll all fit in there."

"You could always stash the excess in the closet," Chance suggested with a straight face.

"I could," she allowed, taking his suggestion at face value. "If it was a walk-in. But it's not. It's barely a hang-in," she quipped.

His eyebrows drew together as he tried to make sense out of what she'd just said. "A what?"

She flushed just a little. "That was a lame joke about there not being enough room to hang more than a handful of clothes in the closet."

That had never been a problem for him. "I never really had more than a handful of clothes at any one time myself."

That fit the image she'd gotten of him. "Of course you didn't. Just your cowboy hat, your boots and your lariat should cover it," she deadpanned.

His eyes crinkled a little in amusement. "You been peeking into my closet, Chloe Elliott?"

The thought of peeking into his living space suddenly made her blush. She struggled to get that under control. "Just making an educated guess."

He wondered if he seemed that predictable to her, or if she was just kidding. Either way, she struck him as a fairly sharp lady. "Well, if that's the kind of thing a degree in counseling gets you, I'd say that it was money well spent."

That being said, he had to admit he was a little leery of psychologists and people who felt all problems could be tackled and solved by delving deeply into people's backgrounds and into what made them tick. That meant hours and hours of talking. He believed in action, not in talking a thing to death.

"But just so you know," he added, "I don't really enjoy having someone poking around in my head, wanting to know if I grew up thinking there were monsters under my bed."

"I don't blame you," she agreed so readily, he found himself believing her. "Neither do I."

Chance jerked a thumb toward the car she had parked out front. "Want me to bring in those suitcases and boxes for you?"

She didn't want him feeling as if he had to do anything for her. And she didn't want him thinking of her as helpless, either. "You don't have to."

"I didn't say I had to. I asked if you wanted me to," he pointed out.

On the other hand, she didn't want to come off like someone who slapped away a helping hand, either.

"Yes, please. That would be very nice of you," she told him.

Chance was out the door before the last word had left her lips. He was back just as quickly, juggling both suitcases as well as the three boxes. It amazed her that he hadn't dropped anything.

"You certainly move fast," she marveled.

"It's a little something you pick up when people are shooting at you," he told her. Looking around the room for a likely spot, he asked, "Where do you want me to put these?"

"Doesn't matter, just any place," she said vaguely. "I've got to empty the suitcases and hang the things up inside that shallow closet." She waved at the small door that was off to one side.

He set the suitcases and boxes down next to the sofa. "Again, that wouldn't be a problem for me—if I had a closet," he added with a hint of a grin.

"You don't have a closet?" Chloe asked, surprised, trying to visualize his living quarters.

"Does a footlocker count?"

"Only if you're in boot camp," she said before she realized that he was being serious.

Chance grinned at the reference. It hit home. "Well, it's kind of like that," he told her.

Picking up one of the suitcases, Chloe placed it on the sofa and snapped opened the locks, then lifted the lid.

Chance caught himself looking into the suitcase. Instead of the jeans and practical shirts he'd expected, he saw that she had packed several very flowery, pastel-colored dresses. The kind, he thought, that seemed more suited to sitting on a porch swing, sipping lemonade, than following around teenage boys as they did their chores on a ranch. From what Graham had explained, Peter's Place had been founded on the idea that the chores were what taught these troubled kids discipline and doing those chores in turn brought order to their lives.

Somehow, that kind of dusty activity just didn't seem compatible with flowing, feminine dresses. At least not to him.

She saw Chance looking rather skeptically at what she'd packed. She could almost read his thoughts by the expression on his face.

He was probably right, she thought. What she'd brought with her wasn't all that sensible. It reflected who and what she was, but it fell short in the practicality department.

Still, as long as Chance didn't bring the subject up, she wasn't about to try to defend her choices.

She thought of something that Chance had said when he brought her suitcases in. Something that had made her think of Donnie. She'd understood her husband's reasons for joining up, just like she understood what Chance had said about it the other day. Fighting for your country were sentiments to be admired. But they were also idealistic and they didn't explain how Chance had dealt with the day-to-day struggle of just trying to survive.

"How did you stand it?" she asked Chance suddenly.

He looked at her, confused. She had him at a complete disadvantage. The question had come out of the blue, and since they weren't actually talking about anything, he really wasn't sure what Chloe was referring to.

"How did I stand what?" he wanted to know.

"When you brought the boxes and suitcases in, you said you learned to move fast because people were shooting at you. How did you stand that?" she asked in all sincerity. "Knowing that any second, no matter what you were doing and how quiet it was, someone could just start shooting at you? Worse, that they might actually wind up killing you?"

"Most of the time I didn't think about it," he told her honestly. "You really can't spend time thinking about it, or it'll wind up paralyzing you. You just hope that when someone does start shooting at you, the bullet won't have your name on it. Or that you get to return fire quickly enough and accurately enough to take out whoever it is who wants you dead." He paused, his eyes meeting hers. "Everyone who goes over there just wants to get home in one piece."

Chance watched as Chloe slowly unpacked, neatly hanging up the dresses. He could easily envision her wearing those dresses, a soft spring breeze flirting with the material, causing it to lightly press against her body in ways that could make a grown man weak.

He felt his stomach muscles tightening and forced himself to breathe.

He had no business thinking like that about her, Chance told himself.

Just like he had no business asking her questions, yet here he was, doing both.

He had to watch that, Chance upbraided himself.

Even so, he heard himself telling her, "You know, whenever you're ready to talk about it, I'm here to listen."

"'Talk about it'?" she asked quizzically. Was Chance just talking in general, or was he somehow intuitively referring to the single loss that had ultimately broken her heart?

Chance felt as if he was getting in too deep, but now that he had opened the door, he had no choice except to continue.

"Talk about whoever it is that you lost," he explained. "I figure it has to be someone in the military. Even with all the communication we have available today, it still has to be tough, being cut off like that. Not knowing what's going on until a lot later—if at all."

He knew he wasn't great with words, but he did have a sense of empathy and he knew without putting it into words what she had to have felt. What she still might be feeling. Because he had gone through the same thing.

"Thank you," Chloe said quietly.

She sounded sincere. Awkward or not, maybe he'd pushed the right buttons after all.

"Then you do want to talk?" he asked.

"No." She'd actually thanked him for the offer, not for the opportunity. "No offense, but I can't. Not yet."

Maybe not ever, she added silently because she didn't know if she actually could. The mere thought hurt too much.

"But if and when I am ready to talk about 'it,'" she said, deliberately using his terminology, "I'll take you up on that offer."

Chance nodded. "Good enough," he told her. "I'll be around." He realized how that had to have sounded, so he amended the last sentence. "At least for now."

That last comment caught Chloe off guard. "You make it sound temporary. Is there a time limit to the job?" she asked, wondering if there was something Graham had said to Chance before they had come out of his den yesterday after the interview.

Chance answered her honestly. "Only the one I set for myself," he said. "I only stay in any one place for as long as it feels right. When it stops feeling right, that's when it's time to go."

That sounded just too nomadic for her. If things were working out, why would he want to leave? It didn't make sense.

"And what makes it time to go?" she challenged.

No one had ever questioned his actions before. But Chloe put him on the spot. Though it made him uneasy, it also had him looking at her in a different light. The woman had spunk, he had to admit.

He shrugged. "Just a feeling. Can't really put it into better words than that," he confessed.

Chloe assessed his words. Was he running from something without realizing it? she couldn't help wondering.

"Maybe that feeling is fear," she suggested. She saw that her suggestion did not please him. But she honestly believed what she was saying to him. She couldn't apologize for that; it would be a lie. Instead, she tried to explain what she meant. "Maybe what you fear is complacency. You get too comfortable, too used to something, and you start to worry that you're losing your edge, that you're getting soft. That the challenge is gone. So you have to leave to find another mountain to climb, another dragon to slay."

Chance looked at her as if she was suddenly babbling nonsense.

"I'm not climbing any mountains, and I sure as hell am not slaying any of those dragons. Anyway, dragons aren't real." He was trying his best not to sound annoyed—but he was.

"No," she agreed, "they're not."

He knew he should just go. Normally, he would have. But something was making him dig in his heels and stay. He wanted to get something straight.

"Is this the kind of stuff you're going to be feeding those boys?" he asked. "Stuff about slaying dragons?"

"No, this is the kind of 'stuff' I'm going to be using

in order to try to understand the boys," she said. "To help them reconnect with the world."

He laughed drily. Still sounded like a bunch of mumbo jumbo to him.

"Well, good luck with that," he told her, shaking his head. "But if you ask me, a little hard work and a little responsibility should help those boys do all the reconnecting that they need."

"Hard work and responsibility," she repeated as if he had just quoted scripture. "Has it helped you?" Chloe asked innocently.

His scowl deepened for a moment, and then he just waved her words away. "Don't try getting inside my head, Chloe Elliott. There's nothing in it for you. I'm doing just fine just the way I am."

She suppressed a sigh. "Okay, as long as you're happy."

Happy? When was the last time he'd been happy? He couldn't remember.

"Happy's got nothing to do with it," Chance answered. "I'm my own man on my own terms, and that's all that really counts."

He felt himself losing his temper, and he didn't want to do that. Once things were said, they couldn't get "unsaid" and a lot of damage could be done. He didn't want that to happen. Not with this woman.

"I'd better go find the boss. Graham said that he wanted to take me around the spread as soon as I stashed my gear."

She didn't want to be the reason he was late. "Then I guess you'd better get going."

"Yeah, I guess I'd better." With that, he crossed back to the door.

He walked out feeling that there were things left unspoken. A great many things. But then, maybe it was better that way. He wasn't looking to have his head "shrunk" any more than it already was. Even if the lady doing the shrinking was nothing short of a knockout.

Some things, he reasoned, were just better off left alone.

Chapter 6

Chloe could feel the butterflies in her stomach. Flexing, but at present unable to fly. They were huge butterflies with wingspans that would make an eagle seriously jealous.

But as she walked to her first meeting with the boys at Peter's Place, she knew that if she gave any indication that she was even slightly nervous—never mind that she was about a minute away from having a full-on panic attack—she was certain to lose any advantage and all credibility. Putting up a calm front was all-important during this first encounter.

She was well aware that this would set the tone for the rest of the visits to come.

No pressure here, Chloe mocked herself.

But she knew that if she didn't project that she was completely in control of the situation, word would spread to the other boys immediately, and then none of them would view her with the respect she needed in order to be of any help to them.

And helping them was why she was here, why she'd become a counselor in the first place.

And maybe, in helping others to heal, eventually she'd find a way to help and heal herself.

When she took the job, she'd assumed that she would be conducting a group session, with Sasha present, in which she'd get to meet all four of the boys at once and learn a little about each of them by the time the session was over.

But Sasha had been concerned that since this was her maiden run, so to speak, she might be a little overwhelmed meeting four teens at once. Graham's wife had suggested that she start out small, talking just to one of the ranch residents at a time.

Naturally, Chloe had agreed. She thought that a one-on-one meeting might work a little more in her favor. Besides, she didn't have a ton of experience. New on the job, she needed to abide by Sasha's wishes. After all, Sasha was the expert here.

So here she was, walking into the small, cheery room that had been set aside in the main house for counseling sessions, doing her best to try to control the squadron of butterflies in her stomach that were morphing into Boeing 747s.

At least the sun was cooperating, she noted, filling the room with warm light thanks to the full-length windows that looked out onto the corral and the stables beyond that.

The sun might be cooperating, but her first patient didn't look as if he was inclined to follow suit.

Brandon Baker eyed her suspiciously the moment he walked into the room less than a couple of seconds after she'd entered. A good-looking fifteen-year-old with dark, almost black hair and brown eyes, he was a lot thinner than he should have been. His stance and his very gait exuded defiance.

His eyes quickly swept around the room. "Where's the doc?" he wanted to know.

Chloe didn't bother asking him if he meant Sasha. That would be stalling. "She won't be joining us for the session," Chloe began.

Brandon made a 180 without missing a step and headed for the doorway he'd just entered through.

Chloe knew she had to say something quickly or he'd be gone in a flash. She called after him. "Mrs. Fortune Robinson thought we could get to know each other better if she wasn't here."

Brandon had his hand on the doorknob and didn't bother turning around. "She thought wrong," he said flatly.

"Come back and sit down, Brandon."

Chloe hadn't raised her voice and she definitely wasn't shouting, but there was no mistaking the firmness in her tone. It wasn't a request; it was an order. She surprised even herself.

Brandon still didn't turn around, but neither did he turn the doorknob and go out. It was as if he was still waiting to be convinced.

"Now, please," she requested.

Brandon blew out a breath, turned around and then walked over to the folding chair that was set up opposite hers.

Chloe gestured toward the padded green chair. "Sit, please." Both words were given equal weight.

After a moment, during which time she had a feeling the boy was mentally going over his options, as well as wondering how far he could push her, Brandon Baker finally sat down.

"Okay, I'm sitting." He looked at her, but she couldn't read the expression on his face. All she knew was that it wasn't warm. "Now what?"

"Now we talk," Chloe told him in as bright and engaging a tone as she could summon.

"Talk?" The single word seemed to mock her, and she saw a smirk on Brandon's sullen face. "Lady, I don't even know you."

"That's where the talking part comes in," she told him in as upbeat a manner as she could project. "We talk so that we can get to know each other."

"And then what?" he challenged cynically. "Become best friends?"

"Maybe," she allowed. "Eventually. If enough time passes."

The scowl on the young face was dark and forbidding. "I don't need any more friends."

"Maybe not," Chloe said agreeably. "Maybe you're one of those people who have all the friends he needs—although I doubt it," she couldn't help adding. A warning look rose in Brandon's eyes. Chloe pushed on. "But it's obvious that you do need a way to get rid of all that anger you're holding on to."

Brandon shifted restlessly, indicating that he had heard all that he was willing to listen to. His eyes narrowed. "Look, lady—"

"Chloe," she supplied. She knew that she should have

told the boy to address her by either her surname or simply "ma'am," but somehow, using her first name just seemed friendlier and she needed to find some sort of an opening if she was going to forge a bridge between them.

Brandon looked bored. "Whatever," he said dismissively. And then, in case there were any lingering doubts about the situation, he told her in no uncertain terms, "I don't know what you thought when you came here, but I'm not some kind of a guinea pig for you to practice on so you can earn your merit badge or whatever it is you're trying to get out of this."

She realized that he was trying to get her angry, angry enough to walk out. She had no intentions of letting him.

"What I'm trying to 'get out of this' is to find a way to help you help yourself," she explained patiently. "No matter how you feel about it, Brandon, I'm not the enemy here."

"Okay, you're not the enemy," he parroted. "*Now* can I go?" he demanded.

Chloe glanced at her watch—as if she wasn't keenly aware of every second that went by. "We've got another forty-five minutes left to the session."

Brandon slouched in his chair, crossing his arms defiantly across his chest as he glared at her. "So you're what, a shrink?" he wanted to know, his hostility almost palpable.

"I'm a counselor," she corrected, fervently wishing she had more ammunition at her disposal for this battle she suddenly found herself in.

"Uh-huh." Hostility momentarily turned to boredom, and he deliberately yawned. "Same difference."

"Not exactly," she told him. In actuality, there was a world of difference, especially in the two disciplines' approaches to the people they dealt with. But she wasn't about to bore Brandon further by explaining them. "Tell you what," she said instead, "why don't I ask you some questions and you can fill in the blanks for me. How would that be?"

He made no answer, other than to scowl and to slouch even lower in his chair, his body language telling her that he didn't care one way or another what she proposed to do.

Chloe had to concentrate not to allow the hand that was holding Brandon's file to tremble. Showing fear was the worst thing she could do, and she knew it.

"According to the information on your entrance form, you had an older brother, Blake, who was killed—"

Brandon instantly sat up, and his body became almost rigid as his eyes blazed accusingly at her. "You shut up about my brother!" he ordered.

She couldn't do that. If she hadn't thought so before, she knew now that Blake was at the root of Brandon's anger. Chloe pressed on.

She understood what he was going through better than he knew, she thought.

"Your brother did a noble thing," she told him in a calm, even voice. "Don't you think that should be acknowledged?"

"No!" Brandon shouted at her. And then he cried, "My brother did a stupid thing! If he hadn't joined the military, he wouldn't have gotten himself killed. He'd still be alive today. He'd still be here! With me!" His voice cracked as he made the declaration.

"Brandon," Chloe continued in a quiet voice, doing

her best to try to calm him, "I know that you're hurting right now—"

His temper flared again. "Don't talk like you know me!" He jumped to his feet now. "You don't know anything about me!" he insisted furiously.

Chloe refused to back down. If she retreated right now, she might as well give up. "I might not know you, but I know how you feel," she told him doggedly as she tried again.

"No, you don't! Don't say that!" The boy looked like he was fighting back tears. "Nobody knows how I feel!"

With that, Brandon dashed right past her and out the door.

He would have dashed down the hall and presumably out of the house if he hadn't run straight into Chance, blindly colliding with the towering cowboy.

The impact might have knocked Brandon to the floor if Chance hadn't reacted quickly and caught hold of the boy by his shoulders.

"Hey, where's the fire?" Chance asked. The next moment, he saw Chloe coming up behind the fleeing boy. He saw the look of concern on her face. "Everything all right here?" he wanted to know.

Unlike his first question, this one was addressed to Chloe.

"Everything's all right," she told Chance resolutely. She caught the surprised look that Brandon slanted her way. "I just decided to end the session a little earlier than planned. Since this is our first session, I thought maybe Brandon needed a little time to digest what we talked about before we could move forward."

Chance looked at the boy he was still holding steady.

He had his doubts about the validity of what Chloe was telling him.

"Is that so?" he asked, looking at the boy.

Brandon shot a look toward Chloe, and Chance could read his thoughts. The teen was calculating his next move, deciding if now was the time to play the odds or to just go along with things.

His gaze flickered as if he'd decided to run with the excuse Chloe had handed him. "Yeah, getting used to someone new takes time. The doc's giving me time."

Chance looked over the boy's head at Chloe. "Is that what you're doing, Doc?" he asked, even though he was highly skeptical about the excuse he was being given. "Are you giving Brandon time so he can get used to you?"

Chloe nodded. "This was an introductory session only," she said, her eyes meeting Brandon's. "The next one will be longer. Right, Brandon?"

Rather than agree, Brandon merely raised and lowered his thin shoulders in a careless, disinterested shrug. "You're the doc," the boy replied.

"Well, since you're free," Chance told the boy, "there's that stall waiting for you to muck out." He saw the face that Brandon unintentionally made. He didn't pretend not to notice. "You know the rules. Chores first, then you can ride—unless of course you want to talk to the doc here some more," Chance said, offering the boy a choice.

Brandon waited, as if he was actually weighing his options for a second. And then he made his choice. "I'll be at the stable."

He walked toward the rear of the ranch house to the exit closest to the stable.

Chance turned his attention to Chloe and saw the disappointed expression on her face. "Didn't go all that well, huh?"

He was kidding, right? "Well, I just took second place to cleaning out manure in a horse stall, so no, it didn't go all that well."

Chance laughed, not at her but at the situation. "Don't take it personally. The kid's mad at the world right now." Graham had given him a quick background summary for all four of the boys. Chance felt for them, even if he wasn't prone to showing it. "He looked up to his big brother, thought of him as invincible. When it turned out that his brother wasn't bulletproof, it threw the kid for a loop. He's still trying to find a place for himself in a world that no longer has his big brother in it. That is *not* an easy adjustment to make," he told her. "Especially at Brandon's age."

"Losing someone is not an easy adjustment to make at *any* age," she told Chance in no uncertain terms. "I was trying to tell Brandon that. Trying to let him know that I understand what he's going through."

Chance was closer to the boy's situation than he cared to admit, so he tried to explain to her just what she was up against.

"He's not ready to hear that," Chance told her. "Right now, he's wrapping himself up in that pain and anger that he feels. That rage. It's the only way he has to cope. Without it, he's afraid that he'll just break down, fall to pieces and never be able to get back up. Being angry is all he has," Chance stressed, trying to make her understand. "You take that away from the boy before he's ready to let it go and, well, there's no telling what can happen."

It was a warning. He didn't want her good heart to accidentally cause her to make a really bad mistake. He had a feeling that she'd never forgive herself.

Chloe laughed shortly. He had a better handle on the situation than she did, she thought ruefully. "You know, you sound pretty wise for a cowboy."

The corners of Chance's full mouth curved just the slightest bit. "I think, on behalf of cowboys everywhere, I should be taking offense at that."

She wasn't getting anything right today, was she? "I didn't mean it that way," she told him apologetically.

He laughed and stopped her before she could launch into a full-scale apology. He'd just been trying to tease her out of her very serious mood. "I know. I'm just having fun with you."

It was her turn to turn the tables on him. "You can do that?" she asked, pretending to be surprised. "You can have fun?"

"I've been known to," Chance deadpanned. "Every once in a while."

It suddenly occurred to her that Chance was standing much too close to her. So close, she wondered if he could hear her heart beating fast. So close that she was sure he could easily kiss her without any effort at all.

And although the thought of being kissed by Chance did instantly raise her pulse rate, Chloe knew that kissing him would be a huge mistake, especially for her. Because being kissed by and kissing Chance would mean opening a door to a place she had absolutely no desire to revisit.

A place filled with feelings.

The very idea of having feelings for someone—*those*

kinds of feelings—much less falling in love with that person, scared Chloe beyond words.

And right now, she needed all her words in order to reach the four boys whose care she had been charged with. That left her no time for anything else, she silently lectured herself. No racing pulses, no pounding hearts. No sexy cowboy to cause her imagination to take flight.

"Um, I'd better get ready for my next session," she told Chance, backing away.

"Who are you seeing?" he asked.

Good. She could talk about work. There was safety in that. "Will Sherman. Hopefully, I'll do better my first time out with him than I did with Brandon."

He'd asked her who she was seeing next for a reason. So he could offer her some help. It was obvious that she needed it.

"That one's got trust issues," he told her. "Because his mother turned on him and beat him so badly, he's closed down. But the good news is that he really doesn't want to be like that. You can make a connection if you're patient enough. Just go slow, and listen. He'll open up eventually."

"Sounds like he already has," Chloe said. "With you."

Chance didn't want her thinking that he was treading on her toes. "No, I'm just good at reading signs," he told her. And then, in an effort to make her understand, he reminded her, "I'm good with horses." It wasn't a boast, just a fact. "They don't talk, either. But if you watch them closely, you get to understand what they want, what they need. Once you know that, gaining their trust is easy and inevitable. Same goes for people, too."

She smiled at him. He'd just summarized an entire

year's worth of studies in a few sentences. The man was a natural, she thought. He should probably be in her place.

But there was no sense in talking herself out of a job she both wanted and needed, Chloe thought. So she simply said, "Thank you. I'll keep that in mind. Now I'd better get ready for my next session."

He nodded. "And that's my cue to get out of here," he said—just before he did.

Chapter 7

The 747s in her stomach were finally down to the manageable size of normal butterflies. Maybe even *small* butterflies, Chloe thought.

She'd been counseling the boys for a couple of weeks now and she was slowly getting used to it, to the routine that Sasha had instituted. After enduring rather tense initial sessions with each of the four boys, she knew what she was up against with them now. They were coming to the office for private sessions three, sometimes four times a week. More if any of them felt they needed it or if they sought a little extra guidance with something they were attempting to work out.

Although conducting a one-on-one had been admittedly scary to her at first, Chloe decided that maybe Sasha was right after all. The four boys had plenty of time to interact with one another while they did their chores and when they spent time riding under Chance's supervision, not to mention that they were always all together at mealtime.

Going with the philosophy that everyone needed their own space and the idea that the boys might be more inclined to open up about something that was bothering them if they didn't have to make a public declaration of it, Chloe continued to see each of them on an individual basis rather than meeting with them as a group.

The two boys who had been at Peter's Place longer were in a better place mentally than the two newer arrivals. Jonah and Ryan had had more time to work out their anger and the issues that had brought them here in the first place. Happily, they both seemed as if they had gotten back on track again after their emotional derailments had threatened to turn them into repeat offenders. Thanks in part to her and to Sasha's joint efforts, both boys were learning how to cope with the curves that life had thrown at them and might very well throw at them again.

None of the battles had been won yet, especially not in the individual cases of Brandon and Will, but Chloe felt that the latter two were definitely taking baby steps in the right direction. It made her proud that she could say that she was a part of their progress, slow though it might seem.

Her own life might still need some work, Chloe thought, but at least she was helping four teens with their whole lives ahead of them work toward fulfilling their destinies. That was definitely something to be proud of, she told herself.

"You look pretty happy with yourself," Chance observed the next time that their paths crossed—which unbeknownst to her was as often as Chance could make happen. Ordinarily, he would have kept to himself the way he usually did, but there was something about this woman that just seemed to burrow into him, to pull him out of the solitary state he'd learned to prefer. She made him remember another time when life hadn't been so deadly serious. When sadness hadn't been his constant companion.

"Actually, I am—kind of," she added, lest Chance think she had an ego problem, or that she was giving herself way too much credit.

Chance read between the lines. "I take it that things are going well on your end with the boys," he guessed. He leaned against the doorjamb to her office. "I don't hear any of them grumbling in the corral anymore. Oh, Brandon still has a bit of an attitude problem when it comes to doing some of his chores, but even he's toned down somewhat in the last week. So I guess whatever it is you're doing here with them, you're doing it right," he told her with an encouraging grin. Then he summed it up simply. "It's working."

He was being kind, she thought. This wasn't just her doing. She really doubted that the tall, quiet cowboy was unaware of the effect that he had on the boys.

"Thanks, but I realize that it's a team effort. What you do with them when they're with you is just as important when it comes to stabilizing their mental health and turning them into well-adjusted young men as what's being said here in this room when the door's closed."

Chloe couldn't help thinking that Chance was the epitome of the strong silent type, enduring things without complaint, and that had to make a real impression on these boys, all of whom were in need of a strong father figure they could look up to and use as a role model. Even if they didn't consciously realize it.

Chance merely nodded, not about to argue with her about it. Arguing had always seemed like a waste of time to him.

"If you say so. Say, are you free now?" he asked suddenly. "I don't know what Sasha's got you doing when you're not counseling the boys, but I'm going to have them out in the corral, exercising their horses in a few minutes, and you're welcomed to come out and watch. Maybe it'll help you with their sessions later on," he speculated. Then a rather infectious smile split his lips. "Who knows, you might even enjoy getting a little fresh air. It might get to be habit-forming," Chance teased.

"Are you hinting that I'm some kind of a hermit?" Chloe retorted. Was that how he saw her? The idea bothered her more than she was willing to admit.

Chance looked perfectly serious as he elaborated. "Not a hermit, exactly. Hermits don't interact with people. But what are those people called? You know the ones I mean," he said, as if hunting for the correct word. "The ones who don't go out in daylight?"

Her eyebrows rose up so high that they all but disappeared beneath her bangs. "Vampires?" she guessed, stunned. "Are you saying I'm a vampire?"

"Well, no, not exactly," he said, backtracking just a little. "You definitely don't suck blood or anything like that, but those vampires you mentioned, they're supposed to have a thing about not going out into the daylight, don't they?"

"I wouldn't know," she informed him a little stiffly.

"Well, I've heard talk," Chance allowed, completely deadpan. But then a smile teased the corners of his mouth, bringing out the same sexy dimples in his cheeks, the ones that made her stare at him, dream about him, even though she told herself not to. "I'm just messing with you," he admitted with a laugh that backed up his words. "But you are kind of pale," he pointed out a little more seriously.

Chloe wanted to protest, but in good conscience, she couldn't. She knew she really was pale, especially in comparison with Chance.

So instead, she inclined her head, conceding the point. "I guess I do stay indoors a lot."

"Well, there's one way to fix that," Chance said, reminding her of the invitation he'd just extended to her a couple of minutes ago. "Come outside to the corral and watch the boys put their horses through their paces. You might even find that you enjoy it. I kind of suspect that the boys will enjoy showing you what they've learned when it comes to handling horses, seeing as all of them were city kids when they came here."

Initially, she'd thought of Chance as being exceptionally closed-mouthed. She was going to have to reassess her original impression of the man.

"You know, for a man who claims not to be much of a talker, you certainly do know how to sell something," she told him with genuine admiration.

He looked at her in all innocence, as if he had no idea what she was talking about.

"I'm not selling anything," he told her. "I'm just telling you the way things are. Nothing more, nothing less. If you're interested in *really* joining in," he went on, "we've got a real gentle mare in the stable named Mirabel. Mirabel wouldn't hurt a fly. You can saddle her up and ride her along with the boys if you want."

Chloe was already vigorously shaking her head. "No, that's okay. No riding. I'll come out to watch the boys, but I'm just coming along as a spectator, not as a rider," she told Chance emphatically.

She'd succeeded in arousing his curiosity. "You ever been on a horse?"

"This is Texas," Chloe told him, as if that fact should be enough of an answer for him.

But he saw what she was trying to do. Chloe was being evasive, trying to use a diversion rather than answering his question outright.

Chance smiled at her. "I know where we are. I didn't ask you that. I asked if you've ever been on a horse. A moving horse," he specified in case she was going to pretend that she thought he meant a merry-go-round or a hobby horse of some sort.

Chloe bristled for a moment. She didn't like being cornered. She also didn't like admitting to any shortcomings, and as she'd already said, this *was* Texas, where everyone was thought to be born on the back of a horse, or at least knowing how to ride one.

For a second, she thought of bluffing her way through this, but then she decided that he was undoubtedly going to find out sooner or later. Better to tell Chance the truth, embarrassing though she felt it was, than be caught in a lie, which, when she came right down to it, was even more embarrassing to her.

"My whole childhood was a hand-to-mouth existence for my late mother and me. Horseback riding was a luxury we couldn't afford—or even have time for, actually," Chloe told him honestly, a solemn look on her face. "I grew up in a run-down section of the city. There was no 'horse next door,'" she quipped.

Chance nodded, straightening. His relaxed stance was gone as his eyes met hers and he looked at her intently. For a moment, she couldn't read his expression.

"So then you don't know how to ride a horse," he concluded.

"I thought that was what I was telling you," she said with a touch of impatience.

He nodded, as if he had just been given a problem to work with. Taking her elbow as he spoke, he carefully urged her toward the doorway, and then guided her out. "We're going to have to take care of that little oversight first chance we get."

The last thing she wanted was to have him see her being inept at something. "I think we both have a lot more pressing things to concern ourselves with than my lack of riding skills," she told him. They were being paid to work with the boys, not to broaden their own skills.

"No law that says we can't do more than just one thing," he replied. Long ago, Chance had learned when to retreat, so for now, he did. "For starters, just come with me to watch the boys. You'll see there's nothing to be afraid of." The easy smile was back as Chance told her, "Think of it as getting two birds with one stone."

She was keenly aware that he'd used the word *afraid*. Was that what he thought? That she was afraid of horses? Afraid of riding?

"I'm not afraid of riding a horse," she protested. "I told you, it's just something I never got around to."

"If you're not afraid, that's good," he pronounced. "That's one less thing for you to overcome."

She'd been so focused on what he was saying—and on trying to dispel this afraid-of-her-own-shadow image he seemed to have of her—that she didn't realize he had brought her out behind the back of the house. They'd gone past the guesthouse, where she was staying, and over to the corral.

All four boys were already there, along with the horses whose grooming and feeding they were each charged with. Five horses were saddled and ready to be ridden, even though the boys still had their feet firmly planted on the ground.

Jonah, who'd been there the longest and in everyone's estimation had come along the furthest, was standing between two horses, the one he had been caring for the last few months and the one that Chance rode when he was out riding with them.

Chance nodded at Jonah in acknowledgment, but before taking his stallion's reins from him, he turned toward Chloe first.

"You'll be all right here?"

She was surprised that he took the time to take her into consideration. "You asking me or telling me?" She couldn't tell from his tone.

That small smile she was growing so familiar with curved just the corners of his mouth. "Asking, mostly," he replied.

She didn't see why he was concerned. For the most part, she was out of the way here. "Sure—unless you suddenly decide to all ride toward me, at which point I'll probably be flattened."

Chance suppressed a wider smile as he shook his head. "Nope, no flattening. Not on the agenda today," he told her. And then he nodded toward the fence directly behind her. "If you want, you can climb up on the fence and straddle it. You'll get a better view that way," he told her.

Chloe looked over her shoulder, glancing at the fence a little uncertainly, even though she told him, "Maybe I will."

He caught the hesitancy and recognized it for what it was. Chloe wasn't one for climbing, he guessed. "Need a boost?" he asked.

Just because he asked, she was determined not to accept it. She tossed her head, sending her blond hair flying over her shoulders. "No, I can manage," she informed him.

But she actually couldn't, she discovered as she attempted to climb up the fence's slats.

Just as she realized she was in serious danger of falling backward and not just embarrassing herself but possibly hurting herself as well, she felt a very firm hand on her backside.

Sucking in her breath, she tried to look over her shoulder only to have Chance chide, "Steady or you're liable to fall. I'm not getting fresh here, I'm just trying to keep you from breaking anything fairly important," he told her. And then the next second, as he helped get her to the top, he declared with a note of triumph, "There you go. Now you've got a better view. Just don't get it into your head to leave before I get back to help you down," he warned.

And with that, Chance headed over to the cluster of boys.

He nodded at Jonah. "Thank you," he said as he took the reins from the group's oldest member. "Looks like we've got ourselves an audience today, boys. Show her what you've learned—and remember, don't embarrass me or yourselves," he reminded them as if that was one of the rules of procedure instead of something he was just now telling them.

"Is she going to be riding with us?" Ryan wanted to know.

"No, Ms. Elliott's strictly here as an observer," Chance answered. "So, no fancy stuff—and no slacking off, either," he told the boys. "Just nice and easy, like I showed you." He glanced toward Brandon, who looked as if he was ready to kick the horse's flanks and lead the others in a gallop around the corral. "Nice and easy, Brandon," he repeated with emphasis. "This isn't the preliminary trial for the Kentucky Derby. Remember, these are horses, not your personal toys," he warned them. "You push your horse too hard and you're back on stable duty—full-time. Are we clear?" he asked, looking around at the four faces before him.

"Clear," they all responded, their young voices blending together.

Chance nodded. "Okay then, let's show Ms. Elliott what you've learned."

Delighted, Chloe watched as the boys put the horses through their paces. The gaits varied from simply walking along the perimeter of the corral, to trotting to finally galloping at a moderate pace. She thought that was the end of it, but then she saw that the boys began leading their horses through several other exercises, one of which involved weaving in and out as if they were following the beat of a song that only they could hear.

When they were finally finished, the four riders lined up next to each other and then, almost in unison, turned toward her to see if she had enjoyed the show they had put on for her.

Chloe applauded enthusiastically. "That's wonderful," she told the boys.

"I wouldn't exactly say *wonderful*," Chance told her, bringing his own horse up to where she was perched on the fence. "But at least they've learned to follow the rules." He paused, looking at the four boys, who brought their mounts closer to where Chloe was sitting. "I'm talking about the boys, not the horses. The horses already knew how to follow the rules. All they needed was to have someone issue them."

Turning in his saddle, he looked at her. "So, how about it?"

His question came out of the blue and caught her completely off guard. "How about what?"

"Are you willing to give it a try now?" Chance wanted to know.

She suddenly realized that there were five sets of eyes turned in her direction, waiting for her to answer.

Chapter 8

It took Chloe a minute before she realized that the cowboy was serious. When she did, she was quick to respond to his question.

"No, not right now," she told Chance, doing her best to avoid looking at the four boys. "I've got all that paperwork I need to catch up on," she added vaguely, coming up with the first excuse she could think of.

With care and effort, she managed to climb down off the fence.

But she found that her exit was blocked, not just by Chance, but by the boys, still on their horses, as well.

"C'mon, Ms. Elliott. Try it. It'll be fun," Ryan coaxed.

"We won't let anything happen to you," Jonah promised solemnly, adding his voice to the others. "Mirabel really *is* the gentlest horse on the ranch, honest."

"And Jonah and I will ride on either side of you, to

make sure you don't fall off," Ryan added, obviously thinking she needed extra convincing.

It was clear that they thought she was inept when it came to horses, never mind that she really was. She didn't want that shortcoming to be general knowledge. That was the sort of thing that would make her stick out like a sore thumb on the ranch.

She looked accusingly at Chance. "What did you tell them?"

"Not a thing," Chance answered. "They're capable of figuring things out on their own."

"Horses aren't anything to be afraid of," Brandon told her, speaking up. Then he glanced at his bunkmate. "Right, Will?"

The latter flushed. When he opened his mouth, it became apparent why. "Hey, when I came here, I'd never been around a horse before." He gestured to the mount he was on. "But I learned how to ride."

"You rode very well," Chloe told him, impressed. She was well aware of the fact that it had taken a lot of work for the boys to be able to ride as effortlessly as they did now. "You all did," she added. And then Chloe looked around at all four of their faces. The light dawned on her. "Oh, I see what you're doing."

The face Ryan turned toward her was one of complete innocence. "What are we doing?"

Like he didn't know. "You're trying to get me so caught up in what you're telling me that I forget all about not wanting to get up on a horse and riding it. *That* horse," she amended, seeing the saddled dapple gray mare that Chance was leading toward her.

"Will you?" Jonah asked.

"We meant what we said. Jonah and I won't let Mirabel run off with you—not that she ever would," Ryan quickly added. "I'm just saying what you're thinking."

"So now I've turned you all into mind readers, huh? I guess the sessions are going better than I thought they were," she told the boys with a grin. She was feeling rather proud of her accomplishments when it came to the teens. Which just reinforced her determination not to look like an inept fool around them.

"Now *you're* doing it," Ryan told her, shooting her a shrewd look.

She looked at him innocently. "Doing what?"

"You're trying to distract us," Ryan told her. "You're getting us to talk about something else so we forget about giving you that riding lesson."

It was like being faced with four tenacious pit bulls. Once they sank their teeth into her, they were holding on for dear life. Well, she could play that game, as well. "I don't need a riding lesson," she protested.

Chance brought his horse closer to her. "I thought those sessions of yours were all about always telling the truth," he said.

They were really ganging up on her, she thought. But she was determined to stand her ground. "They are."

"Well?" he asked, looking at her pointedly. She didn't have to look at the boys; she felt their stares. They were all thinking the same thing, that she wasn't owning up to her shortcoming.

And then it occurred to her how to answer them. "I don't need a riding lesson because I don't *want* to know how to ride. Now if you boys—" she deliberately looked at all of them, including Chance "—will excuse me, I really do have work to do. But good job, all of you," she told them again enthusiastically.

With that, Chloe made her way back to the main house, keenly aware that she was being watched by five sets of eyes as she walked.

She really did have work to catch up on, she thought defensively. It just wasn't as pressing as she made it sound.

What *was* pressing was her need to get away. *Now.*

Chloe wasn't sure if she imagined the knock on her door that evening until she heard it a second time. There was definitely someone at her door.

It was after dinner and rather than linger at the big house with Graham and his family the way she had done on several occasions now, Chloe had left the table early and retreated to her quarters in the guesthouse. She wanted a little time to herself to regroup.

She was still feeling somewhat uncomfortable about this afternoon and the fact that she'd had trouble owning up to not being able to ride.

She had to remember that it was okay not to be perfect, she told herself. It was just that she was trying really hard to present a strong front before these boys.

Maybe, she thought, it was one of them at the door. Perhaps one of them wanted to talk to her about this afternoon. Probably to give her more of a pep talk, she surmised.

Chloe smiled to herself. They were all rather sweet in their own way, and she appreciated that they were trying to be supportive of her.

Maybe she'd just forget about being nervous and throw herself into learning how to ride. It seemed like practically everyone in the state did it, she reasoned. How hard could it be?

It was definitely something to think about.

Tomorrow.

Psyching herself up, Chloe swung open the door. The cheery "Hi" she was about to utter never made an appearance when she saw it wasn't any of the boys standing on her doorstep.

It was Chance.

Ever since she'd lost Donnie, her first thoughts always seemed to entertain a dark explanation. "Is something wrong?" Chloe asked, her heart already lodged in her throat.

Chance's answer was annoyingly vague. "That depends on your point of view."

Damn it, for a plainspoken man he could be maddeningly unclear. "Meaning?" she demanded.

He crossed the threshold, but made no effort to come any farther into her quarters than that. "Meaning that you tried to lie to those boys."

He was referring to her initial pretense of knowing how to ride. She didn't care for his accusation, especially in light of the way things turned out. "Well, they wound up hearing the truth so it's not really lying, is it?"

His eyes pinned hers, making her want to squirm. "What would you call it?"

She could tell him exactly what she would call it. "I'd call it not wanting them to think any less of me."

That didn't make any sense to Chance. "Because you can't ride?" he asked incredulously. Why would they think any less of her for that? "Why? You never told them you traveled with the rodeo as a trick rider."

Why did she think he would understand her motivation? The cowboy had probably never known an insecure moment in his life. He was perfect at everything he did, and he knew it.

"Let's just drop it, all right?" she said shortly.

"Sure," he agreed, then added one condition. "As soon as you come out with me." Just to ensure that she would, Chance caught her hand in his and began to lead her outside.

Not wanting to cause a scene, she went along reluctantly. "Just where are we going?" she wanted to know.

"Don't look so spooked," he said with a short laugh. "I'm not kidnapping you."

Damn it, was he laughing at her? She was *not* going to be his source of amusement just because she didn't measure up to Annie Oakley in his eyes.

"I know you're not kidnapping me and I'm not spooked," she said between gritted teeth. Chloe tried to dig in her heels and found that it was a totally futile act. "But I do want to know where you're taking me."

Chance spared her a glance over his shoulder. "It's not what you think," he assured her calmly, wanting her to know that he had no intentions of getting physical with her in any way.

The problem was, it *was* the first thing that came to her mind. She instinctively knew that Chance was an honorable man, that he wouldn't just drag her off somewhere in order to have his way with her. He just wasn't that sort of person. But even so, she could feel her cheeks getting flushed, heating up and turning a deep shade of red that by no stretch of the imagination was her natural shade.

"Okay," Chloe retorted. "Then you tell me what to think."

She didn't expect him to laugh at that, but he did. "Oh, I doubt very much that there's a man alive who could do that, Chloe."

Maybe she *was* a woman who couldn't be told what to think, but if she was as independent as Chance was giving her credit for, she would have never allowed him to drag her out of her quarters in the first place.

Fueled by that thought, she demanded again, "Where are you taking me?"

"Some place where you can get rid of your inhibitions," he told her simply as he continued to pull her along behind him.

Okay, he was beginning to make her nervous. *Was* he taking her somewhere so that he could—that they could—damn it, how could she be so wrong about a person?

Nervous, incensed, she finally did manage to dig her heels into the ground, making him come to an abrupt stop. When he turned to look at her quizzically, she informed him in no uncertain terms, "I don't want to get rid of my 'inhibitions.'"

"Sure you do," he contradicted. She was about to yank her hand out of his and make a run for the main house when he went on to say, "No self-respecting Texan wants people to think that they can't ride."

"Can't ride?" she echoed. Panic and anger evaporated instantly. "This is about *riding*?" she questioned.

"Not exactly," he amended. "This is about teaching you the fundamentals of riding and ultimately getting you on the back of a horse. If that goes well," he continued, a hint of a smile curving his lips, "then we'll let Mirabel move a little with you on her back and we can call it 'riding' if anyone asks."

He led her to the stables, and when they entered, Chance let go of her hand. There was no need to continue pulling her in his wake. Turning around to face her, he told Chloe honestly, "And if you're going to ask me why I'm doing this, it's because I saw the look on your face earlier."

She didn't know what he was talking about. "What look?"

"The one that you had when you admitted to the boys that you didn't know how to ride. I figured it really bothered you more than you were willing to say. And when something winds up bothering you that much," he told her, bringing her over to Mirabel's stall, "you've got to do something about it or it'll just wind up haunting you." His eyes met hers for a moment. "I know all about things haunting a person," he told her. "Trust me, it's not a good thing."

He cleared his throat, as if that was enough to chase away the emotion that he had accidentally unearthed. He'd gotten very good at blocking out unwanted feelings—except in the middle of the night, when he had no control over them.

He forced himself to focus on Chloe. "Now, take it from me. There's no more peaceful place in the whole world than on the back of a horse, and the sooner you find that out for yourself, the better you're going to feel about the whole experience," he promised.

She was surprised to see that the mare was saddled, as if she was about to be taken out for a ride. Had Chance been that sure that he was going to get her to come here at this hour?

"And we have to do this now?" she asked him.

In response, he offered her that easygoing, sexy smile

that transformed his uncompromising expression into a very compelling one. "No time like the present," he told her.

"Oh, I can think of plenty of other times," she assured Chance. She was doing her very best to hide her nervousness.

Despite her efforts, he saw right through them. Instead of making him feel sorry for her, or stopping him from continuing, it just urged him on. "Which is why this is the best time," he assured her.

The cowboy's reasoning completely mystified her. "How do you figure that?"

"The sooner you get over being afraid of riding," he explained patiently, "the sooner you'll be able to actually ride. And in no time at all, you'll find yourself wondering what the big deal was and what took you so long to get to it."

Chloe looked as if she was trying very hard not to be nervous, and he felt for her, but he also knew that what he'd just told her was true. She needed to meet this fear of hers head-on. He'd learned that firsthand. When he'd first returned to the States, all he'd wanted to do was go off into the wilderness and avoid people altogether. Separation, isolation—he realized that he just wanted to be alone to try and escape from the memories that plagued him of the death and devastation he'd seen. Loss of friends he'd served with, day in and day out had worn his soul to the breaking point—and yet he knew that logically he couldn't completely withdraw from society. He'd compromised by taking ranching jobs but never staying in any one place too long.

For his part, he couldn't see being afraid of riding, but then, except when he was stationed overseas, horses had always been a part of his life. It was like being afraid of the family dog.

"Give me your hand," he told her.

Instead of complying, she did just the opposite and pulled it behind her back.

"Why?" she wanted to know.

"Because I need a third hand," he quipped. Then his expression softened a little. "Just give it to me," he coaxed. "I promise this won't hurt."

Letting out a shaky breath, Chloe hesitantly put out her hand. He took it, covering it with his own, and guided it up to softly stroke the mare's muzzle.

"See, nothing to it," he told her, watching her expression. He was pleased to see her relax a little. Disengaging his hand from hers, Chance said, "Now you do it."

Holding her breath, Chloe did as he instructed, moving her fingertips lightly along the mare's coat. When Mirabel unexpectedly shook her head from side to side, as if tossing her mane, Chloe suppressed a gasp as she pulled her hand back.

"It's okay," Chance assured her. "Mirabel is a horse, not a statue. She's bound to make a few unexpected movements every now and then. She's not rejecting you. She's probably just inhaled something that's tickling her nose."

He paused a moment, allowing Chloe to regroup. "Now try it again," he urged.

It was meant as a suggestion, but to Chloe it sounded just like an order. Orders made her bristle. Still, she didn't want to come across like a coward in his eyes, so she put her hand on the mare's muzzle again and stroked it.

This time, the mare held still.

A smile lit up Chance's penetrating eyes. "See, that wasn't so bad, was it?"

"No," she admitted almost grudgingly, then added, "that was kind of nice."

She wasn't prepared for his question. "Think you'd like to get up on her?" he asked.

Her eyes widened. "You mean like ride her?"

Chance heard the nervousness in her voice and was quick to put her fears to rest. "No, I mean get up into her saddle and just sit still. We're not going anywhere just yet," he told her.

Standing beside the mare, Chloe looked up, judging where she would be sitting. She felt her stomach tightening.

"It's awfully high up," she said. "What if Mirabel decides to take off?"

"Her days of crashing through stable walls are definitely behind her." The second he assured her of that, he realized that Chloe thought he was being serious. "I'm kidding," he told her. "She's never crashed through a stable wall—or anything else for that matter. I'll help you up," he offered.

Chloe really didn't want to do this, but once she looked into Chance's eyes, she had the unerring feeling that he would keep her safe—even high up on a horse. So, reluctantly, she said, "Okay," and had him help.

Chance talked her through it, physically guiding her when he had to. He had her put her foot into the stirrup, then coaxed her through the steps until she swung her leg up over the mare's hind quarters, finally managing to get her other foot into the stirrup.

"You're doing fine," he told her.

"How come I don't feel fine?" Chloe challenged.

Probably because she looked stiff as a board, he thought.

"I've got an idea," he told her.

"I can get off the horse now?" Chloe asked him hopefully.

"No," he told her.

She didn't have very long to wait to see what he was up to. He took hold of the reins and in one fluid movement pulled himself up onto the horse directly behind her.

"What are you doing?" she cried, starting to turn in the saddle and then abruptly stopping because she was brushing up against Chance.

"My best to make you feel safer," he replied.

Having Chance so close that she could feel the heat from his chest against her back made her feel a whole host of sensations—but "safer" definitely wasn't one of them.

Chapter 9

He needed some air. Right now, the scent of Chloe's shampoo was filling up his senses and making him think and feel things he shouldn't be thinking *or* feeling. If he didn't get moving, he was liable to do something one of them was going to regret.

For a moment, in an act of self-preservation, Chance had considered just going ahead and guiding the mare outside. But he had a feeling that it was in the best interests of both of them if he asked her first. He thought it would be better if Chloe was prepared rather than just springing things on her. She seemed to be jumpy enough against him as it was.

"So," he asked her, "are you game?"

For the life of her, Chloe didn't know exactly what he was asking her. She knew what she *wanted* Chance to be asking her, but that would be leaving herself wide open for all sorts of complications that she knew she just couldn't handle.

"Game for what?" she asked uneasily.

"To take a little ride."

"And do what?" she asked suspiciously.

"Ride?" It was more of a question because he didn't know what she was expecting to hear, or what she wanted him to say.

"Oh. How far?"

She felt him shrug against her back. "I thought just around the outside of the stable for tonight. Next time we'll go farther—and on separate horses," he added. She heard the amusement in his voice. And then he asked, "Ready?"

Chloe was ready, all right. To jump off the horse and run back to her cottage. But for some reason she nodded her assent. Whom was she kidding? It wasn't the horse she wasn't ready for. It was Chance.

She wasn't ready to have his arms tighten around her as he took control of the reins, to feel his warm breath on her neck as he coaxed the mare out of the stable, to feel his muscled thighs around hers as they rode the perimeter of the corral. Not at all ready.

Suddenly the evening seemed to get too warm, and she had to steel herself against this man wrapped around her.

"You all right?" he asked her. "You're as stiff as a board."

She gave him the first excuse that came into her head. "Just trying not to fall off."

"You can't fall off," he pointed out. "I have you, and besides, Mirabel isn't exactly trotting. If she were going any slower, she'd be going backward."

Up against him the way she was, she couldn't get comfortable. It would mean lowering her guard, and she couldn't afford to do that. "I had no idea the corral was this large," she commented.

"It's not really. It just seems that way because we're moving around it at a snail's pace. We can go faster," Chance offered, pretending to get ready to kick his heels into the mare's flanks to make her pick up her pace.

"No, no," Chloe protested, raising a hand as if that somehow made her plea more emphatic. "This pace is just fine. Unless you mind," she added, suddenly realizing that riding like this had to be immensely boring to someone like Chance. Given this speed, any second now he was liable to fall asleep.

Mind? Chance thought, astonished that she should phrase it that way. Why would he mind having his arms around a beautiful woman, holding her a hair's breadth away from him?

Being here like this with Chloe reminded him that it had been a long, long time since he had allowed himself to get physically close to someone without worrying about the resulting consequences.

"No, I'm just fine," he assured her. "Matter of fact," he told her as they approached the stable door, "we can go around again if you'd like."

Yes, she'd "like"—which was just the problem. With very little effort, she could just close her eyes and transport herself to another place in time, a time when everything seemed right in the world.

A time when she fantasized about the future that lay ahead of her. A future that included the husband she loved and a family. Having Chance hold her like this made it so easy for her to remember—so easy to yearn.

She had to stop doing that, she silently upbraided herself.

It was time to stop dreaming and face reality—a reality that included neither her husband nor a family.

"No, that's all right," she told him. "Once is enough for now—if you don't mind. We both have things to do," she added, being deliberately vague.

"I don't," he told her honestly. Lord, but she smelled good, even out here with the night air diluting the mind-numbing scent that was still lingering in her hair. "This is the guys' free time," he pointed out, explaining, "They're either doing homework or just kicking back. After I check in on them, the rest of my evening is wide open," he told her.

"Oh, well, mine isn't."

What was with her? Two lies in one day? But she absolved herself of the guilt over this last one. It was self-preservation. She simply couldn't be around Chance in her vulnerable state. There was just something about having him close to her like this with the dusk slipping into nightfall that made her uneasy. Not because she thought that Chance might try something but because she was afraid that *she* might.

"I have to get back," she told him.

"Sure, I understand."

He wasn't about to make things difficult for her, and he certainly wasn't about to press her for details. The last thing he wanted was to make Chloe feel as if he was encroaching on her space or trying to box her in in any sort of way.

After bringing the mare back into the stable, Chance dismounted, then turned to face Chloe and offered her his assistance to get down.

Chloe hesitated, but she knew that she wasn't in any position to attempt a graceful dismount. Not yet. Because she had absolutely no idea how. So she took the arms that were being offered to her and allowed Chance to help her down.

That maneuver involved getting very close to him for another very long moment.

A moment in which her heart seemed to stop even as her pulse accelerated to double time.

Chance picked her up off the mare and brought her down, holding her by the waist and sliding the length of her body down a hint away from his until her feet were finally touching the ground.

He was holding her close enough for her imagination to vividly take flight—and to silently lament when he finally withdrew his hands from around her waist.

When she opened her mouth to thank him, Chloe found that she couldn't speak. Her mouth had completely gone dry, and her words stuck to the roof of her mouth.

Swallowing, she gave communication another try. This time, she did something more than just croak. "Thank you for the lesson."

Chance laughed shortly. "I'd hardly call that a lesson."

"Okay, have it your way," she allowed. "Thank you for the introduction…to horseback riding," she added belatedly, realizing it might sound as if she was thanking him for something entirely different.

"My pleasure," he told her.

It was only after she'd turned from him and began to hurriedly walk away, back to the guesthouse, that she heard him call after her, saying, "This isn't over, you know. I intend to give you that riding lesson."

"When I have time," she tossed over her shoulder without even looking back.

She wasn't about to make promises. She'd had enough of that.

"*Make* time."

It wasn't a suggestion; it was clearly an order.

His order rang in her ears as she all but ran the rest of the way to the guesthouse.

Chance remained outside longer than he knew he should have, watching her and admiring Chloe's form until she was gone from sight.

Nothing wrong with that, Chance told himself as he turned away and went back into the stable. *Just admiring one of the Lord's finer creations, nothing more than that.*

And he would continue telling himself that, Chance thought, until it finally stuck.

"Something on your mind?" Sasha asked her the next day.

Graham's wife had sat in on one of Chloe's sessions with Ryan and then another session with Brandon.

Chloe knew she had to be sporadically supervised, especially since she was so new to Peter's Place. But she still couldn't help being a little nervous.

Added to that was the fact that she kept expecting Chance to come walking in at any moment, announcing that he was going to give her another lesson. Right now it felt as if the last of her nerves had been worn down to a tiny nub. She felt so tense inside that if she were a guitar string, she would have snapped in half.

But she was trying her very best not to appear that way on the surface.

Judging by Sasha's question she wasn't succeeding very well.

"No," she replied, trying to sound laid-back. "Other than doing right by these boys," Chloe qualified at the last moment.

Sasha smiled. "Nice answer but not the one I was looking for." She leaned forward in her chair. "I mean, is there anything else going on? You seem like you're waiting for something to happen."

Obviously, being an undercover spy was never going to be an option for her, Chloe thought.

"No," she denied again. And then she decided to own up a little, hoping that would be enough for Sasha. "I guess being observed puts me on edge a little. I realize that I'm not as good as you are at this, but—"

"Nobody's comparing us," Sasha told her firmly. "We all have our own individual styles. I'm just here to observe whether or not you're connecting with the boys—and I'm happy to say that you are."

The truth was, Chloe was somewhat nervous about measuring up to the woman who had hired her. After all, these had initially been "Sasha's boys" and in a sense, they still were. She'd been rather afraid that both the boys and Sasha would view her as an interloper.

"You don't know how happy it makes me to hear you say that," Chloe told her.

"Then it's mutual," Sasha told her with a warm smile. "Because it makes me very happy to honestly be able to say that." Sasha looked at her a little more closely. "But are you sure there's nothing else? You don't need some time off, do you?"

"Time off?" Chloe echoed. "I just got here." She felt as if she was just beginning to get the hang of the routine. "I've still got a long ways to go before I make a niche at Peter's Place. Why would I want to take some time off?"

Sasha shrugged. "To acclimate yourself to the area a little more. This is different from living in the city," she said sympathetically.

"Amen to that," Chloe said with a laugh. "It's almost too quiet here at night to sleep, but I'm slowly getting used to that, too."

"So you're settling in?" Sasha asked.

"Absolutely," Chloe told her with feeling.

"I'm glad because I can't tell you how nice it is to have another woman around. I mean, I have the girls," she said, referring to her two daughters, "and I love them to pieces, but it'll be a lot of years before either one of them is anywhere near being someone I can actually talk to." She quickly amended, "I mean, Graham is a wonderful man and he's really great with the girls, but well, you know men, there's a lot they don't understand when it comes to the way we women feel."

Smiling at her, Sasha put her hand over Chloe's.

"I just want you to know that if you ever need to just talk—about nothing or about something—I'm here for you."

When Chloe couldn't help but laugh, Sasha looked at her a little uncertainly, wanting to be let in on the joke. "Did I just say something funny?"

"Not exactly." The whole thing struck her as rather ironic. "What you just said to me is what I told all four of the boys after I had my first session with each of them."

"Well, my offer was rendered from a nonprofessional position," Sasha said. "As a friend," she further qualified. And then she continued. "And as a friend, I have to say that being around you right now reminds me of that old adage, the one about being a cat on a hot tin roof."

"I make you think of that?" Chloe asked, secretly wondering if the same thing had occurred to Brandon and Ryan, the two boys she'd seen today for their sessions.

"Well, not exactly," Sasha admitted. "But certainly close to that. Tell me, are you waiting for something to happen, or for someone? Or is it just that I make you very nervous?"

"*You* don't make me nervous," Chloe quickly told her. How could she tell her boss that it was Chance who made her nervous?

It was time to be truthful with herself. To admit that she wasn't afraid of the riding lesson he intended to give her—or the horse—although she wasn't exactly confidence personified when it came to either. What had her feeling so internally jumpy was the man. And the prospect of her next interaction with him.

Her next *solo* interaction with him, she silently emphasized.

Interacting with Chance when there were others around was fine. They were just two employees at Peter's Place with the same prime focus: getting the teens assigned to the ranch to find their better inner core.

She could go on working alongside Chance all day like that.

It was the anticipation of being alone with him that had her acting like that so-called restless cat Sasha had just likened her to. Because being alone with Chance woke things up within her that were better off left dormant and sleeping.

She was certainly better off if they were left dormant and sleeping, Chloe thought.

Looking at Sasha now, she realized that the woman was still waiting for some sort of response from her as to why she was acting so unsettled.

Sasha seemed almost *hungry* for some sort of shared confidence, Chloe thought. She supposed that it was almost cruel of her not to say *something*, even though it was against the privacy she tried so desperately to maintain.

Taking a breath, Chloe made her decision. She'd confide in her half brother's wife. Maybe then they could move past this and get on with her work at Peter's Place.

"Chance wants to give me riding lessons," she told Sasha.

The other woman's face literally lit up.

Chapter 10

"Oh, really?" Sasha asked. If possible, she sat up even a little straighter, her interest unwaveringly engaged. Delight was all but vibrating in her voice.

"Yes," Chloe replied. Her voice was as quiet as Sasha's was vibrant and enthused.

"You don't know how to ride a horse?" Sasha questioned, clearly surprised.

Chloe shrugged. Not wanting to get into a discussion about that, she just said, "The opportunity never came up."

For a second, Sasha was quiet and Chloe thought that, mercifully, that was the end of the discussion on that topic. But then Sasha looked at her, her smile even wider than it had been a moment ago, her eyes dancing.

She clapped her hands together. "This is wonderful!" the woman exclaimed.

"I wouldn't exactly go that far," Chloe protested, not really sure why her newly discovered sister-in-law would be so happy to find out that there was this definite gap in her education. "It just…*is*," she finally said.

This was what she got for trying to be completely honest, Chloe thought a second later. Rather than moving on, she had the feeling that she was about to get sucked down in the ocean by the undertow.

If the gleeful look of anticipation on Sasha's face—the origin of which was a complete mystery to her—wasn't enough, Chance picked that exact moment to walk into the room.

The man had awful timing, Chloe thought, feeling her stomach tighten at the same time that there was this sinking sensation right in the center of it. She was definitely a woman torn.

"Speak of the devil," Sasha declared, amusement as well as pleasure surrounding every syllable that she uttered.

Chance looked just a little taken aback. "Since when have I become the devil?" he asked uncertainly, not quite sure what he'd just walked in on.

Sasha rose from her chair. The binder she'd brought in with her to make notes while observing Chloe's session was in her hands and pressed up against her chest.

"We were just talking about you," she said dismissively. "Well, I'm sure I hear Maddie calling for me so I'll just leave the two of you to it," she said.

Chloe shifted self-consciously. Sasha had all but held up a sign with instructions on it as to what she thought they should do next once she left and they were alone.

One of Chance's eyebrows arched as he turned to regard the woman who was left standing in the room.

"'To it?'" he asked Chloe, torn between being bemused and confused.

"I told Sasha you offered to give me riding lessons." Chloe cleared her throat. She couldn't remember when she had ever felt more awkward. "Sasha thought it was a good idea."

"Oh." He nodded as if comprehending what he had just walked in on—except that Chloe wasn't 100 percent convinced that he wasn't reading a great deal more into Sasha's comment. "Well, it is a good idea," he told her. "Everyone should know how to ride."

"I would think it's more a matter of preference," Chloe countered. "It's not like it's a life-or-death situation, like learning to swim."

Chance wasn't about to get into an involved discussion on the subject. He had a far simpler way to resolve it.

"Wouldn't you rather know how to do something than not know how to do it?"

Chloe suppressed a sigh. She supposed that Chance did have a point. And she didn't want him to think that she was reluctant to broaden her horizons.

"Sure."

She stood up, telling herself she was making way too big a deal out of this. Chance was just giving her a simple horseback riding lesson—same as what he was hired to do with the boys. She had to stop feeling so nervous about it.

So nervous about him.

A thought suddenly occurred to her. "Are you going to be teaching me to ride in the corral?"

Chance hadn't given it much thought. "Yes. That's where I've been doing it with the boys. Why? Would you rather not have your lesson there?" he asked, sensing her reluctance.

She avoided making eye contact with him as she spoke, not wanting to see amusement or something even more demoralizing in his eyes.

"I'd rather we didn't have an audience," she confessed. "Is there any place else that we could go for these lessons?"

"Sure. It's a big ranch," he reminded her. "I just thought you'd rather get your first lessons somewhere where you felt safe."

That was when she finally looked at him. "Why wouldn't I feel safe somewhere else?" she asked him.

"The corral's contained. If I give you riding lessons out in the open, I figure you'd worry that Mirabel could get it into her head to just run off with you on her back."

"Oh." Enlightenment came to her riding a thunderbolt. He wasn't talking about her feeling safer in the corral because she felt he wouldn't try to kiss her in broad daylight in front of possible witnesses. He was talking about the mare running off with her. "You've got the faster horse, don't you?" she asked.

"No disrespect meant for Mirabel, but yes, I do. By quite a lot when you come right down to it."

This time her eyes didn't leave his when she responded. "Then if something happens, say, to spook Mirabel, you could catch up to me on your horse, couldn't you?"

"If it came to that, yes. But from what I've been told, Mirabel doesn't spook easily. That's one of the reasons why I picked her for you."

She believed him. "Then I'd rather you took me

somewhere where no one else can watch and see how bad I am at this."

"You're not bad at riding," he told her. "You just need to learn the right techniques, that's all. It's not all that hard." He tried to soothe her, but he could see his words weren't working. "But if you feel that strongly about it, I know this quiet clearing not too far from the lake that'll do just fine for our purposes."

A quiet clearing by the lake sounded as if it would do fine for other purposes, too, Chloe thought. But she kept that to herself, hoping that the same idea hadn't occurred to him.

Because the lake was some distance from the corral, Chance decided to take her there on his horse. He told Chloe that right now it was safer for her if they rode double on his horse.

"What about Mirabel?" Chloe asked, wanting to be clear on the logistics. "Isn't she coming, too?"

"She'll be right behind us," he explained. "I'll just hold on to her reins so she doesn't get it into her head to hang back."

"And your horse won't mind?" she asked, looking at the black stallion that Chance had already saddled and was waiting for them in the stable. Mirabel was in the next stall, saddled, as well.

Chance unconsciously furrowed his brow. He wasn't sure he understood her question. "Mind what?"

"That we're both going to be riding on him at the same time?" She looked at the stallion doubtfully, worried about the extra weight.

Chance laughed, tickled by what she was innocently

suggesting. "He's fine with it," he told her. "He's not the jealous sort."

Chloe flushed. When he said it out loud like that, she realized that she sounded like an idiot. "I didn't mean…"

He was quick to try to save her from embarrassment. "I know what you meant. C'mon, we're wasting daylight," he urged. "Or was that the idea?" he asked, pretending to look at her as if the light had suddenly dawned on him.

"No," Chloe denied quickly. She wound up sounding almost breathless.

He was going to have to tread lightly with this one, Chance thought. Most of the time, he preferred to keep to himself and not bother interacting with people. It saved time and saved him from spinning his wheels. But he had to admit there was something about this woman that had burrowed under his skin.

He liked seeing the way her eyes flashed and the way she tossed her hair when she was digging in and being stubborn. But for all that, Chloe made him think that he was dealing with a vulnerable, wounded bird.

The whole thing was a revelation to him, he thought. He had never realized until just now that he had any desire to protect a wounded bird.

Or that he rather liked it.

Maybe his soul hadn't died on the battlefield after all.

"Then we'd better get going," he told her. "Come on. Let's get you up there."

The next moment, while Chloe was absently regarding just how much taller his stallion appeared in comparison with her mare, she felt strong hands come around her waist. Suddenly, she was airborne.

As her breath caught in her throat, Chance had her in the saddle in a matter of seconds. She barely had time to suppress the cry of surprise that had all but escaped from her lips.

And then, the next moment, there he was, right behind her. *Snuggly* right behind her, she couldn't help noticing as his body seemed to fit perfectly against hers.

A multitude of sensations went zipping through Chloe, some familiar, some brand-new, all unsettling.

A riding lesson, this is just a riding lesson, she silently insisted.

There was no need for her to react like this to *any* of this. Chance was just doing her a favor, teaching her how to ride so she could go out with the boys. She had to think of it in that light, she told herself.

And *only* in that light.

Chance brought his arms around her, picking up his horse's reins as he formed a protective circle around her.

"You all right?" he asked.

"I'm fine," she answered. *If you don't count the fact that my heart is just about ready to break the sound barrier.*

She felt Chance leaning into her. Her heart raced a little harder.

The next moment he was whispering into her ear. "I guarantee that you'll feel a whole lot better if you breathe."

"Right. Breathing," she agreed the next second.

And then, just to prove that she had heard Chance, she went on to elaborately do just that.

Chloe really didn't remember the journey to the clearing, at least, not when she thought if it in terms of miles or scenery. All she was aware of was how the gentle back-and-forth rocking of the stallion caused Chance's body to move seductively against hers. She was concentrating so hard on not reacting to him that she didn't even realize when they'd reached their destination.

"We're here," Chance announced.

The next second, without any warning, Chance was dismounting. Abruptly deprived of his support and thinking something had gone wrong, Chloe quickly turned to look down at him and wound up nearly tumbling out of the saddle.

"Hey, no sudden trick moves until after I'm satisfied that you know how to ride. We don't want to rush you off to the nearest doctor." He looked up at her face. She'd turned almost completely pale. "Hey, are you all right?" he asked, concerned. "I was just kidding."

"I knew that," Chloe mumbled although she clearly didn't.

"Good." He didn't believe her for a second. Chance extended his arms up to her and said, "Let's get you down from there." Taking hold of her waist, he eased her down until her feet were back on the ground. "This is the last time I'm going to help you dismount," he told her. "I'll teach you and then you're on your own."

He saw the apprehensive look that crept over her face. Rather than being off-putting, he thought she looked even more adorable.

"Don't worry," he assured her. "You'll do fine."

"I wasn't worried," she informed him perhaps a little too quickly.

He graciously accepted her protest, even though he felt he knew otherwise. "My mistake."

Bringing Mirabel closer to Chloe, he announced, “Okay. This is lesson number one.”

And so it began.

Chance patiently kept at it for the next four hours, verbally diagramming every move he wanted her to make so precisely that after a little while, Chloe forgot to be nervous.

Progress came by tiny inches—but it came.

At the end of the session Chloe had a good handle on the basics. He’d taught her how to fluidly mount her horse and how to dismount, as well. He’d taught her how to give the most basic commands to the animal so that the mare knew when she was expected to go and when to stop.

Through it all Chance didn’t raise his voice or lose his temper, nor did he easily dispense praise, either.

He did, however, let her know if she was doing something wrong so that she wouldn’t repeat it. On the few occasions that she did repeat her mistake, he patiently reviewed the steps again, and had her go through the paces over and over until she got it right.

And then, finally, when she thought she was never going to see it again, it happened.

Chance smiled.

“I think that’s it for today,” he told her.

She was exhausted and so ready to go home, but even so, she had to ask him. “That bad?”

“That good,” Chance corrected.

Her eyes fairly danced as she asked, “Really?”

“Really,” he echoed. “And our next session is going to be in the corral,” he informed her, “because you have nothing to be ashamed of. Now, for your reward, I want to take you to see something that a lot of people live out their whole lives without ever being able to see or appreciate."

"Oh? What?"

The nervousness was back in her voice, Chance thought. But he knew just how to put it to rest. Taking her hand, he led her over to the lake.

"Look," he said, pointing out what he wanted her to see.

Once again, Chloe's breath caught in her throat.

Chapter 11

Chance was right. It was glorious.

Chloe had seen sunsets before. They were, after all, a part of everyday life. But she'd never seen one like this.

Standing there with him, at the edge of the lake, she looked up at the sky.

And promptly had her breath stolen away.

There was a multitude of muted colors reaching out to the heavens, as if the sun was having one last hurrah before finally retreating into the dusk and then the darkness, where it would wait for dawn and a rebirth.

"I never get tired of seeing this," Chance told her. "Makes me realize how really beautiful nature is. It also makes me feel that no matter how bad things might seem, in the scheme of things, everything is going to be all right."

Listening to him, Chloe could appreciate the noble

sentiment—as well as the man who uttered it. "It is magnificent."

Maybe it *was* the sunset that did it. Or maybe it was standing here so close to Chance, being infused with a sense of peace she hadn't felt in a long time.

Maybe it was all of the above.

Chloe couldn't honestly pinpoint the reason. All she knew was that when she turned toward Chance, she felt this undeniable, incredible pull within her. Pulling her toward him.

It kept her transfixed so that when Chance lowered his head, bringing his lips close to hers, she didn't move. Didn't breathe.

Didn't do anything—except will the moment to go on forever.

Her wish increased tenfold when he finally kissed her.

The moment their lips met, she could feel something explode within her. Something gleeful and joyous, as if she had been holding her breath, waiting for this to happen from the first moment she'd met him.

Hoping this would happen, she realized.

And yet, it surprised her.

Surprised her that Chance kissed her. What surprised her even more was that she actually *felt* something rather than just the deadness that had existed within her ever since she'd first found out that Donnie was never coming back to her.

Chloe could sense her heart slip into a wild double-time beat when Chance deepened the kiss, when his arms went around her waist and pulled her flush against him.

Almost breathless, she laced her arms around his

neck, leaning into Chance as well as into his kiss. The sun might have been setting over the lake, but right now, it felt as if it was bursting out from within her, sending out long sunbeams to every single part of her.

She was certain that if Chance opened his eyes, he would see her glowing in the dark.

Chance wasn't sure just what had come over him. Yes, it was a beautiful sunset, and yes, he was here sharing it with a beautiful woman, but that alone wasn't enough for him to do what he was doing. They worked together, and he firmly believed that it was never a good idea to mix work with pleasure.

Since he'd come back from the service, he'd been a loner and the first to admit that things ultimately had a habit of not working out in these sorts of situations. When that happened, they wound up turning awkward. He made it a point to never stay in any one place for long, moving on when he grew restless, and he knew that he could do that here, too.

But there was something about this place, about the work that was being done, that appealed to him. That *spoke* to him. Peter's Place was a place he could believe in and for the first time in a long time, he found himself wanting to be a part of it, not just in a cursory way but in a way that actually mattered. That made a difference.

He wanted to make a difference.

That was all the more reason for not getting involved with a woman who worked here, he argued with himself. But again, there was just something about Chloe that reached right into his gut and grabbed him. Something that made him want to protect her, want to be her hero and want to make her smile.

Heaven knew that right now, *she* was making him

smile. Not only that, but it had been a very long time since kissing a girl had actually rocked his world, and she was certainly doing that right now for him.

So much so that he shed his common sense like a snake shed its skin and continued doing exactly what he had been doing.

Chance tightened his arms around her, getting lost in the kiss he had initiated. Getting lost in the sweet, heady fragrance he always detected whenever he was standing anywhere close to Chloe.

He could feel himself wanting her.

If she were any other woman who had crossed his path for the evening, he might have gone on to see where this would lead. But he instinctively knew that Chloe wasn't someone meant for a casual coupling—or even a torrid one. Chloe was the kind of woman a guy brought home to his mother—if he had a mother.

But for him that hadn't been the case for a long time now, he thought. His mother had died six months after he'd graduated high school. His father had died in a hunting accident years before that. Being on his own and alone had been a way of life for him and he'd made his peace with that.

Until now.

He didn't have to be told that Chloe could be easily hurt, and he already sensed that she *had* been hurt—badly—by something or someone. There was pain in her eyes when he looked into them, even when she was laughing at something. He wasn't about to add to that pain. He didn't need that on his conscience.

But he knew that if he continued kissing her like this, he was definitely going to want more, and he also knew that if he pushed, even just a little, he could convince her to make love with him.

But that's not how he wanted it to happen.

And that wouldn't be fair to her. So, hard though it was for him, Chance forced himself to draw his mouth away from hers.

His heart still hammering wildly, he made himself take a step back, although he still kept his arms around her waist, wanting to take comfort in that contact for just a moment longer.

Chloe's eyes sought his, and he saw the question in them. Why had he stopped? He also felt her shudder as she tried to catch her breath.

Chance was coping with a few struggles of his own. He wasn't accustomed to abruptly stopping like this once he'd started kissing a woman. But he knew he had to.

"I think we should be getting back before Graham sends out a search party to come looking for us."

The sun had all but set, taking almost all of the available light with it. But there was still just enough left for him to see that her cheeks had grown appealingly pink.

Had he embarrassed her by kissing her? Or embarrassed her by stopping? He couldn't tell.

"We wouldn't want that," she agreed. She kept her face averted as they walked back to their tree-tethered horses. "Thanks for the riding lesson," she told him, trying to sound casual. "And for sharing the sunset."

Chance laughed softly. "Not exactly mine to keep," he told her. "The sunset," he explained when he saw her looking at him quizzically. "As for the riding lesson, that was my pleasure." Mindful of her still-limited experience, he helped her mount, then swung onto his own horse. "But remember, you're not off the hook yet. I still have a little more to teach you."

As they headed back to the ranch, Chloe felt her thoughts—and her pulse—race. Maybe she was just reading things into what Chance had said, or maybe that kiss they'd shared had changed her focus. Whatever the reason, Chloe caught herself thinking that Chance had a great deal to teach her and riding was only a small part of it.

What's the matter with you? she upbraided herself as they continued riding to the main house. *One kiss and you're ready to forget about Donnie? Forget about what you had with Donnie?*

A shaft of guilt at her disloyalty to her husband's memory shot through her. How could she let herself get carried away like that?

Besides, that kiss probably didn't mean anything to Chance, she told herself. He was just taking advantage of an opportune moment, nothing more.

Just look at him, she thought, slanting a quick glance at him. The man was gorgeous, every woman's idea of the perfect cowboy. He undoubtedly had his pick of women, and that meant he had no need for a permanent relationship. Or any sort of a commitment.

Even if she was, by some wild chance, ready to allow herself to get carried away and start being serious about Chance, she knew she was bound to be hurt.

And the very last thing her heart needed was to be bruised. She already had gone through enough pain to last her a lifetime. There was absolutely no way she was going to set herself up to be hurt ever again—even if Chance was inclined to get involved with her, which she was willing to bet he wasn't.

She had a strong feeling that relationships weren't for him. The man was a loner. He'd all but told her so the first time they'd met.

No, she argued as they rode back, what happened at the lake was an aberration. A lovely aberration, but still just an aberration. And there wasn't going to be a sequel—ever—she told herself.

By now they had reached the ranch and were nearing the stable. Chloe was more than ready to call it a night.

But Chance had other ideas.

"You're not done yet," he told her.

She had no idea what to expect as she finally forced herself to look in his direction. "Oh?"

"I might have saddled Mirabel for you, but now it's time for you to learn how to take care of her. There's more to working with a horse than just riding it," Chance told her as he led the way into the stable. "So, since you're through riding her for the day, you have to unsaddle her. It's like when you were little and had to put away your toys when you were finished playing with them," he added, hoping the metaphor would help her get the idea.

There was just one thing wrong with his analogy, she thought, and she told him so. "I didn't have any toys when I was little."

That piece of information caught him by surprise. Just how poor had she been? At that moment it occurred to Chance that he really knew very little about this woman whom he found himself attracted to.

"No toys? None? Really?" he asked. After all, he knew that she was Graham's half sister. He'd just assumed that all the Fortunes were well cared for. But since there was no reason for her to lie, maybe she'd had it rougher than he'd thought. His heart—a heart he'd thought he'd forfeited on the battlefields of a foreign land—went out to her as he listened.

"Well, I did have one," she admitted. "I had a stuffed bear—Theodore," she told him, recalling the bear's name. "And I took Theodore everywhere, so I guess you might say that I never stopped playing with him. And since I didn't, I never put him away."

"What happened to Theodore?" he asked, curious.

He watched, fascinated, as a fond, faraway smile curved her lips. "I loved him to death and eventually, he just fell apart."

He dismounted before putting his horse in his stall. Chloe followed suit, and he came to join her.

"I guess then being loved by you comes with a price," he said.

She knew Chance just meant it as a joke, but the comment had her thinking of Donnie. And aching—on two counts.

"I guess so," she said quietly.

Her tone made him realize that he'd blundered. Chance quickly changed the subject to something more neutral.

"Because you're new at this, I'm going to walk you through it this time. But from now on, when we go riding, you'll have to saddle and unsaddle Mirabel—or any other horse if you decide to go on to a more lively one," he added.

There was no chance of that happening, Chloe thought. "Mirabel is lively enough for me, thank you," she told him. She was grateful to Chance for switching subjects. "And I'll be happy to saddle her the next time we go out—although I have to say that I'm not too sure how happy Mirabel will be about it."

"You do it right and she'll be fine," he told her. "It's not that complicated." And then he unconsciously went into teaching mode. "Okay, you'll need to loosen the cinch in order to get the saddle off."

"Loosen the cinch," Chloe repeated gamely, looking at the saddle. She had no idea what the cinch looked like or where it was located. Moreover, she was afraid if she did the wrong thing, the mare was going to get skittish. Biting the bullet, she asked, "And how do I do that?"

Chance laughed. "The cinch is right here."

Lifting the stirrup on Chloe's side, he pointed it out. And then he walked her through the entire process, narrating every move he made until he had the horse standing in her stall, sans saddle, blanket and bridle.

He saw that Chloe looked as if she was ready to leave.

"Not yet," he warned her. "You're not finished."

Everything had been taken off the mare except for her horseshoes, Chloe thought. She couldn't see what else needed to be done.

"You going to put a nightgown on her?" she joked.

"No, but you're going to wipe her down—just in case she's wet." He saw that Chloe looked a little bemused. "You're familiar with the phrase 'Ridden hard and put away wet?'" he asked. Then, not waiting for a response, he told her, "Well, we don't do that around here.

"Just in case the horse is wet and the temperature drops at night, your horse might get a chill. No matter what you might have seen in the movies or on TV, horses are a lot more delicate than you might think. They come down with a lot of the same ailments that people do in addition to having their own set of diseases.

"You take care of your horse, and your horse will take care of you," Chance concluded, then stopped abruptly, catching himself. "Sorry, I was giving you the exact same lecture that I usually give the boys," he apologized.

He didn't want her thinking he was talking down to her. It was just that he really cared about the way the horses were treated. Though they were powerful animals, he thought of them as defenseless when it came to being on the receiving end of bad treatment. Any horse in his care had to be treated well.

"That's okay. I like it," she told him truthfully. "And I did learn something," she added.

He looked at her doubtfully. "Don't kiss up to me, Chloe," he told her.

She thought that was an odd phrase for him to use, given what had happened a while ago at the lake, but she let it go, other than to protest, "But I wasn't."

"Oh, in that case, good to hear." And then he handed her a brush with coarse dark bristles.

She looked at it, confused. "Are you telling me that my hair's a mess?"

Chance laughed. "No, I'm telling you to brush the horse."

"Is that part of the ritual?" There were certainly a lot of steps to remember when it came to taking care of a horse, she thought.

"No, but Mirabel likes it, and I thought having you brush her might help build a bond between you two."

Since Chloe still looked just a bit perplexed as she contemplated the brush in her hand, he asked, "May I?"

Chloe was quick to surrender the brush. "Sure."

"You don't want to brush her too hard," he told her. "Just long, even strokes. Think of it like getting a massage."

That didn't help. She shook her head. "Never got one," Chloe told him. Then she looked at him curiously. "Have you?"

The very thought of it made him laugh. "I'm not exactly the beauty spa type," he told her. "I was just trying to find a way for you to be able to relate to the brushing."

Chloe took the brush from him and began to brush Mirabel's flanks. "Like this?"

"Almost." Chance covered her hand with his own and then slowly guided her through the first few strokes. "Like this," he told her, then continued to move her hand beneath his and along the horse.

She knew that technically all they were doing was brushing the horse's coat, but they were doing it in one joint motion, and somehow, it felt rather intimate that way.

She could feel her body heating up, the way it had at the lake when he'd kissed her.

She needed to maintain better control over herself than this, she silently lectured. And part of maintaining that control was not having him get so close to her.

She needed space.

Shrugging his hand off her own, she told him, "I think that I can take it from here now, Chance."

"Go for it," he told her, stepping back. He watched

her for a few moments, and then he abruptly turned away and went into the next stall to take care of his own horse.

And to think about something else other than Chloe. Or try to.

Chapter 12

Chloe finally felt as if her life was slowly falling into place.

She was making decent headway with the four boys who were currently staying at the ranch, albeit at a different pace with each one. Initially, she'd felt as if all of the teens regarded her warily and were keeping up their defenses, but mercifully, that was all changing.

Jonah and Ryan had taken less time to come around than the other two. Since they had already made a bit of progress under Sasha's counseling, it didn't take them all that long to lower their guard and trust her. She was here a few weeks and they had begun to talk to her about things that were troubling them, as well as some things that they were trying to work out.

She found it rougher going with Brandon and Will. Brandon didn't want to risk getting close to anyone because he was afraid of ultimately losing that contact, the way he had lost his brother. As for Will, although he clearly yearned for his mother, because of what she had done, he didn't trust any woman who entered his life.

Although their progress was at slower pace, seeing all four of the teens come around because of her efforts proved to be exceedingly gratifying for Chloe. She felt as if she was actually making a difference in their lives, which in turn added a great deal of significance to her own life. She felt it gave her a real purpose.

And then there were the riding lessons with Chance. She would have never thought, not in a million years, that she'd be proud of the headway she was making with that, but she was.

Chance turned out to be the consummate teacher, which really surprised her. She would have said at the outset of their association that teaching someone to ride wouldn't have made a difference to Chance one way or another. He had struck her as being the poster boy for the quintessential loner. But it turned out that Chance was nothing if not patient with her.

He was patient with the boys, too, she noted whenever she had the chance to observe them together. And she could see that they began to regard him as the father figure they'd lacked in their childhoods.

For that matter, she thought as she finished working on that day's notes and looked out the window at the corral where Chance worked with Will, in a way he was the father *she* had never known, as well.

Except, she reminded herself, she would have definitely never reacted to her father the way she was reacting to Chance.

Chloe sighed.

She was still rather uncertain about all that. Uncertain how she felt about having feelings for him.

She felt as if she was going around in circles.

"You think too much," she murmured to herself under her breath.

But she couldn't help herself, couldn't help analyzing, comparing—remembering. Remembering how it felt to be in love with Donnie—and how that had all ended so heartbreakingly.

Stop it, she upbraided herself. *Just enjoy whatever happens as it happens. For heaven's sake, for once in your life just float, don't plot.*

Chloe shook her head. Easier said than done.

She turned away from the window and went back to her work.

Like a delayed reaction, it slowly dawned on Chance that for the first time since he'd gotten back from serving overseas that he finally, *finally* had a renewed sense of purpose. That was something that had eluded him while he'd been in the military and certainly afterward, when he'd returned stateside.

He supposed that was why he had subconsciously drifted from ranch to ranch and job to job. He'd blamed it on restlessness, but he now realized that he'd been searching for a meaning to his life, some sort of a purpose. Working here, at Peter's Place, with its rescued horses and its rescued kids, was giving him that sense of purpose.

And it felt damn good, Chance thought. The troubled teens he had been put in charge of had essentially come a long way in a short time. He knew in part that was because of Chloe and her sessions with them, but in part it was because of him, as well. And their noticeable evolution gave him a reason for getting up in the morning.

He never thought he'd ever feel that way again. For the longest time he'd believed that opening his eyes each morning, feeling as if his soul had been sucked out by forces he couldn't grapple with, couldn't untangle, was going to be his fate until the day he died.

Now he saw firsthand that it didn't have to be that way. That it *wasn't* that way.

That started him thinking.

If being here, working with both teens and horses that the world had all but given up on, could ultimately rescue his soul, maybe it could do the same for other returning soldiers who were trying—and failing—to find a place for themselves in society.

The thought fired him up.

So much so that he decided to bring it to Graham's attention and see what the man thought of it.

And there was no time like the present.

So, hat in hand—literally as well as figuratively—Chance knocked on Graham's door.

"Door's not locked," Graham called out.

Opening the door to the small bedroom that Graham had converted into his office, Chance made no move to enter. "Mind if I talk to you?" he asked, standing just on the other side of the threshold.

Graham beckoned him forward. "Come on in," he invited warmly, turning away from his computer. "What's on your mind? Everything going all right with the boys?"

"Everything's fine," Chance told him. Then he fell silent. The words he had rehearsed in his head on the way over all seemed to disappear. He mentally shook himself, getting back on track. "That's kind of why I'm here."

But he still stood there like a supplicant before his boss's desk, looking no doubt very uncomfortable.

"Why don't you sit down?" Graham suggested, gesturing to the chair before his desk. "Maybe if you take a load off, you'll find it easier to share whatever's on your mind."

Chance took a seat, but he remained ramrod straight. Graham probably thought he looked like an action figure that had been bent into an uncompromising position.

When Chance didn't start talking, Graham's face took on a serious look.

Other than at the dinner table or by the horses, Chance wasn't used to talking to Graham, and he couldn't read the man's expression. He just had a feeling his boss was about to say something bad.

"You're not leaving us, are you?" Graham finally asked him.

It took a second for Chance to replay the question in his mind. "What? Oh, no, no I'm not—unless you're not satisfied with my work," Chance qualified, wondering if perhaps the man was looking for a way to break the news to him.

"Trust me, I am *more* than satisfied with the caliber of your work," Graham told him. "But something must have brought you in here."

Chance cleared his throat. While he was used to going his own way, he wasn't used to being part of a team, and yet that was what he was right now. Part of a team, and making a suggestion that would in turn affect that team.

Chance began to stumble through a response. "Yes, it did."

"I'm listening," Graham encouraged.

In order to make his point, Chance realized that he was going to have to do something he absolutely hated—he was going to have to talk about himself. But there was no way around it because in order to sell his suggestion, he could use only himself as an example.

"When I was first discharged from the military, because of what I had seen, I kind of came apart at the seams and was pretty much at loose ends." Because the story felt too personal to him, Chance kept the details vague and general. "After having seen combat, after watching more than one person's life wiped out in the blink of an eye, nothing seemed all that important anymore. I certainly didn't feel like I fit in to the world I came back to." He moved closer to the edge of his seat, his eyes intently on Graham to see if he was getting his thought across to the man. "There was no place that felt right to me."

"Go on," Graham urged when he paused.

"But when I came here, when I started working with the boys you had on the ranch, with kids who were caught between two worlds, and working with the rescued horses that you stocked the place with, things began to fall into place for me. They started to make sense." His voice took on volume as he warmed to his subject. "I knew why I came back when so many of the other soldiers I shipped out with either didn't come back at all, or came back with their bodies and spirits maimed and damaged. I found my purpose here."

"I'm really glad to hear that," Graham said, and Chance could hear the man's sincerity.

Then Graham leaned forward in his desk chair. Chance had the feeling he knew that Chance wasn't finished, that there was more to the reason why he'd come into his office this afternoon.

Chance ran his tongue along his dried lips, stalling. "So I was thinking..."

Graham was the soul of encouragement. Nodding, he said, "Yes?"

Chance took a deep breath. "I was thinking that if I could feel this way, working with kids who needed help and horses that needed their own form of rehabilitation, maybe in the long run this could work for other soldiers, as well."

Graham kept his gaze even. "Go on."

He'd come this far; he couldn't just let his courage flag now, Chance thought. "What would you think of the idea of opening up a Peter's Place for returning vets?" he asked. Then the next moment, not wanting to put pressure on the man who had given him a second chance to live his life, Chance shrugged evasively and murmured, "It's a dumb idea, huh?"

"No," Graham told him with feeling, "I think it's a great idea."

Chance was as close to being dumbfound as he'd ever been in his life. He felt his excitement growing. "Really?"

"Absolutely." Graham nodded. "In all honesty I always thought that the work we did here could have other uses. Not just for troubled teens. Give me a while to see if I can either find funding for a separate place, or if there's a way to build on to Peter's Place. You know, incorporate the vets and the teens."

This was more than Chance had hoped for. He'd

come in expecting Graham to at least listen to his idea, but not to jump on it like this. He was more than delighted.

Apparently so was Graham, as he went on enthusiastically. "The Fortune Foundation's already given us funding to expand the original Peter's Place—that's why you and Chloe are here. Maybe I can talk to the people who hold the foundation's purse strings while they're still feeling generous and see if I can get them to part with a little more money for this added venture. I certainly think it's worth a try—and definitely worthy of consideration."

Graham took a deep breath as he leaned back in his chair. "You have any other suggestions?"

"No, fresh out," Chance told him, spreading his hands out in front of him, a pleased expression on his face. "That was it." So saying, he rose, ready to leave.

"Well, what you came up with was damn good," Graham assured him. "But like I said, let me see what I can do on my end and whose cage I can rattle. And, Chance—?"

Chance stopped on his way out the door, half turned and looked at his boss over his shoulder. "Yes?"

"If you have any other ideas, be sure to come see me with them. I'd be more than happy to hear you out."

Chance grinned broadly, really pleased with how well this had gone. He'd had bosses who had looked upon him as nothing more than a big dumb cowboy. Muscle on horseback. Any minor suggestions he'd tried to make regarding running the ranch had been quickly disregarded. It was nice to be working for someone who regarded him as a person. "Yes, sir, I will. Thank you, sir."

"It's Graham," Graham said, calling after him. "Graham, not 'sir.'"

"Got it," Chance called back, although he had to admit, if only to himself, that it was hard to think of his boss in terms personal enough to refer to him by his first name.

That just wasn't the way he operated.

"Well, you certainly look happy," Chloe observed when Chance walked into the stable a little later that day.

She had arrived a few minutes ago and was saddling her horse. When she hadn't seen Chance here, she'd begun to wonder if maybe he was tired of mentoring her and spending his late afternoon riding with her.

For her, these riding lessons had become the highlight of her day, but she could well understand if Chance was viewing them as time-consuming nuisances.

Then again maybe she was worried about nothing, Chloe thought, because he was here now and he was smiling.

"I am happy," Chance declared, still running on the energy generated by what he felt had been an extremely successful pitch. It amounted to his first small victory in a long, long time.

He was still flying so high on his earlier exchange with Graham that he completely forgot all about being on his good behavior with Chloe—something he'd instituted for himself after that long kiss at the lake. Instead, he took hold of her shoulders and kissed her before he could think to stop himself.

He kissed her hard and with enthusiasm that melted into something more, something meaningful and soul searing. It was only after Chance unlocked his brain and began to think that he realized he'd done it again. He'd gotten carried away.

Chloe made it all too easy to do that.

Releasing her shoulders, Chance still didn't step back immediately. Instead, he forced himself to look into Chloe's eyes, half afraid he would see condemnation there, but nonetheless hoping against hope that what he would find there would be acceptance.

Having been soundly kissed by this handsome cowboy, Chloe found that, just like the first time, she had to struggle to get air in, struggle not to sound as if she were some addled-brained, incoherent groupie who had just been kissed for the first time.

It took her more than a second to find her mind, which had temporarily gone MIA. When she and her mind were reunited, she was finally able to question him. "Mind if I ask what's made you so happy?"

"I just talked to Graham about the possibility of establishing another center like this one, to help returning veterans. You know, the ones who feel like they're caught between two worlds and don't really belong to either."

It sounded like a noble suggestion to her, and she was proud of him for making it. "What did Graham say?" she wanted to know.

"That he'd look into it." The paltry sentence didn't begin to cover the hope he had attached to the proposed venture.

Chloe felt torn. Torn between being happy for Chance and being unhappy for herself. Because if this suggestion of his worked out and Graham went ahead with establishing a new companion facility to Peter's

Place, this one strictly for veterans, she knew that she'd lose Chance. He'd move on, just as she had been afraid he would.

She admonished herself for being selfish. This would help a lot of servicemen if it came to fruition. But she couldn't quite help her emotions.

Feeling almost disloyal, she still had to ask, "Does that mean that you'll be leaving here?"

He honestly hadn't even considered that possibility. He just assumed that if the center he'd suggested turned out to be a separate one, it would still be built somewhere within the area. It had to be, he silently insisted.

"What? No," he told her. "I don't want to leave here."

"But if you wind up running this new center for Graham," she began, "wouldn't you have to?"

But there was so much up in the air that Chance didn't want to talk about it right now. And he silenced Chloe the only way he knew how.

By kissing her.

Chapter 13

That kiss by the lake hadn't been a fluke, Chloe realized. It hadn't been just a one-time exhibition of fireworks going off within her and somehow managing to light the darkening skies. Because whatever she'd felt that evening when Chance had kissed her, right now she was feeling that and more.

So much more.

She was feeling almost too much, Chloe realized, a sliver of panic burrowing its way through to her consciousness.

Because of that, *she* was the one who called a halt to the kiss by drawing her head back. Pulling in air, she put her hands up against his chest to serve as a wedge between them.

When Chance looked at her quizzically, undoubtedly wondering why she'd stopped him, Chloe grasped at the first excuse that she could think of.

It was also true.

"Someone might walk in and see us," she warned him breathlessly.

Chance blew out a breath. She was right. What had come over him? They were both in positions of authority when it came to the boys at the ranch. If one of the boys accidentally saw them behaving like hormone-driven teenagers, that wouldn't exactly be the best kind of example for them.

"Right," he murmured, striving to regain control over himself. He flashed her an apologetic look. "Don't know what I was thinking."

Actually, he knew *exactly* what he had been thinking. What he was *still* thinking. That more than anything, he wanted to take Chloe to his bed and make love with her.

But he wasn't about to force his will on her, and if Chloe wasn't interested in making love with him for one reason or another, then that was that.

End of story.

But was it? He couldn't help thinking about that sunset on the lake—and the kiss they'd just shared now. He was certain that he wasn't imagining things. Chloe had kissed him back—with as much feeling as he had experienced himself.

He was just going to have to be patient, he told himself.

"You were probably thinking that we're both human," Chloe said, answering his rhetorical question. "But right now we have to be more than that—for the sake of the boys," she added emphatically. "They look at you as a father figure, you know," she told him.

Since both horses were saddled and ready to ride,

Chloe swung onto Mirabel's back and pointed the mare toward the open stable doors.

"Father figure? I wouldn't go that far," Chance told her, easily mounting his stallion and following her out through the doors.

"I would." She knew what it was like to desperately want a father figure in her life and was acquainted with the signs. She saw them in the four teens at Peter's Place, in the way they interacted with Chance. "Because it's true. I think it's a good thing," Chloe went on, seeing she needed to convince him. "All of them need a father figure in their lives. It's an awful thing for a kid when that space is left empty."

He was only vaguely aware of her backstory, her connection to the Fortunes. None of it was his business, he knew that, but he had the feeling that she wanted to talk, so he asked, "You lose your dad early?"

She laughed and he thought the sound was a bit hollow. It made him wonder about what she'd gone through, growing up.

"Yeah, *really* early," she emphasized. "My father was gone before I was born."

"Sorry for your loss," Chance told her, echoing the phrase that people somehow thought was supposed to make up for the pain and cover every sentiment in between mourning and anger. He knew her father wasn't dead, but if he'd been an absentee father, in a way, that was even worse.

Chance sounded genuinely sincere, Chloe thought, and she appreciated it. But the whole tale was just too sordid to get into right now. She was trying to find her purpose here, feeling better about herself because she was reaching out to these boys. For the most part, until just now, she'd managed to focus on the present and not the past.

"It wasn't my loss, it was his." Chloe said. "The man just ran for the hills when he found out my mom was pregnant with me, and he was never heard from again."

She saw that Chance was struggling to find something appropriate to say to her—as if there was such a thing. Which there wasn't.

"It's okay," she assured him. "I got over it. For a while there, I harbored hopes that he'd just come walking back into my life someday, like a scene in one of those 'feel good' movies—you know, the kind that never really happen in real life. But to be honest, I did miss having a father," she admitted. "Until I turned about twelve."

"What happened when you turned twelve?" he asked before he could stop himself.

He realized that perhaps this was going to get way too personal and she was going to tell him about some traumatic event that was better left unsaid. He didn't feel he was equipped to offer her the kind of comfort she might deserve.

She tossed her head almost defiantly, sending her hair flying over her shoulder. "I decided that it was his loss if he wasn't there, not mine."

There was admiration in Chance's laugh. "You know, you turned out to be a lot feistier than I first thought you were."

"That's what happens when you've got only one parent and you have to half raise yourself," she told him. "Don't get me wrong," she quickly added. "I didn't have the kind of childhood that Will had. I adored my mother and she was my best friend until the day she died. Heaven knew she tried her best to be both mother *and* father to me. But there were times, more than a few," she admitted, "when I was acutely aware that I could have used having a father around, the way a lot of the other girls did."

"So, does it feel any better now?" Chance wanted to know.

"Now?" she questioned, not sure what he was asking her.

He would have thought it was the first thing that came to her mind.

"Well, you're part of the Fortune family now," he reminded her. "That has got to feel different to you, doesn't it?"

"It does," she agreed. "In a way." Chloe searched for the right words to make him understand what was happening and how she felt about it. "But to be honest, I'm not exactly being embraced by one and all and pressed to the bosom of my family."

"Graham hired you." He'd just assumed that was a sign that she'd been accepted.

"Yes," she allowed. "And being a Fortune no doubt had something to do with that. But some of the others—the ones I met at a family dinner at Kate Fortune's last month—they regard me as an outsider, an interloper they made clear they were on their guard against. I got the feeling they thought I wanted more from them than just their acceptance." She was thinking of Sophie Fortune Robinson. The woman had been especially accusatory and downright unkind. Chloe was still trying to get over that ill-fated meeting because it had hurt so much.

And then it dawned on Chloe that she was talking too much, admitting too much. She didn't ordinarily open up like this. Attempting to cover up her feelings, she shrugged.

"That's okay," she said, affecting a careless attitude. "I've been on my own for the most part for so long, I'm pretty used to it. It's nice to have a family, but at this point, if for some reason that changes, I'm okay with that, too."

Chance wasn't buying the nonchalant act. There was a look in her eyes, a distant, wary, hurt look that he didn't know if she was even aware of. But he was. And what it told him was that she had her guard up.

What it didn't tell him was why. He had a feeling that it had something to do with whoever it was whom she had lost—he remembered the one time that she'd let that slip—but until she trusted him enough to really open up, he wouldn't know anything for sure.

"Well, this still looks like a good spot," he said when they came to a stop by the lake—the same exact place he had brought her to that day he'd first kissed her. "Feel like stopping here for a while?"

"Sure, why not?" Chloe thought it looked as perfect now as it had the first time, and it was quickly becoming her favorite place. Dismounting, she saw that Chance had already gotten off his horse and held a blanket in his hands.

"I thought we could just sit here and enjoy the sunset," Chance told her, spreading the blanket on the ground.

"I guess we think alike," she told him. When he stopped to look at her, a question in his eyes, she told him, "I packed a couple of sandwiches for us." She took them out of her saddlebag, along with bottles of water.

They sat down on the blanket. Facing the lake, they

watched the sun going progressively lower in the sky as they ate.

When they were finished, Chloe rolled the sandwich wrappers into a transparent ball. "It almost looks like the sun is sinking into the lake, doesn't it?" she observed in hushed awe as she looked on.

"Just gets better every time I see it," Chance admitted.

His words seemed to linger in the air as he turned to look at her.

She told herself that she was imagining things, but it almost sounded as if Chance was applying the words to her as well as to the sunset.

She couldn't help the flash of excitement that went through her veins.

"Does it?" she asked in a hushed whisper.

Chance started to answer.

Or thought he did.

But what he wound up doing was framing Chloe's face with his hands and turning it up to his.

The next moment, he was kissing her again. Kissing her and losing himself in the taste of her mouth, the scent of her breath as she exhaled. Losing himself in the very essence of her.

The sun continued dipping down lower in the sky until it looked as if it was gracefully dancing along the lake's edge, savoring one last moment before it finally vanished completely into the water.

Despite being in the presence of a magnificent display by nature, Chance was aware only of the woman in his arms. How she felt, how soft her lips were, how inviting the press of her body was against his.

And how much he wanted her.

The kisses grew longer.

And deeper.

As did his desire.

His body urged him to go faster, to take what was right there in front of him. But with effort, Chance forced himself to go slow, to not just enjoy her, but to give Chloe the opportunity to consider what was happening between them—and to say no at any point if it came to that for her.

Although he fervently hoped that she wouldn't.

It was inevitable. The more he caressed her, familiarizing himself with every soft, inviting curve of her body, the more he wanted her.

His heart was hammering wildly as he drew Chloe beneath him on the blanket, slowly exploring every inch of her, finding pleasure in every inch of her and giving her the same pleasure.

And she loved every second of it.

Still, Chloe tried very hard to resist the allure of what Chance promised. Not because she didn't want this to happen, but because she did.

And because she wanted it, guilt hovered on the edges of her consciousness, threatening to break in and shatter everything. That guilt reminded her that she'd already given herself to a man. A man who was no longer able to claim her.

But this feeling that was traveling through her—the desire, the heat, the passion—was exquisite, and she had missed this feeling oh, so much. For the very first time in two years, Chloe felt like she was alive, and she'd missed that feeling.

Missed making love and being made love to.

Her heart was racing like a car at the Indianapolis 500 as her desire for more of Chance's kisses, his touches, just kept increasing at a stunning rate.

She didn't remember tugging off his clothes, didn't remember him pulling hers off, either. But somehow, it had happened because they were on the blanket, naked, their limbs tangled around one another as they lay beneath the full moon, each trying to get their fill of the other.

Each deeply involved in pleasuring the other.

She bit her lip to keep from sighing with delight as she felt his sensual mouth almost artfully glide along her skin, silently claiming everywhere he touched, everywhere he kissed.

Chloe let herself absorb each and every sensation that went spiraling through her body in response to the almost magical things this cowboy was doing to her.

Till her very core felt like an inferno.

She had trouble catching her breath. Her mind scattered in a thousand different directions—which was just as well. She didn't want to think because thinking was bad. Thinking brought guilt, and all she wanted to do was feel. Because in feeling, there was freedom, and what she was feeling had her soaring above the clouds, above everything. As free as a bird.

Finally pulling in a deep breath, she turned and rose above Chance, doing her best to give him back a little of the intense pleasure he was giving her. She'd had only one other partner her whole life, while she was certain that Chance had had many, but she did her best to show him her gratitude for this timeless gift that he was bestowing on her.

After a few moments of reciprocation had passed, he pulled her beneath him again.

He slid his body along hers, sending electric currents of anticipation surging all through her.

Her heart raced faster, all but stealing her breath away.

His eyes met and held hers, communing with her even though not a single word was exchanged. And she answered his unspoken question in kind.

Chance kissed her, then kissed her again. She could feel her body priming.

Waiting.

For him.

When his knee parted her legs, she was ready for him. And then they were joined together, one heart, one mind and one desire overseeing them both.

His body rocked against hers, and then began to move in the timeless rhythm she'd been waiting for.

She moved with Chance, her hips all but sealed to his. The movements grew quicker, stronger as each seemed to anticipate the other, and suddenly they were racing to the end goal, to the explosion that was waiting for both of them.

It seemed to take forever and yet was only as long as a blink of an eye. When it came, rocking them both with its explosion, they clung to one another as if letting go meant extinction.

She could feel her body shuddering, could feel the fireworks receding, ushering in an aftermath awash with a feeling of well-being. She lay there, cradled in the crook of his arm, wondering just how things had come to this moment in time.

She was too tired to come up with an answer, even if it was just for herself.

The sounds of nature were soothing, and she found herself relaxing.

If only for the moment.

Chapter 14

Chloe felt a hand on her shoulder, gently shaking her. Startled, she opened her eyes. Until that moment, she hadn't realized that her eyes had closed or that she'd wound up falling asleep.

"Chloe?" She detected concern in Chance's voice. "Are you all right?"

Embarrassed, flustered, for a second Chloe was at a complete loss for words. They'd made love, and then she'd fallen asleep. What had to be going through his head about her right now?

"I'm okay," she mumbled.

The smile she saw on his lips was totally unexpected. "You're a lot better than 'okay,'" he told her, his smile widening. "But I thought maybe you were upset, you know, now that everything kind of settled down." It was obvious that he must have thought she was only pretending to be asleep.

Chance had never been much for small talk, or really any sort of talk at all. He was a man who believed in doing rather than talking, and as far as he was concerned, his actions—and hers—had done all the talking that was necessary this evening.

But he wasn't so naive or obtuse to believe that men and women thought alike when faced with the same situation. That meant that what was "fine" with him most likely wasn't that way for a woman. Specifically, for Chloe.

So he pressed the matter a little further. "You're not upset or anything, are you?"

"Because we just made love?"

He would have said "had sex," but Chance left it her way and nodded. "Yes."

Chloe took a breath, stalling as she tried to gather her thoughts into a coherent whole. She didn't know what she felt.

Falling asleep beside Chance had to mean that she trusted him, right?

She could see that he was still waiting for an answer. "Well, it wasn't exactly something I'd planned to have happen, especially out in the open like this, but no," she told him honestly after considering the matter, "I'm not upset."

That was a relief, he thought. Out loud, he said, "That's good, because I wouldn't want you to be upset." Replaying his own words in his head, Chance flushed a little. Talking was definitely *not* his strong suit. "Guess that sounds kind of lame to you."

That more than anything else—except for perhaps the way she'd seen him interacting with a couple of the boys—really touched her. Instead of feeling awkward or embarrassed, she felt her heart swelling.

"No," Chloe said, reaching up and lightly caressing his cheek. "As a matter of fact, I think it sounds rather sweet."

"'Sweet,'" Chance repeated, bemused. He laughed shortly. "I don't think anyone's ever called me that before."

"Maybe nobody's ever taken the time to get to know you before," Chloe said. The next second, she realized how that had to sound to him. "Not that I think I know you all that well. I mean—" She was floundering and she knew it. "This isn't coming out right."

Damn, there was just something about her, about the way she talked, even about the way she made mistakes that kept drawing him in.

"I think it came out just fine," he told her right before he kissed her.

He was doing it again, Chloe thought. He was making her head spin. Making her body heat.

It took Chloe several moments before she could finally force herself to draw her mouth back, away from his. It definitely wasn't easy.

"We start doing that again and we're never going to get back to the ranch. Graham's liable to send a search party out for us come morning."

"Wouldn't want to be found like this," Chance agreed. Even to his own ears he didn't exactly sound as if he really meant what he was saying.

She looked beautiful in the moonlight, he thought. So beautiful that everything he'd felt earlier just before he made love to her was coming back in spades. You'd think that having consumed the forbidden fruit would have negated the overpowering desire for it. But in Chloe's case, it seemed to have just the opposite effect.

Having made love with her had just whetted his appetite for her, because Chance now knew just what was waiting for him.

Rather than let her start getting dressed, the way he knew he should have, Chance lightly brushed his lips against her bare shoulder, sending shock waves through himself—as well as through her.

"One more for the road?" he asked, a very sensual look in his eyes.

The question, so guilelessly asked, had laughter bubbling up in her throat.

"I guess it can't do any harm," she replied, her heart already revving up.

"None whatsoever," he agreed as he pulled her back into his arms.

It began all over again, the thunder and lightning, the excitement, all culminating in a breathtaking shower of stars.

Chloe thought it might prove awkward, running into Chance, having their paths cross half a dozen times a day, not to mention at the dining room table for meals, but it was just the opposite.

It was nice. Very, very nice.

Neither one of them took any liberties with the other or resorted to private jokes or secretive looks that left the others on the ranch guessing. But there was still something enormously comforting about just being around one another.

She wouldn't have given that feeling up for the world.

For one thing, Chloe felt a great deal less alone now.

She was still Graham's half sister and Gerald Robinson's offspring, for whatever that was worth, but neither of those two things made her feel as if she was actually part of anything, as if she was connected to anything, despite the implications and despite what Graham had told her when he'd first called her.

But being around Chance and catching glimpses of him during the day *did* make her feel as if she was part of something larger than herself. Something larger and oh, so emotionally comforting.

Chloe knew she was letting herself get carried away and that all this was just temporary, but for now, for this tiny space of time, it didn't matter. She was determined to enjoy this for however long it lasted.

"A family picnic?" Chloe repeated, looking at Graham after he had called her into his small office.

A couple more days had passed and things had been going very well at work as well as during her free hours, but admittedly, in that same time she had barely socialized with her half brother and his family. Despite the fact that they shared some of the same DNA, she still tended to think of Graham more as her boss than as her kin.

And now, out of the blue, Graham had sought her out to invite her to a family picnic he was planning for that Sunday.

Recalling her last venture into a family function, Chloe had some grave doubts about the invitation. "Are you sure you want me to attend?"

"It *is* a family picnic," he pointed out. "That means it's for both the Fortune family and my work family," Graham explained. "And you actually qualify as both, so yes, I want you to come. Sasha and I both want you to come. Besides," he added, "you're good with Sydney and Maddie."

Now it was starting to make sense to Chloe. "If you need a babysitter—"

Graham was quick to cut her off. "If I wanted a babysitter, I would have said so," he told her. "I was just trying to tell you that the girls would love to see you there, not that we require your services in any other capacity than as an attendee," he said pointedly. Then he added what he felt would cinch the deal for Chloe. "Oh, and Chance should be there."

Chloe looked at him in surprise. "He already agreed to come?"

Graham paused a moment. "He will if he knows that you're going to be there," he admitted. "So what do you say? I'd really like you to come. I'm inviting the boys, too," he added, hoping that would convince her to attend.

Chloe surrendered. She really didn't want to drag her feet about this. "Can't say no to my boss—or to my half brother."

"How about you just call me 'brother'?" Graham suggested. "'Half' brother makes me feel like I've been sliced in two and you get to pick which half you want to deal with. It's not exactly a flattering image," he added.

Chloe grinned. "Well, that's easy enough..."

Graham raised his hand to stop her right there. "I think I'll quit while I'm ahead—provided you did just agree to come to the picnic."

She laughed, knowing that she'd been set up. "How can I say no now?"

"Good, then my plan worked." He picked up the landline receiver and pulled over a list of phone numbers he'd written down. "Now I have to corral the rest of the people for this picnic."

That caught her by surprise. "I'm the first one you asked?"

"Not exactly," Graham admitted. "I did ask Sasha first. Actually, it was more of a discussion as to what day would be the best to have the picnic. So, in a way, I guess you are the first one." He saw the surprised look on her face. "Why?"

Chloe thought of waving the whole exchange away, but decided, in light of everything, she owed her new-found brother the truth. "I'm used to being the last one asked—to everything—so thank you for that."

"No thanks necessary, Chloe," he responded, already tapping a phone number into the keypad.

Chloe walked out of the office smiling.

When Chance was invited, Graham asked him to extend the invitation to the boys. Like him, they were surprised to be included and at first, all four seemed hesitant to attend what was going to be, after all, a family gathering.

"Why? You need us to act as servers when the food's brought out?" Brandon wanted to know, reverting to his old chip-on-his-shoulder attitude as he posed the question to Chance.

"If you want to help out, that's fine," Chance told the teen, then looked at the other boys who were gathered around him in the stable. "But nobody expects you to. You're just welcome to join in—as guests, just like everyone else."

"Is it mandatory?" Will wanted to know, shifting restlessly from one foot to the other as he eyed Chance.

"It's an invitation, not an order."

"Don't be a jerk," Jonah told the two younger residents. "It's a chance to eat some really good barbecue and be around regular people. Relax. Nobody wants anything from you."

Color crept up Will's shallow cheeks. "I guess you're right," he conceded.

Chance knew the comment from their peer would carry some weight, but he was still grateful when he saw Chloe stepping out of Mirabel's stall, no doubt having heard the entire conversation. He knew she'd add her two cents to the persuasive argument—but only if she felt that he might need backup.

Evidently, she decided he did.

"Old habits are hard to break, aren't they?" Chloe asked knowingly.

The boys turned, almost in unison, to the sound of her voice. From the looks on their faces, she judged that they hadn't realized that she was anywhere in earshot.

"Sometimes people do things just because they want to be nice without expecting anything in return," she told Brandon and Will. "Get used to it. You'll find that it happens a lot more frequently than you thought—once you put your guard down.

"So," she concluded, looking around at all four of the teens. "Are you guys in?"

Will raised and lowered his thin shoulders in an indifferent shrug. "I guess so."

"Sure," Ryan chimed in with a ready grin.

"I'll be there," Jonah assured them.

"How about you?" Chloe asked Brandon when he kept his silence.

After several beats, Brandon, like Will, shrugged, Unlike Will he avoided looking at either Chloe or Chance when he answered.

"Yeah, I guess so," he mumbled.

"Enthusiasm," Chloe teased, putting her arm around Brandon's shoulders and giving him a quick hug.

Brandon's shoulders were stiff, but she noted with pleasure that he was forcing himself to relax them a little.

Progress!

"I love it," she added.

"Yeah, whatever," Brandon mumbled. For the moment, he let her keep her arm where it was.

"Baby steps, Brandon," Chloe whispered into his ear. "Take baby steps."

"Uh-huh." He shrugged her off, but the moment had lasted longer than Chloe'd expected. "Well, I got chores to do," he announced to no one in particular.

"Then you'd better get to them," Chance told the boy. He looked at the other three. "How about the rest of you? Stalls cleaned?" he wanted to know.

"Cleaner than our bunks," Ryan volunteered, speaking for the others.

"Then maybe you'd better see about those bunks," Chance suggested pointedly.

The quartet dispersed immediately, one going deeper into the stable, while the other three went to the bunkhouse where they stayed.

"I think that they're coming along pretty well," she said to Chance once the boys were well out of hearing range. She turned toward him for an answer. "What do you think?"

"There's still a lot of work left to do," Chance replied.

He had never been one to allow himself to be overly enthusiastic about something, especially when it was still a work in progress. And that was exactly what he considered the evolution of the four teens to be—a work in progress.

He saw that Chloe was still looking at him, obviously waiting for a positive response.

He sighed, giving in. "But yeah, I think they're coming along. I have to admit that I'm kind of surprised that they're willing to go to this picnic," he told her, lowering his voice in case Brandon could pick up on their conversation.

"Well, I think that it's a hopeful sign," she told him in all sincerity.

He wished he could be as optimistic as she was about this. But life had knocked him around too much. Because of that, he always anticipated the worst.

"Maybe you should keep an eye on them just in case," he suggested.

She wanted to ask in case of what, but there was a bigger question in her mind than that at the moment. "Why? Aren't you going to be there?"

She couldn't think of any other reason for him to say that. Had he changed his mind about going? She was sure that Graham had convinced him to attend. What happened?

"It's a family picnic," he told her, as if that explained everything.

"Not *strictly* family," she reminded him. "Besides, as Graham pointed out, he considers the people at Peter's

Place family, too. That means the boys. *And* you," she said pointedly. "Why don't you want to come?"

He frowned slightly, wishing she hadn't put him on the spot like this. "I don't do well in crowd scenes."

That was a lot of nonsense, she thought. "You were in the military. That was a crowd."

"Yeah, and I did my time," Chance pointed out, as if that ended the argument.

Refusing to give up, Chloe tried another tactic. "You can't insult your boss by not showing up. Remember, you're still waiting for his decision on that expansion for a center to help returning vets." She pinned him with a look. "You have to come."

Chance laughed quietly as he shook his head. The woman just didn't give up. There was a time, not all that long ago, when he would have found that to be annoying. But for some reason, not when it came to her.

"You do know how to present a convincing argument," he commented, surrendering.

Chloe's eyes were shining as she replied, "I do whatever I have to do." Then, patting his cheek, she walked out of the stable humming to herself.

Chapter 15

He had told Chloe the truth. He had never really been all that fond of crowds. Wide-open country where a man could travel all day without running into anyone else held far more appeal for him, which was why he preferred spending most of his time on the back of a horse rather than at a table, talking to people he didn't know.

But he had to admit that lately, he had begun to broaden his horizons just a little more. The work he'd been doing with the boys, taking sullen, angry-at-the-world teens who felt that they had been cheated by society and helping them turn their lives around—both by working with them and by his example—had made him reevaluate his take on the world at large.

And then, of course, there was Chloe, Chance thought. He couldn't very well do what he'd done with her on the back of a horse. Not without one of them hurting themselves, he tactfully amended.

Still there was a world of difference between being around Chloe or the boys and these wall-to-wall—or more accurately, he thought, tree-to-tree—people he was looking at today. People who seemed to come in all sizes and shapes, united only by their last name—or at least the DNA that ran in their veins.

Apparently, Gerald Robinson had been extremely generous with his seed, if at times not so generous with his name, Chance thought. The former Jerome Fortune had fathered eight children with his wife, Charlotte. Apparently, that hadn't been enough to satisfy the man. He also snuck around procreating more children—Chloe being one of them—with unsuspecting, easily infatuated young women, leaving them high and dry—and pregnant—as soon as the time seemed right to him.

Chance had to admit that he was surprised to see just how well-adjusted a lot of these people seemed to be, given their background and their father's less than Boy Scout–like history.

But well-adjusted or not, this gathering of Fortune Robinsons and their extended family was just no place for him, Chance decided.

After less than half an hour into it, he began searching for the best time to make his unobserved getaway.

As he moved about, trying his best to look unobtrusive and blend in with the background, Chance suddenly felt someone slip their arm through his. Caught entirely off guard, he turned his head to find that Chloe had quietly walked up behind him.

Chloe returned his rather startled look with a smile. "I know what you're thinking," she told him.

"Oh? And what is it that I'm thinking?" Chance wanted to know, rather impressed by the confidence he heard in her voice.

She knew because in his place, she would have thought the same thing. "You're thinking that it's so crowded here, you could just easily slip away and nobody would notice that you're gone."

She was good, he thought.

"The thought did cross my mind," Chance admitted in a conversational tone.

"Well, they would notice. *I* would notice," she told him, looking at Chance pointedly.

That look in her eyes had him remembering the way she'd been at the lake the other night. And the memories had him fervently wishing they were there alone again right now, instead of milling around in a crowd of people.

"You're just saying that," he told her.

"No, I'm just meaning that," Chloe insisted. "You forget, aside from Graham and Sasha and their kids—" she pointed at the small quartet out in the center of a larger circle of people "—you and the boys are the only other people here I really know."

Something wasn't quite making sense to him. "I thought you said you met these people at a big dinner party at Kate Fortune's ranch last month ago."

"I *saw* them at a big dinner party a couple of months ago," she corrected. "There's a big difference between seeing and knowing. I just recognize some of these people by sight. That's not the same thing," she stressed, wanting him not to feel as if he was the only outsider here.

Still, Chance looked unconvinced by her argument.

"Recognizing some of these people by sight is a start," he pointed out.

Chloe laughed as she picked up a paper cup filled with diet soda from one of the smaller tables that had been set up. "Don't try to snow me with rhetoric, Chance. By your own admission, you're not all that good with words."

"No," he agreed, then spared her a meaningful look. A look that instantly made her feel warm and wanted. "I have other talents."

She blushed, unable to stop the surge of color that raced to her cheeks.

"Yes, you do," she quietly admitted. "And I'd really like it if you and your 'talents' stayed awhile longer. And the boys would like it, too."

She pointed them out for his benefit.

He was surprised to see that all four were not that far away from them, caught up in a conversation with one of the other Fortune Robinson family members.

"They're finally beginning to learn how to adapt to people," Chloe told him. "This is very good for them."

He saw her point about how being here was good for the teens, but he didn't see the dots connecting in his case the same way that she did. "Don't see what my leaving or not leaving has to do with them."

Some people needed to be hit by a two-by-four before they understood things, she thought. Chloe tried her best to get her point across. "Don't you see? You're their leader. They look to you to set an example. You leave, it won't be long before they leave."

It was a hell of a burden she was putting on his shoulders, Chance thought. "What about you?"

"I'm not leaving," Chloe answered, deliberately tightening her arm around his.

"No, I mean, you interact with them. They come to you for advice on top of those counseling sessions you have. Why can't *you* be their leader here?" he wanted to know. That made sense to him.

But Chloe had no intention of giving an inch in this matter. "Sorry, the role of leader's already been cast, and it's you," she told Chance, patting his arm with her free hand. She smiled up into his face. "Deal with it." Chloe gestured toward the barbecue grills that had been set up. "Have a burger, have a beer. *Smile.*" The last seemed almost like an order.

He moved his lips spasmodically in response to the last word.

Chloe laughed. "That'll do for now."

"Who *are* all these people, anyway?" he asked her, looking around at the sea of people, both pint-size and adult.

Chloe looked around, trying to see them through his eyes. She could understand how all this might be kind of overwhelming to a loner like him. Being a part of this family was still overwhelming to her, too.

She took a breath, wanting to get the names and faces straight in her mind before answering him.

"Well, I don't know all of them," she qualified. "But over there, next to Graham and Sasha and the girls, are Ben and Ella Fortune Robinson and their newborn, Lacey. Well, she's not a newborn anymore, she's two months old—"

"Practically old enough to go to work," Chance joked.

Relieved that he seemed to be in a better mood, Chloe pointed to another couple.

"That's Ben's brother, Wes, and his new wife, Vivian. Over there—"

She stopped as she suddenly recognized the young woman who had made her feel so unwelcome at the last gathering. For a split second, Chloe thought of turning around and leaving herself—but after what she'd just said to Chance, she knew she couldn't do that. So instead, she mentally regrouped and tried again.

"Over there," she told Chance, "is Sophie Fortune Robinson, and her fiancé, Mason Montgomery."

As covertly as possible, Chloe turned the other way so that Sophie wouldn't see her face if she looked in this direction. All Sophie would see would be the back of her head. One blonde was more or less like any other, Chloe reasoned.

"Now, right over by the lake is Zoe Fortune Robinson. Except she's married now. That's her husband, Joaquin Mendoza, with her."

Because she'd started this, Chloe continued to systematically identify the next cluster of people she recognized even though she suspected that Chance would be perfectly happy if she just stopped right here.

She pointed to the next four people. "That's Olivia and Kieran, two more of Gerald Robinson's legitimate children. And that guy with the British accent is Keaton Fortune Whitfield. He's one of the…" She hesitated, then added, "…well, illegitimate offspring, like me. And that's his fiancée, Francesca Harriman."

She looked around but didn't find the last Robinson daughter. "Seems the only one missing is Rachel. Graham told me she lives in Horseback Hollow with her husband."

Chance nodded. They were nothing but names to

him, but because it meant so much to her, he mentally reviewed the people she'd pointed out. He noticed the expression on the man she called Kieran. "Now, there's a man who looks as unhappy about being here as I am."

Because she'd named so many for him in quick succession, she wasn't sure whom Chance was referring to. "Which one?"

He didn't want to come right out and actually point to the man. That seemed kind of rude. But he had been paying more attention than Chloe probably thought he was.

"That guy you called Kieran," he told her.

She had to admit that Chance had surprised her. She looked over to the man he'd singled out and saw that Chance was right. Kieran did look exceedingly unhappy. Pausing, she recalled what Sasha had told her about his situation.

Things fell into place.

"He's not unhappy because he's here," Chloe told him. "He's worried about Zach."

"Zach," Chance repeated. Another new name. This was getting really complicated. "Maybe I should be taking notes here," he said sarcastically.

She could understand Chance's confusion. There were a lot of names, a lot of details to keep straight. She gave him a quick summary. "Zach is Kieran's best friend, and Zach's been in a coma for a week now, ever since he was thrown by a horse. He suffered a skull fracture. Obviously, not everyone can become one with a horse the way you can," she couldn't help adding.

Chance's immediate response was one of sympathy. "Poor guy." And then he asked, "Is he going to be all right? The guy who got thrown, I mean. Zach," he finally remembered.

"Nobody knows," she told Chance. "But we can ask for an update on his condition."

Taking his hand, she urged Chance to come with her as she drew closer to Kieran.

Chance was reluctant at first. After all, this wasn't any business of his. He didn't know either of the two men involved. But he did know what it was like to be worried about a friend, worried about that friend not making it. That memory would always be very vivid for him, he thought ruefully.

That got the better of him, and he came along with Chloe.

As they drew closer to Kieran, she overheard one of the other people at the gathering asking him about Zach's condition before she had a chance.

"It's the same," Kieran answered. He was toying with the glass of lemonade in his hand, but he had yet to drink any of it. "He hasn't opened his eyes in a week. I've been in the hospital with him every day, and I keep waiting for Zach to sit up and laugh, 'Gotcha!' but he just goes on lying there."

"What about his three-year-old?" someone else spoke up, wanting to know about the man's daughter. "Rosabelle, right? He's the only one she has."

That only added to the sad scenario, Chloe thought.

"Zach's parents have been taking care of her while they've been praying for a miracle. We've all been praying for a miracle," Kieran murmured more to himself than to anyone around him.

"What if there is no miracle?" This question came

from Francesca, who looked deeply moved by what she was listening to. "What happens to Rosabelle then?"

Kieran took a deep breath, as if that would give him the strength he was looking for in order to reply. But it wasn't enough. His voice came out quiet, distant. It was obvious that this was not an outcome that he welcomed.

"Then Rosabelle comes and lives with me. Zach asked me to be her guardian." Kieran shook his head. "He must have been out of his mind," he said sadly.

"Or maybe just very intuitive," Chloe told him, speaking up.

Kieran flashed her a grateful, albeit sad smile. "I doubt it," he replied.

"That was a nice thing to say," Chance told her as they moved away from the cluster of people who were around Kieran.

She shrugged off his compliment a bit self-consciously. "That would be what I'd like someone to say to me under those circumstances," she confided. "Maybe it would even make me feel better."

To Chloe's relief, as the afternoon wore on, Chance no longer looked as if he needed to be tethered in place to keep him from fleeing the premises. And once he relaxed, that in turn had an effect on her, and Chloe felt herself relaxing, as well.

The picnic seemed to go on forever, but it was the good kind of forever, the kind that wound up being one of those memories people looked back on fondly over the passage of years.

Consequently, she and Chance were still at the picnic as the day tiptoed toward twilight.

The conversation, which had revolved around a whole

host of different topics, turned to Ariana Lamonte, a reporter, Chloe discovered, who was systematically interviewing various members of the family for a piece the woman was writing entitled "Becoming a Fortune."

From what she was picking up from various family members, it sounded to Chloe like a huge invasion of privacy.

"I don't particularly like her angle on this," Sophie was saying. "She's been doing a lot of hinting that our mother—well, the mother of some of us," Sophie amended, trying to be as tactful as possible given the situation. Taking a breath, the young woman started again. "She's broadly hinting that Charlotte," she said, referring to her mother by her given name, "knew quite a bit more about Dad's cheating on her than she admits to."

"Well, that's because your mother's a smart woman," Sophie's fiancé said. "Let's face it, unless he kept her drugged or locked in a closet, she had to know something."

Chloe caught the indignant look that Sophie shot at Mason, but then she noticed Sophie's face soften. Perhaps because she felt Mason was right, Chloe thought. What Gerald Robinson had done was nothing short of terrible. He had willfully broken his vows and slept with every woman who apparently wasn't smart enough to run for the hills when she met him. Including her own mother.

"Guess we're kind of a sorry bunch," Sophie said to the others.

"Hey, I'm not sorry," Keaton told her. "Because no matter how I got here, I *did* get here," he said with emphasis. "And it doesn't matter who sired you or how.

You're here, you're breathing and the rest is up to you from here on in. You've got your own future in your hands," Keaton maintained. "That's not to say that you can't look to family for a little backup," he added with a grin. "And there sure is a lot of family to look to around here."

"I still feel bad about Mother," Sophie told the others.

"Don't," Zoe said. "I'm sure she feels more than compensated for her 'pain and suffering' whenever she takes a look at the bank account balances, or goes shopping in one of those high-end department stores she loves so well."

"That's terrible," Sasha said to Graham, apparently not quietly enough because she was overheard.

"That's life," someone else countered. "Not everyone's a romantic at heart like Sophie."

Appalled at the criticism of a woman she'd never met, Chloe spoke up. "But money doesn't keep you warm at night no matter how much there is of it."

"But it can certainly pay for a really good heating system," one of the other people pointed out, laughing at their own joke.

This was a conversation Chance felt he had no right to be part of, as well as no interest. No doubt it had to be disturbing Chloe, too.

Feeling protective of her, he took Chloe's hand and guided her away.

"C'mon, let's see if we can find something sweet to take the bitter taste out of my mouth," Chance urged, nodding toward some of the tables that were set up beyond the grills. Sasha had several different desserts arranged there, and there were still some left.

Chloe looked around at the picnic gathering. Despite

some of the differences of opinion that had been thrown out over the course of the last few hours, she was beginning to believe that maybe, just maybe, she could have it all. A career, a family that numbered more than just one other person and, most important of all, love.

She slanted a look toward Chance, her heart swelling with hope. "Sounds like a good idea to me," she agreed.

Chapter 16

"Chloe, could I speak to you for a minute?"

About to go with Chance to get some dessert, Chloe was stopped dead in her tracks by a familiar voice. The last time she had heard that voice, she was being reviled for having the nerve to crash a family celebration, pretending to be Gerald Robinson's daughter. More things had been said, but Chloe had tuned them out, leaving the party soon after that.

With effort, Chloe forced herself to turn around and face Sophie Fortune Robinson. Although she was doing her best to hide it, an awkward feeling immediately wrapped itself around her. The exact same feeling that she'd experienced at the dinner party when Sophie had cornered her only to give her a complete dressing-down. Gerald Robinson's youngest legitimate daughter had been furious with her.

Bracing herself for the worst, Chloe said, "All right, I'm listening." *Which was more than you did*, she added silently.

Looking rather uncomfortable herself, Sophie glanced in Chance's direction. "Alone?" she requested.

Chance took his ground. "I can stay with you if you want me to," he told Chloe, deliberately not looking at Sophie. "Or I can wait for you over there." He nodded toward the dessert tables. "Your call."

The fact that he had volunteered to remain with her and was willing to do whatever she wanted heartened Chloe. It also gave her the strength to face whatever it was that Sophie had to say.

Chloe squared her shoulders. "It's okay. Just don't leave," she added as a coda, afraid he might take this opportunity to walk away from the picnic and go back to the bunkhouse.

"I'll be by the dessert table," Chance promised. And then he slanted a glance at Sophie before adding, "Within earshot if you need me."

With that, he walked away.

Stepping over to an area that was temporarily devoid of any picnickers for the moment, Chloe told Sophie, "All right, we're alone—or as alone as we can be at a family picnic." She pressed her lips together, centering herself before asking, "What is it that you want to tell me?"

It took Sophie several moments before she finally said the words Chloe never figured she'd hear.

"I'm sorry."

Chloe didn't know if she was being set up, or if she'd missed something. Sophie had looked almost hostile when their eyes had met that night at the dinner party. She assumed that nothing had changed. Or had it?

"Excuse me?"

"What I said to you the night at Kate Fortune's ranch… Well, I was out of line and I'm sorry. But you have to understand, it was a huge shock to me."

"Finding out that Gerald Robinson was my father?" Chloe asked. "Think how I felt," she pointed out.

Sophie nodded. "All I could think of was how *I* felt. And it wasn't just about finding out about you. It was finding out that the father I grew up adoring was nothing like what I thought he was. That the man I thought was so honorable couldn't seem to remain faithful or true to anyone." Her voice trembled as she spoke. "I was angry, I was hurt and I felt betrayed. And I'm afraid that I took it out on you." She looked at her, clearly embarrassed. "And for that I'm very sorry. I shouldn't have been angry with you. We were both in the same boat."

"Actually, we weren't in the same boat," Chloe politely corrected her. "Yours was a luxury liner. Mine was a leaky rowboat," she said, referring to the fact that while Sophie's childhood was spent in the lap of luxury, hers had been more of a hand-to-mouth existence because her father had deserted her mother.

Sophie's discomfort seemed to increase. "And that makes me feel twice as bad," Sophie told her.

"That wasn't your fault," Chloe pointed out. "That was your father's fault. When my mother finally told me who my father was—that he wasn't her high school sweetheart who was killed in a car accident before he could marry her, which was the story she'd told me all along—she admitted that she'd loved him a great deal.

And she told me how devastated she was when he just up and left her."

Chloe felt emotion choke her, and she cleared it from her throat before she continued. "Anyway, that practically destroyed my mother—but she realized that she had to go on living because I needed her, so she pulled herself together and created a life for the two of us.

"Because of the strength she displayed, my mother made me see that we each have the ability to be the masters of our own destinies. That means we can't put the blame on some outside forces that might or might not come swooping in."

As Chloe spoke she saw the shift of emotion on Sophie's face. Her expression went from sorrowful to hesitant and now hopeful. "So does that mean you forgive me?"

"There's nothing to forgive," Chloe told her, wanting to put the matter to rest.

But Sophie wasn't finished atoning for what she'd done. "Still, it took a lot of courage for you to come meet us the way you did, and then having me jump down your throat like that had to have made you feel just awful."

"Well, it didn't make me feel good," Chloe admitted. Since Sophie had apologized, she didn't want the other woman to continue feeling badly. "But if I were in your place, maybe I would have said the same thing."

Sophie shook her head. "No, you wouldn't have—but thank you for saying that," she told Chloe as she hugged her.

A smile bloomed on Chloe's lips. It looked like she was finally being accepted, not just by one or two members, but by the whole family in general.

It felt wonderful, Chloe thought.

Disengaging herself from Sophie, she pointed behind the young woman. "I think someone's waiting for you to get back to him," she told her half sister.

Sophie turned around to see that Mason was standing off to the side, patiently waiting for things to be resolved.

"He's been my rock through this whole thing," she told Chloe. Releasing her, Sophie lingered a moment longer. "We need to get together again—soon," she emphasized sincerely.

"It's a deal," Chloe told her, relieved that Sophie no longer looked upon her as some sort of a troublemaking agitator.

Chloe breathed a sigh of relief as she turned around to look for Chance.

He was waiting for her exactly where he said he would be—at the dessert table.

As she joined him there, Chloe had the impression that he had been watching her the entire time she'd been interacting with Sophie.

When she approached, he said, "I guess you didn't need rescuing after all."

"No, it turns out that I didn't," she told him. "Sophie came to me to apologize."

Ordinarily, he never asked for more information than was offered. But this time, he made an exception. Since he was in the dark about the whole incident at the previous dinner party, Chance asked, "What was she apologizing for?"

Chloe filled him in on the details.

"And she just apologized to you now for having a bad attitude?" he asked.

"I think, in part, she was apologizing for accusing me of lying about the whole thing. I get the impression that until the man's numerous partners came to light, Sophie thought her father walked on water." Chloe shook her head. "I guess it kind of goes along with the way my mother felt about him.

"When she finally told me the truth about who my father was, my mother admitted that she'd literally worshipped him—right up to when he walked out on her and broke her heart." Chloe frowned, thinking back over the years. So much made sense now. "I guess that's why she never got married or even had a relationship. She couldn't bring herself to trust another man enough to let her guard down."

Chance shook his head. He didn't say what he was thinking. That in his opinion, after what Chloe's father had done and all the people he had hurt with his behavior, Chloe's father should have been horsewhipped—at the very least.

"How many illegitimate kids did you say this man has?" Chance asked her.

Chloe sighed. She honestly had no idea how many there were. It was an odd thing to admit about her own father.

"The final count isn't in yet," she told him when she saw that he was waiting for an answer. "A couple of my half brothers are still trying to track down other potential siblings."

"Damn, that's really one for the books, all right," Chance commented.

It certainly was, Chloe thought, growing quiet. Gerald or Jerome or whatever he chose to call himself now was still her father, but she felt no affection for the man, no desire to be protective of him. She did, however, feel protective of her late mother, and she felt that to criticize the man her mother fell in love with, even temporarily, was to criticize her, and Chloe wouldn't allow that.

When Chance commented on the fact that she had grown very quiet, she deliberately changed the subject by suggesting they find the boys to see how they were faring at the picnic.

It took some looking, but when they did find all four of them, the teens were apparently having a good time, mingling with the younger people who had been brought to the picnic. They were also getting along with one another rather well.

When she saw that, Chloe felt warm all over. She'd been right to talk the boys into coming.

The way she saw it, the picnic, by almost all accounts, was a success.

There was only one downside to the picnic, and it was only a minor by-product, affecting no one but her.

She'd been riding high for almost the entire duration of the picnic. First because Chance had stayed, as she'd asked him to, and then because he had acted like the perfect hero, offering to stand by her. But now Chloe began to examine her feelings for Chance as well as what she'd hoped was her developing relationship with him.

The conclusion she came to was that any way she looked at it, Chance was too good to be true.

The phrase stunned her, echoing in her brain.

She realized that these were the exact same words her mother had used to describe the man who was her father. The man who had ultimately just run out on her, disappointing her so badly that he had crushed her young heart and prevented her from ever venturing to love anyone again.

That had to have been so emotionally crushing for her mother, Chloe thought. Even so, her mother had refused to crumble. Instead, she became a strong woman who had gone on to make a life for the two of them.

Admittedly, Chloe didn't know what she would have done if she'd been in her mother's place. What she did know was that she never *wanted* to be in her mother's place.

Too good to be true.

The phrase continued to echo in her head each time she looked at Chance. How could she expect a man like him to remain with her? To love her?

She knew the inevitable answer to that.

There was something she needed to do, Chloe decided, if she didn't want to be hurt the way her mother had been. She needed to make a preemptive strike in order to save herself.

The thought haunted her for the next few days, growing progressively larger and larger in her mind until it felt as if there was nothing else on her mind except for that.

"Miss Elliott? Are you okay?"

Chloe realized that she'd allowed her thoughts to get the better of her—again. It had been happening to her for days. In this case, instead of listening to Will and responding, she'd drifted off.

She looked at the boy apologetically. She couldn't afford to jeopardize the progress he and the others had made by allowing herself to become obsessed with her personal life. That wasn't fair to the boys, and it just wasn't right.

"I'm sorry, Will. I'm afraid I was just thinking about something."

"Yeah, I can tell." A shy smile curved the boy's mouth. "I asked you a question three times and you didn't answer."

Chloe looked at him, appalled. "Three times? That's unforgivable," she told the teen.

"Well, maybe it was two," he admitted, shrugging his thin shoulders. "But you did look like you were really far away. Anything I can help with?"

How far the teen had come, she thought. She was proud of having had a hand in his progress. She didn't want to be the cause of its undoing. "No, but you're a doll for asking."

Will flushed. "You're not going to call me that in front of the other guys, are you?" he asked, clearly horrified at the possibility.

She struggled not to laugh at the look on his face. "Your secret's safe with me, Will," she assured him, then, in case there was a question, she added, "*All* of your secrets are safe with me. You know that."

Will nodded. Their session was over and he had homework waiting for him, so he needed to go.

"Yeah, that's what you said when we started these things," he said, referring to the sessions as he got up. And then he stopped to look at her. "Um, Miss Elliott, you know that goes both ways, right?"

"I'm not sure I understand, Will," Chloe admitted.

Rather than just retreat, the way he would have a few short weeks ago, Will tried to explain. "What I'm trying to say is that if you've got something you want to talk about to someone, you can talk to me. I'm a good listener," he told her. "And I won't tell anyone anything. I promise."

She was tempted to hug him, but she knew how fragile teen egos were. She didn't want him thinking she regarded him as a child. He was a budding adult. So she kept her arms at her sides and simply told him, "I appreciate that, Will."

Even so, she wasn't about to tell him or any of the boys what was on her mind, especially since it involved Chance.

"But there's nothing I need to talk about," Chloe said.

There was something, though, she thought, that she needed to *do.* And soon.

But it wasn't going to be easy.

She'd agonized over it the entire day, until it was finally time for what had become a minor ritual: going out riding with Chance at the end of the day. She knew she couldn't put this off any longer. Because the longer she did, the harder it was going to be for her.

When Chance walked into the stable, expecting to go riding with Chloe as he did every late afternoon, he was surprised to see that although she was there, her horse wasn't saddled yet.

"You just get here?" he wanted to know. Even that was unusual for her. Punctuality was a thing for Chloe. She didn't like being late.

As he looked at her, he sensed the tension in the air and couldn't help wondering what was wrong. Rather than push, he waited for her to answer.

"Actually, I've been here for a while, waiting for you." Every word felt as if she was dragging it out of her mouth from the very depths of her soul. And every word tasted bitter on her tongue.

Her answer didn't make any sense to him. He frowned. "But your horse isn't saddled. Something wrong?" he asked, subconsciously trying to brace himself.

She didn't answer his question directly. Instead, Chloe went on to say the hardest words that she had ever had to say. "I don't think that we should go out riding together anymore."

"Okay." He regarded her warily as he spoke. Still, he had to go on as if everything was all right. Because he really wanted it to be. "You want to do something else instead?" Almost every time they went out, they returned to end their day in the guesthouse, enjoying each other's company to the fullest.

He had a feeling that wasn't going to be the case today, but he still had to ask.

She shook her head. "No, you don't understand. I don't think we should do anything together—including what we do after we go riding," she added, deliberately being vague because she didn't think she could say anything more specific without breaking down. As it was, she was fighting back tears. Her throat felt as if it was closing up.

She was looking away. Gently taking her face between his hands, Chance forced her to look up at him. "Have I done something to offend you?"

"No, you've been perfect," she cried, pulling back. Needing to put distance between them. "You've always been perfect."

It almost sounded like an accusation, he thought. One that just didn't make any sense at all. "I don't understand."

Tears were welling up in her eyes, and she looked away, not wanting him to see her cry.

"Please, don't make this any harder than it already is. I just can't see you anymore."

"Did Graham say something?" he asked, trying to make sense out of what was happening. Was there some sort of nonfraternizing rule in place that he didn't know about? If there was, then he'd quit. She meant that much to him.

For the first time in years, he'd been able to get beyond himself, and it was all because of her. And now she was pulling back. It didn't make sense to him, and he needed to know why this was happening.

"No, nobody said anything, and it's not anything you did." Her voice cracked and she tried again. "Please, Chance, don't ask me any more questions."

He felt as if he had been sliced in half, and he had no idea why or even what had gone wrong. All he knew was that he needed to get out of there now, while he could still function.

Before he couldn't move.

"All right," he told her stiffly, "I won't."

It was the last thing he said to her before he walked out.

His voice echoed in the stable long after he left. Just as long as she went on crying.

Chapter 17

It's better this way. It's better this way, you know that. Better to stop this now, before you give away your heart. You know what happens after that.

Chloe kept telling herself that over and over again, and while she believed she had done the right thing, that still didn't make it any easier for her to live with. She tried to keep as busy as possible, but a sadness saturated her every waking moment.

Especially the evenings, which now seemed to last twice as long as they used to.

But the hardest part was running into Chance. Their paths seemed to cross a lot less than they used to, but when they did, she felt an unbearable pain, as if she'd been stabbed by a sword with rusty, jagged edges every time she realized that he was there, somewhere near her space.

When was it going to get better? When was the pain going to go away? She had broken things off with Chance to avoid being hurt and yet, that was exactly what was happening. Pain, raw and devastating, was eating her up from the inside out.

In its own way, this was every bit as difficult to endure as when she'd found that Donnie was no longer going to be part of her life, that he'd never be coming back to her.

Chloe began to second-guess herself. Had she acted too rashly? In trying to avoid heartache, had she unwittingly opened the door and allowed heartache to come into her life?

Chloe had no answers, only more questions.

"How come you don't go riding with Ms. Elliott anymore?" Brandon asked out of the blue one afternoon as he and Chance were in the corral, working on taming a new addition to the herd that Graham had just bought.

Chance had picked Brandon to help him because the teen showed the most promise when it came to working with the horses. His hostility finally under control, Brandon was usually on the quiet side. But that obviously wasn't the case today.

"That's not a question you should be asking me," Chance told him.

"I thought you told me that I could ask you anything," Brandon said innocently.

The horse was fighting the bit he was trying to put into its mouth. For the moment, Chance stopped to look at Brandon. "About your own life, not mine."

"Well, since I've been here, you've become part of my life," Brandon pointed out. "You and Miss Elliott."

Determined to get an answer, he tried again. "So how come you don't go riding together anymore?"

"It's just better this way," Chance told the teen dismissively, hoping that would be the end of it.

It wasn't.

"Doesn't seem better," Brandon observed after several minutes. He stroked the stallion's muzzle, doing what he could to keep the animal calm as Chance made another attempt to put the bit into the stallion's mouth. "Seems like both of you look real unhappy. If things were better, you two wouldn't look like that."

Chance sighed. *No arguing with that*, he thought. "It's complicated."

"That's what people say when they don't want to talk about something—or admit that they're wrong about something," Brandon added. "From where I'm sitting," he continued when Chance made no comment, "it doesn't look complicated at all. You were happy riding together, and now you're not riding together and you're not happy. Seems to me like you were both better off riding."

The third attempt to get the horse to accept the bit succeeded. Chance paused, not wanting to rush things with the stallion.

"Yeah, well, that's not going to happen," he told Brandon as he fed the horse a lump of sugar. "Get the blanket."

Brandon did as he was told, hurrying to the fence where the blanket hung and then back again. He held it out to Chance, along with more advice. "You could tell her you're sorry."

Chance handed the reins to the teen and spread the

blanket on the horse's back. The stallion remained relatively still. "What?"

There was a warning note in Chance's voice, but Brandon pushed on anyway.

"If you made her angry," Brandon explained, "you could tell her you're sorry. Women like it when you tell them you're sorry."

The assertion by one so young made Chance laugh. "And how would you know that?"

"That's what my brother told me," Brandon said matter-of-factly. "You know what else he told me?"

Chance paused. He realized that this was a breakthrough for Brandon. Up until now, the teen hadn't talked about the brother he'd lost. He'd acted on the anger he felt because of the loss, but he had never mentioned Blake in a day-to-day context, never even referred to him.

There was a momentary tug-of-war within him, and then Chance decided to set aside his need for privacy, putting Brandon's need to heal and progress ahead of his own. "No, what else did he tell you?"

A distant, wistful look came over the teen's face as he no doubt thought of his brother. "That if you want something, sometimes you've got to fight for it. That if something just falls into your lap, it doesn't mean nearly as much as it does if you have to go out and fight for it."

Brandon grew very solemn as he recalled his brother's words. "That's what Blake told me when I asked him why he enlisted instead of going to college like he was supposed to. He said he had to fight for what he believed in. Maybe that's what you need to do," Brandon concluded, looking at him. "Maybe you need to fight for Miss Elliott."

Chance shook his head. "I don't think Miss Elliott wants me to fight for—"

"I think she's looking pretty sad lately," Brandon stressed. "And Will said she keeps losing her train of thought during his sessions. Ryan says the same thing," he added. "Maybe like she's always saying, you need to talk about it. About whatever it is that made the two of you stop doing what you both liked doing." The teen gave Chance an encouraging smile. "Might make you both feel better about things if you clear the air."

Chance looked at the boy he had been trying to reach for weeks now. The boy who had just now tried to reach him instead.

"It just might at that," he agreed. "But right now, we've got a horse to work with."

"I don't think he'd mind waiting," Brandon speculated.

"Get the saddle." He indicated where he'd placed it on the top rung of the corral. "Always finish a job you start."

"That's a good one," Brandon said, nodding with approval as he went to fetch the saddle. "You might want to remember that one when you go talk to Miss Elliott later," he suggested.

Chance grinned as he took the saddle from Brandon and placed it carefully on the stallion's back. The horse tried to pull away, but Brandon was holding firmly on to the bit, keeping the animal in place. Chance slowly tightened the cinch, watching the horse intently.

"I might at that," Chance agreed.

For the first time since he'd arrived at Peter's Place, he saw Brandon grin.

* * *

"Come in," Chloe said in response to the knock on the door of her small office.

When she looked up from her work, she was surprised. Expecting to see one of the boys coming in for what she assumed was an extra session, she found herself looking up at Chance instead.

Her heart leaped, and she felt the definite rush of adrenaline surge through her veins before she managed to tuck it away and get it under control. She wasn't supposed to be reacting to Chance like this anymore, she upbraided herself. Especially since in the days that followed her breaking it off with him, Chance hadn't attempted to approach her, not even once. That convinced her that her so-called preemptive strike in pushing Chance out of her life before he walked out on her had been the right move. Because if he'd actually cared about her—even a little—he would have at least *tried* to get back into her life, tried to get her to give him a second chance.

But he hadn't.

Instead, he'd kept his distance. Even at the table, when they took their meals, he didn't say even two words to her. A man who cared didn't behave that way.

A man who was glad things were over, however, did.

Not waiting for Chance to say anything that she might not want to hear, she took the lead. Doing her best to sound cheerful, she said, "I hear congratulations are in order."

For a moment, because he was still trying to sort his thoughts out and find the right words to say to her,

Chance didn't know what she was referring to. He looked at her, puzzled. "For what?"

"For getting Graham to approve your idea. He seemed very enthusiastic about it," she added, recalling the look on her brother's face when he told her the news.

Because of what he'd been going through, Chance had almost forgotten that his proposal had been approved. Graham had gotten the funding, and plans were under way for expanding Peter's Place to include a military equine therapy center for returning vets. "Oh. Right. Thanks."

She would have thought that he would be happy about his victory. Why wasn't he? "Well, you don't sound like you're nearly as excited about it as Graham is," Chloe observed.

"Right now, that's not the main thing on my mind," Chance admitted, his eyes meeting hers.

She wished he wouldn't look at her like that. It made her remember. And yearn. She had to keep herself from squirming.

"Is there something I can help you with?" Chloe asked stiffly.

She sounded like a robot, Chance thought. Was it because he was here? He began having second thoughts about the whole thing. Maybe this wasn't such a good idea.

But he *was* here now, so he might as well say what he'd come to say. He knew Brandon would ask him about it. Just as he knew that he had to give this one final try so that he knew he had done all he could before giving up on the situation.

On her.

On them.

Here goes nothing. "You can help me understand why you suddenly decided to pull back. I thought things were going pretty well," he told her, forcing himself to be honest about his feelings. "I realize that I don't measure up to your late husband, but—"

She stared at him, stunned. "Wait, what? Who told you about Donnie?" she wanted to know. She had never said anything about her late husband to Chance, never mentioned how distraught she'd felt about losing him. How had he found out?

Chance didn't see how that was the point, but he answered her question. "Sasha told me. Don't blame her, I made her tell me. I asked if you were involved with anyone. I thought maybe that was why you didn't want to go riding with me anymore. Or anything else for that matter," he added meaningfully.

He'd missed being with her more than he could possibly say, but it was hard for him to actually admit that. "She told me that you were devastated by your husband's death."

He'd done his homework, contacted people he knew, people he hadn't spoken to in years and asked questions about the man.

"I know I don't measure up to him in your eyes, but I don't want to take his place. I just want to be with you." She was seated at her desk, and he stood over her now, looking down into her face as he searched for an answer. "Why can't I be with you?"

"Because you're perfect," she blurted out, "and before long, you'll realize that you can do a lot better than me and you'll move on. I just can't take dealing with loss again," she informed him, sadly adding, "This way is better."

His thoughts had come to a grinding halt several sentences ago. "Hold it. You think I'm *perfect*?" he questioned incredulously. "You're pulling my leg, right? I mean, you can't be serious." He was as far from perfect as a man could be, Chance thought.

"Of course I'm serious," she told him. "Why wouldn't I be?"

"Well, for one thing, because I'm not perfect," he told her with a disparaging laugh. Thinking back on the image he'd portrayed to her, he realized how he might have misled her. "I just wanted you to see the best in me because a really classy lady like you isn't going to want to be with any ol' cowboy, especially one that's got his own set of demons."

Despite everything, she couldn't help the smile that rose to her lips. Couldn't keep it from curving the corners of her mouth.

"Haven't you heard?" she asked him. "That's what I do. I exorcise demons." Her smile faded a little as she grew more serious. "But you never indicated that you were anything but a tall, silent cowboy, the kind that used to be in all those old Westerns that they made in the fifties and sixties."

"A cowboy, yeah," he scoffed. "A cowboy who fought overseas."

Why would he think that changed anything in the way she saw him? "At least you got to come back."

He didn't see that as a plus. It was more like his cross to bear. "At times, I really feel that I shouldn't have."

That made absolutely no sense to her. "Why?" she cried.

He told her what weighed most heavily on his conscience, something he hadn't shared with anyone since he'd returned stateside.

"Because I couldn't save my best friend," he confessed. "Evan and I had been friends since grammar school. We enlisted together, did everything together." His mouth felt dry as he relived his friend's final moments. "Evan got between me and enemy fire. He died in my place, in my arms. And I haven't been able to find a place for myself since." Chance took a breath, and then he looked down at her. She had made the difference in his life. "Until I met you."

"But when I said that we shouldn't be together, you just accepted it," she pointed out. "If I meant that much to you, why did you just back off and not even *try* to get me to change my mind?"

He wasn't the type to push himself on anyone. "Because that's what I thought you wanted, and I wanted you to be happy even if I wasn't."

That sounded like him, she realized. "What changed your mind?"

He laughed softly to himself before answering. "Brandon."

"Brandon?" she repeated. Brandon hardly talked now that he had stopped being angry at the world. "What could he have possibly said to change your mind?"

"He noticed how unhappy I looked. How unhappy we both looked," Chance emphasized. "Then he told me something his brother told him."

"His brother? He opened up about Blake?" Chloe asked, stunned and excited at this breakthrough. Brandon had been her last holdout.

"Yes, he did. He told me that his brother told him very simply that if he wanted something, really wanted it, he should go for it. Fight for it." Chance paused, looking at her pointedly. "So this is me, 'fighting for it.'" He took her hands in his and brought her up to her feet. "Fighting for you." He drew her into his arms and bent his head, kissing her.

Chance's kiss felt as if the sun had suddenly come out after days of being hidden behind a dreary rain cloud. This was what she'd missed, what she'd longed for.

What she'd *needed.*

She kissed Chance with all the bottled-up passion she'd been trying to convince herself she no longer felt. Wrapping her arms around his neck, she clung to him for a moment, her lips sealed to his.

When he finally drew back, he smiled into her eyes.

"Does this mean you'll go riding with me again?" he asked. There was a trace of mischief in his eyes.

"It does," she told him.

Maybe he was pushing his luck, but he still wanted to ask. "Does this also mean that you'll—"

Her eyes danced as she cried, "Yes."

He laughed. She was getting ahead of herself. "I haven't finished asking you the question."

The smile that lit up her features was warm, sunny. And oh, so relieved. "I have an idea I know what's coming."

"I have an idea that you don't," he told her. He knew he had to get this out before his courage deserted him, and he really wished he had something to give her to seal this moment. "Chloe Elliott, I don't have much to offer you—"

How could he even think that? "You're wrong," she told him. "You have a great deal to offer."

"Don't interrupt," he said. "I have to get this out before I lose my nerve."

"All right," she told him, her heart pounding madly. It wasn't easy for her to keep quiet, but she did her best. "Go on."

He started again. "I don't have much to offer you, but I love you and I'll do everything in my power to make you happy—and to never regret marrying me." He stumbled a little, his thoughts getting in the way of his tongue. "That is, if you *want* to marry me." He blew out a breath. "This isn't coming out the way I want it to. Talking isn't what I do best."

She was nothing if not encouraging. "You're doing great so far."

He took a long breath. If he talked any more, he'd mess it up. "I'm finished," he told her. "You can answer now if you'd like."

"I like," Chloe told him with all sincerity. "I like very much."

Maybe this wasn't a total disaster after all. "So will you marry me?" he wanted to know.

Her eyes crinkled as she laughed. "What do you think?"

She was drawing this out, and he couldn't stand the tension pulsating through him. "I think I'm going to have heart failure if you don't answer me in the next couple of seconds."

She kept as straight a face as she could. "I don't know CPR, so I guess I'd better say yes." And then every single part of her being grinned. "Yes, I'll marry you. Yes, yes, yes," she cried, throwing her arms around his neck again.

"I heard you the first time," he answered, gathering her in his arms.

"I wanted to be sure you did."

"I did," he answered, then added, "I do," before he kissed her again.

And, just to be sure that she wasn't going to change her mind, he went on kissing her for a long time.

Epilogue

"So, how did it feel to find out that your father is one of the famous Fortunes?"

The question came from Ariana Lamonte, the magazine writer and blogger who had already interviewed several of Gerald Robinson's children.

They were sitting in the living room of the guesthouse where Chloe was presently living, and the vivacious reporter had already asked her a number of probing questions.

At first, Chloe had thought she was just going to avoid the woman, but after the reporter had called her a number of times in the last few days, Ariana didn't give her the impression that she was about to give up until she got what she wanted. And besides, submitting to the interview seemed almost like an initiation into the family. Others had done it, and if her responses and feelings were put down on record, then by all rights that made her a part of the family, as well.

"It felt strange," Chloe admitted, answering Ariana's last question.

The woman's fingers flew over her small laptop, making notes as thoughts occurred to her.

She looked up at Chloe, giving her a sympathetic smile. "That's right, he was AWOL for most of your life, wasn't he?"

"Not most," Chloe corrected. *"All."*

Ariana nodded, her keyboard clicking rhythmically as she made more notes. "So what did you think of him when you two finally met?"

"We haven't." When Ariana looked at her sharply, she added, "Yet."

"But you're going to, right?" the woman with the long brown hair and the animated, deep brown eyes pressed. "Now that you know who he is, you can't just *not* meet the man," Ariana insisted.

"There's been talk about setting something up, yes," Chloe replied vaguely.

And there was. Gerald Robinson had actually reached out to her. But, still harboring anger over the way the man had treated her mother, Chloe was in no hurry to meet her father face-to-face. She had stalled.

"Aren't you at least curious what he's like?" Ariana wanted to know.

She supposed she was somewhat curious. She wouldn't be human if she wasn't. "Maybe a little," she admitted.

Ariana laughed. She paused and reached over to lightly touch Chloe's hand. "Well, if it were me and my absentee daddy had all that money—"

"I don't care about the money," Chloe told her, cutting the woman off.

Ariana could only shake her head. "Well, you're a better person than most," she confided.

Chloe set her jaw. "There are some things that money can't pay for. But I will give him a chance to explain why he did what he did—if he actually has a reason."

Ariana smiled warmly at the young woman sitting across from her. "You're a good person, Chloe Elliott. Or would you rather I called you Chloe Fortune? Some of your siblings have taken on the name," the reporter said.

"I'd rather you just called me Chloe," she told the reporter.

"I think I'd like that," Ariana replied. She closed her laptop. "Well, I think I have everything I need," she said, concluding the interview as she rose to her feet. "If I think of any further questions, I'll give you a call. And after you meet your father face-to-face, I'd appreciate it if you give *me* a call," she requested.

Chloe accompanied her to the door.

"Thanks for your time," Ariana told her. "I'll email you a copy of the interview when it's finished."

As she began to walk out, the woman nearly collided with Chance, who was just about to knock on Chloe's door.

"I can see why you were in a hurry to wrap this interview up," Ariana said, looking appreciatively at the tall cowboy, then gave Chloe a grin. "Maybe I'll see you again."

The moment the reporter crossed the threshold and left the house, Chance closed the door behind her. He flipped the lock in place.

"So, how was it?" he asked Chloe, turning to face her.

"Not as bad as I thought," Chloe confessed. "She was nice. She asked a lot of questions, but I think that I managed to hold my own."

"I knew you would," Chance told her. He pressed a kiss to her temple as he gave Chloe a quick, warm embrace.

"Well, that puts you one up on me." She looked away from the door and turned her face up to Chance. She knew he had just come from a meeting with Graham about the planned expansion. "So, tell me," she urged, waiting for him to share his news.

"Everything's in motion," he told her happily. "With any luck, the military *equine*—" he deliberately drew the word out to emphasize it "—therapy center will be opening ahead of schedule. I can't tell you how good that makes me feel."

"Oh, I think I can guess," she told him, amusement dancing in her eyes.

He knew he needed to put this in perspective for her. He wanted her to understand just what she meant to him. "Almost as good as knowing that you're actually going to be marrying me. You still are, aren't you?" he asked, closing his arms around her.

Chloe's smile was wide and warm. "Try to stop me," she told him with a laugh.

"Now, why would I want to do that?" he questioned as if she had just suggested something completely absurd. "My mamma didn't raise any stupid children."

"Good. Neither did mine. Wanna go for a ride?" she asked him.

"Why don't we skip going for a ride today?" he suggested. "And just go straight to the good part."

"I thought you once told me that riding was the good part," she reminded him.

"I did and it was—until I met you and found a whole other way to feel good." He pulled her tighter. "No more talking," he said as he lowered his mouth to hers.

One touch of his lips had desire streaking through her. "No more talking," she agreed.

So they didn't.

* * * * *

Though her name is frequently on bestseller lists, **Allison Leigh**'s high point as a writer is hearing from readers that they laughed, cried or lost sleep while reading her books. She credits her family with great patience for the time she's parked at her computer, and for blessing her with the kind of love she wants her readers to share with the characters living in the pages of her books. Contact her at allisonleigh.com.

Books by Allison Leigh

Harlequin Special Edition

Return to the Double C

A Weaver Christmas Gift
One Night in Weaver...
The BFF Bride
A Child Under His Tree
Yuletide Baby Bargain
Show Me a Hero
The Rancher's Christmas Promise
A Promise to Keep
Lawfully Unwed
Something About the Season
The Horse Trainer's Secret
A Rancher's Touch
Her Wyoming Valentine Wish

Visit the Author Profile page
at Harlequin.com for more titles.

WILD WEST FORTUNE

Allison Leigh

For Susan and Marcia.
Nobody keeps our Fortune world together
better than the two of you!

Chapter 1

"Girl, this is not good."

Ariana Lamonte made a face as she looked out the windows of her car. She hadn't seen another vehicle for more than an hour. Grassland whipped in the wind all the way to the horizon in every direction. The same wind rocked her little car where she was parked on the dirt shoulder, and sent the thick clouds overhead racing across the sky. "Not good at all," she repeated to herself.

She fished her cell phone up from the passenger side floor by the charging cord tethering it to her dashboard. Using the GPS on the phone always drained the battery quickly, so she'd at least been prepared on that score when she'd set out from Austin that morning. But she sure wished she'd been better prepared with the address she was seeking. There was a dot blinking on her phone screen, right atop a barely discernible line that indicated the laughable excuse for a road on which she sat.

But that was it. No town. No other roads.

Nothing. Nada.

For the third time, she checked her notes and verified the address she'd put into her GPS app. Everything matched.

Which meant she ought to be sitting in the middle of a place called Paseo, Texas.

Instead, she was sitting in the middle of…

"Grass," she muttered, looking out the windows again. "Nothing but grass and more grass." And she'd wasted nearly an entire day getting there.

The wind howled and her car rocked again. She studied her phone for a moment. The GPS dot blinked back at her, but there wasn't a strong enough cell signal to even make a phone call or send a text message. Not that she particularly wanted to advertise to anyone that she wasn't really home in her apartment where she was supposed to be working on an assignment for the magazine.

Instead, she'd set out on yet another wild goose chasing down facts for the real life story behind Robinson Tech's founder, Gerald Robinson. The real life story that would prove once and for all that Ariana Lamonte wasn't just an internet blogger who'd more or less stumbled into print journalism. That she deserved her own spot on the map.

Preferably a better map than the one her GPS was currently providing.

She dropped the useless phone on the passenger seat and opened the thick pink notebook on the console, clicking her pen a few times before sighing and drawing a line through the address as she thought about Gerald Robinson.

For one thing, he was a tech industry giant. A household name well beyond the city limits of Austin, Texas, where Robinson Tech was based and where Austinites tended to follow his family like the Brits followed the Royals.

On the surface, the billionaire had everything. Money. Power. Success. He was the father of eight children thanks to his long-standing marriage to a woman who didn't seem outraged at all over the fairly recent revelation that he'd also fathered more than a few illegitimate children during that marriage.

But what made the situation particularly interesting to Ariana was that Charlotte Prendergast Robinson had also been resolutely closemouthed since the truth came out a year ago that the very *identity* of the man she'd married was a fiction. Gerald Robinson was a creation of Jerome Fortune. A black-sheep relative of an immensely wealthy, immensely powerful family who'd all believed Jerome to be dead.

Half the world had collectively gasped when that came out.

But not Charlotte. It was as if there was nothing on earth capable of shocking or surprising Gerald's wife.

Though that wasn't exactly accurate, either. If it weren't for Charlotte, Ariana wouldn't be trying to find Paseo.

She flipped a page in her notes, chewing the inside of her cheek as she studied Charlotte's photograph. Presumably, she enjoyed the perks of her position so much that she'd rather stand by her husband's side than publicly express even the slightest hint of outrage and possibly hinder those perks.

But would they really be hindered?

Charlotte was clearly the injured party in the Robinson marriage. Ariana had found no record of the couple ever having a prenuptial agreement. Their marriage predated Robinson Tech's astronomical success. Success that hadn't been hurt in the least by Gerald's scandals. If anything, the company was stronger than ever. If Charlotte chose to walk away from a philandering husband, she'd be walking away with at least half of their fortune. The luxurious lifestyle to which she was accustomed wouldn't be changed in the least.

And it wasn't as if the children she and Gerald had together would necessarily be affected. They were all accomplished adults in their own rights. Ariana had profiled many of them, as well as some of Gerald's illegitimate offspring, in her series, "Becoming a Fortune," for *Weird Life Magazine*.

As she'd gotten to know them, she'd formed the opinion that Charlotte was hardly the most loving mother in the world. The woman seemed more involved with her charity work than she was in their lives—even when they had been much younger. Admittedly, none of them had derogatory things to say about their mother. They were too classy for that. But Ariana still sensed there *was* some curiosity regarding their mother's steadfast loyalty to their father.

And Ariana was pretty curious, too. Particularly after she'd managed to get a moment alone with the excessively private woman at one of Charlotte's recent fund-raisers. All Ariana had asked her for was a little clarification about a newspaper article she'd found at the

Austin History Center. Not once had Ariana seen the woman look even remotely rattled until she'd grabbed Ariana's arm, escorting her personally from the function with the warning that she was not going to treat kindly anyone digging up useless old dirt about Paseo.

So far, Charlotte had said, she'd tolerated Ariana's vacuous magazine series, but it would be an easy matter for her to have a "little talk" with the local magazine about the harassment her family was receiving at the hands of Ariana. After all, she and the publisher sat on a few boards together.

Ariana could have argued the harassment point, but she'd chosen to leave instead. The tacit threat about her job would have been more worrisome if not for the fact that she had bigger fish to fry than the magazine where she worked. Now she had a book deal. The kind of deal where Ariana could really make her mark as a biographer.

But she hadn't left empty-handed. Because not once had Ariana ever mentioned Paseo in any of her pieces. She hadn't even heard of the name before. It hadn't been in the article Ariana had uncovered. That had simply been a decades-old society feature about Charlotte and Gerald's wedding.

And Ariana wasn't even certain now that Mrs. Robinson had meant the *town* of Paseo. It could just as easily be a person's name. Maybe the name of a company…

Ariana looked out the window again. Not that the town seemed to exist outside of a map.

Which meant she'd have to go back to the drawing board where Gerald's life was concerned. She wanted to tell the story that no one else had already told.

Yes, Gerald had been born as Jerome Fortune. Yes,

he'd cut his ties with his real family so decisively that he'd even faked his own death. Then he'd effectively disappeared from all existence until one day springing forth as Gerald Robinson. And soon after, he'd made Charlotte Prendergast his bride.

It ought to have been a grand love story. Gerald and Charlotte went on to have eight children together, for heaven's sake. There'd been countless articles and news stories about them. Yet now it came out that Gerald had consistently strayed. Even during the earliest years of their marriage, he'd been off Johnny-Appleseeding with other women.

Was it simply a character flaw? He wasn't the first brilliant, powerful man to have a weakness for women. Or was there something deeper? Another secret that motived him?

What had really happened between Jerome's "demise" and Gerald's explosive success in the tech field?

That was a big black hole into which her book would shine a good, long light.

And that was why she was sitting on the side of the road in the middle of Grassland, USA.

She rubbed her face and wished she hadn't finished her Starbucks coffee two hours earlier. It would take her hours to get back to Austin. She'd do better to just keep plowing onward. She knew she had to be close to the state line by now, which would put Oklahoma City much closer.

A decent hotel bed. A lot of fresh coffee. Then she could hop on the interstate and drive back to Austin in the morning. It would still take five or six hours, but at least she'd be driving faster than the snail's pace she'd had to use during today's wasted trek. She'd be home in plenty of time to finish up her article about the grand opening of Austin Commons, Austin's newest multiuse complex scheduled for the end of the month. She wouldn't even have been assigned the story if the project's architect hadn't been Keaton Whitfield. He'd been one of her first "Becoming a Fortune" subjects.

She sighed and tossed aside her notes, peering through the windshield again. The clouds were angrily black, and lightning flashed in the distance.

A sharp crack on the side window made her jump so hard she banged her elbow on the steering wheel.

The sight of a man standing on the road right next to her car, though, made her nearly scream.

She reared away from the window, slamming her foot on the brake and jabbing the push-button start.

"Whoa, whoa, whoa," the man yelled through the window. From the corner of her eye she saw him tip back his black cowboy hat. "Don't run me over, honey! Just checking that you're all right."

Hesitating was stupid. Every single thing she'd ever read or written about a woman's personal safety told her that. Her heart was lodged somewhere up in her ears, pounding so loudly she felt nauseated.

The wind ripped, yanking the hat off the man's head, and she heard him curse before he jogged after it.

She could have driven off right then, but the sight of him chasing after his hat, reaching down more than once trying to scoop it up as it rolled and bounced along the road, kept her in place.

That, and the sight in her rearview mirror of a shaggy brown-and-black dog hanging its head out the window of the dusty pickup truck parked behind her.

Did ax murderers tie bandanna kerchiefs around their dogs' necks?

"Get a grip, girl." She put the car in gear but kept her foot on the brake. The guy finally caught his cowboy hat and jammed it back on his head as he strode back toward her car.

This time, when he leaned down to look in her window, he kept his hand clamped on top of his hat, holding it in place. "Got a bad storm coming, ma'am. I can give you directions if you're lost."

"I'm not lost."

He squinted his clear brown eyes at her, clearly skeptical.

Her heart was back in her chest again, pounding harder than usual, but at least in the right sector of her body. She need only hit the gas to drive off.

And she'd already wasted a whole day…

She surreptitiously double-checked that her doors were locked and squinted back at him. If he was an ax murderer, he was a fine-looking one. And what his rear end did for his plain old blue jeans was a work of art. He wouldn't have any difficulty getting a woman to follow him most anywhere.

Not her, of course. She was too smart to get bowled over by a stranger just because he happened to be—as her mama would have said—a handsome cuss. If he was an ax murderer, he was going to have to work a little harder than that.

She reined in her stampeding imagination and wondered if she should give writing fiction a try, since she was so far doing such a bang-up job on the biography.

Despite common sense and caution, she rolled down her window. Her hair immediately blew around her face.

She grabbed her phone and held it out for the stranger to see the map displayed on the screen. "I'm looking for a town called Paseo. Paseo, Texas," she elaborated just in case she *had* crossed into Oklahoma without knowing it.

He ducked his head when another dirty gust blew across them. "What kinda business you got there?"

She squinted at him. "Well, that's *my* business, isn't it?"

He yanked off his hat, evidently tired of trying to keep it in place. The wind chopped through his brown hair and pulled at the collar of his gray-and-white plaid shirt, revealing more of his suntanned throat. "Gonna be my business if I have to haul your toy car here out of a ditch when this storm gets worse." He thumped the top of her car with his hand. "You want Paseo, you almost found it. Up the road a ways, you gotta cross a small bridge and then you'll see the sign. But you'd better get your pretty self going before those clouds open up. This isn't a road you want to be on in a storm."

"So you live around here?"

"Yes, ma'am." He stuck out his hand toward her. "Jayden Fortune."

The phone slipped out of her fingers.

He caught it. "Whoa, there. Looks too expensive to be tossing around on the highway." He held it toward her.

"Not much of a highway," she managed as her mind spun with excitement. Could it be so easy? *Fortune?* "There are more dirt ruts than pavement."

The corner of his mouth curled upward. "Well, we're not exactly looking for strangers around here. Which—" he ducked his head against a gust of wind accompanied by a crash of thunder "—pleasant as this may be, *is* what you are."

She was blinking hard from the dust blowing into her eyes. "My name is Ariana Lamonte. From Austin. I'm working on a magazine article." It was true. Just not the whole truth.

"A magazine article about Paseo?" He snorted, looking genuinely amused. "Don't want to disappoint you, ma'am, but there isn't a damn thing interesting enough around these parts to merit something like that."

"I don't know about that. Considering a Fortune lives here." She yanked her hair out of her eyes, holding it behind her head so she could see him better. If this man was one of Gerald's illegitimate offspring, then he'd be the first one she'd encountered who already *knew* he was a Fortune. Or maybe he wasn't even illegitimate. She'd already entertained the idea that Gerald could have had a family before his Robinson one. There were certainly enough missing years in his life to allow for one. And it would definitely account for Charlotte's antagonism toward Ariana bringing up the past.

Could there have been another wife? Maybe one whom Gerald had never even bothered to divorce before he'd married Charlotte Prendergast?

The wheels in her head spun fresh again as she gave Jayden a closer look.

"The name Fortune doesn't mean I possess one," he was saying. His smile was very white, very even, except for one slightly crooked cuspid that saved him from looking a little too perfect. Maybe there was a resemblance to Gerald Robinson. Or maybe that was just hopeful thinking on her part.

He rested his arm on top of her car and angled his

head, his gaze roving over her and the interior of her car. He glanced over the empty coffee cups and discarded fast-food wrappers lying untidily on the floor as well as the thick notebook laden with news clippings and photographs spread open on her passenger seat.

"Only thing I'm rich in is land, and land round here isn't all that valuable, either. So what's interesting enough about Paseo to bring a reporter like you all the way from the big city?"

Her car rocked again and several fat raindrops splattered on her windshield. "I'm not a reporter for the local news or anything. I'm a journalist."

"There's a difference?"

"If I was a news reporter, I'd probably have a better salary," she admitted ruefully. She casually closed the notebook as she reached behind her seat and grabbed the latest edition of *Weird Life Magazine* and passed it through the window. A photograph of Ben Fortune Robinson—Gerald's eldest son, who was the Chief Operating Officer of Robinson Tech—was on the cover. "I'm not just writing an article. I'm working on an entire series about the members of the Fortune family, actually, for *Weird Life Magazine*. You have heard of Gerald Robinson, right? Robinson Tech? His real name used to be Jerome Fortune." She watched Jayden's face. But the only expression her admission earned was more humor.

"Then you're really gonna be disappointed," he drawled, barely giving the magazine a glance before giving it back to her. "I'm not related. My last name might be Fortune, but only because my mom made it up."

The sky suddenly opened up in earnest and he shoved his hat back on his head. "Storms around here're pretty unpredictable, ma'am. Last year we had hail that damaged the town hall so badly it looked like a bomb had hit it. Might be best if you come with me."

She rolled up the window, stopping shy a few inches, but rain still blew in. Just because he had the last name Fortune—which she wasn't ready to attribute to coincidence no matter what he said—didn't mean she planned to get into his truck. The weather hadn't worried her before, but the rain was coming down so hard now, she could barely see out the windshield. "I'll follow you."

He was already drenched, rain sheeting off the brim of his hat. He looked like he was going to argue, but then just tilted his head. "Suit yourself."

She closed the window the rest of the way and switched on her windshield wipers, watching through her rearview mirror as he yanked open his truck door. Even the bandanna-wearing dog had ducked back inside the cab of the truck.

The car rocked again, whether from the vibration of another violent thunderclap or the wind, she couldn't tell. "Not good, Ariana," she muttered. "Not good at all."

The truck passed her, and even through the curtain of rain between them, she could see Jayden Fortune looking at her.

A shiver danced down her spine.

Okay. So not *all* not good.

She gave him a thumbs-up sign and steered back onto the road to follow him.

Less than a mile had passed before she was starting to wish she'd taken his offer and left her car on the side of the road. It might have washed off in the deluge but at least she wouldn't have been in it. As it was, she'd nearly driven off the side of the road twice, her wheels slipping and spinning in the slick mud.

Her knuckles white, her windshield wipers going full blast, she followed as closely as she dared. She didn't want to lose sight of his taillights, but she was also afraid of running right into the back of his truck.

"Times like this make you want to be a waitress again," she muttered, then screeched a little when she felt her tires sliding sideways again. Her heart in her throat and her father's lectures spinning inside her head, she finally regained traction only to see Jayden's truck had turned off the highway and those red taillights were getting fainter by the second.

She couldn't tell where the road was that he'd turned onto, but she followed him anyway, her chest knocking the steering wheel and her head hitting the headrest as she bounced down a small hill.

"Next time just get in the dang truck," she said loudly when water splashed up over the hood of her car, dousing her windshield with mud.

The only saving grace was the force of the rain that washed away the mud and allowed her a moment to see the road—yes, it *was* a road—in front of her and Jayden's taillights still ahead.

She exhaled loudly, focusing on them like a lifeline as they drove onward. It felt like they'd been driving for miles when the rain suddenly eased up, and she spotted buildings nearby that soon became distinct enough to identify as a two-story house and an enormous barn.

"Thank you, God," she breathed, unclenching her fingers as she pulled up next to where Jayden had parked. She jabbed the ignition button and her car went still.

She hadn't even had time to unbuckle her seat belt when she saw him streak from his truck to the side of her car again, yanking open the door.

"What—"

"Hurry up."

Ariana automatically reached over for her phone that had once again fallen onto the passenger side floor.

"Leave it." His voice was sharp and her hackles started to rise.

She deliberately closed her hand around the phone before straightening in her seat once more. Annoyed or not with his tone, she still needed to explore this whole Fortune thing. And a girl usually got further with honey than she did with vinegar. "I appreciate your—"

"Sweetheart, in gear. *Now.*" He grabbed her arm, practically hauling her out of the car.

Horror mingled with annoyance as she struggled against his iron grip, nearly tripping before she found steady footing. If it weren't for her high-heeled boots, he would have towered over her. As it was, her forehead had a close encounter with the faint cleft in his sharp chin. "I don't know who you think you are, but—"

"I'm the guy who's trying to get us to cover."

She dragged her blowing hair out of her eyes again. "Are you going to melt in the rain? Seems to me you're already soaked through."

"No, but I don't want a house coming down on those ruby slippers of yours." He gestured and her mouth went dry all over again at the sight of the funnel cloud snaking downward from the clouds.

"Oh, my God!" She grabbed his wet shirtfront. "That's a tornado? Is it coming this way?"

"Let's not wait around to see, okay?" His hand was

like iron as he pulled her along with him—not toward the nearby stone-sided house surrounded by a wraparound porch, but well off to the side of it in the direction of the barn. He stopped halfway there, though, letting go of her long enough to lean down and pull open a storm-cellar door angled into the earth. "Get in."

She looked nervously from the house to the barn, then stared into the black abyss below the cellar door. Ax murderer? Tornado? It was no time to weigh odds, but she couldn't help herself.

"Sweetheart, I'll carry you down those steps myself if you don't get your butt moving." He whistled sharply, making her jump. But the bandanna-clad dog simply trotted past her, brushing against Ariana's leg before sniffing the ground in front of the cellar entrance. "Steps, Sugar," Jayden said and the dog hesitantly took a gingerly step down into the darkness. "She's mostly blind. Don't trip over her on your way down. There's a handrail. Use it."

A blind dog.

She couldn't have made up such a detail if she'd tried.

She held her arm around her head, trying to keep her hair from blowing in his face as well as hers as she took the first step beyond the wooden door. "Is that, uh, that door going to keep out a tornado?" The wood was faded nearly gray and looked to be a hundred years old. It was a fitting complement to the steep stairs, which seemed to be carved from stone.

"Guess we'll see, won't we." He was right on her heels, pulling the door closed as he followed her.

"I've never been in a tornado." Or gone down into a dark storm cellar with a blind dog and her handsome cuss of an owner.

"I have. There's usually a flashlight right here by the door, but I'll find one soon as I can. The walls are stone, but the floor's dirt. You'll feel the difference when you get to the bottom."

She did, but was glad for the warning. She felt as blind as Sugar and leaned over to pet the dog, who seemed to plant herself immediately in front of Ariana's shins. Then she felt Jayden brush against the back side of her as he, too, reached the base of the steps.

She straightened like a shot.

"Sorry," he murmured. His hand cupped her shoulder as he sidled around her. "No electricity down here."

She wasn't so sure about that. Both her butt and her shoulder were tingling from his brush against her, even after his touch left her and she heard him moving around.

A deafening clap of thunder made her jump. Sugar whined and she knelt down to rub her hand over the shaggy dog, all the while looking up at the wooden cellar door. She had some serious doubts about that door. "Was that tornado a few years back in Paseo? Are we even still near Paseo?"

"My address says so." She heard a few clanks, and then a narrow but reassuring flashlight beam shone across the floor as he moved back to her side. "Here." He handed her the sturdy, metal flashlight and retreated once more to what she could now see were shelving units lined up against two walls. "And there *was* a tornado around here a few years ago, but I wasn't here for it. Shine that up here, would you?"

"Sorry." She immediately turned the flashlight in his direction again. But she'd seen enough of the rest of the cellar to know that it was larger than she'd expected. Her vivid imagination was conjuring any number of creepy crawlies hanging out in the far corners of the dirt-floored cellar.

She realized her flashlight was trained squarely on his extremely excellent rear end and angled it upward where his hands were. "So where were you, then?"

"Two years ago? Germany. The close-up brush I had with a tornado was further back than that. In Italy."

He spoke with a distinct Texas drawl that said he'd grown up here. "World traveler?"

He shot her a grin over his shoulder. "Courtesy of the United States Army, ma'am."

She was glad he quickly turned back to his task. His grin was positively lethal.

She sat down on the bottom step and rubbed Sugar's warm head when the dog rested it on her lap. It was hard not to keep looking up at that cellar door. It was hard not wondering what unmentionable creatures they were disturbing in the dirt cellar with their very presence. "You don't look like a soldier." She jerked the flashlight upward again and jumped at another crack of thunder.

"I'm not anymore. You don't look like a reporter."

"I told you. I'm a journalist."

"Working on a magazine article. I remember."

Which brought her mind squarely back to her purpose for being there in the first place. She blamed the fact that she'd been even momentarily sidetracked by the storm.

She jerked the flashlight—and her gaze—away from his butt when he turned with a lantern in his hand. She'd seen ones like it pictured in the advertising section of *Weird*. She herself, however, had never had any personal experience with the things.

Primarily because her idea of roughing it meant being somewhere without a handy Starbucks.

Or traveling to a tiny map-dot called Paseo, Texas, where cell phone signals were apparently unheard of.

Along with the lantern, he'd also found a box of kitchen matches. But instead of lighting a match by scraping it against the box, he just scraped his thumbnail over the top. Then he set the flame to the lantern, and a moment later, another source of light countered the gloom. He set the lantern on the floor near her feet. "Turn off the flashlight. Might as well save the batteries."

She turned it off before handing it to him. He stepped around her, going up a few stairs before tucking the flashlight between the wall and the handrail near the door. "That's where we usually keep it." She leaned to one side for him to go past her again as he came back down.

Then he picked up the lantern, holding it high as he looked around the rest of the room, making a satisfied sound as he headed into one of those far corners. When he came back into the small circle of light, he was carrying a puffy, orange sleeping bag that he flipped open a foot from her toes.

Her alarm level started rising again. "We're, uh, not going to be down here all day, are we?"

"Probably not." He set the lantern on the floor next to the brightly colored bag and disappeared into the shadows again. He came back with another sleeping bag, though he left this one rolled up and tossed it down on the one he'd spread out. "There used to be a small table and a couple chairs down here. Don't know what happened to them. But we might as well be a little more comfortable while we're here." Suiting action to words, he knelt down and stretched out on one side of the opened sleeping bag and propped the rolled-up one behind his head.

Then he patted the area beside him. "C'mere, girl."

Her mouth went dry.

Then she felt her face flush when Sugar sniffed her way along the edge of the sleeping bag before circling a few times next to Jayden's hip and lying down.

Of course he'd meant his dog.

"Room for you, too," he said.

She pressed her lips together in an awkward smile and shook her head. She was twenty-seven years old. Hardly inexperienced when it came to men. But lying on the floor next to a soaking wet stranger—even a handsome cuss of one—was not exactly in her wheelhouse.

Though it had been over a year since she'd broken up with Steven—

The thought blew away when the cellar door suddenly flew open.

Dirt and debris rained down the stairs and she shot off the step where she'd been sitting. She would have collided with Jayden, who'd bolted upright to his feet, if not for the quick way he set her aside.

She wrapped her arms around her midriff, but that didn't really help the quaking inside her. She didn't know how it was possible, but the sky outside was even blacker than before. So black that she almost questioned the time of day, even though logic told her it was still afternoon. "Can I help?"

He was halfway up the stairs, reaching out of the cellar opening to grab the door that kept slamming against the ground. "Stay there." His voice was terse.

It seemed the nerves inside her stomach had found a whole new set of hoops to toss around.

The wind was whipping down the stairwell so violently that it blew his shirt away from his back like a maniacal parachute. The end of the sleeping bag flipped up and over her boots. Her hair felt like it was standing on end and Sugar shot off to hide in one of the dark corners.

She sat down on the sleeping bag and patted her hands together. "Come here, Sugar. It's okay." After a moment, the dog slunk back. Her tail was tucked. Her pointed ears were nearly flat against her head. She was more terrified than Ariana. She put her arm around the dog, wanting to bury her face in the dog's silky fur.

Then Jayden finally won his battle with the door and it slammed shut with such force that even more dust came down, settling over his head.

He secured the latch again and jammed the flashlight through it as well.

"Is that going to hold it?"

"It'll hold the latch." He came back down the stairs. "Whether the door holds together is another matter."

Sugar whined.

Ariana wished she could, too.

"Hey." He crouched down next to them both. "Don't worry. Everything's going to be fine."

The door blew again, metal and wood seeming to scream against the pressure.

"You don't know that," she told him.

"You're too pretty to be so pessimistic." He put his arm around her and his dog.

She didn't move away. Because, whether she wanted to admit it or not, just like Sugar obviously did, she felt safer with him right there even though the wetness of his clothes seeped through hers.

Still… "There's a tornado out there," she said, as if she needed to point that out to him.

"Not yet. At least I didn't see the funnel cloud again. Hopefully, it's just one hellacious storm."

Right on cue, thunder shook the very walls. She couldn't help flinching. "I never liked thunderstorms, either," she admitted.

His hand squeezed her shoulder. "I don't know. This one's not so bad."

She huffed out a disbelieving laugh. "Right."

"It brought you, didn't it?"

Chapter 2

Jayden felt Ariana stiffen next to him and wished he'd said just about anything else.

That was the problem with his propensity for voicing blunt truths.

He pushed to his feet. He was soaked to the skin but he ignored the annoyance. "If I remember, there ought to be some stuff to eat and drink down here. Interested?"

She rubbed her hands up and down her arms. "If it's a hundred years old like that cellar door, I don't think so."

He chuckled as he went over to the shelves. They were crammed with everything from tools to packing boxes that had been there since before his mom had ever set foot in Paseo. Which dated them more than thirty-six years, since he and his brothers hadn't yet been born. In the years he'd been gone in the army, the shelves had only gotten more jumbled.

"The door's old," he allowed. "But not a hundred years old. It's just the Paseo sun that makes it look that way." He pushed aside a stack of newspapers. Who kept old newspapers these days? To him it was sort of like saving string.

Outside, the thunder had settled into a continuous rumble. He hadn't lied to the lovely, young Ariana Lamonte. Aside from that one sight of the funnel cloud, he hadn't seen it again when he'd been fighting with the damn cellar door. But he still wasn't inclined to leave the safety of the cellar just yet, either. Not when the sky had that ominous blackish-green hue. Just because he hadn't seen a funnel didn't mean there wasn't one. And he had no desire to tangle with a tornado.

As far as storm cellars went, this one was pretty old. Back in the day, it'd been used more as a root cellar than anything. Nowadays, it was the place where old crap—like thirty-plus-year-old newspapers—went to die.

He didn't find the box of crackers he'd been hunting for, but he did find an old radio. He switched it on.

"Is that a radio?"

He didn't want to dash the hopefulness in Ariana's voice, but truth was truth. "There are only a few radio stations with a strong enough signal to reach Paseo. Television's even worse. Hated it when I was young."

"That's what cable and satellite dishes are for."

He chuckled. "No cable out here. And satellite was *way* too expensive. At least it used to be." They had satellite television now, primarily so his mom could keep up with Grayson's rodeoing when she wasn't traveling with him. But when the weather was bad, the first thing it did was lose its signal. He held up the radio that emitted only static no matter how many times he turned the dial. He turned it off again and stuck it back on the shelf.

"And no cell phone signal, either," she said. "Which I discovered for myself already."

"Nope. No cell signal." He shrugged and moved a cardboard box full of toys he vaguely remembered from his childhood. If he was really lucky, he'd find some old towels.

"Any internet?"

"The library in town has it. They're only open on Wednesdays, last time I checked." Admittedly, that had been a good year ago, when he'd been ironing out leftover details from leaving the service.

"This is Texas," she muttered. "Not a third-world country."

He smiled faintly. "We are kind of off the grid," he allowed. "But I've traveled the world. Seen the best and more often the worst of people along the way. So I've come to appreciate Paseo's peacefulness."

The cellar door shuddered again.

"Usual peacefulness," he amended, resuming his search for the crackers. From the corner of his eye, he watched Sugar cuddle up close to Ariana.

The dog was ordinarily wary as hell around strangers. But he couldn't exactly blame Sugar.

The reporter—*journalist*—had curves just meant to be cuddled up close against. She had rich brown hair that reached halfway down the back of the artsy black-and-white sweater she wore open over a clinging gray top. Her snug jeans showed off shapely thighs before they tucked in impractical knee-high red boots. They ought to have looked ridiculous, those boots. Like they belonged on a fashion runway. On her, though, they were just plain sexy. Combined with darkly lashed brown eyes that had sucked him in the second she'd turned them his way out on the highway, Ariana Lamonte definitely made an impact.

And her presence now was only serving to remind him just how long it had been since he'd enjoyed an attractive woman's company.

He'd hooked up a time or two right after things ended with Tess in Germany, but that was it. Grayson had told him he was turning into a hermit and suggested he meet some of the buckle bunnies always following him around. Jayden had bluntly told his brother to stuff it.

He finally spotted the old-fashioned metal container that held a sealed box of saltine crackers. "Ah. Success."

For all he knew, they were the same ones he'd put there when he was eighteen, but he was hoping they'd been refreshed somewhere along the way. He pulled the tin off the shelf, as well as the dusty bottle sitting behind it—definitely not his doing when he'd been eighteen. He'd been a hell-raiser, but even he hadn't had the nerve to keep a bottle of whiskey in the cellar right under his mom's nose. She'd have tanned his hide, regardless of his age. He'd never met a fight he didn't like—except when it was against his mom.

Carrying both the tin and the bottle, he went back to sit on the sleeping bag.

Sugar lifted her head and shuffled over to him, curling up against his thigh and going back to sleep.

"How old is she?"

He rubbed the dog's ruff. "About three. I brought her back from Germany with me when I got out of the army." He left out the part that he'd basically stolen her from his master sergeant. The man had gotten Tess. As far as Jayden was concerned, he hadn't deserved to have the dog, too.

"Was she born blind?"

"No." He ignored her curious expression and peeled open the cracker box. Fortunately, it looked relatively new. And the outer metal box had done a good job keeping bugs from getting at the cardboard inside.

The storm was howling worse than ever outside. Rain had started lashing against the door and he hoped to keep Ariana distracted from it as much as he could. "Here." He set a sleeve of crackers on the sleeping bag between them and wiped off the dusty bottle with his wet shirttail. "No glasses, I'm afraid." He held the bottle closer to the lantern so she could see the label he'd exposed. "You are legal, right?" For all he knew, she could be a twenty-year-old journalism student.

She let out a soft, sexy laugh and leaned forward to take the bottle. Her fingertips brushed his. He wasn't sure if that made more of an impression on him than the way her long, tangled hair formed a curtain around her. "More than legal," she assured him. "I'm twenty-seven."

Older than she looked, which was a relief. "I've got nine years on you."

"Not exactly a generation gap," she offered drily. She twisted off the cap from the bottle of whiskey, took a sip and promptly coughed. "Potent," she finally managed. She set the bottle next to the crackers and peeled off her sweater.

The clinging shirt beneath possessed no sleeves. Just two narrow straps over shoulders that gleamed ivory-smooth in the lantern's light. His gaze started to drift over the shadowy cleavage also on display beneath her collection of thin gold necklaces, and he grabbed the whiskey bottle for himself.

Hell of a time for that dead feeling inside him to be shocked back to life.

"Potent," he agreed after he took a healthy swig. The liquor burned all the way down, joining the heat already pooled inside him.

Fortunately, she seemed to take his comment at face value and fiddled with her cell phone. "I couldn't function without the internet," she said. "How do you stand it?"

"Just fine," he drawled. "What do I need it for?"

"Keeping up with the world?"

He smiled slightly. "Hear everything I need to know at the feed store in town." It was an exaggeration, but not that much of one since he, personally, wasn't all that inclined to ever turn on the television. Not when every time he did, all he saw were politicians arguing and neighbors shooting neighbors. He'd seen enough of that in the service. "What do *you* need the internet for?"

She'd been sitting cross-legged and she shifted, straightening out her legs, too. "My job, for one thing. Research. Filing stories." Her lips twitched. "Keeping up with the world."

"I kept up with the world plenty thanks to fifteen years with the army."

She set aside her phone and lifted her hair off her neck with both hands. "It's warm down here."

And getting warmer. He wasn't entirely certain that his clothes hadn't started steaming. "Blame it on the whiskey." Personally, he was blaming it on *her.*

"It's June but the rain still ought to cool things off." She twisted her hair, managing to tie it into a knot atop her head. She inhaled deeply and Jayden did blame the whiskey then, because he should have looked away from the lush curves pushing against that thin excuse for a shirt, but he didn't.

And the heat inside his gut just increased.

The only thing that distracted him was the thumping of the cellar door as the storm buffeted against it. It sounded like it was hailing, but in the lantern light, he could see the glimmer of rain dripping through the slats of the wood door.

If he'd met Ariana Lamonte under just about any other circumstance, he wouldn't hesitate to pursue the attraction. But she was in his storm cellar. Essentially under his protection.

Which changed the rules entirely.

Or should.

"So what do you do in Austin when you're not chasing around stories for your magazine?"

She shrugged a shoulder. "The usual. I have friends. Parents." As if she realized the spare details were hardly the way to keep a conversation going, she pushed to her feet and paced the short distance to the shelves, arching her back a little as she stretched. Then she bent over in half, her bracelets jingling softly, and pressed her fingers against the dirt floor.

He damn near swallowed his tongue.

The knot in her hair wasn't holding up. As he watched, it seemed to uncoil in almost slow motion. Then she straightened again, caught her hands behind her back and stretched once more.

He closed his eyes, stifling an oath. "Grow up there?" He had to raise his voice over the noise from outside.

"In Austin? Born and raised. Same as my mom and

dad before me. I love the city. I have an apartment that overlooks the skyline. Ridiculously expensive, so I barely have it furnished, but I can walk or ride my bicycle to work if I want. I can get most anywhere I want, really, without even taking out my car."

He looked at her again and was both relieved and chagrined that she'd stopped stretching and was pacing once more. "Except here," he said drily.

Her lips curved. They were full and luscious, like the rest of her. Not overblown. Just…right.

Exactly right.

"Except here," she agreed. "What about you? Did you grow up in Paseo?"

"Born and raised," he parroted. "Right here on this very ranch."

She propped her hands on her hips and looked at him. "And your parents?"

He wasn't accustomed to telling strangers his business. But she was easy to talk to. And it kept her from turning to see the water that had begun streaming down the steps.

The cellar had stone walls and a dirt floor. He'd never known it to flood more than a foot. Still, if it got worse, he was already figuring they'd have to leave the shelter. In a flood, being inside the house higher up was better than being below ground. If there really were tornadoes in the area, they'd have to take their chances. His mom's bedroom closet in the house would be the best bet. First floor. Interior room.

There wouldn't be much space for the two of them. It would definitely be close quarters—

"Never knew my father," he said, pulling his thoughts away. "My mom was pregnant when she came to Paseo."

Her expression shifted a little. "So your *mom* is a Fortune?"

"Not one of *those* Fortunes," he reminded her. "The ones you've been writing about for your magazine. Like I said. The name's just a coincidence. So if that's what brought you to Paseo, you've wasted a trip. My mother's definitely not related to them."

She tilted her head slightly. "It's not that common a name."

"It's the one my mom decided on when she was making a fresh start here. She wanted a new life. A new identity. Said my brothers and I were the only fortune she needed. Thus the name. I'm pretty sure she was running from the guy who'd gotten her pregnant. She could have chosen any surname she wanted." He raised his voice over a crack of thunder. "Always figured Fortune was better than Smith."

Ariana jerked to attention at his words. *His mother had been running?*

"It's just thunder." Jayden's deep voice was calm. The kind of voice to inspire trust. "It can't hurt you."

"The lightning that causes it can." Much as she disliked thunderstorms, she was glad to blame her reaction on it. "So why do you think she was hiding from him?" she asked casually, concealing her intense interest. Gerald Robinson had a history of being a womanizer. But not a violent one. Even now, in his seventies, he was a compellingly attractive man. She'd only had a few brief encounters with him—he was *not* a proponent of her magazine articles, to say the least, and had no idea about the book of course—but it wasn't difficult to understand how women had flocked his way.

But none of the women—even his wife—seemed to hold his heart.

Some said that Gerald Robinson didn't really have one.

But maybe he'd had one and left it in Paseo.

"Was your mother afraid of your father?"

"I probably should have phrased it differently." He adjusted the rolled sleeping bag behind him, stretching out even more fully on the one spread beneath him. He tore open the sleeve of crackers and fed one to Sugar. "I think she was running from a broken heart. And that's it."

Another frequent refrain when it came to the women in Gerald's past. The only heart that seemed to have not broken along the way belonged to his wife.

Then she realized what else Jayden had said. "You have brothers?"

He'd uncapped the whiskey again and held up two fingers as he took a sip. When he was finished, he held the bottle toward her.

Even though she knew she oughtn't, she took the bottle again and this time managed not to choke on the alcohol as it burned down her throat.

But she dropped the bottle completely when a loud crash vibrated through the very walls, making even the metal shelving shudder and squeal.

She froze, forgetting entirely her interest in his brothers, and warily looked up at the low ceiling, half-afraid it was getting ready to collapse in on them. It was covered in wood. But above that, she really had no idea what was there. Except earth and that awful, awful howling wind. "That was not thunder."

He'd sat up, too, and shook his head. He righted the

whiskey bottle she'd dropped. "No, it wasn't." He went up the stairs and pried the flashlight out of the metal latch where he'd jammed it. Only then did she realize the stairs were flowing with water.

"Are you sure you should go out there?"

"No, but I want to know what the hell that noise was. I'm not worried about the house—nobody is here but us—but I've got horses in the barn." He pushed up on the cellar door and swore.

Her stomach curled in on itself nervously. "What's wrong?"

"Something's blocking the door." He put his shoulder to it and heaved.

The door that had blown open from the wind now stayed stubbornly closed.

She felt like choking on a whole new lump of misgivings. "So we're trapped?"

"I wouldn't say that."

She picked up the lantern and carried it with her up a few steps until she was just below him. In the light she couldn't see the faintest glimmer of anything between the wood slats. She could, however, see the muscles standing out in his arms as he pushed futilely against the door. And she could also see the stream of water pouring steadily down the stone steps. How it was getting around whatever blocked the door was a mystery.

But water had a way of going where it wanted.

Take the Grand Canyon, for example.

"What *would* you say, then?"

His answer was curt. And unprintable.

Her mouth went dry. She backed down the wet steps.

He followed her and took the lantern from her fingers that had gone numb. "Don't look like that."

"Like what?" She wrapped her arms around herself. It was humid and warm in the cellar but she suddenly felt cold. How much water would the dirt absorb before it started to fill the cellar? "You just said nobody was here but us."

"Not for a few days."

She gaped. "A few *days*? So someone will find our bodies sooner or later?"

He set the lantern on the ground and put his arms around her. "You do have an imagination, don't you?"

She nodded against his shoulder, breathing in the warm, comforting scent of him. "My teachers always told me that was a good thing. But this is not at all how I expected this day to go."

"Me, either." His hands slid down her spine. "We'll get out of here before we're reduced to *bodies*. The cellar has never flooded much more than ten, twelve inches before."

The details were not a comfort. "I don't know how to swim."

"You're not going to need to," he promised.

She tilted her head back, looking up into his face. It really was a cussedly handsome one. From the cleft in his chin to the straight brows over his level gaze. "My mother will never forgive me for not giving her grandchildren." Karen Lamonte had been going on about it ever since Ariana had broken off with Steven.

His eyebrows shot up and the corner of his lips lifted. "Pretty sure that's not going to be decided here and now, sweetheart."

She really didn't know what was wrong with her. She'd never particularly been prone to panic before. But she'd also never found herself stuck in a storm cellar in a town nobody could seem to find except for those who actually lived there, in the company of a man who might or might not be another son of Gerald Robinson, but who definitely had an overwhelming appeal for her personally.

And focusing on Jayden was far preferable to thinking about what could happen if that water kept coming down the stairs.

"You have a scar," she murmured inconsequentially and touched the faint white line above his eyebrow. "Right there."

"Bar fight." His lashes drooped and she knew instinctively that he was looking at her lips.

Without conscious thought, she moistened them. His fingertips were tracing her spine, setting off all manner of sensations inside her. "Are you, ah, in a lot of bar fights?"

"One or two. I stopped more of them." He shifted slightly, pulling her in closer till her breasts were pressed against his chest. "I was an MP in the army."

Her breasts were pressed against his chest. "MP?" Her voice was little more than a whisper.

"Military Police." His head dropped toward hers. "Former badass Sergeant First Class Fortune at your service." As he said the words his head lowered toward hers. His breath fanned her mouth as he said, "I'm going to kiss you, you know."

Heat flushed through her veins, collecting in her center. Her head felt heavy as she looked up at him. Any hope of maintaining a professional distance had gotten washed away. "Former Sergeant, I sure hope so," she breathed.

One of his hands left her back to slide along her jaw.

Her lips parted and she drew in a deep breath. She felt the way he went still when she slid her hands around his neck. His thumb brushed over her lower lip and she couldn't help the soft sound that rose in her throat.

"Damn," he murmured. And then his mouth found hers.

His kiss didn't feel damned. If anything, his kiss felt glorious.

And if she was going to go in a storm cellar, at least she was going to go like this.

He lifted his head way too soon. His eyes were dark and unreadable in the dim lantern light, but the searching in them felt as real as the moisture leaching from his clothes into hers.

She pulled his head down. "If you're going to kiss me," she said as she caught his lower lip between hers and lightly tugged, "*kiss* me."

He groaned, kissing her even more deeply. His hands traveled down her back, down her hips, her rear, pulling her up and into him. He was hard and her head whirled even more. All she wanted to do right then and there was twine herself around him and he seemed to know it because he yanked his mouth away from her and lifted her right off her feet.

"Put your legs around me."

She didn't need the request. She was already linking her boots behind him and wishing there weren't two layers of denim between them. She couldn't do anything about that at the moment, but she could do something about his shirt. She yanked it upward, hearing a few buttons scatter before he let out a low, groaning laugh and managed to pull it off his head.

She pressed her open mouth against his collarbone,

tasting the moist, salty heat of his skin. He cradled her backside as he crouched down, finally lowering her onto the sleeping bag. One corner of her mind wondered if the thing was floating in water yet, but that didn't stop her from reaching greedily between them for his belt.

He jerked and caught her hands in his, pinning them above her head against the sleeping bag.

"Don't tell me you want me to stop." In any other world, she'd have been shocked by her own boldness. But this wasn't any other world. The only world that existed was contained in a flooding dirt cellar from which they had no way out. She angled her hips against his. "I can feel what you want."

"Yeah?" His hair brushed her cheek as he kissed the side of her neck. "Does that mean I have to hurry?" His mouth burned along the curve of her shoulder. Over the thin strap of her camisole and down to where her achingly tight nipples pushed against the cotton fabric. "You're not wearing a bra."

Was there any point in explaining the built-in shelf bra? "Maybe you do need to hurry, if we're going to be flooded in this cellar."

"We're not getting flooded," he said again.

"How do you know?"

"Because I know." Still holding her wrists above her head with one hand, he peeled down the top of her camisole with the other, until she felt his breath on her bare breasts. She was coming positively unglued, anticipating the brush of his mouth, the slide of his tongue—

But instead of tasting her, he lifted his head a little. "What is that?" He reached for the lantern, pulling it near so he could look more closely at her exposed breasts. "A butterfly?"

She groaned, twisting beneath him. "Yes, it's a butterfly." All of an inch big in pale pink and black, tattooed on the upper curve of her right breast when she'd been twenty-one. She still couldn't free her hands, so she arched her back, rubbing her rigid nipples and the tattoo against his hard chest. "You were in the army, Sergeant Fortune. Surely you've seen tattoos before." In the scheme of things, her little butterfly was hardly a record breaker. Neither was the floral curlicue on her left shoulder blade.

His teeth flashed. "Sweetheart, I've seen things that would turn your hair white." He ducked his head and kissed the point of her shoulder. Then the butterfly.

Heat flowed under the surface of her tingling skin and she bit back a moan when his lips finally surrounded her nipple. Even though she twisted her wrists, halfheartedly trying to free them, he kept them bracketed. She pressed her face against the top of his head. "Jayden, please," she breathed.

In answer, he pushed his thigh between her legs and palmed her other breast.

Pleasure rocketed through her and she cried out.

Jayden made a low sound. Utterly male. Utterly triumphant. Then his mouth was on hers again, and her wrists were finally free, and he rolled over, pulling her over him.

Noise seemed to rage beyond the storm cellar, but she was far more aware of her heart pounding loudly inside her head, of the low sounds coming from Jayden, of the clink of his belt when he finally loosened it. Breathless, she braced one hand on the floor, reaching to undo her own jeans with the other. But instead of dirt, her hand sank into mud. "Jayden, the water—"

"I know." He cursed and kissed her hard again while the pounding outside the cellar door got even louder.

Then suddenly, he went still. "Wait." He sat up, dumping her somewhat unceremoniously onto her butt as he stood. Instead of finishing the job of undressing, though, he fastened his belt and headed up the stairs. He pounded on the door. "Nate," he yelled. "That you?"

Ariana hoped she wasn't hearing things when she heard a faint, indecipherable response.

"Yeah, we're stuck," Jayden yelled, pressing his head close to the wood.

Once again, her adrenaline seemed to want to blow the top of her head right off. She wiped off her muddy hand and scrambled up the few steps behind him. "Who's out there?"

"My brother Nathan. So you, uh, might—" He gestured and she flushed, realizing her camisole was bunched around her waist.

Suddenly embarrassed, she turned and tugged the stretchy fabric back where it belonged, hiding her still-tight nipples and the butterfly tattoo. She would have put on her sweater for good measure, except when she picked it up from where she'd left it bunched by the base of the stairs, it was soaking wet.

As was her cell phone.

She grimaced. It was supposed to be waterproof, but she wasn't sure that meant it could withstand sitting in several inches of water. She was drying it off the best she could against her jeans when Sugar started barking, pacing back and forth across the sleeping bag, leaving muddy paw prints all over it.

"Sugar, come here." Ariana reached out so the dog could sniff her hand and then closed her fingers around the bandanna to hold her still. "Good girl." She tucked the phone in her back pocket and looked back at Jayden. "I can't hear what your brother is saying. What's blocking the door?"

"Your car."

"What?"

"It's on its side." He pressed his ear against the door again. "Yeah," he shouted. Then he looked back at her. "He's hooked up the winch from my truck to drag it off."

She hadn't even had the car for three months yet. She'd bought it outright with her book advance. Her savings account wasn't quite sucking air, but it was close. What if she had to pay for car repairs? "Is it going to be damaged very badly?"

"I doubt the winch will do anything worse to it than the wind that turned it on its side in the first place."

She grimaced, knowing it had been a foolish question.

Jayden was listening again at the wood panels, and then he backed down the steps, sliding his arm around her waist to pull her away as well. "Sugar, come on." The dog moved also, sitting against his leg, thumping her tail and looking up at him with an adoring expression on her pointed face. "Just to be safe," he told Ariana and brushed his lips over her temple.

She closed her eyes for a moment, fighting the strong urge to put her arm around him, too.

"Relax," Jayden said. His long fingers squeezed her hip. "Everything's going to be fine. We're getting out."

She smiled weakly. She was relieved about that. More than she could say. But it also meant that getting carried away like she had with Jayden *Fortune* could not happen again. Not when she was far from convinced his name was merely a coincidence. Getting personally involved with someone she was writing about was out of the question.

"I thought you never had any doubt about us getting out."

"I didn't." He gave her a quick wink, and then they both went silent as they heard what could only be the sound of her car being dragged away from the cellar door.

A few moments later, the door was opened from the outside. Rain pounded through the opening and then a drenched man appeared, shining a heavy-duty light down on them. "Well, well, bro. Glad to see you still like bringing the pretty girls to see your underground bachelor pad."

Ariana flushed. She had no right to feel jealous of what Jayden had done in the past or would do in the future with anyone. But that didn't stop her from feeling it anyway.

Jayden grabbed her hand and started up the stairs. "Be careful," he warned her. "The stones are slippery as hell."

She found that out quickly enough when Sugar slipped and lost her footing. Jayden immediately let go of Ariana to pick up the dog and carry her up the rest of the stairs.

Grabbing hold of the handrail, Ariana followed. She was soaked even before she accepted the hand that Jayden's brother offered when she reached the top of the stairs.

"Out you go," Nathan said, practically lifting her right out onto the ground. "You guys all right?"

Ariana nodded. Even though it was pouring buckets and it was nearly dark, the sky no longer had that terrible, angry black look, as if it were ready to explode. "Thank you." He'd set the big flashlight on the top of her car—make that the *side* of her car, because she saw right away that it was, indeed, lying on its side. "How could this happen? Was it a tornado after all?" She looked up into Nathan's face, and now that the flashlight wasn't shining in her face, she nearly did a double take. "You're twins?"

Nathan grinned. "Triplets, actually. But I'm the best-looking one of the lot."

Jayden let Sugar jump to the ground. The dog, mostly blind or not, raced immediately across the muddy ground toward the house. "I'll disagree with that," he said, reaching out to give his brother's hand a pump. "But I'm glad as hell that you're the most unpredictable of us. Thought you were still in Oklahoma City."

Nathan shrugged, offering no explanation.

Ariana took the flashlight to shine it over her car.

Not only was it sitting on its side, but half the windows were broken out. The copy of the magazine was gone. Worst of all, though, her thick notebook was nowhere in sight.

She'd had nearly a year's worth of research packed in that notebook. It had contained everything that her laptop—which was sitting safely in her apartment back home—did not. And the thought of losing it was almost overwhelming.

"It's not so bad," Jayden said. "We'll get it turned right side up and replace the windshield—"

She nodded and blinked her eyes hard.

"Hey." Nathan took the flashlight from her nerveless

hand. "I'm used to being waterlogged, but maybe we could get out of the rain and take this inside the house."

"Getting out of the rain sounds good," she agreed.

She followed the two men who were so alike that they were two peas in a pod. And evidently, there was a third pea from that pod as well.

Multiple births ran in Gerald Robinson's family. His two eldest sons with Charlotte were twins.

Ariana didn't need her notes to know that.

She didn't need her notes to know a lot of things.

But she honestly couldn't recall from her biology classes whether multiples happened from the mother's side or the father's. Which meant she needed to do a little research.

The very thought of it energized her.

Her car would get fixed. And her notes could be recreated. When it came to some things, she had an excellent memory for detail.

Maybe Paseo wasn't turning out to be a wild-goose chase after all. She'd just found three more sons of Gerald Robinson. *Possibly* three more sons.

That in itself was huge.

But Jayden and his brothers were also thirty-six. Which meant if Gerald was their father, they were his eldest heirs.

Was that the reason Charlotte Robinson had shown her fangs to Ariana?

Because she knew?

Chapter 3

"Still dead?"

Jayden nodded as he hung up the wall phone. The dead line wasn't surprising, considering the weather. He didn't particularly care, except it meant if their mom heard about the storm, she might be concerned.

He pulled a mug from the cabinet and tossed Sugar a treat that she snagged when it landed on her bed, then sat down at the kitchen table across from his brother.

From over their heads, they could hear the sound of a shower running.

"She's a looker," Nathan said.

It took no effort at all to imagine Ariana standing beneath the running water.

It took considerable effort to squelch the inevitable result of that image. He grabbed the coffeepot his brother had set in the center of the table and filled his cup. "True enough." He considered warning Nathan off, but decided against it. His brother would probably make something of it.

"Didn't mention you were having company when I talked to you last week."

"Didn't know I was going to have company."

"Sure about that? You guys were looking pretty cozy down in the cellar. Makes me wonder if my timing couldn't have been a little better."

Jayden ignored the devilry in his brother's eyes. What he and Ariana had been doing in the cellar was none of Nathan's business. "She's a journalist from Austin," he said. "She came to Paseo for some magazine she works for."

Nathan gave a bark of laughter. "Paseo? What the hell is interesting around here?"

"She's writing about the Fortune family. The real one. With all the money over in Austin."

Nathan made a face. "Only one in the money around here is Grayson and he doesn't even use our last name. Disappointing for her, I guess. What's she been doing? Going through all the Texas phone books looking up anyone with the last name Fortune?"

Jayden sipped the coffee. Grimacing, he got up to get some milk from the refrigerator. Usually, he liked his coffee black, but Nathan made the worst coffee in the world. "I don't know how she knew about us. Doesn't matter, anyway. I told her the truth. Mom made up the name when she had us." He dumped milk into the mug, then added a spoonful of sugar. "When did you get back from OK City?"

"Ten minutes before I saw that dinky red car sitting on its side."

Jayden was the eldest of his brothers by a matter of minutes. "You shouldn't have been driving in this weather."

Nathan gave him a look. "Dude."

"I don't care if you used to be a SEAL or not. It was stupid." He glanced up at the ceiling when the sound of the shower cut off.

He'd put a clean towel in the bathroom for Ariana to use. About now, she'd be running the pale blue terry cloth over that sexy little butterfly. Then, when she was all nice and dry, she'd be pulling on a pair of his sweatpants and one of his T-shirts.

He buried his nose in his coffee mug, taking a big swig of the nasty stuff. He choked it down and it was almost enough to overpower the images in his head. He should have found something for her to wear from his mother's closet. It would have made more sense. And he wouldn't be thinking about her skin, bare and soft, beneath his own clothes.

Banishing the image, he asked his brother, "Did you notice any other damage around the place?"

"Barn's damaged on the north side, but the roof's intact. Horses were restless, but okay. Haven't checked anywhere else. I saw your truck. When I realized you weren't in the barn or the house—" His brother didn't finish. Just shrugged.

He didn't need to finish. Nathan had come looking for Jayden. Period. Everything else could wait.

Through the window over the sink, he could see Ariana's car. The wind was finally gone, but the rain showed no sign of slowing. Rivers of water had formed, crisscrossing the saturated ground around the storm cellar.

Well beyond the cellar was the barn. Only the corner of it was visible from where he stood. He was glad the barn roof was okay. But even gladder that the horses were okay. Property damage was bad enough without adding damage to their livestock.

"We'll need to check the rest of the stock," he said.

"I've spent enough time in the water for today. I never saw any cows flying through the air, so I figure it can wait until the rain lets up."

His brother hadn't been joking. Still, Jayden found himself smiling a little. "Weird, isn't it?"

"What?"

"You went to the navy. I went to the army. Neither one of us wanted to be here."

"And we both came back," Nathan finished the thought.

Jayden knew why he'd come back. So far, though, Nathan wasn't saying much about his reasons. Since he himself didn't feel inclined to talk about his military separation, his brother's similar silence didn't strike him as particularly unusual.

"We should check and make sure there are no broken windows in the house."

"That your way of getting rid of me so you can go on about entertaining your…journalist?"

He'd never known not having brothers. But there were moments when the idea was more than a little appealing. He lifted a brow and looked over the coffee mug.

Nathan didn't bother hiding his amusement. "Hey. I think it's great. About time you showed some of the old Jayden spirit." But he pushed away from the table anyway. Like Jayden, he'd already changed into dry jeans and a shirt. “I’ll check this floor. You can check upstairs.”

It hadn’t been Jayden’s plan to go upstairs anytime soon. Keeping a little distance between him and Ariana didn’t sound appealing, but he knew it was only smart.

She’d been panicking in the storm cellar. Before he’d fallen for Tess, he’d been no saint when it came to women. But taking advantage of the situation with Ariana like he had was all sorts of wrong.

Not that he had even been thinking real straight at the time. Soon as she had tried undoing his belt, his resistance had been laughable. And when she’d come apart the way she had—

“Jayden?”

He jerked slightly, realizing that his brother had left the kitchen and Ariana had entered it. And the way she was looking at him made him suspect she’d been there for more than just a second.

He dumped the rest of the undrinkable coffee down the sink, trying not to dwell on the way the V-neck of the white undershirt he’d loaned her hung off one of her bare shoulders. On her, the shirt was loose, thank God. Way too loose to give any hint of the gorgeous breasts he knew were beneath.

“Shower okay?”

Her wet hair was slicked back from her face and twisted in a thick braid down the center of her back. “Yes, thank you.” She held up the towel in her arms and he realized she’d wrapped it around her wet clothes. “Do you have a washer and dryer I could use?”

“Sorry. I should have thought of that already.” His wet clothes were still lying in a heap on the floor in his bedroom.

"Why?" Her face was shiny and clean, yet she still had the thickest, darkest eyelashes he'd ever seen. And they surrounded the brownest gaze he'd ever fallen into. "We've both had a little distraction lately." She moistened her lips. "What with the, uh, storm. So—" She lifted the bundle slightly.

"Laundry room's back here." He led the way from the kitchen to the mudroom in the back where the washer and dryer sat. "Grayson bought 'em for my mom a few years ago, so they're fairly new." His neck went a little hot. Like he was bragging or something.

She slid around him and pulled open the washing machine. "Grayson?"

"My other brother. He's gone a lot. Rides rodeo."

She chuckled. "There's a famous rodeo rider who goes by just Grayson."

At his silence, she looked up at him.

His neck felt even hotter.

"Wait a sec. Your brother?" She looked astonished. "He's *The* Grayson?"

"Guess you've heard of him."

"Well, yeah. One of my coworkers does a blog for *Weird Life* entirely devoted to rodeo. She never stops talking about it."

"Blog?"

"Online journal. You know."

"I guess. Never been particularly interested in that sort of thing. And around here…no internet."

"Except for at the library."

He smiled slightly. "Right." He reached above her head to open the cabinet. "Soap and stuff. Use whatever you need."

She shook her wet things out of the towel into the machine. Thin excuse for a shirt. Jeans. One red sock. One blue sock. A tiny scrap of something white that caught on the edge of the machine before she flicked it inside with the towel and hastily closed the door.

He looked at her bare feet below the rolled-up legs of the sweatpants he'd provided. For some reason, he'd expected her toenails to be painted some bright, shocking color. But they were naked. No color at all.

And who knew why, but the sight of her entirely naked feet turned him on all over again.

God, he was a head case.

"I should check for storm damage upstairs," he said abruptly. And take his own damn shower. An icy one. "You need anything else?"

She looked a little startled. "I appreciate everything you've already done," she said swiftly. "I'll be fine. Do what you need to do." She tugged at the neckline of the shirt, pulling it up her shoulder where it promptly slid right back down again. "Go."

"Look, about what happened—"

She shrugged, which sent the shirt sliding even farther. She reached up to snatch the oversized bottle of laundry soap from the cupboard. "There's no reason to talk about it. We're two consenting adults—" Her eyes rounded and she gave him a quick look. "And *unattached* adults…right?"

"I sure hope so." Tess hadn't been unattached at all. She'd just neglected to share that fact with Jayden.

Ariana looked away from him again, nodding. "So, no harm, no foul. It's not like we, uh, actually—" She broke off and cleared her throat slightly. "You know."

Not for lack of wanting, he answered silently. Particularly after she'd writhed against him the way she had, making the sexiest sounds he'd ever heard. Sounds that were sure to haunt his sleep for some time to come.

"I mean, I don't sleep with men I don't know," she added. She filled the soap dispenser and jabbed a few buttons on the front of the fancy machine. "I imagine you're more discriminating than that, too."

He took the heavy soap bottle from her and replaced it in the cabinet. "I don't sleep with men I don't know, either."

"Sweetie," she drawled sweetly without missing a beat, "if you swing both ways, I'm not going to judge."

He let out a bark of laughter. "Do *you*?"

Her face was rosy, belying her seemingly bold expression. "As a matter of fact, I don't, but—"

"Neither do I," he assured her. "I like women." Despite his better intentions, he moved closer to her. Crowding her back against the machine. Standing close enough to smell the minty toothpaste on her breath and inhale the warmth from her smooth skin. "Particularly the one I'm looking at right now."

Her lips parted like she was struggling to breathe. He knew she wasn't, though, because he could feel the rise and fall of her breasts against him just fine.

"You smell like toothpaste."

"I didn't use your toothbrush or anything." Her voice was faint. "I…made do without."

He wasn't sure he'd have cared all that much if she had used his toothbrush. "Sweetheart, I was in the army a long time. I know all about making do. I am a little sorry my brother found us when he did," he murmured. "Another hour—"

"Hour?" She pressed her lips together again and looked away. Her cheeks were even redder.

"Okay." He smiled slightly. "Fifteen minutes."

She let out a breathy laugh and shook her head. She crossed her arms between them. He didn't have the heart to tell her that only plumped up her creamy, butterfly-kissed breasts, making them plainly visible for him within the neck of the loose shirt.

"I thought you had things you needed to do," she prompted.

He nodded. "Things I should do." Because he couldn't resist, he grazed his knuckle across that small butterfly. "Things I want to do."

She inhaled sharply. Her eyes met his.

A noise from the kitchen startled them both.

"There you are." Nathan stepped into the mudroom with a bland look that didn't fool Jayden for a second.

His brother always did have a twisted sense of humor. And impeccably annoying timing.

"Window in Mom's room needs to be boarded up," he said, pulling out the toolbox from where it was stashed in a bottom cabinet. "I wiped up the water already, so hopefully the wood floor'll be okay."

Ariana had looked down at her feet. She shifted slightly.

Jayden stifled a sigh. "Plywood's in the barn. I'll get it." If he didn't have a cold shower, he guessed the still-falling rain outside would do the job just as well.

Ariana chewed the inside of her lip, staring at the screen of her cell phone.

It was useless. She could get it to turn on, but it just as quickly turned itself right back off. And she didn't know if that was because the battery was dead or because of the soaking it had gotten in the storm cellar.

She tossed it onto the nightstand and threw back the sheet, pushing off the bed. It was his mother's room, Jayden had told her. She'd protested, but he'd insisted. Deborah Fortune was gone for the week, anyway. Off with Grayson. Evidently she acted somewhat as his third brother's manager when he was touring.

Then Nathan had chimed in with that strangely unholy innocent look he seemed to possess, saying that Ariana could either use their mother's room or she could use Jayden's.

She could envision sleeping in Jayden's bed all too easily. Which was—as she had to keep reminding herself—completely out of the question.

So Mrs. Fortune's bedroom would have to do.

Even though Ariana wanted to, she couldn't look out the window, because the two men had already boarded it up, along with several more around the house. Then, after they were satisfied with their makeshift repairs, Jayden had dumped a loaf of bread and a collection of sandwich meats on the table for supper.

Now it was the middle of the night.

The rain had finally stopped. The house was dark and quiet.

And she was ensconced in the bedroom of the woman who might have been—if the article from the Austin History Center was on the mark—the cause of the broken heart Gerald had supposedly been nursing when he'd met Charlotte.

She paced around the bedroom.

It wasn't large. There was the bed, modestly sized and covered with a faded quilt. Below the boarded-up window was a set of dresser drawers. A tall, narrow chest stood against another wall. There was a lamp on the single nightstand, and that was it. Plenty of framed photographs were scattered around—all of them featuring her sons.

It was easy to pick out which ones were Jayden. The army uniform helped when he was wearing it, but even without it, Ariana was already able to tell him apart from his brothers. It wasn't just the scar on his brow or that slightly crooked cuspid. It was an attitude that sat on his shoulders.

She picked up the largest photo of the three brothers. They were just summertime kids, grinning into the camera. Skinny, bare chests and lanky legs stretched out beneath swimming trunks. But even then, that attitude seemed to shine from the boys' faces.

Jayden's was challenging.

She was pretty sure it was Nathan on the left of Jayden. In one sense looking like butter wouldn't melt in his mouth and in another sense like he held that stick of butter behind his back. Which left Grayson as the boy on Jayden's right. Smiling head-on into the camera with a smile that already packed a lot of wattage.

What had their life been like, growing up in Paseo? Three sons with no father. On a ranch that was basically in the middle of nowhere. In a house that was certainly comfortable but by no means lavish.

Without question, it had to have been the very antithesis of what it had been like for Gerald and Charlotte's children, growing up at their palatial estate in Austin.

She set down the picture frame and pressed her lips together.

The idea of hunting around Deborah Fortune's bedroom for some hint that she'd known Gerald before he'd become Gerald had already occurred to Ariana. And she'd dismissed it.

For one, she wasn't that unethical. For two, she figured the odds were minuscule anyway of Jayden's mom keeping something around that would identify her sons' father, since she had never told them who he was in the first place.

Ariana picked up her phone again and tried once more to power it up. Not that it would do her any good, anyway. If there wasn't a strong enough signal to make a phone call, there certainly wasn't a strong enough signal to send an email or get online.

Feeling frustrated and hemmed in, she left the phone on the bedside table and quietly opened the bedroom door, stepping out into the dark hall. Deborah's room was on the main floor of the house. The rest of the bedrooms were upstairs and she was fairly certain Jayden and his brother had gone to bed some time ago.

Still, she didn't want to chance disturbing anyone as she crept barefoot down the hall toward the faint light coming from the kitchen. It was empty when she got there, though the light over the stove had been left on just as Jayden had said it would be. Sugar's bed was empty and the room was cooler than it had been earlier. Probably because of the breeze she could feel drifting through the wooden screen door.

Feeling thirsty, she took one of the mugs hanging below an upper cupboard and filled it with water. She stood there at the sink and drank it, looking out at the sight of her tipped-on-its-side car.

She still didn't want to think about all of her research notes being lost. If they'd scattered in the wind, the rain would have surely ruined them.

She chewed the inside of her lip, then abruptly set the mug in the sink and quickly returned to the bedroom. Her clothes were dry from when she'd laundered them earlier, but she was still wearing the oversized T-shirt Jayden had loaned her. It practically reached her knees and she'd justified that it served as a good nightshirt.

But mostly, she just hadn't wanted to take it off, enjoying too much the feel of his shirt against her.

She made a face at the dampness still clinging to her suede boots when she pulled them on. She'd already decided not to snoop through Deborah Fortune's room, and opening the woman's closet to see if there were some shoes to borrow felt almost as invasive. So Ariana's own damp boots would have to do.

She walked on her tiptoes back to the kitchen and, as quietly as she could, let herself out of the house through the wooden screen door.

The air smelled wet, and the breeze tugged at her hair and the hem of the T-shirt around her thighs. There wasn't much moonlight, but as her eyes adjusted, she could tell that the layer of clouds overhead had broken up enough to let an occasional star shine through.

Hoping that she wouldn't step in a big puddle of mud, she picked her way to the car, slowly circling it until she was standing by the roof.

Not entirely sure what to expect, she set the flat of her hand on the roof and gave a cautious push.

If the car had been likely to tip back onto its wheels or, heaven forbid, roll right onto its roof, it probably would have done so when Nathan had pulled it away from the cellar door using the winch on Jayden's truck.

She put her other palm against it and slowly leaned her weight against it.

No movement.

The heels on her boots gave her extra height, so it was easy enough to see and reach the car door handle. Getting the door to open, however, wasn't easy at all. No matter how she pulled or pushed, she couldn't get the darn thing to open more than an inch. The only solution would be to climb up on the top—

"You don't have the right leverage."

She snatched her hand back from the car at the sound of the voice behind her and whirled around to see Jayden sitting on the kitchen porch step.

He was shirtless, and he looked like he'd been sitting there for some time.

She dropped her hand from where she'd pressed it to her pounding heart. "How long have you been sitting there?"

"Long enough."

Which told her nothing.

"What's so important inside the car?"

"Nothing." Her heart still pounded. Only now it had a distinctly guilty quality to it that she hated. It was her car, after all. If she wanted to look inside it, wasn't that her right? "I just, uh, couldn't sleep. Couldn't stop thinking about my car."

"So you figured you'd go for a drive?"

She was glad it was dark. It would hide her hot cheeks. Of course, that same darkness hid the expression on his face just as well. "I suppose it's silly of me, but I never thought to ask my insurance company whether my coverage extends to, well, *weather*. No pun intended."

He stretched out his long legs and crossed his ankles.

Unlike her, he hadn't put on boots. Or any other type of footwear, for that matter.

His feet were as bare as his chest. Logically or not, it made her tend to think he hadn't expected to encounter her, either. "What's got *you* up in the middle of the night?"

"Couldn't sleep."

Unlike her, he didn't offer a reason or an excuse and the silence that followed felt awkward. She moistened her lips and swallowed. Then the breeze tugged again at the hem of the T-shirt and she pushed it down. "I must look ridiculous."

"My mom's got shoes in her closet. You could've borrowed something better suited to tramping through the mud."

"I know." She really didn't want to explain her reasoning. "I'm imposing enough already." He also hadn't disagreed that she looked ridiculous. Given the circumstances, she had no right whatsoever feeling vaguely offended. "I should've given you back your shirt and sweatpants after I got my clothes out of the dryer."

"What's stopping you?" He splayed his fingers across his bare abdomen. "God knows I can't go another minute without that T-shirt."

Heat went from her face straight to her stomach. She wondered what he would do if she pulled it off right then and there and handed it to him.

But then again, she didn't really wonder.

She knew exactly what he'd do.

And even though there was an aching, soft spot inside her that wanted that very thing, she turned on her heel again and looked at the car. "I thought about climbing up on top of it so I could get the door open."

"What stopped you?"

She propped her hands on her hips and shook her head. "Afraid I'd tip the car over."

"I doubt it would tip. When Nathan hauled it away from the cellar door, it dug into the mud pretty well."

She hadn't thought about that. "So, you think I *could* climb up—"

He made a sound.

She looked over her shoulder at him again. "What?"

He rubbed his hand over his head, then pushed to his bare feet. He braced his arm against one of the thick wooden posts supporting the overhang of the porch roof. "Just because you could doesn't mean you should. The car's not going anywhere. The insurance policy or whatever you're so anxious to look at is not going anywhere. We'll get the car back on its tires when it's daylight and then we'll see about getting it fixed."

"Is Paseo even large enough to have an automotive repair shop?" The damage might not have affected her ability to drive it, but she couldn't go anywhere with the windshield in the state it was in.

"There's a guy who does work."

She chewed her lip, managing to keep her "Is he qualified?" contained within her own thoughts. She didn't think she was a snob and she certainly didn't want to sound like one. Even if she did have some doubts about the availability of services around here. How could she not?

"You're right. There's nothing that can't wait until daylight. Do you suppose the phone lines might be working again by then?"

"Might be. We're remote, which makes a working

phone line pretty important to everyone in the area. You have someone you need to call?"

"Sooner or later. I do have people who'll wonder where I am." Her parents. Her work, particularly if she couldn't deliver her piece about the grand opening of Keaton's office complex.

She pushed his shirt back down again when it fluttered around her thighs and walked back toward the porch. The entire house was perched on a stone-covered foundation that was at least two feet high. If she'd bothered putting on her jeans—or the sweatpants he'd loaned her—she could have stepped from the ground straight onto the porch without using the three stairs he was blocking.

But she hadn't put on her jeans. Or the sweatpants.

And the only things she had on beneath the shirt was the skin she'd come into the world with plus a pair of seriously skimpy white panties that she'd be embarrassed for her mama to know she'd ever bought.

Which he would most certainly see if she took that two-foot-high stretch.

Instead, she put her boot on the first step. Then the second. The third.

He still didn't move.

She swallowed and had to force the words through her tightening throat. "Excuse me."

He shifted to one side, though he didn't move entirely out of the way. Instead, he lifted his hand and put one finger beneath her chin.

She froze in place, her nerve endings suddenly fizzing. He stood so close to her that she could feel the warmth emanating from his bare skin. Could smell the same scent of soap on him that was on her own skin.

"I can think of one thing that can't wait until daylight," he murmured.

She waved her hand a little desperately at the house. "Your brother—"

"Sleeps like the dead. A skill he learned with the teams. Nothing wakes that guy up these days." He pressed her chin up an inch.

She was having the hardest time breathing. If she leaned forward, she could touch her mouth to the hard line of his collarbone. Taste that warm, smooth skin one more time. "Teams?"

"Navy SEAL."

"My dad was in the navy for a few years. Surprised your other brother isn't air force."

He smiled slightly. His fingertip lifted another inch. "So about that thing that can't wait."

Her lips tingled, already anticipating his kiss. "Yes?"

His finger slid down her throat. It seemed to linger over the pulse she could feel throbbing there, then slid farther, slowly tracing down one side of the V neckline to the lowest point in the valley between her breasts, then even more slowly up the other side and back to her pulse again.

She shifted from one foot to the other, feeling herself leaning closer to him. If her pulse beat any harder she might well pass out. "Jayden."

His head dropped toward hers until his lips were a breath away from hers. "The shirt."

"Hmm?"

"Turns out I can't go without it after all."

She knew he wasn't serious about the challenge, because she could feel the curl of his smile against her mouth.

But it was enough to bring her to her senses.

At least a little.

Because she'd rarely been able to resist a challenge. And this one—right or wrong—was too irresistible to ignore.

She pulled back a few inches and gave him a long look before turning away from him. She reached out and pulled open the screen door. But before she let it close, she tugged the shirt off her head and tossed it over her shoulder at him.

She heard his muffled exclamation as the door closed between them.

Chapter 4

"Sleeping beauty finally awakens."

Ariana smiled ruefully at Nathan's greeting and let the screen door close behind her as she walked out onto the porch. The sun was bright and warm and halfway to noon and the sky was entirely cloudless, as if it were completely innocent of the mayhem it had so recently caused. "I didn't intend to sleep so late," she admitted. "I can't remember the last time I slept until ten in the morning."

Jayden's brother was leaning over the opened hood of her car. Jayden himself, however, was nowhere in sight.

Considering the outrageous way she'd walked away from him in the middle of the night wearing nothing but her panties and boots, his absence—however brief it might be—felt like a good thing to her.

She squinted against the sunlight and went down

the steps, crossing to her car. "How hard was it to get it back on four wheels?"

Nathan shrugged. He was wearing a dark T-shirt and disreputable-looking cargo shorts. "Bitty car like this? Not hard. We can be glad the twister didn't carry it farther than it did."

"It *was* a tornado, then? How'd you find out?"

"Phone line's fixed. Neighbors have been calling all morning wanting to talk about it."

"I hope nobody was hurt."

He shook his head. "But it ran along the highway for a good while. Ripped the heck out of the highway bridge just outside of town. Tore down a farmhouse back the other way."

She swallowed.

"All things considered, we got off lucky." He focused on the car again. "This thing's got one of those hybrid engines."

She nodded even though it hadn't been a question. Rather, judging by the face he was making, it was more of a condemnation.

That was okay. Her father thought her choice of vehicle was ridiculous, too. But then, aside from his four years in the navy right out of high school, he'd spent his life working for a gas company. She made a mental note to check in with her mother as soon as she could and gestured at the car.

"It's quite a mess, though." She stated the obvious. Mud was caked against the passenger side of the vehicle, pressed into every crevice from the wheel wells of the two flat tires to the door handles to the cracked windows. She walked around to the driver's side. It was cleaner, but not by much. At least the windows and tires looked to be intact.

She pulled open the door. She'd never had the chance to lock it when Jayden had pulled her to the storm cellar the day before, and it opened easily at her touch.

She swiped a few inches of dirt off the seat the best she could and sat down behind the steering wheel.

"Couldn't find your key," Nathan said.

"It takes a keyless remote. I keep it in my purse."

"That's what we figured. We looked."

Her nerves tightened. She'd been so preoccupied with her notes. "I hadn't even thought about my purse." No purse. No key.

And how on earth was she supposed to get back home again without her key? Without her wallet? Her money? Her everything?

"You never know," he said. "With a tornado? Sometimes things get found hundreds of yards away."

"Like my purse?"

"Stranger things have happened." He was silent for a moment. "But I probably wouldn't get my hopes up, if I were you."

"Great." She couldn't see him because of the upraised hood in the way. She felt under her seat, then the passenger seat and came up with nothing but a crinkled receipt from the coffee she'd bought before leaving Austin the morning before.

She got out and opened the rear door. There was glass on the seat and the floor from the back window.

But nothing else.

Trying not to succumb to the panic bubbling around the base of her stomach, she sat back behind the wheel again and leaned over to paw through the glove box.

At least there, among a jumble of receipts she needed for her expense report at work, she found her insurance policy information right where it belonged in its little plastic sleeve.

It was one sign of normalcy. As was the wrapped chocolate bar also sitting there.

Coffee was a daily necessity. Just thinking about her lack of it was almost more than she could stand. Which meant if ever there was a time for emergency chocolate…

She pulled out the candy bar and peeled back the wrapping, took a bite off the corner and let it sit on her tongue to dissolve.

"Not the healthiest of breakfasts."

She jerked upright, banging her elbow on the console, and looked at Jayden, standing next to her opened door with Sugar by his side. Unlike his brother, he was dressed in faded jeans and a white T-shirt.

For all she knew, the same white T-shirt from the night before. On him, the plain white cotton seemed stretched to capacity across his wide shoulders.

She swallowed the melting bite and swiped her mouth just in case she'd been oozing chocolate bliss. She broke off another corner and offered it to Jayden while she reached out to let Sugar sniff her fingers and accept a few pats. "Never knock chocolate."

"Or accept candy from strangers." He smiled slightly as he took the small wedge. "But then, can you really be considered a stranger after everything?" His voice dropped a notch and his eyes were wicked. "I mean, I have seen two of your tattoos." He popped the chocolate in his mouth, seeming to savor it. "Makes me wonder if there are more."

She flushed, but figured she deserved to after her behavior the night before. “There aren’t,” she said briskly.

She rewrapped the chocolate bar and closed it once more in the glove box. But she kept hold of the insurance card and got out of the vehicle. Sugar was working her way around the car, sniffing at the tires. “I’m going to need to use your phone.” She wiggled the plastic-covered card between her thumb and forefinger. “I don’t think they’ll pay for a towing company all the way back to Austin, but it doesn’t hurt to ask.”

At that, Nathan pushed the hood down and it shut with a noisy bang. “Don’t need to tow it anywhere except to Charlie’s.” He propped his hands on his hips, not seeming to care that there was grease on his fingers.

Jayden was nodding. “And you don’t need to hire a towing company for that. We’ll just hook ’er up and take care of it ourselves.”

A mental image formed of her poor car being dragged along behind Jayden’s pickup by a rope. “I don’t want to cause you any more work.”

“No work,” he assured her.

She lifted her eyebrows and gestured toward the barn behind them. “Really? So that wall over there on the barn is supposed to look all caved in like that?”

“She’s got you there.” Nathan started toward the house. “But before we do anything, I need more coffee.”

Amen to that. Coffee sounded good to her, too. Ariana swung her arm, following Nathan’s progress toward the two-story house with its patchwork of boarded-up windows. “It looks like you and your brother are facing a lot of extra work already without worrying about my car.”

Jayden's arm brushed hers as he pushed the car door closed. "Do you know how to make coffee?"

It wasn't exactly the kind of response she'd expected. "Of course. Who doesn't?"

"Nathan," he muttered. "I don't know what the hell he does to it." He wrapped his warm hand around her bare elbow and drew her around the car. "You take over coffee and I'll be happy to tow your car all over the state if necessary. It's a fair trade. Trust me."

It was a warm summer morning. Much too warm for the sweater she'd been wearing the day before. But at least if she'd been wearing it now, his hand wouldn't be in direct contact with her skin, setting off all sorts of little fires beneath the surface.

He evidently took her agreement for granted, because she didn't even have a chance to respond before he called his brother's name.

Nathan had just opened the screen door and he looked over his shoulder at them.

"Ariana offered to make it," Jayden said quickly.

She did?

She looked from Jayden's blithe expression to smile brightly at his brother. "It's the least I can do." And all of this talk about coffee had her coffee buds jangling more than ever, anyway. She quickened her step and Jayden's hand fell away before she darted up the stairs and through the screen door that Nathan was still holding open.

Her shoulder brushed against him as she slipped past him. "Excuse me." The two men looked identical. But there was zero effect when it came to Nathan.

To her way of thinking, it was irrefutable proof that physical chemistry wasn't only about looks.

One portion of her mind wondered if there could be an interesting blog about that as she stopped in the middle of the kitchen. There wasn't a coffeemaker visible on the scarred butcher-block counters. "Just point me in the right direction."

In answer, Jayden opened a cupboard and pulled down a huge can of ground coffee that he set on the counter. And Nathan plucked an old-fashioned coffeepot from the sink.

He sniffed the inside, then set it next to the can of coffee. "Go for it."

So much for a coffeemaker.

She eyed the pot. It was tall, white and blue. "My grandmother used to have one like that." Her grandma's hadn't been blackened around the base, though. Nor on the inside, as she saw when she picked it up and looked in. "But then, when she was alive, I wasn't anywhere close to coffee-drinking age."

"Long as it doesn't taste left over from when your grandma did make it, we're in for an improvement," Jayden murmured. "Make as many pots as you want."

"You don't like my coffee, *you* fix it," Nathan said, looking annoyed.

"*I'll* fix it," she said quickly. She'd never once made coffee without a coffeemaker, but she wasn't going to let that stand in her way. She'd simply Google—

The thought screeched to a halt.

Without internet, she wouldn't be looking up how to do anything at all. Not on Google or any other search engine. "Just go on and do your thing and I'll bring it when it's brewed."

Nathan immediately pushed open the screen door

again. "Sounds good to me," he said as he left. She heard his whistle and Sugar's answering bark.

Jayden didn't go so quickly, though. "You sure you don't mind—"

"I'm not exactly a guest. If it weren't for the weather, you wouldn't be saddled with me at all."

"Don't hear me complaining, do you?"

She chewed the inside of her lip, wallowing a little in pleasure.

"Seems to me my brother and I are the ones benefiting all around." He peeled the plastic cover off the coffee can and the smell of ground coffee filled the room, tantalizing her taste buds. "But you've got a crunched car and nothing for that magazine article of yours."

At the reminder, her pleasure stepped right into a pothole, tripping all over itself.

She set her insurance card on the counter. Until she had more information one way or the other about Jayden and his brothers' "made up" Fortune name, she needed to focus on more immediate matters.

Like coffee.

"On the other hand, I wasn't alone and out on the road when my car decided to tangle with the wind." She had to wait out the sudden tightening in her chest. "And for that, I have you to thank," she finished huskily. "Seriously, Jayden. Who knows what might have happened if you hadn't stopped to check on me. Thank you."

He waited a beat. Then two. And when he spoke again, his voice was low and impossibly deep. "My pleasure."

She moistened her lips.

Nathan's impatient shout from outdoors felt like a bucket of cold water being thrown in her face.

And judging by Jayden's rueful expression, she was pretty sure he felt the same. He angled his head toward the screen door. "I'd better make sure he doesn't tear down half the barn while he's at it."

She nodded quickly. "Of course. I'm not a guest, remember?"

His beautiful mouth twitched. "Maybe not. But you're sure the prettiest thing the wind's ever blown in."

"You're the pretty one." The words came out before she could stop them.

His eyebrows shot up. He let out a short bark of laughter, and shaking his head, he followed his brother's path out the screen door.

The second it banged softly back in place, Ariana exhaled shakily and leaned back against the counter. "Not good, girl," she whispered to herself. "Objectivity is key. So you can't go falling for someone you're writing about."

And if you're not *writing about him?*

She shook off the notion. The storm had complicated things for her, but she still had a book advance to earn. She'd do well to remember it.

Then she turned and stuck the coffeepot under the sink faucet.

She didn't know how to make coffee in it, but she was pretty certain that she wanted the thing to at least be clean inside when she started. Then she'd just use the old-fashioned rotary-dial phone hanging on the wall to call and ask her mom what to do with it.

Her car didn't need to be dragged by a rope behind Jayden's truck after all.

Turned out the brothers had a flatbed trailer on which

they loaded her car later that day. And the trailer was hauled behind Jayden's truck.

When he'd asked if she wanted to accompany him for the drive into town, she'd eagerly agreed.

Only because of her curiosity about Paseo in general, of course.

Not because sitting beside him in the front of his pickup truck going anywhere at all was too tempting to pass up. No, not at all.

Nor did she feel like a teenage girl on her first real car-date with the high-school quarterback, either.

She could feel a wry smile determined to work its way loose and turned to look out the side window as they drove down the highway. Once again, all she could see for miles was grass, grass and more grass. It undulated this way and that in the breeze in a mesmerizing manner. One way, nearly golden. The other, nearly green. Then *swoosh*, back again.

"What're you thinking about over there?"

Nothing that she felt compelled to admit. Yet she still couldn't wipe off the smile that she knew was on her face as she looked back at him. He'd tossed his hat on the dashboard and his short hair was ruffling in the warm air blowing through his opened window. "Just thinking that there is sure a lot of open space."

"Yep."

Looking at him was too enjoyable to stop. "What made you decide to leave here and go into the army?"

"The opportunity to leave." He had a few laugh lines radiating from the corners of his eyes. She'd noticed the faint lines when his expression was serious because they were slightly lighter. Which made her think he spent a lot of time outdoors either laughing in the sun or squinting in it. Right now, his amusement evident from the glint in his eyes to the slant of his lips, she figured the odds were about even, either way. “Like you said. Lots of open space around here.”

“Too much?”

“For a restless eighteen-year-old kid, yeah.”

“You enlisted right out of high school?”

“I wanted to. My mom had a fit. She insisted on college first.”

“Where’d you go?”

“TJC.”

Tyler Junior College, she deciphered.

“You?”

“University of Texas.”

“Journalism, I’m guessing.”

She shook her head. “Advertising at first, actually. Only I never quite fit.”

“Why not?”

“I don’t know. I guess I wasn’t comfortable enticing people to want what you’re selling even if you don’t happen to believe in it yourself.”

“And you think journalism is more ethical?”

“I don’t think there’s anything unethical about either. As long as it’s done with integrity. Advertising is an interesting mix of science and art. But the further along I got in school, the less satisfying it felt.”

“Journalism satisfies you?”

“It’s getting there.” Her book deal certainly didn’t hurt on that score. “I like writing,” she said honestly. “I like people. I like learning about their lives and interests and understanding what makes them tick.”

“Surprised you didn’t switch to psychology, then.”

She chuckled. “I minored in sociology. That’s close enough for me. What’d you study in Tyler?”

His smile widened. “Girls.” He shrugged. “Criminal justice. But only because I had to pick something.”

She was surprised, though she probably shouldn’t have been. He’d told her already that he’d been an MP in the army. But she had no idea if that was something a person sought out or if it was assigned. “Did you want to be a cop?”

“No. I just wanted out of Paseo. TJC was as good as any other place and it was affordable. It was far enough from home that I finally got the dirt out from under my nails and the smell of hay off my skin. And the second I graduated with an associate degree, I trucked on down to see the recruiter. Two years later than I’d originally wanted.”

“Do you feel like your time at Tyler was wasted?”

His smile kicked up again. “Nah. There were the girls, after all.”

She laughed and realized they were slowing. Since they’d gotten on the highway, they hadn’t passed a single other car. “Was there anyone serious?”

“Not serious enough to keep me from enlisting.”

“And after that? You were in the army for fifteen years.” She caught the look he gave her. “What?”

“Good memory.”

“I like to think so, but you told me that just yesterday when we were in the storm cellar.”

“Yeah, but a lot’s happened since then. Seems longer than just a day.”

Heat flowed swiftly in her veins from thinking about how much had happened. It wasn’t just the storm. It was *him*.

"Well, I don't worry that you're an ax murderer anymore," she admitted.

His concentration was forward as he turned off the highway onto a narrow paved road, but he shot her a quick look. "Ax murderer?"

"You never know." She raised her eyebrows right back at him. "A complete stranger on a remote Texas road? Blockbuster slasher movies have been made on less." When her mother had heard about the situation, she had been nearly apoplectic until Ariana told her that Jayden and his brother were *The* Grayson's brothers.

Evidently the fact that Karen had heard of the rodeo rider lent some legitimacy to Ariana's situation.

"Maybe I figured *you* were an ax murderer," Jayden countered.

She shook her head immediately. "Statistics are all wrong. Eighty-seven percent of murders are committed by men."

"Should I be alarmed that you can pull that stat out of your head?" He shot her an amused look. "You don't have to tell me what men are more capable of doing. But trust me. Women don't get a pass, either."

"Didn't say that they did."

"So if you were so worried I was the next character out of a horror flick, why go with me at all?"

"Sugar. What can I say?" she added at the expression that earned from him. "You'd tied a bandanna around her neck for a collar."

"Because crazed people never have dogs?" His tone was dry. "Frankly, I was glad that you had the sense to show some caution." He'd reached a run-down-looking house. He propped his arm over the top of the steering wheel and peered through the windshield. "Should have shown more, probably."

She looked skeptically from him toward the house. It was surrounded by a chain-link fence behind which a growling white pit bull was racing back and forth along the rut it had worn among the weeds. "Where you're concerned or where this place is concerned?"

Unlike Jayden's stone-fronted home, which had a comfortable and welcoming demeanor, this place practically shouted "stay away."

"If I had a sister, I'd want her to assume every man wanted something from her they shouldn't."

"I'm not your sister."

His gaze dropped to her mouth for a moment. Then he grabbed his hat off the dash and planted it low over his forehead and pushed open the truck door. "Thank God for that," he said as he climbed out.

She started to open her own door but stopped when she realized he was coming around to open it for her. "The only man who always opens my door for me is my father," she said as she hopped out.

"I'm not your father."

She couldn't stop her smile. "Thank God for that."

The frenzied dog's growling had graduated to barking, and the racket drew a short, skinny man wearing denim overalls and a stained ball cap from around the side of the house. "Betsy, shut up," he yelled and the dog's barking immediately subsided to a yip. She reared up on her hind legs and hung her front paws over the top of the fence.

Ariana almost wished she'd stayed inside the truck. "She's not going to jump the fence, is she?"

The man in the overalls had reached them. "Nah,"

he drawled. "Less'n you give her a reason to." He stuck out a hand that was missing half a forefinger toward Jayden and grinned as they shook briefly. He had a lined, weathered face that could have put him anywhere between fifty and eighty. "She's got a real soft spot for Sugar."

"Last time I brought her with me to see Charlie, it took us a whole day to track them down," Jayden said. "Learned the hard way that I had to leave her at home whenever I come here." He introduced her. "Ariana Lamonte, meet Charlie Esparza."

"Fool pooches were halfway to the next county." Charlie doffed his cap, revealing a shock of white hair that he dipped in her direction in a vaguely quaint, courtly manner, even though he was a good head shorter than she was. "Pleased to make your acquaintance, miss. Sorry it's because of that tornado." He looked back at Jayden. "Glad to hear things weren't torn up too bad over at your place."

"Nothing we can't put back together again with a few days' time. Unlike the Ybarras' house. Figured we'd stop by there on our way back home," Jayden told him. "See how they're doing."

That was news to Ariana, but obviously not surprising to Charlie, who nodded. "'Spect they'll have a lot of people callin'. Damn shame about their farmhouse." He gave Ariana an apologetic look. "Pardon my French, miss."

She couldn't help her bemusement. "Ariana, please."

"That's a real pretty name, miss."

"Thank you."

"Watch out for Charlie here." Jayden clapped the man on the shoulder. "Besides his considerable skill at flirting, he's been fixing up everything on wheels around these parts ever since I was a kid."

"Since before you wrecked your first car, that's for sure." He replaced his ball cap and walked to the trailer and her car. "Looked a lot worse than this little doll, if I remember rightly."

"And I was driving that old Mustang for another couple years."

"Until he wrecked it again," Charlie told Ariana in an aside.

"I've never even had a fender bender," Ariana admitted. "What caused your accidents?"

"Fool-headedness," Charlie said before Jayden could.

She looked from the older man to Jayden. He'd reached one hand over the fence to pet Betsy's head. Gone were the ferocious teeth she'd been baring, and instead, her long tongue hung out of her triangular face as she panted. It almost looked like the dog was smiling.

"Racing a friend out on the highway." He rubbed the dog's floppy ears and Betsy's eyes rolled in pleasure. "Fool-headedness, just like Charlie said."

"The first wreck or the second?"

Jayden's lips twisted wryly. "Both." He gave the dog a final pat, much to Betsy's obvious dismay, and moved over to the car as well. He propped his hands on his lean hips. "So what do you think, Charlie?"

In answer, the man nimbly climbed up on the trailer, working his way around the car. "Gonna take some time. Parts for these hybrids are harder to come by than some."

She may not have had experience with vehicular accidents, but she did have some dealing with auto repair shops since the car she'd owned before this one had broken down more often than it had run. "Where do you do the work, Mr. Esparza?"

"Charlie," the man corrected her, hopping down to the ground next to her. "Back in the garage." He gestured vaguely in the direction of the house. "Drive 'er on back," he told Jayden. "We'll get 'er unloaded."

"I have insurance," she said quickly. "They'll want an estimate before they'll pay for work. And I don't know if Jayden told you, but I can't find the key—"

Charlie waved off her words. "Sure 'nough, miss. We'll get all that official stuff taken care of. And I can get a replacement key just like the rest of the parts, no problem. Just takes time, like I said. Don't worry yourself none. Everything'll be fine." He looked at Jayden. "Pull up by the back bay," he said and started walking away.

Jayden opened Ariana's door again and she climbed in.

Then he drove around the run-down-looking house and she spotted the garage. It was easily four times the size of the house and not run-down in the least. "Wow."

"Yeah." Jayden clearly understood her surprise. "What Charlie doesn't put into his house, he puts into the garage. It's his one true love. Guy does everything from bodywork to building cars from the ground up."

He backed the trailer up to one of the several oversized garage doors. They were all closed, but as Charlie neared, the one behind them began opening and Ariana could see inside the cavernous space that already housed a sports car with its hood up, a fancy-looking boat on a trailer and a half-dozen motorcycles in various stages of assembly.

"Looks like he does more than just cars. There's enough water around here for a boat?"

"If you don't mind a bit of a drive." He got out of the truck. "Charlie's got an office inside on the other side of that tire rack if you want to go over and wait while we get your car unloaded."

She'd already taken her insurance information out of the glove box. Aside from the clothes on her back, at the moment, the insurance information and her still-inoperable cell phone comprised all of her personal effects. With both in hand, she walked through the spotless garage into the office. It had a glass door and she could see Jayden and Charlie make quick work of unloading her small car. Then the two men started toward the office, stopping along the way to check out one of the motorcycles.

Ariana couldn't hear what they were saying, but she couldn't help but chuckle at the sight they made. Physically, the two men couldn't be more different. But their expressions as they lovingly examined the bike were exactly the same.

She was still smiling when they pushed through the glass door. Charlie shuffled around to sit behind a metal desk that had only a single in-box sitting on its surface, squarely aligned in one corner, while Jayden sauntered to where Ariana was sitting in one of the black-and-white-checked chairs lined against the wall beside a small, also spotless, restroom.

Ariana had to admit that Charlie's garage was the cleanest one she'd ever been in.

"What're you sitting there smiling about?" Jayden pulled off his cowboy hat as he sat beside her and hooked it over his bent knee.

"You guys drooling over that Fat Boy out there."

He raised his eyebrow. "You know your Harleys?"

"I did a blog a year ago on men's love affairs with their motorcycles." It had actually been about men's love affairs with their toys superseding their love affairs with their mates, but that was beside the point.

She could smile about it now. Which meant the cathartic blog had done its job. Hadn't hurt that her readership had skyrocketed, either. That was when her editor at *Weird Life* had first assigned her to interview an up-and-coming architect from London named Keaton Whitfield…who also happened to be the illegitimate son of Gerald Robinson.

And her series "Becoming a Fortune" had been born.

Jayden's booted toe was bobbing in her peripheral vision and her sense of well-being wilted.

The series might have become the delight of the magazine's readers, but it wasn't always to the delight of her subjects whether they were one of Gerald's legitimate *or* illegitimate progeny. She'd also never exposed anyone as being one of his offspring. By the time she'd interviewed Keaton—and subsequently, his half sister Chloe Elliott—they'd already learned elsewhere that Gerald was their biological father. They'd had time to adjust. Sort of.

"Miss?"

The same couldn't be said for Jayden and his brothers, though. The truth—if it was the truth—would blindside them.

Ariana realized that Charlie was speaking to her. She looked over at him, dragging her thoughts into the present.

"You all right?" Jayden's head was angled as he studied her from those steady brown eyes.

It was never her intention to cause harm in her writing. But it was her intention to be truthful.

And some truths were harder to swallow than others.

"I'm fine," she lied. "Just got to thinking about what a hassle it's going to be replacing my driver's license and everything else in my wallet. I don't even have my credit card with me to pay the insurance deductible to Charlie."

Jayden's hand covered hers and squeezed. "You're not worried about that, are you, Charlie?"

"Nah." Charlie had pulled a paper form onto his desk and she could see that he'd completed some of it. Now he extended the pen he'd been using toward her. "Only need your signature, miss, and we'll settle up the score later."

Jayden squeezed her hand again. "Sound good?"

"Sounds good," she repeated dutifully and reached for the pen.

She just wished she were certain that settling the score with Jayden wasn't going to cost her more than whatever she ended up owing for her car.

Chapter 5

"There you have it." Jayden braked in the middle of the road and gestured at the cluster of buildings ahead of him. "Downtown Paseo in all its glory. Bet you've never seen anything quite like it. Outside of a spaghetti Western, at any rate."

He was determined to put the smile back on Ariana's face. The smile that had been absent since she'd signed the paperwork in Charlie's office.

The smile that was still absent as she looked through the windshield of his truck at the town he called home.

"I've never seen anything quite like it," she agreed. "What's the population?"

"Last census had us just over a couple hundred. Of course, that includes the surrounding ranches." He took his foot off the brake. "Let me give you the tour. Don't blink now. If you do, you'll miss it."

That, at least, earned a twitch of her lips.

It was progress.

"That's the town hall." He gestured to a square brick building that was under construction.

"It's still being repaired from the hailstorm last year. You mentioned it," she reminded him when he showed his surprise.

He kept forgetting her attention to detail. She had a singular ability to listen and listen well.

It wasn't a trait he was all that used to when it came to women. Or at least when it had come to Tess, he supposed.

Fortunately, Ariana wasn't Tess.

"The construction isn't from those repairs, though that did take a while. What they're doing now is expanding to accommodate the library." He pointed to the RV sitting in the town-hall parking lot as he slowly trolled past the building.

"That motor home is the library? It's a bookmobile?" She looked at the vehicle with a hopeful expression. "I wish this was one of the days it was open. I could sure stand a little time with the internet."

"Thought you called your boss before we left."

"I did. But I've also got to get the ball rolling on replacing my driver's license and such."

He shook his head. "Ball is still going to have to wait. Library's not open on Saturdays. And it's not exactly mobile. The RV is just a shell. Doesn't run."

She made a face. "Well, that's my luck lately. So, is the existence of a library new around here?"

"Nah. But it used to be just a wall of books in the gas station. The RV was donated by the Ybarra family a few years back. Same Ybarras who just lost their farmhouse."

He poked his thumb in the direction of said gas station. "You can get your gas and your groceries there. Or if you're feeling in a festive mood, you can sit down in the Mexican restaurant they run in the back."

A humorous light filled her chocolate-brown eyes and the twitch on her lips had turned into a soft curve. She didn't have on a lick of makeup but she couldn't have been prettier if she'd tried.

"Sounds tasty," she drawled.

"Don't knock it until you've tried it. Rosa—she owns all three businesses—makes some mean carnitas. Better than I've had anywhere else."

"I'd offer to take you in return for giving me shelter during the storm, but—" She spread her hands and the bracelets around her wrist sparkled. "I have no way to pay."

He grinned. "Play your cards right, and maybe I'll take *you*."

"Careful. You'll turn my head with such fancy offers." Smiling fully, she pointed at another building.

"Hardware store," he provided. "Sells bits of everything from farm equipment to bolts of fabric."

Her eyebrows immediately went up. "How about a cell phone charger?"

He doubted it. "Let's check and see. I need to stop anyway and order the replacement window glass we need cut."

She smiled winningly and quickly unclipped her seat belt, hopping out before he had a chance to get around to her side. He followed her into the store and couldn't help but chuckle at the amazed expression crossing her face.

"I'll go ask about the charger," he offered, but she was already setting off for the nearest aisle. He couldn't imagine what would be so interesting about stove parts and cast-iron cookware, but he followed her through the aisles anyway.

Watching her explore fascinated him. She stretched up to look at a dusty copper bracelet display and crouched down a few steps later to examine a metal water trough. When he plucked a wind chime off the shelf, she gave him a surprised look. "Wind chimes with little fairies on it?"

He didn't care about the fairies. He cared about the tones it made. "We lost the set of wind chimes that usually hangs by the kitchen door. They help orient Sugar when she's outside."

Her eyes softened.

They made it around the entire store, never having encountered another person. Much to his surprise, though, she had found a section of electronics and had pounced on one package in particular with glee.

Until she'd rolled her eyes and shook her head, muttering to herself as she put the package back on the shelf.

It didn't take a genius to figure out why. He handed her the package. "You can owe me if it makes you feel better."

She told him it did, and she clasped the package to the front of her thin excuse for a top as if it were precious and carried it there through the rest of the store, not setting it down until they reached the checkout counter at the front. "Is there anyone even here?"

He'd begun wondering that himself. Admittedly, Paseo wasn't a hotbed of crime when it came to shoplifting. But there was usually someone around the store, either the owner, Harvey, or one of the local kids he hired. "I'll check the stockroom." He headed to the back of the store again, pushing through the swinging door there and calling Harv's name.

The two teenagers getting busy on a camping mattress in the back sprang apart.

Jayden gave the boy—Harvey's grandson—a look. "Kind of hard to watch the store when your eyes are closed, son."

The kid flushed, though Jayden privately gave him props for trying to shield his nearly naked girlfriend from view.

"Need some window glass cut." He pulled a folded paper from his pocket and set it on the shelf just inside the swinging door. "Those're the measurements. I'll be back tomorrow to pick them up."

He returned to the front of the store, dropped a fifty-dollar bill on the counter for their two items and steered Ariana out of the store.

"I can't believe someone would leave the store open like that without anyone there," she said as they climbed into his truck once more.

"Someone was there," he said wryly. He tossed the wind-chime box in the backseat. "Just...otherwise engaged."

She looked up from peeling open her cardboard package.

"Sex," he elaborated as he pulled a U-turn on the empty street. There were other highlights the town possessed besides a town hall and a hardware store, but it was getting late and the clouds on the horizon had started climbing high in the sky with what would likely become another thunderstorm before too long. And he still wanted to get by the Ybarra place. "Two kids in the storeroom making the slow day pass by a lot more quickly."

He watched her cheeks flush. Which was interesting, because in their limited but eventful time together, Ariana had not struck him as being either shy or prudish. "Never made out in the back of a store when you were a teenager?"

She rolled her eyes, shaking her head. "Never worked in a store when I was a teenager."

"So, what *did* you do when you were a teenager?"

"Daydreamed." She gave him a wry smile, looking vaguely chagrined. "Babysat. Helped out at the front desk at the dental office where my mom still works." She lifted her shoulder. "Cheerleading."

"No kidding?"

She did a sort of rah-rah thing with her arm. "Go Cougars."

"Suppose you dated the captain of the football team, too."

"Briefly." She pulled the contents from the box and held up the car adapter. "Do you mind?" When he shook his head, she leaned forward and plugged it into the cigarette lighter, then sat back and attached it to her cell phone. "Whoahoa!" She held up her phone. The surface of it was black, but a small light on the corner was blinking. "We have liftoff."

She was clearly delighted, so he didn't remind her how useless he figured the thing was in their corner of the world.

She rolled down her window, propping her elbow in the opening, and her long hair streamed away from her face. “Anyway, the quarterback’s name was Scotty. We lasted all of two weeks.”

“What ended the great romance?”

“Juliette Wysocki. My next-door neighbor, head cheerleader and chief easy-pants of the school.” She waited a beat. “Not that I held a grudge or anything.”

He laughed. “Easy-pants, huh?”

“Better than calling her Empress of Slutville. Though I’ll tell you that particular shoe is one she’s still wearing.” Her eyes danced as she looked at him. Then she seemed to realize that her long hair was blowing across his shoulder and she gathered it together, holding it in one hand.

He’d been a long way from complaining about it. Ariana had amazing hair. Thick. Lustrous. He couldn’t look at it without wanting to wrap his hands in it.

He dragged his mind out of that particular puddle.

“So you lost out to Juliette’s seductive ways. What happened then?”

“I swore off boys for the rest of the year, graduated *almost* at the top of my class—that honor went to Simon Mendivil—went to New York City on a two-month internship and came back home to start UT a few weeks later.”

“What’d you think of New York City?” He could imagine her there.

“Vibrant. Crowded. *Way* too expensive. Have you been?”

He nodded. “Always on my way to somewhere else, though.”

“Well, while I was there, I shared a one-bedroom apartment with four other girls. Cozy, to say the least.”

“What was the internship for?”

"Working at an advertising firm. It was interesting and I was even offered a longer-term stint, but I couldn't afford to stay on the pittance I was earning, and I didn't have time enough after hours to get another job. So—" She shrugged. "I came back home." She peered through the windshield. "That's not another storm, is it?"

"Supposed to be the tail end of the season for storms, but I figure anything's possible. Clouds are pretty far off yet." He flipped through the radio dial, finding a handful of talk shows in Spanish, a fuzzy country station and a pregame for the Astros. No weather at all. He turned the volume down, but left the baseball station on.

She was chewing her lip.

He reached over and caught her hand. "Don't look so worried. Watching the rain from our front porch is one of the most peaceful things in the world."

"So long as it's only rain," she said.

But she'd stopped torturing her soft lower lip.

And she'd left her fingers curled around his.

Even though Nathan had said the tornado had torn down a neighbor's farmhouse, until Ariana saw it for herself through Jayden's windshield as he slowly rolled to a stop in front of it, she had no real conception just how devastating the sight would be.

"Oh, my God," she murmured. She couldn't tell if the house had been a single story or a multistory. She couldn't tell if it had been painted white or yellow or purple.

If it weren't for an avocado-green refrigerator with the door half torn off lying on its side in the midst of the pile of sticks and lumber and debris, she wasn't sure she would have even known it had ever been a house.

Someone's home.

"That poor family."

Jayden's expression was solemn as he pushed open his door. "You want to come or wait here?"

Beyond the group of camper trucks and SUVs clustered together, she realized that someone had erected a pop-up canopy midway between the remains of the house and a tall white barn, and there was a group of people milling around it. "I'd like to come if I won't be intruding."

"When it comes to Paloma and Hector Ybarra, nobody is an intruder."

She pushed open her own door. "They're the owners, I take it?"

"Yes. Be careful," he warned. "Don't get close to the house."

She nodded and went around the back of the truck to join him on the far side. He pulled a five-gallon jug of water out of the truck bed that she hadn't even noticed before and propped it on his shoulder before taking her elbow as they walked toward the tent. Which was good, since Ariana could barely tear her attention away from the destruction of the house and she nearly tripped over a broken roof tile in her path.

It didn't matter how many news stories she'd ever watched about tornadoes and the damage they caused. It was positively eerie seeing the house leveled, while a couple hundred yards away, the barn looked blissfully untouched.

"Jayden." A diminutive white-haired woman broke away from the group under the tent and approached them. She was smiling and her arms were held wide.

"What a welcome sight you are. I see you brought us more water."

Jayden let go of Ariana and set down the heavy water container to hug the tiny woman. "*Lo siento*, Paloma."

"Ah. Thank you, *mijo*. But it is a house. Hector and I are the home." She patted his cheek, looking past him with bright brown eyes to Ariana. "And who is this?"

Jayden's gaze moved over Ariana, setting off a sweet warmth inside her. "A new friend. Ariana Lamonte, this lovely lady is Paloma Ybarra. One of my most favorite people on earth."

Ariana held out her hand and found it clasped warmly between both of Paloma's. "I'm so sorry to meet you under these circumstances, Mrs. Ybarra."

"Better to meet than not to meet, isn't that right, Jayden?" She smiled up at Ariana. "Come and meet my Hector." Still holding Ariana's hand, she also grabbed Jayden's arm and tugged them toward the canopy. She called out something in Spanish and a teenage boy trotted past them to take the water and add it to the collection of supplies that Ariana could see under the canopy.

"Graciela is here," Paloma was telling Jayden. "She and Tomas arrived this afternoon." Her eyes bounced back to Ariana. "My daughter and her husband. They live in Mexico City. Tomas is an attorney there."

"She definitely moved up from the likes of me," Jayden said with a smile. His eyes met Ariana's over Paloma's head. "Graciela was the girl who got away."

"He is teasing you, Ariana," Paloma assured her. "Jayden was only a boy when my daughter finished high school."

"Yeah." They'd reached the tent and Jayden gave Ariana a quick wink. "The unattainable older woman."

He moved away from Paloma and Ariana to kiss the cheek of a strikingly beautiful, dark-haired woman who threw back her head and laughed throatily over whatever it was he said.

Even with that wink of his, Ariana still felt a curl of jealousy. She clamped down on it witheringly.

Oftentimes when people were displaced from their homes because of some disaster, local charities lent aid. But in such a remote area as Paseo, Ariana had a feeling those services were probably hard to come by.

"Mrs. Ybarra, do you and your husband have some place to stay?" Admittedly, she hadn't seen all of the businesses in Paseo, but considering its size, she doubted there was a motel of any sort. "Do you have more family in the area?"

"Graciela is our only child." Paloma patted Ariana's hand. "But Hector and I have each other." She gestured toward the barn. "We have shelter." She nodded toward Jayden, who was working his way through the dozen or so people there, greeting them all. "We have friends. We are very blessed."

Ariana wasn't sure how many people would feel so blessed when confronted with similar circumstances.

Because Paloma didn't let go of her hand, she found herself pulled along, being introduced to everyone. "This is Jayden's new *friend*," Paloma would say. Emphasis on the *friend*. As if it weren't all that ordinary to be introducing a female fitting that particular category when it came to Jayden Fortune.

Someone started moving the folding lawn chairs, and before Ariana knew it, she was sitting in one squarely between Hector and Paloma with a plate of coleslaw and corn bread on her lap and a bottle of beer in her hand. Paloma's husband mostly smiled benignly at everyone, Ariana included. Whatever he didn't have to say, his wife more than made up for it as she chattered on about Paseo, about the weather, about God and the Devil and just about everything in between.

"He was a wild one, your Jayden," Paloma said after finally pausing to draw breath.

Ariana had been fascinated by everything Paloma had said. But she really needed to correct this misapprehension about her and Jayden. "Mrs. Ybarra, Jayden's not my—"

"Never deliberately chased a fight," Paloma said right over Ariana's attempt to correct her. "But he never turned away from one, either. Oh, how his mama used to worry about him. He's told you about his mama, *sí*?"

Ariana glanced his way. She had the feeling he'd just as easily stand out among five dozen people as he did in this small gathering. And as if he felt her attention, he turned his head and looked at her.

His lips tilted up and the lines beside his eyes crinkled.

Her nerve endings fizzed.

Lord, the man did have a smile.

Then he turned back to the three teenagers he was speaking with—Hector's second and third cousins who were both named Arturo and who also lived in Mexico—and Ariana belatedly focused on Paloma. She casually set the beer bottle on the ground next to her boot. "Jayden's mother? He, uh, he hasn't said a lot." *Just that Deborah supposedly made up the surname of Fortune.* She ignored the voice inside her head.

"Raised those boys all on her own." Paloma hadn't waited a beat. "Course, she had a little help early on from the Thompsons. Earl and Cynthia. Deborah was a comfort to them, sure enough, after they'd lost their only daughter that horrible way just a few months before." Paloma nodded as if all of these were details that Jayden's *friend* undoubtedly already knew. "But even in tragedy there is blessing. Earl and Cynthia took in Deborah when she was in a bad way. Traveling like she was, so pregnant and all. And my, they loved those little babies when they were born a little while later. If it hadn't been for them, I'm not sure what Earl and Cynthia would've done. And vice versa. They had someone to pass on their ranch to, and those babies had a safe and happy place to grow up in." She set her wrinkled hand on top of Ariana's and patted it gently. "Life tends to work out the way it's supposed to if we don't let ourselves get in the way." Then she pushed herself off the chair, because another car had driven up and she was heading toward it.

"My wife likes you," Hector said in a low, raspy voice.

"She's lovely," she told Hector truthfully. "But I have the feeling your wife would like everyone she meets." Paloma obviously would find something good to say about anyone. Even the Empress of Slutville. She shoveled some coleslaw in her mouth and popped her plate into the opened trash bag that Graciela's handsome husband was offering to everyone. "Mr. Ybarra, I don't want to intrude, so please tell me it's none of my business if you like. But where will you and Mrs. Ybarra be staying?" All of their relatives seemed to have come from miles and miles away. Which also had her wondering where they would stay.

"Right here, girl." His arm encompassed the devastated house, the temporary canopy and the barn all in one.

"But it's going to rain again soon." The clouds on the horizon were nearing and they were obviously carrying rain.

Hector looked amused. "Roof on the barn's still sound. Was last night. And will be tonight."

"You're sleeping in the barn?"

"Unless it's clear. There's nothing like sleeping under a Paseo sky." His eyes shifted to Jayden for a brief moment. "Ask him. He'll tell you the same." He looked back at Ariana. "Been living on this land since I was born. Not going to leave Paseo just because of some wind and rain. Stole my wife from her family in Mexico when she was just seventeen. Been married more 'n fifty years now and every night of that's been spent here on this land whether we were under what used to be that roof or not."

She smiled at him. "Mr. Ybarra, I write for a magazine in Austin. Nothing you would have even heard of here in Paseo, but I'd really like to do a piece about you and your wife."

His bushy gray eyebrows shot up. "The heck you say!"

"I think our readers would be inspired by your story."

He laughed and shook his head. "If that ain't *loco*. Long as you don't say something untrue, I guess I don't see the harm. Paloma'll be real pleased, I'm sure."

"Hector," Jayden drawled as he stopped in front of them, "you married the prettiest woman already. Then Graciela didn't wait for me to get out of short pants before she married Tomas. So don't be smiling like that at the next beauty to come along."

Ariana laughed at that. She had never made the mistake of considering herself beautiful. She was reasonably passable when she had a bag of armor to brighten up her face and plenty of hair products to tame her unruly, long hair. But that was okay, because she was generally comfortable in her own skin. A trait that made the people she talked with more comfortable in theirs.

"Mr. Ybarra has agreed to let me write a story about him and his wife for *Weird*," she told Jayden.

"Weird?" Hector looked suddenly alarmed. "What kinda magazine is that?"

She smiled reassuringly. *"Weird Life Magazine,"* she clarified. "It's a lifestyle magazine published in Austin. It's named after 'Keep Austin Weird'—the town's unofficial slogan. Trust me, you have nothing to worry about."

He looked somewhat appeased. "You vouch for your girl, Jayden?"

It felt like a rope suddenly sneaked its way around Ariana's throat.

"Sure I do, Hector." Jayden grabbed her hand and pulled her to her feet. "Nathan and I will come by tomorrow and help with some of the cleanup. You and Paloma can talk yourselves hoarse with Ariana then."

The older man pushed to his feet and shook Jayden's hand. Then he bowed slightly over the one Ariana offered, as if he weren't particularly accustomed to shaking women's hands.

Paloma was in the clinch of a sausage-curled woman wailing about the tornado when they started to leave. Paloma just spread her hands behind the woman's stranglehold and smiled as she caught their eye. Then she patted the woman's back. "It's all right, Molly," they heard her soothe. "Don't upset yourself this way."

"I think Paloma must be a saint or something," Ariana said in a low voice once she and Jayden returned to his truck. "I'm pretty sure I wouldn't be up to comforting someone else if my house was a pile of kindling around my feet."

"They're good people." He pulled open the passenger door for her and she climbed up inside. "You really want to write a story about them?"

She nodded. Her gaze went from the destroyed house to the canopy. "I really do." She picked up her cell phone. It still looked like it was charging, though nothing happened when she pressed the power button. "Hopefully, this thing will be working again and I can record the interview and take some photographs of them. Whether I can use it as a phone or not, it has a really good camera."

She'd love to take a photograph of Jayden, too, but she kept that tidbit to herself. Particularly considering she wasn't sure if she wanted it for personal reasons or professional.

"I'm surprised you didn't have a laptop or something with you. But you never mentioned one getting lost in the storm."

She waited until he got behind the wheel. "I only use my laptop when I actually get down to the business of writing. I had one crash on me once without a backup—my fault entirely—but it made me superstitious, I guess. I take most of my notes by hand."

"So you're not tied quite so much to technology as I had you pegged," he drawled.

She smiled and turned her hands upward. "We'll see."

He worked their way around the collection of haphazardly parked vehicles and it dawned on Ariana that, while Hector and Paloma slept in the barn, many of their callers were probably sleeping in those campers.

A fact that Jayden confirmed when she voiced it. "Unless it's clear out and they'll move their sleeping bags under the stars."

She couldn't help but smile, thinking of what Hector had said.

"So what other kinds of stories do you write? Besides your Fortune thing and guys' fixations on things that go zoom."

She grabbed her hair before it could start blowing around too much from the opened windows. She was already going to have a heck of a time getting a comb through it. "I mostly do human interest stories." That was entirely true. Even her bio on the magazine's website said so. It just didn't say a thing about her current pursuit into one man's secretive past.

She shifted in her seat, pulling the shoulder belt a few inches away from her chest because it felt strangely tight.

"Mostly?"

She reminded herself that she wasn't really hiding secrets. Jayden already knew about her "Becoming a Fortune" series for the magazine. And when it came to her book, she'd deal with the facts as she learned them.

She realized she still hadn't answered him and shifted again. "I still do a weekly blog on the club scene around Austin. That's pretty much how I started out. With the blog, I mean. I check out popular venues.

Grand openings. New concerts. New shows. That sort of thing. I was supposed to do a place called Twine last night. I have a couple of friends who bartend there. Surprisingly enough, my editor hadn't reassigned it to someone else when I called in yesterday."

"Lot of competition among the writers?"

"Enough to keep you on your toes." Enough to know that her book deal would add considerable weight when it came time to negotiate her next contract with *Weird Life*. "So you had a crush on Graciela? She's very beautiful."

"That's a quick change of subject."

"What can I say? People interest me, obviously."

"That's all it is?" A small smile played around his lips as he shot her a quick look. "Professional interest?"

He charmed her way too easily.

"I'm not going to answer that," she said calmly.

His laugh was low.

It still managed to send shivers straight down her spine that didn't ever really stop, not even when they arrived back at his ranch almost an hour later.

They did beat the clouds back to the ranch, but not by much. Nathan and Sugar met them when Jayden drove up and it started to rain as the two men unhitched the trailer.

Hovering around watching them only meant getting wet or getting in their way, so she headed back to the house. She plugged her phone into one of the kitchen outlets and left it on the counter to charge, then went into the bedroom and sat on the bed to pull off her boots.

Mismatched stockinged feet freed, she dropped the boots on the floor and lay back on the mattress, wiggling her toes and rotating her ankles. "Oh, yessss."

"I suppose it would be wrong of me to take that as an invitation."

She looked to where Jayden was standing in the open doorway. His shirt was speckled with raindrops. And she had to fight the strong urge to hold out her hand to him in invitation.

Instead, she rolled onto her side and propped her head on that hand just to make sure it didn't do something it shouldn't.

"Unless you're offering a foot massage," she said drily, "yes, it would be very wrong." She leaned over and picked up one of her bedraggled-looking boots. The red color had turned patchy and the suede itself was flattened and shiny. "Aside from the sad state of the suede, these boots weren't quite made for walkin'. At least not anymore."

"They have kind of taken a beating."

"That's one way to put it. I don't know if they shrank after getting wet, but they sure fit tighter now than they did before yesterday's storm." She let the boot drop back onto the floor next to its mate and swung her legs off the bed and stood.

Lying there didn't feel all that wise. It was too easy for her mind to skip down seductive paths.

"That's why you pretreat suede," he said, walking past her to open the closet door. "So it doesn't shrink. Doesn't stain, either." He gestured at the interior of the closet. "Find something in there that'll be more comfortable. Shoes. Clothes. Whatever. I doubt anything of my mom's clothing is going to be too small for you. She's taller 'n you. And she wouldn't mind," he added before she could open her mouth to protest. "That's what people do in these parts, in case you missed it. We look out for each other. It's a necessity when there're so few to depend on. Hell, that's how Mom came to settle in Paseo in the first place. Depending on the kindness of strangers." He gestured again at the clothing. "Find some shoes. Then come on outside. I'll get the grill going soon for supper. You like steak?"

"Couldn't call myself a Texan in good conscience if I didn't."

He grinned and left the room.

Ariana drew in a deep, needy breath that was owed entirely to the wallop packed into that grin.

Even though she still felt strange about it, she crouched down and plucked a pair of faded black tennis shoes from the neat row on the closet floor and pulled them on.

Jayden had been right. They were at least one size too large. She tied them tightly, but still had to be careful not to step right out of them as she left the room.

She found him and his brother sitting in two of the wooden rockers that were scattered along the wraparound porch. Sugar, sprawled between them, lifted her head as Ariana approached, sniffed a few times, then lowered her head again to her paws and closed her eyes.

Jayden pulled a third chair closer to him. "Sit."

She sat. She stretched out her legs and crossed them at the ankles the same way the two men were doing.

"Now just watch," he said. "And listen."

So she did.

Beyond the overhanging roof, the light rain fell. She could hear the sound of it striking the roof, pinging on the gutters, splashing on the stones. The air filled with the redolent scent of moist, rich earth.

She wasn't going to think about Gerald Robinson.

About Deborah Fortune. What their relationship might have been and what, if anything, Charlotte had known about it. Not while Ariana was wearing Deborah's shoes and sitting beside two of her sons.

Ariana drew in a deep breath and let it out.

She felt Jayden's dark gaze on her and looked his way.

He smiled slowly.

Warmth—comfortable and sweet—seemed to fill her, rising right up through her from the soles of her feet to the top of her head.

He was right.

Watching the rain from Jayden's porch was about the most peaceful thing in the world.

Chapter 6

The following day, after Jayden and his brother had already spent several early-morning hours working the cattle—whatever *that* meant—Ariana went with him again back into town to retrieve the window glass he'd ordered.

While he was busy with that, she made a beeline for the aisle two rows over from where she'd found the cell phone charger. There, she flipped through the neatly folded pile of neon-colored tie-dyed T-shirts emblazoned with *Paseo Is Paradise* that she'd seen the day before and found two size mediums at the very bottom. She took them both. Then she found a tube of lip balm and a travel toothbrush in the camping supply aisle and was just thinking wryly how lucky she was not to be needing any type of feminine supply items anytime soon when Jayden found her.

"Find everything you want?"

She nodded and followed him to the checkout counter where his panes of window glass were already waiting, padded and packed in wooden crates.

"I'm keeping a list," she said once he'd paid and was strapping the crates upright in the truck bed. To prove it, she showed him the screen of her cell phone, which had finally powered up even though she still couldn't use it to make calls. "I'll pay you back every dime."

His lips twitched and his eyes squinted against the bright morning sun. "Or we *could* work it out in trade."

"Tempting though that may be, I'm not taking that particular bait," she said drily.

She pocketed the phone, and while he finished tying down the windows, she got in the cab, deftly pulling one of the T-shirts over her head and down her chest. Watching him through the side-view mirror to be certain he was otherwise distracted, she pulled the straps of the camisole off her shoulders and worked it off through the neck of her T-shirt, then hastily shoved her arms through the sleeves just in time before he got into the truck.

He took in the bright pink, orange and green T-shirt and the camisole bunched in her fist. "You're a quick-change artist in addition to everything else?"

"It's a skill that comes in handy sometimes." She shoved the camisole in the hardware-store bag and tossed it onto the backseat next to the notepad she'd borrowed from him before they left the ranch. She often recorded interviews but was equally comfortable going old school with pad and pencil. As evidenced by the notebook she'd lost from her car. Which was still something she didn't like thinking about. "I've changed into cocktail dresses in my car before when I've had to run from one club to another for my blog."

He gave her a sidelong look that had her nerves fizzing and thoughts about anything besides him flying out the window.

"Are we stopping anywhere else?" The plan was to meet Nathan—who was bringing the front loader from the ranch—at the Ybarras' after Jayden had picked up the windowpanes.

"I doubt you'll find a pair of shorts to go with that T-shirt anywhere in town, if that's what you're hoping." A smile flirted around his eyes. "Pretty sure those shirts were left over from a fund-raiser the school had when *I* went there."

She plucked at the hem of the cheap tie-dyed cotton. If she were honest, it wasn't all that far a cry from her usual style, which admittedly leaned toward the Bohemian. "I don't care how old it is. At least it's not borrowed." That made her wonder about the Ybarras again. Their entire house had gone the *Wizard of Oz* way. Would they be dependent upon the donations of other people's clothing while they put their life back together? "I hope the Ybarras have good hazard insurance."

"I guess you can ask them when we get there."

"I imagine that I will." She chewed the inside of her cheek as she thought about the questions she planned, absently noting the half-dozen vehicles pulled up at the gas station. "Looks like there's a run on gasoline today."

He followed her glance. "Sunday-after-church grocery shopping, more like." This time, he wasn't hauling a trailer on the back of the truck, and as soon as he left behind the town, he picked up speed.

In the side-view mirror, she could see the wind blowing at the crates holding the window glass. "Who will do the window work for you?"

"You mean replacing the panes? We do it ourselves."

She watched him thoughtfully. "Did you and your brothers come out of the womb just naturally self-reliant?"

He chuckled. "It's kind of do-it-yourself 101, sweetheart."

"Maybe for some. My maintenance and repair skills reach as far as replacing the bag on my vacuum cleaner."

"If you're interested, I'll give you a lesson on glass repairs for the next time you're stuck after a tornado."

"At least I'd be of more use to the people saddled with me."

"You've said that before. And if you'll remember," he said, his voice deepening as he gave her a steady look, "I said it was my pleasure."

She was vaguely shocked to feel her skin tightening the way it was. To feel her nipples peaking under the cheap cotton shirt that was all that covered them. She wasn't a prude by any means, but she'd never met anyone besides Jayden who elicited such a visceral reaction from her.

And without so much as a single touch.

She swallowed and struggled not to moisten her lips.

His gaze dropped to them anyway. Then, for an infinitesimal moment, it dropped to her breasts before he focused again on the road ahead of them.

Feeling hot, she rolled her window down a few more

inches and stared out at the passing landscape. It was all she could do not to cross her arms over her chest and squirm in her seat, and she had never been so grateful to get somewhere as she was when they arrived at the Ybarra place.

It meant she could throw her focus entirely on someone other than Jayden. At least for a little while.

It was a good idea. In theory.

But after she'd spent the afternoon talking with Paloma and Hector about their life together in Paseo—interrupted by family members and friends who presented them with pieces of personal property they'd salvaged from the tornado wreckage as they helped clean up—Ariana had to admit defeat.

To herself, at least.

No matter what she did, how truly interesting she found Paloma and Hector to be, she was never able to completely move Jayden out of her mind.

The task certainly hadn't been helped by the fact that he was within Ariana's eyesight almost every minute of the afternoon. Even when she and Paloma and Hector left the shade of the canopy—where a camp kitchen had been set up, to Hector's delight—into the barn to show off their makeshift living quarters—complete with a portable potty, to Paloma's delight—Ariana had been able to see him through the wide-open barn doors. He sat there shirtless and sweating atop the tractor as he drove it back and forth. Slowly and inexorably and with the help of many hands, he cleared away the destruction until all that remained were a huge pile of bricks and a farmhouse-sized patch of bare earth.

Everything else had been loaded onto trailers and a roll-off Dumpster that had appeared since the day before.

If she hadn't seen it for herself, she would have found it difficult to believe that so much work could be done in such a short amount of time. And without a lot of heavy equipment. She'd captured some video of it on her phone, knowing it would be a good online tie-in for the article when she wrote it.

By the time the work was done, somebody had brought trays of carnitas and tortillas from Rosa's in town. The helpers, who had worked for hours in the hot Texas sun, tucked hungrily into the food, and although they had to be exhausted, they broke into song and dance when someone produced some loud Tejano music. They hung around making merry until the only light there was came from the moon and the two strands of red and green Christmas lights Tomas and Graciela hung from one edge of the barn to the corner of the portable canopy.

Ariana was so moved by the whole thing she had to break away from the crowd just so she could wipe her wet cheeks in private.

"Talk about the human spirit, eh?" Jayden—shirt back in place—found her standing in the shadows of the barn.

"Yes." Her voice was husky. "Last I saw, you were dancing with Graciela." If not for the fact that every time Graciela looked at Tomas it was with adoration in her expression, Ariana might have been eaten up by jealousy. Because Jayden most definitely was not in short pants anymore when it came to women.

"Last I saw," he returned, "you were sitting with the two Arturos eating some of Rosa's killer flan."

"I was."

He angled his head slightly. "Everything all right? I should have offered to take you back to the ranch. It's been a long day."

"Please." Teary-eyed or not, her toe was tapping inside her too-large tennis shoe in time to the rhythmic music. "Do you think I'd have taken you away for even an hour this afternoon? I didn't work anywhere near as hard as most of you did." Not to mention the hours he'd put in at his own place even before she'd rolled out of bed.

"Your interview was good?"

"Very." Somehow, the distance between them was shrinking and she wasn't sure if she could lay the blame on him. "But I think it was less an interview *I* conducted than keeping up with them as they just talked." She'd gone with her instincts, knowing the second she suggested recording them that they'd have gotten self-conscious. So she satisfied herself instead with taking a few notes that she would elaborate on when she was alone. If she needed to clarify any particular facts later on, she could.

"Do you know Paloma said she wasn't afraid when the tornado was blowing through? That she and Hector waited it out in their storm shelter playing cards?" If Ariana hadn't spent as many hours with the couple by now, she'd have found it difficult to believe. "When it was blowing over us while we were in your storm cellar, I was terrified."

He lifted his hand and tucked a lock of hair behind

her ear and her heartbeat stuttered. "Guess I should have tried playing cards with you."

Her laugh sounded breathless even to her own ears. "You were plenty distracting."

His lips stretched into a smile as his head lowered closer to hers. "So were you." He slid another lock of hair behind her other ear and she felt rooted to the earth when his mouth grazed lightly over hers. "You're still distracting," he murmured.

She could hear her blood rushing through her head. But she still managed to pull back. "Jayden, this isn't a good idea."

"Afraid someone will see?" He wrapped his hand behind her back and started moving faintly to the music.

Before she could even think, she was moving along with him. She only realized he was dancing her farther away from the twinkling red and green lights when they circled around the side of the barn and out of sight entirely. "No one can see us now." His voice was low. Deep.

And she was dissolving on the inside.

"It's still not a good idea," she managed and slid out from between him and the wall of the barn behind her.

But he still held her hand and he followed, pressing close against her back. He pushed her hair away from her neck and kissed the side of her throat. His fingers were linked with hers and he pressed them flat against her belly, still swaying slightly with the music. "Sure?"

The only thing she was sure of at that moment was that she could feel every inch of him pressed against her, burning from her shoulder blades to her rear. She turned her head toward him and his lips grazed her ear.

The music carried easily in the night, but she could still hear the faint sound of his breath. And heaven knew, she could feel the warmth of it. She turned her head a little more and his lips brushed over her cheek. When she tilted her head back against his chest, they found her jawline.

She stared blindly at the stars overhead. There was a carpet of them, and they blurred together when his palm slid beneath the front of her T-shirt and pressed flat against her belly.

He had large, calloused hands. His splayed fingers stretched from below the dip of her navel to the valley between her breasts. And oh, she longed for him to move his fingers over her. It was an acute ache inside her, centering with a ball of heat beneath his palm.

"I haven't wanted a woman this badly in a long time." He pressed even closer against her and she wondered vaguely if this was what it felt like to *swoon*. Then his mouth slid from her jaw to cover hers. And for a mindless moment, her lips clung to his.

When he turned her into his arms, she hauled in a fast breath. Grasping for common sense felt like trying to hold sand in a sieve. But she shook her head, pressing her hand against his chest. "We can't."

His strong hands circled her hips, fingertips kneading. "Not here, I know."

Her head was too heavy for her neck. She let her forehead fall against his chest. He smelled of heat and sweat and smoky carnitas and the wide, wide land around them.

And she'd never been more aroused by a scent in her life.

"It's not that." It seemed to take a ridiculous amount of willpower to lift her head. To look up into his shadowy expression. "But there are reasons—"

She broke off at the pounding of footsteps. They had only a moment to step away from each other before the two Arturos came skidding around the barn, running past them, laughing hilariously as Tomas chased them, threatening bodily harm for some transgression.

The trio was long out of sight before either one of them moved. And then it was Ariana, who took another step away from him, tucking her thumbs in her back pockets as she stared down at the ground. Everything inside her wanted to move back into his arms. To forget her ethics and everything else but him.

"You told me you weren't attached," he said.

Genuinely surprised, she looked up at him. "I'm not! I don't cheat. I haven't been involved with anyone for more than a year."

"That's a long dry spell," he murmured. "Or did he break your heart?" He rubbed his thumb down her lower lip and she darn near drooled.

But she *did* have ethics. Not everyone might agree or like them, but they were hers. And if she crossed the line once with him…

So she pulled back an inch. Just enough for his hand to fall away. "I've never had a broken heart," she admitted huskily. Not even after Steven and his obsession with motorcycles. But having met Jayden, she finally had some inkling of how easily it could happen.

"Then if it's not someone else, what's stopping us?"

She exhaled. She'd never ever let herself be in this position before. "I told you I was writing about the Fortunes." She had to push the words past the constriction in her throat. Because even though that part was true, there was so much more beneath the surface that she hadn't told him. "I shouldn't be getting involved with you at all. Not…not like this."

"Try again, sweetheart. I told you the name's pure fiction. There's no 'Becoming a Fortune' for us. I thought I'd made that clear already."

She moistened her lips, swallowed hard for what felt like the tenth time and lifted her chin. "What if it's not pure fiction? What if there's actually more to your name than what your mother told you?"

In an instant, his expression went hard. So hard that she could suddenly see the military man in him.

"Is that what you're hoping? That why you're batting those big brown eyes at me, showing off your little butterfly tat? You want to seduce a story out of me?"

He could have slapped her and not shocked her more. Her teeth clenched so tightly, she could barely manage to speak. "Is that what you really think of me, Jayden? *Really?*"

He was silent for so long that she wasn't sure he intended to respond at all. "No." The admission was grudging. "But my mom's the straightest shooter I've ever known. If she says she made up the name, then she made up the name." His tone was inflexible. "Far as I'm concerned, the bastard who knocked her up could be alive or dead. I don't care either way. Pretty sure my brothers feel the same." He shoved his fingers through his hair and took a step back. The gap was only a foot and a half, maybe, but it felt so much wider. "So the sooner you take your Fortune hunting down the road and leave us the hell alone, the better."

She was shaking with anger, but she still winced.

He took a few steps away from her, back toward the corner of the barn, and she could see the silhouette of him more clearly in the faint light coming from the other side. She could see the rise and fall of his shoulders as he took a deep breath.

Then he gestured sharply with his hand. "It's late. Time we get going."

She managed to keep it together as she went to thank Hector and Paloma again for their time. They were sitting together, their fingers linked, and even though she insisted they remain where they were, they both stood and accompanied Ariana and Jayden halfway back to Jayden's pickup.

She realized Nathan must have left with the trailer and the front loader while she and Jayden had been—

She closed her eyes for a moment, then quickly walked around to the passenger side of his truck and pulled open the door before he could even try.

They drove back to the ranch in silence.

He stopped near the house, engine running. Taking her cue, she climbed out with the bag from the hardware store and her notepad.

He drove off the second she pushed the truck door closed again.

Even though she could see he was only moving the truck down toward the barn where he usually parked it, she still felt like he was driving away from *her.*

Rather than be caught watching, she quickly turned. The wind chimes that Jayden had bought the day before were hanging next to the door and they clinked musically as she went inside.

There was no sign or sound of Nathan as she walked back to her borrowed bedroom, but Sugar got up from her bed in the kitchen and padded after her.

"At least you still like me, Sugar."

She turned on the lamp and sat on the edge of the bed. The dog hopped up to lean against her, swiping her tongue over Ariana's hand.

She rubbed the dog's silky head and looked into her dark, sightless eyes. "He never did say how you went blind. But I don't think he's going to tell me now, do you?"

Sugar's tongue came out, catching Ariana's chin.

"You're a sweet girl." Ariana pressed her face against the dog's head for a moment. Then she got off the bed, changed into the robe hanging on the back of Deborah's door and went down the hall to the bathroom. She heard Jayden's footsteps on the staircase as she was hand-washing her stretchy knit cami and panties in the bathroom sink and wasn't sure if she felt more like screaming or crying.

She did neither, of course. No matter what he thought about her, she was under his roof. At least for one more night since he hadn't kicked her out.

Yet.

The bathroom downstairs didn't have a tub or a shower, so she made do with the washcloth and a sink full of water. She worked the comb she'd found in the medicine cabinet through her tangled hair and wove it into a long braid. She didn't have a band to fasten it, but the braid would hold for a little while. Then she used her new travel toothbrush, rubbed lip balm on her lips and returned to the bedroom where she hung her wet things off the closet doorknob. They would both be dry long before morning. She'd washed her jeans the night before last. She figured she could stand another day in them while she figured out just how she was going to take her Fortune hunt down the road, when she was currently stuck and dependent only on Jayden's once-good graces.

She pulled on the sweatpants he'd already loaned her and tugged the second tie-dyed hardware shirt over her head. Sugar was still lying on the bed, so after returning the robe to the door hook, Ariana left the door ajar in case the dog wanted to leave.

Then she climbed in bed with her notebook and tried concentrating enough to expand on her notes with the Ybarras. It was difficult. Because she would never be able to think of the couple without also thinking about Jayden.

She flipped to a fresh page and drew a line across it. At the left end of the line, she wrote "Jerome." At the right end, she wrote "Gerald." Then she made little hash marks along the line, dividing it into segments. She marked the point when Jerome had faked his demise. Then at the midpoint of the timeline, she wrote "Charlotte." After that, she filled in the names of all the children so far accounted for.

It made for a busy, congested timeline to the right of Charlotte.

And like it always had before, it made the area to the left between Charlotte and Jerome's supposed death look very, very empty.

She bit the end of the pen, her gaze roving around the bedroom. Then she made another hash mark in the bare zone and wrote Deborah's name above it. Quickly scrawled in Jayden and his brothers.

She sighed as she circled Jayden's name a few times.

Then she scratched her pen back and forth across the entire page as if to erase it and turned back to her notes from the Ybarras.

He couldn't sleep.

And lying there in bed, tossing and turning because he couldn't sleep, was just pissing him off.

He threw back the sheet and got out of bed, pulling on a fresh pair of jeans before stomping down the steps.

Ever since Ariana had challenged the facts as he knew them about his family name, he'd been angry. And he didn't much care if he disturbed anyone else in the house.

Petty? Maybe.

But wasn't a man's house supposed to be his castle? Or some such thing?

At the base of the stairs, he looked toward the end of the hallway where his mother's bedroom was located. The door was ajar and a triangle of gold light shone onto the hallway floor.

Ariana was still awake.

His jaw tightened and he turned away, heading into the kitchen. Sugar's bed was empty, but as soon as he yanked open the refrigerator door hard enough to make the bottles inside rattle, he heard the dog's paws on the hallway floor.

"Hey, Sugar." The dog walked over to him and leaned

against his leg. "Where you been, huh?" Usually, the second he went to bed, the dog followed right on his heels. Not tonight.

He fed her a treat, then grabbed a beer and twisted off the top, tossing it onto the counter.

She followed him when he went out onto the patio and threw himself down on one of the old chairs. She propped her head on his knee, working her wet nose under his hand, and flopped her tail against the stone porch. "I wish everything was as simple as pleasing you, mutt." He patted his knee and she gathered herself, hopping nimbly onto his lap.

She was too big to be considered a lapdog. But she didn't know it. She just propped her front paws on his shoulders and stuck her nose in his face. He tolerated a few messy kisses across his forehead before angling his head away. "Yeah, I love you, too." He patted her back and she gave a sigh, finally settling her head on his shoulder where she breathed noisily against his ear. "What're we gonna do about her, huh?"

Unfortunately, his dog gave him no helpful answers.

He finished his beer and nudged at Sugar until she reluctantly hopped off and allowed him to stand. Back in the kitchen, he refilled the water bottle that kept her bowl always full and then started for the stairs.

Instead of following him, though, she trotted confidently to the end of the hall, passing through the triangle of light and nosing her way into the bedroom.

Jayden wasn't a man accustomed to hesitating. But he found himself doing so, one bare foot on the first stair tread and one bare foot still on the scarred wood floor as he looked toward his mother's bedroom.

He'd been too harsh with Ariana at the Ybarras'. But knowing it didn't make it any easier to swallow what she'd suggested.

Or swallow the fact that he had his own sliver of doubt.

He was thirty-damn-six years old.

He didn't want to think about the man his mother had always refused to discuss. Deborah Fortune was made of leather and steel. She'd had to be to raise three sons on her own in an area of Texas that people tended to forget existed.

And the only time he'd ever seen tears in her eyes had been when he was little. When he'd complained once too often about Nathan and Grayson and him not having a dad the same as other kids around Paseo did.

He exhaled roughly and pulled his foot away from the stair tread and soundlessly followed Sugar's path to the triangle of light. The dog never slept in his mom's room.

"Ariana." He pushed lightly on the door, opening it wider.

She was sprawled on her back, sweatpants hanging low over her golden-hued hips and a pad of paper lying on her belly. She didn't move even when Sugar, who'd hopped onto the bed, circled a few times as she sniffed her way around and knocked the pad aside before settling on the pillow next to Ariana's head.

He gave the dog a look. Even though she couldn't see him, he knew she'd interpret his vibes. But she only turned her head and flopped her tail a few times.

He put his fingers together, intending to snap them.

But he didn't.

Instead, he walked into the room. Silently he picked up the notepad. It was covered in almost indecipherable handwriting, but *Ybarra* was clear enough. He set it on the nightstand.

And still, Ariana didn't waken. Her lashes looked darker than ever against her cheeks. Her soft lips were parted faintly. The rise and fall of her breasts beneath the T-shirt were even.

Much as he wanted to stay there and look at her, he reached out and shut off the lamp.

Then he turned around and went to bed.

Chapter 7

She didn't intend to oversleep. But once again, when Ariana opened her eyes, she was dismayed to see that it was already the middle of the morning.

Maybe it had something to do with the total lack of sunlight coming into the bedroom since plywood was still secured over the window. When she was sleeping, it was fine. But now that she was awake, it made the otherwise comfortable room feel more like a cell. And a warm one, at that.

She rolled off the bed, scrubbing her face, trying to remember how late it had been before she'd stopped working and turned off the light. But she couldn't.

She picked up her notepad, feeling a little bleary-eyed as she read a few lines of her notes from the Ybarras.

Then she tossed it down on the nightstand and stuck her head out into the hallway.

She couldn't hear a sound, so she ventured into the kitchen. The blue-and-white coffeepot was sitting on the unlit stove. It was half-full and barely warm, but she filled a mug from it anyway, then nearly choked on the first sip and hastily leaned over the sink, spitting it back out.

"Good grief."

She rinsed out her mug with water, then did the same with her mouth. When Jayden had said Nathan's coffee was the worst, he hadn't been exaggerating. And obviously, the reason couldn't be attributed to the cleanliness of the coffeepot, because she'd cleaned it to spotless herself only two days ago. And it had been just as clean when she'd made a pot the day before.

She dumped the coffee into the sink and was refilling it with clean water when she spotted Jayden and Nathan through the window, unloading bales from the same trailer they'd used to haul her car. They were both dressed in jeans and short-sleeved T-shirts, with heavy gloves on their hands. The sheen of sweat on their roped arms was visible. But even from her distance and despite the straw cowboy hats on their heads, she could tell them apart.

She'd been born and bred in Texas. Had been around men in cowboy hats and jeans all of her life. Some wore them as a fashion statement. Some wore them simply because it was who they were.

These two men—whether they'd spent years in military service or not—were definitely in the latter camp.

The shrill ringing of the telephone nearly made her jump out of her skin.

She looked at it and wondered if she ought to answer

it. But given Jayden's attitude the night before, she decided it probably wouldn't be appreciated.

She left the coffeepot in the sink and turned away from the window. At the moment, the men were entirely occupied. She went down the hall and grabbed up her clean clothes, the toothbrush and comb, then dashed up the stairs. She was going to take a real shower while the taking was good, because she had no idea when the next opportunity would come.

Ten minutes later, after the fastest shower in her personal record, she was once more in the kitchen.

There was no sign of the guys through the window now, and she finished putting the coffee on the stove. The temperature in the kitchen was already excessively warm. She had no idea if the house came equipped with central air-conditioning, but it wasn't her business if it did or did not. In any case, she still wanted coffee, even if she ended up putting it on ice. And when she'd fixed it before, Jayden and Nathan had finished off the entire pot. So they obviously didn't reserve drinking the stuff for cooler temperatures, either.

She left the water to heat and returned to the bedroom and made up the bed. She found cleaning supplies and quickly cleaned the hall bathroom as well as the one upstairs. By the time she was done, the coffee water was boiling away. She mixed up the coffee grounds in a bowl the way her mother had described with an egg and a piece of the shell. She dumped the grounds into the pot, watching to make sure the water didn't boil over. After a few minutes, she pulled the pot off the heat, poured in another cup of cold water and watched the mucky mess of coffee grounds that had amassed in a froth at the top of the water sink like magic to the bottom.

"Coffee makes everything better," she murmured, standing over the pot and inhaling the aroma. "Please make some miracles now, too."

The wind chimes outside the door jangled softly and she looked over her shoulder in time to see Jayden coming through the door.

He had one finger of his leather glove between his teeth as he tugged his hand free and he stopped short at the sight of her.

She leaned back against the sink because the impact of him pretty much in full-on cowboy mode was almost overwhelming. Her knees, quite literally, had gone weak.

"I made coffee," she said stupidly, because of course he could see that. "I hope you don't mind."

He finally yanked his hand free and slapped the glove against the other that was clutched in his fist. He didn't take off his cowboy hat. "Make it whenever you want. Already told you that."

Yes, she thought. But that was before she'd dared to suggest that his mother had lied to him.

"It's hot in here." He sounded—and looked—peeved. "Why didn't you turn on the air?"

"One, I didn't know if you even had air-conditioning." She spread her hands. "And two, I wasn't particularly inclined to snoop in order to find out. Shocking to you, no doubt. I know you want me out of your hair at the earliest opportunity."

His lips compressed. She could see a muscle work in his jaw, and for a moment, she thought he intended to say something, but then he just strode out of the room.

A moment later, she heard the distinctive clicking sound of a central air-conditioning unit coming to life.

Then he came back and shoved the kitchen door closed.

"Thermostat is in the living room." He slapped his gloves against his palm again. "Look. About last night—"

She shook her head quickly, raising her hand. "No, wait."

His eyebrow went up.

"Please," she added. "Let me say what I've, uh, got to say and then—" She broke off. They both knew what she'd been about to say. *"—and then you can kick me to the curb."*

His lips compressed again. He waved the clenched gloves. "Go ahead, then."

He didn't look particularly pleased and she wished at that moment that she were better at expressing herself verbally. But she'd always been better with the written word and that fact wasn't going to magically change right now just by wishing it.

So she just dived in.

"I shouldn't have pushed the issue about who your father is." The words came out in a rush. "You told me from the beginning that I was on the wrong scent and I should have left it at that." She wasn't going to mention her book deal. She'd decided the night before that as long as she was under his roof, she had to forget *any* kind of research about Jerome.

"Because that's what journalists do? Give up at the first roadblock?"

The accusation stung. "Do you want my apology or not?" Then she winced. "Sorry." She looked away from his face, staring into the clear brown brew inside the coffeepot. It was the exact shade of his eyes.

She looked back at him. "Look, I didn't come to Paseo specifically hunting for Fortunes to feature in my 'Becoming' series. Believe me or not, but it's still the truth. I never expected to meet someone who actually had the name. And frankly, coincidences like that are pretty suspect in my line of work! So of course I was interested."

"Except you didn't come here to find Fortunes," he scoffed.

"I *didn't*. If I had been, would I have told you right up front about my series?" She pressed her fingertip to the pain that was suddenly throbbing in her temple. "All I came here to do was try and establish whether or not Jerome Fortune had ever been in Paseo. If he had any ties here."

"Why don't you just ask him? According to you, this Jerome guy is Gerald Robinson. You know where *he* is at. Hell, everyone in the country probably knows where he is at. The guy's always in the news."

"He refuses my requests for interviews."

"Imagine that."

Her lips tightened. She reminded herself that she was the interloper. This was Jayden's home. Jayden's space.

"Why do you think he might have been here, anyway?" His voice sounded grudging.

"I don't necessarily think he was. Not for certain. I was trying to figure that out."

"Sounds like you're grasping at straws to me."

"Maybe I am." Maybe it was wishful thinking on Ariana's part. But why would Charlotte have mentioned Paseo when the only thing in the article from the Austin History Center had been about Jerome's new bride, Charlotte, healing his broken heart?

"Did you ask Hector or Paloma about him?" Jayden's voice hardened even more. "They've lived in Paseo as long as anyone has. Is that what that interview was really about?"

"What? *No!*" The pain in her temple deepened. She still hadn't gotten to the point of what she was trying to tell him. "That interview was exactly what I said it was. Nothing more. Nothing less." She lifted her chin. "I don't lie to people in order to gain their trust. And I don't manipulate situations to my advantage. Not with you. Not with the Ybarras. Not with anyone. You couldn't have shocked me more by telling me your name was Fortune than if you'd poked me with a cattle prod. I didn't plan to get stranded here any more than you did. And the second I can leave, I will." The phone rang again, making her jump.

His gaze pinning hers in place, he reached out a long arm and snatched the phone off the hook. "Fortunes," he snapped.

Then he angled his head and she could no longer see his eyes below the brim of his hat. "Hey, Mom." His tone had turned neutral. "Yeah. No. Everything's fine here." The brim of his hat lifted an inch and his eyes fixed on hers. "Just still cleaning up the mess from the storm."

She exhaled shakily and left the room.

Jayden's grip tightened on the telephone receiver as he watched Ariana walk away, her head not ducking quickly enough to hide her pinched expression.

All he'd meant to tell her was that he was sorry for being too harsh the night before. But every time he opened his mouth, he seemed to dig himself in deeper.

His mom was still speaking—something about Grayson's tour—and he focused in on her with an effort. "You'll be gone another week, then? Yeah, no problem." In fact, it was better than that. Because Ariana's car should be fixed by then and she'd be long gone before his mother came back to Paseo.

There'd be no reason for Deborah to ever even know about Ariana Lamonte and her damn Fortune hunt.

After he hung up, he went in search of Ariana.

She was sitting on the front porch with Sugar in her lap. The dog was spread across Ariana the same way she'd been on his lap just the night before.

He shoved his gloves in his back pocket and stepped out the door.

Ariana looked warily at him over his dog's head. "If you don't mind me using your phone, I'll call someone in Austin to come and get me."

His jaw tightened. "That's not necessary."

"Well, I obviously can't stay here."

"Why not?"

Her eyebrows went up. "Seriously? You don't want me here anymore. You were pretty clear about it, Jayden."

"I was frustrated." On more than one level. "That doesn't mean you have to get somebody to drive all the way from Austin to take you home."

"Well, I'm not going to ask you or Nathan to do it," she muttered. "You've already got enough on your plate as it is. You haven't even had a chance to do your own repairs around here except for boarding up the broken windows."

He couldn't argue with her on that score.

She nudged Sugar off her lap and stood. She was

wearing her jeans and that skin-hugging camisole that showed off her sleekly toned shoulders and full breasts. But it was the wide brown eyes she trained on him that caused the knot in his gut.

"I can't pretend I don't have an interest in all things Fortune," she said. "But as long as I'm stuck here, I promise not to bring it up again. Not in any way. That's what I was trying to tell you before your phone rang."

"That's what you were trying to say?"

She huffed. "Next time I want to say something important, I'll send you a letter."

"What?"

She lifted her arms to her sides. "I'm better on paper!" She dropped her arms. "So can we call a truce or not? Because if not, maybe Nathan could drop me off at the Ybarras' and I can camp out with them."

"Nathan can do what, now?" The brother in question had come around the corner of the house, bearing a couple of sawhorses over his shoulder. He looked at Jayden. "Thought you wanted to get started on the windows."

"I do." It had only been a couple of days but he was already sick of feeling penned in in his own dark bedroom. It reminded him too much of sleeping in army barracks.

He looked at Ariana again and wondered when he would manage to stop feeling his gut tighten every time she blinked those brown eyes at him, or if he was going to be plagued by the problem until she left for good.

"You're not going to go camp out with the Ybarras, or anyone else, for that matter." He knew all the irritation he felt came through loud and clear. Particularly when Nathan shot him a sideways look. "Just...just go find something else to put on."

Her cheeks turned red. He wasn't sure if it was embarrassment or fury.

But she ducked her head and rushed past him, slamming the door so hard after her that the windowpanes in it shook.

So, fury then.

"I see you still have the magic touch when it comes to the ladies," Nathan drawled. "Ever thought about giving classes?"

"Shut up."

His brother chuckled as he set down the sawhorses and walked away. He was still shaking his head when he returned with the toolbox and power drill. "Well? You just gonna stand there, or are you going to give me some help here?"

"I hate having brothers," Jayden muttered.

Nathan wasn't fazed. He just held out the power drill toward Jayden. "Preaching to the choir, bro."

He grabbed the tool and stomped down the front steps and around to the plywood they'd fastened over their mother's bedroom window. He attacked the screws while Nathan set up the sawhorses and got the rest of the supplies ready for the first windowpane.

Then the two of them lifted the plywood away from the window.

Ariana was on the other side, sitting on the foot of the bed watching.

Obviously waiting.

Not only had she pulled on one of her virulent *Paseo Is Paradise* shirts, but she'd topped it with that artsy sweater she'd been wearing when they'd met.

"Is this better?" Her tone was dulcet.

A more god-awful combination of colors had never existed.

The base of his spine still tingled. His gut still tightened.

"It'll do." He slammed his hat harder on his head. At least he didn't have her hard little button nipples staring at him through that sleeveless excuse for a shirt. "Do you want to see how this is done or not?"

She stood. Her eyes were practically shooting sparks, but the smile on her face was demure. "How could I resist such a charming invitation?" She turned with a flip of hair and left the bedroom.

"She's gonna get heatstroke wearing that sweater this afternoon," Nathan warned conversationally. He laid the plywood on the horses, giving them a flat surface to work on, and then turned back to start removing the window sash. It was a large window. Even though it meant a little more prep work, glazing the window flat would be easier than doing it with the sash still in place. "Guess if she passes out, you'll have a reason to try mouth-to-mouth."

It would be about the only reason she'd let his mouth get close to hers again, Jayden figured. Not that he appreciated his brother's dig. "When did you get to be such a chatty Cathy?"

Nathan didn't answer. He just smiled slightly at Ariana when she joined them. She'd pulled off her sweater before coming outdoors and she had her cell phone in her hand.

"Don't mind if I take a few pictures, do you?"

"Gonna write an article about home DIY projects?" Better that than some damn thing suggesting his mother had once been one of Gerald Robinson's playthings.

It made his blood boil every time he considered the possibility. The unlikely, ridiculous possibility.

"A DIY article could come out of this. You never know." Ariana had moved around to the other side of the sawhorses, as if she wanted to keep a physical separation between them.

Or maybe he was letting his imagination go berserk and she simply wanted to stand in the shade afforded by the Texas Ash that his mom had planted several years ago.

"So, Nathan," she said with annoying cheer. "Tell me about yourself. Jayden said you were in the navy. A SEAL. Was that as exciting as it sounds?"

"Don't go asking my brother a bunch of questions."

Ariana gave him a wide-eyed look. "I'm sorry, Jayden. Are *all* questions off-limits? I didn't realize." She looked back at Nathan and gave an apologetic shrug. "Clearly even navy SEALs need protection from me."

Berserk was right. "Dammit, Ariana—"

"Okay, kids." Nathan set the putty knife and screwdriver he'd been using on the makeshift plywood table. "Choose your weapons. I'm outta here." He strode off.

Ariana's lashes swept down, hiding her expression. She pushed her phone into the back pocket of her jeans.

Jayden yanked off his straw hat and swiped the sweat from his brow. He was letting good air-conditioning literally blow right out his mother's window.

"Ever been on a horse?"

Her lashes lifted. "Sorry?"

"Horse. You know. Long nose. Four hooves. Sometimes wears a saddle. A real one."

"I know what a horse is, thank you."

"So? You know how to ride or don't you?"

"No, I do not know how to ride."

"You don't swim. You don't ride. And you call yourself a Texan?"

Her chin went up a notch. "Not all Texans grow up on ranches or around horses."

"That's true. And you're a city girl if ever there was one." One who changed into cocktail dresses inside her car whenever the need arose.

"I'm not going to apologize for the way I grew up, if that's what you're expecting. Just because you're spoiling for a fight—"

"I'm not spoiling for a fight."

"Then what *do* you want?"

"Dammit, I want you!"

The bright color faded from her cheeks, making her eyes look even darker brown. A swallow worked down her long, slender throat, as if she was bracing herself for what she was about to say.

"I want you, too." Her voice was husky when she finally broke the ringing silence. "But I can't change anything. I can't change the fact that I've written nearly a half-dozen articles in my 'Becoming a Fortune' series. I can't change the—" She broke off and twisted her fingertips through her hair, drawing it off her face and neck. "I can't change anything."

"I can't change the fact that my mother chose *Fortune* for our names."

"If she'd chosen *Smith*, things would've been a lot simpler, that's for sure. I'd just be me. You'd just be you. And—"

He almost felt a click inside his head because it suddenly seemed so simple.

He stepped forward, shoving out his hand. "Jayden Smith, rancher. Nice t' meet you."

Her lips parted. Those mesmerizing eyes of hers softened.

Then she stepped forward also and slowly placed her hand in his. "Ariana Lamonte, writer. Nice to meet you, too."

He tightened his grip, fighting the impulse to draw her closer and nearly losing. But then he heard Sugar barking and he let go of Ariana's hand.

He gestured at the window. "Since we ran off the big, brave SEAL, first thing to do is get the sash out."

Her eyes clung to his for a moment. Then she suddenly rubbed her hands down her thighs, as if she, too, had made a decision. "Tell me what to do to help."

So he did.

And he quickly learned that whatever Ariana lacked in knowledge, she more than made up for in willingness.

Soon, he had the sash removed and laid out on the plywood. He and Nathan had cleared all the broken glass before they'd boarded it up with plywood. But there was still old glazing to clean away from the wood and Ariana attacked it with fervor. Once she'd scraped one section clean, he sanded it down to bare wood. When they were done, he brushed on a fresh coat of primer.

"The window sash looks practically brand-new," she said when he finished cleaning his paintbrush. "So now what? We put the glass in the grooves?"

"Putty first. Then the glass. But the primer needs to dry before we can putty." Which would only take a few hours, considering the heat. "Time for lunch."

She didn't argue.

When they went inside, the temperature was cool and comfortable. He went upstairs to wash up first, but when he got back down to the kitchen, she'd already assembled sandwiches and had them grilling on the stove.

"I hope you don't mind." She gestured at the frying pan with the slotted metal spatula in her hand.

"Toasted ham and cheese? What's to mind?" He filled a water glass and chugged it, then filled it again and took it with him to the table and sat down, watching her. The only woman he could remember ever cooking in this kitchen was his mother. "You know how to cook anything else?"

"A few things."

He nodded toward the coffeepot that was sitting on the rear burner. "You made a huge improvement over Nathan."

"If his coffee is so bad, why don't you just make it yourself?"

"Because even his bad coffee is better than having to do it myself." He grinned faintly. "Gotta have something to complain about."

Her lips twitched. "Well, that's honest, I guess." She flipped one sandwich, then the other. She glanced at him and then away. "I could do the cooking for you guys." Her suggestion sounded diffident. "You know. If I'm going to stay here. At least then I'd actually feel like I'm doing you a service in exchange for—" she waved the tip of the spatula in the air "—the roof over my head and all."

"There's no *if* about it. So is that what cleaning the bathroom upstairs was all about?"

She looked surprised.

"I'm not such a slob that I don't appreciate a clean bathroom mirror when one magically appears."

"You're not a slob at all." She lifted her shoulder and *Paseo Is Paradise* shifted softly. "For two men living on their own, this place is surprisingly tidy."

He was a grown man. He knew that openly staring at a woman's chest was against the rules of common politeness. But it was damn hard when he also knew the only thing beneath Ariana's ugly shirt was some seriously beautiful flesh.

"You forget," he said a little absently. "Nate and I were both military. Order is the rule. Grayson, now?" He shook his head. "He's another story."

"Speaking of the military—" She peeked at the bottom of one sandwich and turned off the gas flame. "And assuming this isn't an off-limits topic, after fifteen years of service, why get out?" She transferred the sandwiches to two plates, sliced them quickly in half and carried them to the table. "Why come back to this place when you'd been so anxious to leave it when you were young? Were you just burned out or what?"

"The woman I was sleeping with was engaged to my master sergeant. My boss," he translated. He wasn't sure whom he'd surprised more with the admission. He wished he could retract it, but it was already too late.

"He found out?" Her brows pulled together and she almost looked outraged. "Did he *make* you quit?"

"No." He bit into the crispy sandwich. Ariana had browned it perfectly. "*I* found out. You wouldn't think a thing like that could be kept secret so easily, but you'd be wrong." Especially on an installation where the population easily exceeded twenty thousand. "I've done a lot of things, but I don't mess around with another man's woman. Not knowingly, anyway. And I damn sure don't forgive a woman lying to me like that."

"Couldn't you have sought a reassignment? I mean, after all those years in the army, to just give it up—"

"I didn't give it up because of Tess. She was just the final straw. I gave it up because I knew I was never going to get any further." He rubbed his jaw. "Eventually, even in the army, there's a game to getting advanced and I didn't particularly like the rules." He gave her a twisted smile and the same excuse he'd given his mother when he'd shown up on the doorstep two years ago. "Besides, I was sick of wearing the uniform."

"I'm sorry." She reached across the table and lightly touched his hand. Just for a moment, before sitting back and snatching up her sandwich. "Not about the army. If you were ready for a change, you were ready. But it still can't have been easy."

"Easier than considering proposing to a woman only to learn she's already got another man's ring on her finger." What the hell was wrong with him? One compassionate look from Ariana and he was totally spilling his guts.

Her sandwich paused halfway to her mouth. "So it was more than just sleeping with her. You loved her."

He'd thought he had. He and Tess had been together for more than a year before she'd confessed the truth. But even from the first, Jayden couldn't remember her affecting him as easily as a single glance from Ariana could.

He was no stranger to lust. But that was controllable. And nothing had felt particularly controllable these last few days. Add to that the fact that he couldn't keep his mouth shut about details he hadn't even shared with his own family?

Hell. Maybe he wasn't berserk. Maybe he was having a damn midlife crisis.

"Are you still in love with her?" Ariana had set her sandwich back on her plate. She was looking down at it, picking tiny pieces off the corner.

"No." He could see that now, with a clarity he hadn't possessed even two weeks ago.

She got up from the table suddenly, but only to open the kitchen door and let Sugar inside. "You said you brought Sugar home from Germany?"

"She belonged to Tess's fiancé." He held out his palm and the dog nuzzled against it. "He never took good enough care of her."

"Tess or Sugar?"

"I came home with Sugar, didn't I?"

She smiled faintly.

She hadn't sat back down at the table and he moved his hand from Sugar to Ariana's hip. Then he slid his hand around to the small of her back, pulling her toward him.

She didn't resist.

He pressed his forehead against her chest, and after a moment, he felt her fingers sliding through his hair. She leaned over him slightly, and he felt engulfed by her warmth.

"Sex is off the table," she whispered.

"Okay." He slid his other arm behind her. His palms fit perfectly over the curve of her rear.

She shifted and curled her arms even more around his head. "I mean it, Jayden."

"Okay." He was so hard, he hurt. But he still turned

his head slightly, feeling the soft give of her warm flesh beneath her shirt.

She made a low sound as she flexed her fingers against his head. “You’re killing me.”

“Tell me about it,” he said darkly. Ironically.

She exhaled. He felt it in the faint sway of her breasts against him as she lowered her head toward his.

“I ache,” she whispered near his ear. “If you really want to know, I’ll tell you all about it.”

His comment had only been sarcasm. Directed squarely at himself. He hadn’t expected her to take it literally.

She ran her hand along his arm, circling his wrist with her fingers and pulling his all-too-willing hand around to the front of her. “Here.” She pressed his palm against her belly. Then she pushed it even lower, right at the juncture of her thighs. “Here,” she breathed.

He nearly ground his teeth together, fighting the urge to push her back on the kitchen table right then and there.

Instead, he let go of her like he’d been burned and shoved his chair so hard, it slid back more than a foot.

Her dark, dark eyes were fastened hungrily on his face. Rosy color rode her high cheekbones. And her pointed little nipples were clearly stabbing through her shirt.

He pointed at her. “You said sex was off the table.”

“You said okay,” she retorted swiftly, jabbing a finger in the air right back at him. “You don’t get to pull out all the seduction stops and expect me not to give it right back to you!”

He nearly choked. He wasn’t sure what to make of

her. He wasn't sure about much of anything except that she had him twisted in knots. She had since the tornado.

He stood, muttering an oath because he had to adjust himself just so he could stand. "Be careful playing with fires, sweetheart."

She lifted her chin and raised an eyebrow. Though she didn't exactly look right at him, he noticed a fresh blush of pink on her cheeks. "Burn goes both ways, *sweetheart*."

Then she reached behind her for his plate. "Now, are you going to finish eating this? Or can we go finish the window? Because the day's not getting any shorter, and by my count, there are still three more windows to go. And I, for one, would like to see moonlight outside the window when I go to bed tonight. Wouldn't you?"

What he wanted to see when he went to bed that night was her.

And that was something that was just not going to happen.

Because his last name wasn't Smith.

Fiction or not, it was Fortune.

Chapter 8

"Mom. I'm fine here. Last time I called, you promised you were going to stop worrying about me."

"How can I stop worrying about you?" Karen's voice sounded loud through the receiver against Ariana's ear. "Your father wants to drive out to this Paseo place and bring you home. You've been there nearly two weeks, honey! There's no reason why you need to keep imposing on those people while you wait for your car to be fixed. How are you going to pay your bills when you're not even working? How are—"

Ariana barely had a chance to register that Jayden had walked into the kitchen, where she was using the wall phone, before he reached past her and plucked the receiver from her hand.

He raised his eyebrows at her. "Y'mind?"

She couldn't have responded if her life depended

on it. Primarily because she was too busy staring at his bare chest above the faded blue jeans hanging low around his lean hips.

Since the "day of the windows," as she'd come to think of it, they'd both been careful to keep to their respective, circumspect corners. She knew the only reason *she'd* been successful at it was because he hadn't so much as brushed against her, even inadvertently.

Not once. In ten whole days.

Even now, while taking the phone right out of her hand, he managed to do so without touching her.

He put the receiver to his ear and walked far enough away that the coiled phone cord stretched out to its full length.

But that just left Ariana's eyes free to explore the sculpted lines of his back. To study the stark line of demarcation just visible above the waistband of his jeans. To admire the tanned skin above and the paler skin below.

And to pick out the few droplets of water that were still clinging to his shoulder blades from the shower he'd obviously taken.

The shower was part of his routine. Get up before the sun, work until the afternoon heat got really serious, then come in and shower away the sweat and grime that went hand in hand with repairing barns and fixing fence and working cattle. Over the last few days she'd learned that meant anything from giving inoculations to tagging ears to weighing to castrating. This time of year, though, he'd said they were mostly working with the calves that'd been born in the spring.

She'd also learned that if she timed it right, she could

often catch a glimpse of him on the back of one of his horses as he came back in for the day.

She'd even managed to snap a few photos of him with her cell phone without him noticing.

But even though she'd learned his routine well over the past two weeks, this was the first time he'd strolled into the kitchen looking half-naked.

She quickly swiped her hand over her forehead and hoped her cheeks didn't look as hot as they felt while she listened to him speak into the phone.

"Mrs. Lamonte, this is Jayden Fortune. Sorry to hijack your phone call, ma'am, but let me assure you that Ariana's not imposing. Fact is, she's been real helpful lately."

She glanced his way and his carefully neutral gaze roved over her face.

"That's right, Mom." Despite her better intention, she stepped over to him, speaking loud enough for her mother to hear. She held up her palms as if Karen could see the bandage strips there. "Jayden put up a new barn wall this week and I helped." Helped as much as she could, at any rate, once he'd shown her how to hammer a nail without hitting her own fingers. She'd hammered so many nails she'd earned blisters even through the work gloves he'd given her to wear.

"I appreciate your hospitality on my daughter's behalf," she heard her mom say, "but would you put her back on the line, please?"

"Yes, ma'am." He set the receiver on the countertop and stepped around her.

Ariana picked up the receiver and told herself that it was her imagination that the hard plastic felt warm from his brief grip on it. "I'm here, Mom."

"Seriously, Ariana. About your work? You haven't been online anywhere. You didn't put up a fresh magazine blog this week or last. Mrs. Wysocki was in for her teeth cleaning this morning and she just couldn't wait to pump me for the reason why."

"Mrs. Wysocki needs to worry less about what I'm doing than what the Empress of—than what her own daughter Juliette is doing. She has to testify soon in Judge Rivera's sexual-misconduct trial, if I remember." From the corner of her eye, she watched Jayden flipping through the pile of mail on the kitchen table.

As if he were aware of her attention, he angled his head and gave her a sideways look.

She tucked the phone in the crook of her neck and studiously picked the corner of one of the bandages on her palm. "And I haven't posted anything online because the library internet has been down. But don't worry. I still have a job. People are covering for me at the magazine and I got my latest story submitted on time just like usual." She'd had to dictate it over the phone, which had been a pain, but it still had worked. Which meant she didn't have another column to write until next month. At which time, she would certainly be back home again.

The thought of getting back home, of getting her life back on its usual track, ought to have been a relief.

"And what about that book of yours?"

Ariana stiffened, holding the phone more tightly against her ear. She hadn't told anyone at work about her book deal but she had told her parents. How could she not have shared that momentous news with them? The day she'd been offered the deal had been one of

Ariana's proudest. But she didn't want Jayden overhearing something that would only end up upsetting him.

"It's coming along fine, Mom." If *fine* could be described as not having done one single thing.

Her mother's sigh was noisy. She clearly wasn't convinced. "Well, what about your car? How's that coming along? Daddy and I were concerned when you paid for it outright with your book advance. It would have been wiser to put some of that money in your savings. Or at least you could have bought some furniture to replace the hand-me-downs you've had since college."

Again with the book? "My furniture is fine, Mom. And so is the investment in my car. Charlie—the guy who's doing the work—was still waiting on one last part when I talked to him Wednesday." Jayden had given Ariana the keys to his truck to drive into town and use the library. She had stopped to see Charlie on her way back.

The boat had been gone from his garage, only to be replaced by a showy new pickup truck and a John Deere tractor. Charlie had shown her the progress he'd been making on her car, though. And he'd tried to explain about the mechanical damage he'd discovered once he'd started working on it. Everything he'd said had gone over her head. But he'd assured her that her insurance had approved the work and all he was waiting on was the part, which he didn't expect to get for another few days.

"So you'll be driving home soon." Ariana's mom was still talking in her ear. "Daddy will be awfully glad about that. He's not at all comfortable with you staying under a strange man's roof. Of course, he thinks all men are just after one thing where his baby girl is concerned.

The only reason he can sleep at night is knowing you've got a built-in chaperone from that SEAL boy." As if Ariana were still seventeen instead of twenty-seven.

Ariana thought it best not to share the fact that Nathan hadn't been around for the last few days. And even when he *had* been around, he hadn't been the least bit chaperone-y.

"Just make sure you let us know this time before you get on the road," Karen continued pointedly.

"I will, Mom." Ariana let the cord re-coil itself as she walked back toward the phone's base on the wall. "I've got to go now. Love you." She quickly slid the receiver onto its cradle.

Jayden was tearing open one of the envelopes and he glanced up at her. "Everything good on the home front?"

If he'd been able to hear her mother's comments about the book, he didn't appear interested.

"Same as usual." She headed for the refrigerator and pulled it open. When she'd first blown in with the tornado, the refrigerator had been stocked to the gills. In the two weeks since, it had become nearly empty. Which meant that figuring out things to fix was becoming increasingly challenging.

She ought to have stopped at the gas station for some groceries when she'd gone into Paseo the day before yesterday. But she'd already been feeling foolish for reminding him that she'd lost her driver's license in the storm, so she really shouldn't be caught driving anywhere until she got it replaced. He'd just given her a look and dropped his truck keys on the table in front of her.

Having to ask him for money on top of everything

would have been just too much. And he hadn't remembered to offer.

Which was why the refrigerator was now in its current state.

No milk. He was a grown man, but he still drank gallons of it.

No eggs. She'd learned straight off that he and Nathan could plow through a half dozen a day before taking off at the crack of dawn.

No bread. Deborah Fortune made it from scratch and even the frozen loaves were gone.

No fresh lettuce or tomatoes or fruit. Though Ariana had discovered a garden near the house, it had been leveled by the storm.

And she suspected that the half carton of cottage cheese on the bottom refrigerator shelf was growing the world's next great antibiotic.

On the positive side, there was a slab of leftover rib eye, from when Jayden had grilled the night before, and an onion.

She pushed the refrigerator door closed and pulled open the metal bin partially filled with potatoes that she'd discovered the week before.

She could make a hash with the potatoes and steak, she supposed. Though it would be better with fried eggs on top—

"Forget the food."

She looked over her shoulder at Jayden. It was silly to feel light-headed just from the sight of his bare chest. She'd seen bare chests before. Had even been up close and personal with a few of them. What was the deal with Jayden's, then?

"So? Do you want to go or not?"

The owner of said chest was giving her an impatient look and she felt her face flush. She'd completely missed whatever it was he'd said and had no idea where he'd asked her to go. Still, she answered, "Uh, yeah. Sure." No matter what it was, she was determined to pick it up in context.

Only Jayden just continued standing there. Watching her. And after a moment, his eyebrows went up. "You going to change?"

She looked down at herself.

Despite her reluctance to invade his mother's clothes closet, necessity had simply won out. She could only wear the same combination of jeans, cami and two tie-dyed shirts for so long without losing her mind. Which was why she was currently wearing one of his mother's long-sleeved denim shirts. She had the sleeves rolled up. And even belted around her waist, the long shirt-tails made for an adequate dress. It covered her more than some of the sundresses hanging in her apartment closet. Plus, it was cooler than her jeans. "I know it's hardly high fashion, but—"

"But you'll be more comfortable on horseback wearing jeans," he said drily.

She hid her surprise behind an obliging smile. The only time he'd asked if she knew how to ride a horse had been on the day of the windows. "True. I was just waiting for you to, uh—" She gestured toward him with her hand. "You know, change also." She hoped her face hadn't turned as red hot on the outside as it felt on the inside. She turned on her too-loose, borrowed tennis shoe and inadvertently stepped right out of it.

She barely managed to keep from pitching forward onto the kitchen table and scooped up the offending shoe during the momentum. "Your mom has big shoes to fill," she said breathlessly.

"I'll tell her you said so."

It was too hard keeping a smile in place, and it died the second she ducked out of the kitchen.

Whether they'd reached a truce or not, she seriously doubted that Jayden intended to tell his mother one single thing about Ariana, once she was out of his hair. And she knew, without question, that he particularly wouldn't say anything about her so-called Fortune hunt.

She closed herself in Deborah's bedroom and quickly pulled on her jeans. She'd washed them that morning and had taken them from the dryer while they were still damp. They were dry now. But barely. Then she pulled on the closest thing she had to a real bra—the shelf-lined cami. She was just reaching for one of the hardware-store T-shirts to pull over the cami when Jayden knocked on the door.

She pulled it open.

His eyes skimmed over her from her face to her bare toes and back up again. His gaze left a trail of heat in its wake as surely as if he'd physically run his fingertips up and down her. "I just came to tell you to wear a pair of boots. Mom's boots," he added, as if she didn't have the sense to know he hadn't meant Ariana's high-heeled red ones.

"Fine."

His eyes roved over her again. "And put a shirt on over all that." His fingers waved. Evidently meant to encompass her "that" which she'd intended on covering anyway.

An unwise spurt of contrariness bubbled inside her.

"You're going to stand there half-naked, but I have to wear a nun's habit?"

He snorted, and before she knew it, he'd slid a finger beneath one of her cami straps. "Habit?" With a quick tug, he pulled the scooped edge of her cami down just far enough to reveal the wings of her butterfly tattoo. "Not even close."

She yanked her strap back over her shoulder. If she could only hate the way her skin was tingling, things would be ever so much easier. But she didn't hate it.

She longed for it.

And whether she was awake or sleeping, she couldn't get away from the intensity of it.

"Don't make the mistake of thinking I'm easy on top of everything else," she warned.

"Believe me, sweetheart. Nothing's easy about you."

Her skin prickled even more. She abruptly turned away and snatched up the shirt she'd fully intended on wearing to begin with and yanked it over her head. She looked back at him as she worked her hair free. "Satisfied?"

His gaze roved over her and she actually felt dizzy.

Then he suddenly cleared his throat and turned on his heel. "Don't forget the boots," he said as he walked away.

Ariana's breath rushed out. She leaned against the tall chest of drawers for a moment. When she felt a little steadier, she pulled on her mismatched socks and opened Deborah's closet door again.

Jayden's mom had several pairs of cowboy boots. Ariana chose the most worn-looking pair and sat on the edge of the bed to pull them on.

They were just as loose on her feet as the tennis

shoes, but at least they weren't so easy to step right out of. The fact that she had to tuck the legs of her narrow jeans inside them didn't hurt, either.

She rubbed the dwindling tube of lip balm over her lips and left the room.

The kitchen door was open when she got there and she went outside, spotting Jayden. He was pulling on a blue plaid shirt and it flapped loosely around his lean hips as he disappeared into the barn. Sugar was trotting along at his heel.

Her heart did a slow cartwheel inside her chest at the sight.

There just was no way to deny it.

She pulled the kitchen door closed behind her and followed after them.

Even though she'd spent hours this past week working on the barn wall repairs with him, her first step inside the barn had her nose wrinkling. Not because the smell was unpleasant. Far from it. There was the expected smell of horseflesh, yes. But even more, it smelled like fresh wood and hay and the cleanser Jayden used when he swept down the aisle at the end of nearly every day.

There were two fans at either end, suspended from the rafters. They helped keep the air flowing and the flies down, and as she walked down the center aisle, she could feel the air tugging at her hair.

At the moment, none of the horses were in their stalls. Nathan, she knew, had taken two of them with him when he'd gone out on the range earlier that week. Two others, she saw through the open door at the other end of the barn, were tied to the railed fence surrounding the pasture.

Since she'd been at the ranch, she'd gotten close to the horses only a few times, and that had been to feed them carrots over the top of the sturdy fence standing between them. And even though she'd sooner choke than admit it, the thought of getting up on the back of one now was more than a little daunting. But she wasn't going to give Jayden another opportunity to point out what a city girl she was.

Not if she could help it, anyway.

"You going to stand there chewing your lip all afternoon?"

She looked over to where he was pulling a saddle from the rack. "Maybe," she admitted.

His eyes crinkled slightly. "Ridin's easy."

"Says the man who grew up doing it." She rubbed her hands down the sides of her jeans. "What do I do?"

"Carry this on out to Daisy and Jobuck. You can hang it on the rail." He set the saddle on her outstretched hands.

"Holy mama." The weight was unexpected and she had to hurriedly adjust her grip or drop the unwieldy saddle right on her feet. "How much does this thing weigh?"

He'd grabbed two saddle pads in one hand and hung a second saddle from his shoulder. "That's Mom's saddle. It's a light one," he said, leading the way from the barn. "Less 'n thirty pounds."

"So much for thinking I work out at my gym often enough," she muttered. He'd buttoned up his shirt and shoved one tail of it haphazardly into his jeans, which left her plenty of rear-end beauty to ogle as she followed. It helped distract her from the fact that for every step she took, she had to sort of push the saddle along with her thigh. It made for a Quasimodo kind of pace.

At the fence surrounding the pasture, she managed to heave the saddle onto one of the rails like he did without sending it toppling onto the other side. Then she started gnawing the inside of her cheek as the horse closest to her turned its head toward her and gave a loud snuffy huff.

"Think she smells good, do you, Daisy?" Jayden rubbed his hand over the horse's back and looked at Ariana where she was hovering. "Come closer. She'll sniff you up real well but she's not going to bite." He matter-of-factly took Ariana's hand in his and set it on the horse's warm back. "See?"

"Sure." Between the supple feel of the short, coarse hair under her palm and the warmth of his calloused one holding it in place, she was awash in sensation. And the way Daisy swung her head around to eyeball Ariana made her wonder if the horse knew it, too.

He stroked their hands across the horse a few times. "All smooth. They're already groomed, but you still always want to check and make sure nothing's there to irritate her when she's saddled."

His hand left Ariana's and he stepped away for a moment, and she quickly swallowed, sharing another look with Daisy.

Then he came back with the saddle pad, and once he'd shown Ariana how to make sure it was placed correctly, he grabbed the saddle and gently situated it on top of the saddle pad.

Explaining all the while, he fastened the front cinch. Then the flank cinch. He glanced at her where she was standing next to Daisy's enormous head. "I'm not using a breast collar." As if Ariana even knew what that was. "And we don't really need the flank for where we're heading this afternoon, but it'll make things feel a little more secure for you."

"Ah. Thank you?"

His lips twitched and he looped the reins over the horse's neck with one hand and hung his other fingers on the stirrup. "Come on. Left foot up in the stirrup if you can reach it. I'll tighten things up a little more once you're up."

Nervousness fluttered up her chest. She stroked Daisy's cheek. "What if I fall off?"

His lips tilted. "Then you'll get back on." He moved, gesturing for her to take his place standing next to the saddle. "But you won't fall off. Daisy's the steadiest ride we've got. She's been around a long time." He scratched the horse beneath her neck as they switched spots. "Haven't you, girl? Not that it's polite to talk about a lady's age, but she's twice as old as Jobuck."

Ariana blew out a puff of air. She stretched her foot up and was grateful not to hear one of her seams rip as she fit the toe of her boot through the stirrup.

"Okay. I s'pose you could find a hundred people to tell you a hundred ways to mount a horse, but here's how I learned." He moved her left hand from where she'd grabbed the saddle horn and placed it instead near the horse's mane not far from the edge of the saddle pad. "Usually you'd have the reins in your hand like I do." His left hand nudged hers. Then he guided her right hand to the back of the saddle. "Some people grab the far pommel. Some the cantle. This is the cantle. You're only looking for balance when you push yourself up.

Not pulling. Pushing. Keeping your weight toward the horse while you're doing it. Got it?"

She let out half a laugh. She felt like she was being stretched on a rack. "Sure. Right."

When he'd been saddling the horse, she'd noticed that one of his hands had maintained contact with Daisy the whole while. And when his hand left Ariana's to find her waist, she realized he did the same thing with her.

She couldn't decide if it was unsettling or comforting.

"I'll give you help if you need it," he said. "Once you're off the ground and feeling balanced standing there in the stirrup, swing your right leg over. Try not to kick Daisy in the process. She doesn't like that much."

"Who does?"

He laughed softly and the sound of it was almost music to her ears. He hadn't laughed like that since… well, *since*.

"Get some good spring going here." His hand touched her thigh. "It'll help a lot. And *push*."

She pushed, barely feeling his hand fall away from her waist as, by some miracle, she swung right up into the saddle, completely bypassing the whole stand and balance part, but nevertheless ending up with her butt where it belonged.

She laughed, surprised by the exhilaration she felt. Not to mention being able to look down on him for once.

It was a novel experience.

"I feel very high up here," she admitted.

"You're a natural." His hand left her boot and he ducked under Daisy's head and checked her right foot in the stirrup after she'd stood up in them when he requested. "You're shorter than my mother." He ducked back under again and adjusted the front cinch some more. The process had him standing distractingly close to Ariana's thigh. "I figured I'd need to shorten the stirrups, but I don't."

His brown hair was slightly lighter on top. Sun kissed. She caught herself just in time from reaching out to ruffle her fingers through the short, thick strands. His hair wasn't much lighter than Daisy's but she knew very well that it was so, so much softer.

"Long legs, I guess." She absently pressed down one of the bandages striping her palm.

His gaze lifted, catching hers for a moment that seemed to stretch. "Yeah."

Then he took a step back, breaking the moment.

He scooped up the cowboy hat he'd left hanging over a fence post and put it on his head. "Just get used to the feel of Daisy under you for a few minutes."

"Mmm-hmm."

She watched him stride back into the barn and leaned forward over Daisy's neck. "Be gentle with me, okay, girl?" Daisy shook her head and shifted, and Ariana quickly straightened, grabbing the saddle horn as she rocked. "I hope that's your way of saying yes."

The horse standing next to them—Jobuck—also shifted, tossing his head and pulling against the rope tethering him loosely to the fence rail, and Ariana gave him a wary look. "Behave over there, would you, please? I'm still new in town, remember?"

Then Jayden returned carrying a coiled rope, a canteen and a longish pouch from which he pulled a pair of leather gloves. He handed them to her. "They're the softest ones I could find," he said a little gruffly. "But they'll give your hands a little more protection."

Stupidly touched, she pulled them on.

In a matter of minutes, he had Jobuck saddled. The younger horse didn't stand quite so placidly in place as Jayden worked. "Cut it out," he said easily as the horse seemed to deliberately bump against him. Jayden just pushed back with his shoulder against the horse and he settled.

It was a reminder that Ariana didn't really need that the horses could run the show if they so chose. "Have you ever been hurt by a horse?"

"Not intentionally." He looked up at Ariana as he fastened the bag to the back of his saddle. Next came the canteen and the rope. "Don't worry about Jobuck. He's just feeling frisky."

"What's the rope for?"

"In case."

"In case of what?"

His lips twitched. "In case you don't behave yourself."

She made a face and his smile widened. "In case," he said again.

She supposed when it came to a rancher, "in case" probably covered a lot of possibilities.

He replaced the horse's halter with the bridle and reins. But instead of mounting Jobuck, he led both horses around to the front of the barn, not stopping until he'd practically reached the storm-cellar door.

Ariana pointed toward it. "Did it get all dried out down there?"

He glanced at the cellar door. "Probably by now. Haven't worried about anything down there enough to look."

He checked the cinch on Ariana's saddle one more

time before handing her the reins. "Hold 'em in your left hand." He showed her. "You want 'em easy and loose for Daisy, but not so loose she worries you're not in charge. Yep. There you go. Keep 'em up like they're a cup of coffee you don't want to spill."

"Coffee!"

His eyes glinted. "Figure that might resonate more than the usual ice-cream-cone comparison. Drape the rest over on your right. You're green, so you can hold the horn if you need to. Otherwise just let your free hand relax."

"Relax. Because that's so easy to do."

He was smiling as she watched him swing up onto Jobuck's back and she nearly swallowed her tongue.

How on earth had she gone her whole life without realizing just how sexy the sight would be of a man climbing on a horse? Even though she knew Jayden had worn an army uniform for most of his adult life, at that moment it was hard to picture it. Not when he looked so completely and utterly where he belonged on the back of a horse.

His smile widened and his eyes glinted. "Ready?"

Her stomach danced around. And she knew at that particular moment that it had absolutely nothing to do with a horseback ride and everything to do with him.

"Yes." The word slid from her lips. "I think I am."

Chapter 9

They rode through grass. And more grass.

And Ariana realized that she'd been wrong when she'd first thought that it all looked the same. In the thick of it, there seemed to be an endless variety of colors and textures and smells.

And the sounds. She wasn't sure why she'd ever thought of the country as being so quiet.

There was buzzing. There was chirping. There was the quick rush and flap of wings as birds scattered almost from beneath their hooves when Jayden decided it was time for her to trot. At which point she was pretty sure that the loudest sound in the entire county was her teeth clanking together as she bounced ungracefully in the saddle. She didn't know what to grab. The saddle horn to help the jouncing or her chest to stop the bouncing.

"Relax your knees," Jayden called. "Squeezing with your legs isn't going to help. Lighten up your spine and let your hips rock more. Sorta like you're bouncing on a yoga ball."

She couldn't help it. She laughed. "Yoga ball?"

"You've been on one, haven't you? You look like the yoga sort with the way you go around exercising every morning."

She hadn't thought he'd noticed anything she did in the mornings. Aside from keeping food on the table and the coffeepot brewing. "Yeah, I do yoga." She nodded, only to bite her tongue. Which, strangely enough, just made her laugh that much harder. "This is awful!"

He was grinning. "How do you think it feels from Daisy's perspective?"

"Oh, great. Now I feel guilty for hurting her, too."

He pulled up Jobuck and Daisy slowed as well, taking a couple of steps, then just stopping altogether.

"She's patient," he assured her. "She knows you're learning." He brought Jobuck closer until there was only a few feet between them. He pulled off his hat and reached over to plop it on her head. "Your nose is getting sunburned."

She pushed up the brim so she could see from beneath it and warned the pitter-pat going on inside her chest not to get too excited.

"When we start trotting again, imagine keeping your seat bones in contact with the horse. Then once we do a slow lope, you'll feel more of a wave motion and it'll get easier. Graciela once told me she thought sitting the trot was sort of like learning to follow your partner during sex. Close your eyes if you have to."

He was waiting for a response. She merely nodded. It

was all she could manage because she suddenly couldn't seem to think a single, coherent thought.

His eyes crinkled and they set off again.

When she felt Daisy picking up speed beneath her, transitioning from that easy, swaying sort of walk into another trot, she had to clap one hand on his hat to keep it from blowing off her head.

She closed her eyes.

She didn't know if she bounced any less, really.

But she certainly enjoyed the image of him behind her closed lids.

She wasn't sure how long they rode, but she was pathetically grateful when they finally stopped in the shade of the trees surrounding a large, meandering pond where an old-fashioned-looking windmill slowly turned.

The hot sunshine had sent sweat dripping down her spine. Even inside the gloves, her hands were so wet that when she peeled them off, the bandages on her palms dropped off, too.

"Here." Jayden leaned toward her from Jobuck's back, offering the canteen.

"Thanks." She was breathless. She'd lost count of how many times Jayden had her move in and out of a trot. In and out of a lope. Enough times, though, that she'd actually felt like she was getting the hang of it. "I didn't know riding a horse was such a workout." She twisted off the cap and drank thirstily. The water was cool. Vaguely metallic. And entirely refreshing.

"That's how Nathan and I keep our girlish figures."

She coughed a little as she swallowed. The day Jayden Fortune and his brother were in any way girlish would be the day the earth started spinning in the opposite direction. Even though she hadn't met Grayson, she figured he had to have been cut from the same cloth, too.

She swiped her arm over her mouth and took another drink, then screwed the cap back on.

Jayden had already dismounted and led Jobuck near the edge of the water, leaving the reins loose.

"You're not afraid he'll run off?"

"I'll keep an eye." He walked back toward her and took the canteen. "But he's usually pretty good being ground tied. Particularly when Daisy's around." He pulled off the cap and tilted his head back as he drank.

His throat was tanned and sheened with sweat.

And she felt desperately in need of something to fan herself with, just from watching him.

Then he looped the strap of the canteen over a tree branch and took the reins that she'd draped around her saddle horn and walked Daisy nearer to Jobuck. "Need help getting down?"

She shook her head. "I don't think so."

"Just go in reverse pretty much. Get your right foot out of the stirrup. This time grab the horn with your right hand. It'll keep you from getting anything hung up on it as you come down."

"What would get hung up?"

He waved vaguely. "Your, uh, shirt."

She frowned.

"Just trust me," he said. Then he sighed a little impatiently. "Graciela once got hung up on her bra," he said abruptly.

She raised her eyebrows. It was difficult being blithe when she felt more like baring her teeth. "Just what exactly went on between you and Graciela? I thought she was supposed to be the older woman who got away?"

"Nothing to write home about." He gestured to the horse. "Swing your leg over." He waited while she did it. "And now lower it on down." His hands surrounded her hips when her foot hit the clover-covered ground and she slid her left toe out of the stirrup. "Good job."

Daisy's warm body was in front of her. Jayden's warm body was behind her.

It was safer to focus on the horse. She patted the side of Daisy's neck and pulled off Jayden's cowboy hat. Even though it was straw, her head immediately felt cooler from the fresh air and she shoved her hand through her hair, flipping it away from her neck. "Is the pond deep enough to swim in?"

"Thought you didn't swim."

"I don't."

"Well, as it happens, it's only a few feet deep, anyway. Good for wading in, but that's about it." His hands fell away from her as he gave her space. "Though if you want to strip off and give it a shot, don't let me stop you."

She gave him a look.

He spread his hands. "I'm just a guy, sweetheart."

"You're not *just* anything."

His smile was faint and entirely wicked. "It's fresh water, though. That old windmill's been pumping up water since the fifties."

She looked up at the metal-framed structure situated on a slight rise above the trees. The fan part of it was turning slowly with a distinctly rhythmic squeak.

In conjunction with the buzz of bugs and the chirping of birds, it was almost musical.

"Fifties, huh?" She tucked the gloves in her back pocket and yanked her T-shirt off as she walked toward the water's edge. "That was before your mother came to Paseo." She crouched down and swished her shirt through the clear water, glancing back at him.

He'd hooked his thumbs in his front pockets. His shoulders seemed particularly massive and his expression had closed. "So?"

She swallowed a sigh and straightened. Every muscle in her legs protested.

"I'm not digging for details," she assured him evenly. "Paloma told me about your mother and the Thompsons. Irv— No. Earl. Earl and Cynthia Thompson. They're the ones who took in your mom before you and your brothers were born."

"Yeah. So?"

She wrung the water out of the T-shirt and pulled it back on over her camisole.

The cooling relief it brought was immediate.

She swished her legs through the short, thick grass growing at the water's edge as she walked along it. There were a few boulders along the pond bank that would have made a decent enough spot to sit, except her butt didn't feel ready for contact with anything just yet. Especially a hard piece of rock. "So, nothing. I was just wondering if the Thompsons were the ones who put in the windmill, that's all."

"Yeah. They were." His thumbs came out of his pockets and he pulled down the canteen from the tree branch. "They were like grandparents to us. They both died when we were in high school. Within a year of each other." He waved in the direction of the windmill. "There's a small cemetery over there. That's where they're all buried."

"Do you know what happened to their daughter?"

He took a swig of water. "Car accident is what most people say. Suicide by car was more accurate, though. Earl told me about it one night."

"How terrible."

"She was pregnant, too. Like Mom."

Ariana winced. "So, not just one life lost, but two."

"Yeah." He tossed the canteen strap over the branch again and moved around the horses where they were chowing down on the bright, green grass to sit on one of the boulders. Apparently a couple of hours in a saddle were nothing to him. "I used to wonder if Mom would have stayed here like she did if things had been different. If Earl and Cynthia hadn't needed us all so badly to fill the void after their daughter died."

She imagined him as the boy he'd described. The one who'd wanted to be anywhere other than tiny little Paseo, and her heart squeezed. She perched gingerly beside him on a slanted rock. "Did you ever ask your mom?"

"She said the only family who mattered was the one we'd made here."

So many questions. Questions she couldn't ask because she didn't know what might or might not lead to the matter of Jerome Fortune. And more than anything, she didn't want that ruining their time together.

"I never knew my grandparents," she told him. "It was always just my folks and me."

"No wonder you're spoiled."

She gaped. "I'm not spoiled!"

His coffee-colored eyes were lighter than usual because of the bright sun. And when they looked right into her, the world stopped.

I love this man.

The realization flowed through her.

But then he was speaking again, his smile widening. "Okay. You're not spoiled."

The world started up again. She managed to lightly roll her eyes, even though inside she felt like she was reeling. "Darn tootin' I'm not. I've been living with one pair of underwear here. No makeup. No cell phone. No internet. Have you heard me complain?"

He scooped up water in his hand and splashed it around his neck. "No underwear. Hadn't thought about that."

She cursed her thoughtless tongue. At least her red face could be attributed to the hot day. And just because she couldn't get the notion of loving him out of her head didn't mean he had to know it.

She grasped for a change of subject. "How, uh, how long do you think it will be before the Ybarras can start rebuilding their house?"

"They've already started."

"What?" She wobbled a little on her perch and instinctively grabbed his arm to steady herself. She felt his muscle flex, and then he stood, whether needing or wanting to put some space between them, she didn't know.

Then she told herself she was being overly sensitive, because all he did was head over to retrieve the canteen.

"Nathan was over there before he headed out to check the north section," he said before taking a drink. Once he capped it again, he held it out toward her. "He told me they'd already poured a new foundation and started the framing."

Her fingers brushed his as she took the container. "Amazing."

"Even in tiny Paseo, things *can* get done quickly."

"Clearly." Just not when it came to getting parts for her car. She had no complaints on that score, though, as it gave her a reason to still be there. She had her back to the water and she stretched out her stiff legs as she sipped the water. "So, seriously. About Graciela..." A bee buzzed by her face and she jerked back, swatting at it.

Unfortunately, she didn't factor in the angle of the rock on which she sat and she felt her butt sliding back. Her arms sawed and her legs went up.

She had only enough time to see Jayden's startled expression before she hit the water. It sloshed up over the rocks, splashing her in the face, and she had a moment's panic before she realized just how shallow the pond really was. Her rear end was on the bottom, her face well above the surface.

She sat in deeper water when she was in her bathtub at home.

She swiped the water from her face and looked up at him.

At the edge of the pond, he stood there with his hands on his hips and a broad grin on his face.

Dry.

"You all right?"

She finished capping the canteen that she'd somehow managed to keep aloft the pond water and tossed it onto the grass. "Aside from busting my dignity?" She put her hands down in the water, prepared to push herself upright, but they slipped against the slick bottom and water splashed up and over her shoulders. “I don’t know what’s growing on the bottom here, but may I just say *ick*?”

He laughed outright. “It’s just grass, sweetheart.”

“Easy for you to say.” Stupidly, something sweet was jiggling around inside her chest from the sound of his laughter. She tried finding some purchase with her boots, but the heels just seemed to sink farther into the bottom of the pond. “Sure there isn’t quicksand under here?”

Still chuckling, he leaned forward, stretching out his hand. “No quicksand,” he promised. “Maybe some frogs and water bugs. A snake or two.”

She grimaced, tried scrambling out of the water, only to land yet again with a splash. Not even a beautiful, graceful splash. Just an unbecoming flop. Because, naturally, that’s what would happen when you realize you love a guy.

“I was kidding about the snakes.” He was still grinning. “Come on, city girl. Give me your hand.”

“I guess I should be glad you’re not going for your ‘in case’ rope to haul me out.” She held out her hand and he caught it, circling his long fingers around her wrist.

She yanked.

He snorted, easily planting one foot in the water to keep himself from being pulled down into the water beside her. “Nice try. You think it’d be that simple? Other hand now.”

She made a face but gave him her other hand and he hauled her clean out of the water. She bumped flat against him and his hands went to her waist.

Before her nerve endings had a chance to fire too brilliantly, he pivoted to set her on the dry grass.

"There you go. No harm done. Except for a little pond scum." He pulled a long, slick piece of grass away from her neck and tossed it back into the water.

She smiled. And gave him a healthy shove.

Healthy enough to unbalance him and watch him land on his butt with a big splash.

She laughed as she propped her hands on her soaking hips. "Watch out for us city girls."

He angled his head, giving her a considering look. "I suppose you think we're even now."

She nodded. "I suppose I do." She scooped up the canteen and took another drink. Then she capped it once more and eyed him. "You just going to sit there among the water bugs and frogs?"

"Maybe I'm enjoying the view."

There was no question he meant *her*.

She resisted the urge to look down at herself, because she knew what she'd see. The human equivalent of a drowning rat. "Sure you are. Because this is a really attractive look." She squished her way to the flattest boulder and sat on it to pull off the boots. She upended them and water poured out. "I hope I haven't ruined your mom's boots, too."

She heard him splashing and looked over to see him standing in the pond and sloshing his way to the edge.

"Y'ought to worry more about ruining mine." Unlike the rest of him, his voice was dry. And somewhat muffled by the shirt he was taking off. He didn't even bother with the buttons. He just pulled it straight over his head. Then he tossed it at her and it landed with a wet slap against her chest.

It was almost impossible not to ogle him when his body was just so impossibly perfect. "Your boots got soaked the day we met," she reminded him. "They survived that, didn't they?" She threw the shirt back at him.

He caught it in midair long before it could hit him. "You do realize that we still have to ride *back* to the ranch, right? If you were feeling saddle sore before, it's nothing compared to how you'll feel after riding in wet jeans."

"I would've been riding in wet jeans whether you took a little bath in there or not."

"Except I could have given you my dry shirt to wear."

"With wet jeans."

"Not if you took them off."

She raised her eyebrows. It was all she could do to keep it light. "Riding in just my dainties? You must be joking."

His eyes were amused. "We are gonna have to get our jeans dried out, though. Unless you'd rather walk, we'll both be in for a pretty uncomfortable ride."

Being soaked from the pond had momentarily taken her mind off her stiff legs. "So walking, we'd probably get back around midnight?"

He chuckled. "It wouldn't take that long." He spread out his shirt over a tree branch, then sat on a rock and worked off his boots. Then he pulled off his socks that she could tell were nowhere near as wet as hers. Then he stood and started unfastening his jeans.

She couldn't help the strangled sound that emerged from her throat and flushed when he looked at her. His eyebrows rose a little. "Something wrong?"

"Aside from you having way too much fun at my expense?" She pointed an accusing finger at him. "That's what you're doing."

He spread his hands. "Considering history, you've shown an aptitude for taking off *your* clothes." Then his grin broke loose and his hands fell away from his pants. "Truth is, I don't know if our jeans'll dry faster with us wearing them or not." He walked barefoot through the soft grass over to where the two horses were still grazing and unfastened the bag from his saddle.

He came back and handed it to her.

"It's like a fanny pack," she said, unzipping the nylon bag to find a collection of granola bars and a small first-aid kit inside.

"Cantle bag," he corrected her, looking like he wanted to laugh.

"Well, you attached it to the fanny part of your saddle." She pulled out one of the bars and tossed the bag back to him. "Thank you. Aside from the failure to pack a spare change of clothing, you're very prepared."

"Thank the army." He sat down on the grass, then took a bar for himself before lying back. He had one leg hitched over his other upraised knee. "Wet jeans or not, this is the life," he murmured. He tore open the wrapper and bit off half the granola bar.

He'd made himself similarly comfortable that first day in the storm cellar and she couldn't help smiling a little at the sight. She tore open her own bar and took a bite. "Did Graciela really get her bra hung up on a saddle horn?"

"She really did."

"And she really said…what you said she said about the trotting thing."

He'd finished his granola bar and he rolled onto his

side, propping his head on his hand. The muscles in his arm bulged. "She really said what I said she said."

He was laughing at her. No question. And she was still left wondering what had really gone on between him and the beautiful older woman.

"Did you ever sleep with her?"

His eyebrows shot up. "You don't hesitate to ask questions, do you?"

"Not usually," she admitted.

He rolled onto his stomach, propping himself on his arms.

There was no real reason for her mouth to run dry, but it suddenly did. "Well?"

"Yes, I slept with her."

Her jaw went tight.

"I was all of six years old and she was babysitting me and my brothers," he added. "Why's it bother you so much?"

"Who says it bothers me?"

He just looked at her.

She focused on the faint scar above his eyebrow. "She's very beautiful now. I can only imagine what she was like when she was younger."

"She didn't hold a candle to you."

There were probably a hundred books written about the wisdom of trusting a handsome cuss's flattery. She'd written a blog or two about it herself.

But he wasn't just any handsome cuss. Not anymore.

"I'm not fishing for compliments."

"Generally speaking, truth is rarely complimentary. It's just truth."

Something inside her chest squeezed.

"Come here."

She hesitated. But it was a lost cause. It had been from the first time he'd smiled at her. She moved off the rock to sit on the grass growing around the base of it.

"Closer." He extended one arm toward her, his palm up, fingers curled slightly.

She focused on his palm, on the ridge of calluses that were plainly visible.

He had a working man's hands.

Without thinking about it, she found herself moving closer to him. "When's the last time you slept under the stars?"

Instead of looking surprised by the odd question, he just slowly slid his palm over her forearm, setting off a rush of heat through her veins. "About a week before I met you."

"Out camping or something?"

He shook his head and drew his hand down to hers. He slowly pressed his larger palm against hers and her head swam.

"Out, uh, checking your cattle like Nathan's been doing?"

He shook his head again and steadily separated her fingers with his.

She swallowed and moistened her lips. "Then why?"

His eyes lifted to hers. They were clear brown and so much more addictive than any amount of coffee could ever be. "Because there's no place better than being beneath the Paseo sky."

"To sleep?"

He reached out his free hand and slid it along her jaw. His thumb slowly brushed against her cheek.

She felt herself being drawn down toward him.

"Just to be," he murmured.

Then his mouth slowly brushed against hers.

Tasting.

Tempting.

And no matter how smart she wanted to be where he was concerned, she couldn't stop herself from leaning into him. From tasting him in return. From parting her lips when his kiss deepened. From winding her arms around his back when he drew her down onto the soft, fragrant grass with him.

She couldn't stop herself from sucking in a quick breath when his hand slid over her belly, pulling up both her soaking T-shirt and the cami beneath. Or from threading her fingers through his hair when his lips followed his hand.

"If you're going to stop me, say so now," he murmured as he worked his way upward, pulling the elastic-edged shelf bra above her breasts.

She couldn't find words if her life depended on it. She lifted up enough to finish pulling everything off over her head. And then it wasn't his hands running over her but his gaze, and she felt weak from it.

He leaned over and kissed her butterfly tattoo. Slowly he worked his way to one nipple, then over to the pulse pounding madly at the base of her throat.

The grass beneath her tickled her back and the heat from the afternoon sun beat down from above, glowing even when she closed her eyes.

She wrapped her hands around his head and pulled him up to her, pressing her lips to his. "Jayden—"

He went still. Then he levered his chest up from hers. "You want to stop."

She shook her head as she opened her eyes and looked up into his face. The sun was behind his head and the aura surrounding him was nearly blinding. "I want you to never stop," she whispered.

He was silent, while all around them, the sound of nature seemed to get louder. The buzz of grasshoppers. The warbling and chirping of birds. The squeak of the windmill.

Then his lips brushed against her cheek. "I'll do my best," he murmured against her ear, before his lips burned their way once more down her neck. Past the pulse. Beyond the butterfly. He slowly kissed his way along her breasts, down the center of her belly to her navel, not stopping until he reached the button of her jeans. He freed it with a soft pop. "Lift."

She raised her hips and he peeled the soaking jeans and her frivolous white panties away.

"Don't leave me here like this alone." She managed to slide her fingers beneath the waistband of his jeans and he caught her fingers, dragging them away. He kissed the tips of them before letting her go long enough to work out of his own wet things.

And then he was settling against her, and she exhaled shakily, because she had never felt anything quite so momentous in her life as the weight of him. The heat of him. The need for him. As if her entire life had simply been marking time until this very moment.

She slid her hands over his wide shoulders, down his back, all the while hovering on the agonizing precipice of waiting as his strong fingers gripped her hips, staying her motions.

"You're sure?"

She twined her legs around his and nodded, pressing her mouth against his because she wasn't sure that she could hold back words that she didn't dare admit.

Fortunately, it was answer enough and she shuddered when he slowly pressed into her, filling her so perfectly she wondered how she would ever be the same again.

Then his hands slid up to find hers again, their fingers meshing. "I knew it." His voice had gone rough. Husky.

She could already feel herself tightening around him. She could hardly manage to form words as he rocked against her, making the pleasure inside her build and build.

"Knew…what?"

"How you'd feel." Then his breath hissed between his teeth as she arched sharply, winding her legs even more tightly around his hips. "Perfect."

But she was already beyond hearing as he emptied himself inside her and she cried out, startling a nearby bevy of quail into scattering.

All she knew was that he was right.

There was no more perfect place than being beneath the Paseo sky.

With him.

Chapter 10

Jayden's cotton shirt dried long before hers did and he pulled it over her head. "More than your nose is getting sunburned."

"And you're not getting sunburned?"

"I'm already mostly leather," he murmured, kissing her shoulder through the shirt.

She smiled, because she knew better. His upper torso was deeply tanned and felt like satin covered muscle. "Not your under-the-swimsuit bits," she said.

He gave a choked laugh. "Bits?"

She lifted her shoulder and twisted her fingers through his.

They were picking their way barefoot through the clover around the pond. And even if it ought to seem odd that he was wearing only his still-damp jeans and she was wearing only his wrinkled plaid shirt over her panties that had quickly dried in the sun, she didn't care.

"I suppose you'd prefer something a little grander sounding."

"I'd prefer words other than *little* and *bits*," he allowed wryly.

She laughed and he suddenly pulled her around to face him, twisting his hands in her long hair as he kissed her.

Despite the lethargy still clinging to her, she felt heat streak through her and she swayed unsteadily when he finally lifted his head and started walking again.

They passed the windmill and she stopped to look up at the tall structure. She reached up and wrapped her hands around one of the horizontal bars running between the corner pieces. The pipe running straight down from the top slowly moved up and down and connected to another series of pipes near the ground, one which clearly ran toward the pond. "Considering the noise this thing makes, I thought it would be rustier."

"It's not rust that's squeaking. It's the sails and the sucker rod." He stopped close against her and set his hands on either side of hers. "We've gotta keep it running. Can't depend only on rain that's either too little or too often." He tapped the metal bar. "This baby keeps the place irrigated and the cattle from drying up. We have three more mills farther out, too. Nathan'll be checking on 'em while he's out. Make sure they weren't damaged during the storm that delivered you."

She leaned her head back against his chest as she squinted up at the slowly revolving fan blades. Sails, he'd called them. Such an evocative term. "It's kind of beautiful, isn't it?" The afternoon. The windmill. *Him.*

"Mmm-hmm." He lifted the plaid shirt and slid his arm around her bare waist. "Only times it's not real beautiful is when we have to climb up and repair something." His fingers grazed her breasts, circled her eager nipples. "View's great, but it's still a pain in the butt and seems to only happen when it's either hotter 'n hell outside like today or cold as a witch's heart."

She was having a hard time breathing. Particularly when his leg slid between hers and she felt him, hard and insistent against her backside. And even though she felt a rush of dizzying want all over again, she closed her hand over his, stilling his motions. "I want to." How badly she wanted to.

"But?"

She rubbed her temple against his chin. Despite her cautioning hand, his thumb still managed to taunt her sensitized nipple and heat collected low inside her. "But I'm too sore," she admitted in a raw breath.

"You'll get used to saddles and horseback riding." He slid his hand from beneath hers.

Regret was like a physical noise, joining the cacophony of sound around them. "I'm not talking about being sore from the horse."

He dipped his head and kissed the side of her neck. "Guess that makes up for the *bits* bit," he said in a low voice. His hand didn't leave her, though. It slid leisurely over her rib cage.

She exhaled shakily and rested against him, feeling more than a little mesmerized by the motion of the windmill. The turn of the sails. The up-and-down glide of the rod. The no-longer-random trajectory of his fingers. "Jayden—"

"Sshh." His hand covered hers where she was still

holding on to the metal bar. His other hand—the provocatively tempting one—moved inexorably southward. "Just let me do this."

She inhaled sharply as his fingers breached the edge of her panties. She wrapped her fingers around his strong wrist. Whether to stop him or urge him on, she wasn't sure. "But what about you?"

His fingers delved between her legs, gliding slickly. He made a low sound of pure appreciation that rumbled from his chest, through her spine and straight to her heart. He pressed his mouth against her shoulder and his voice dropped even deeper. "This is for me." His clever, marauding fingers swirled against her and she couldn't hold back a sigh of pleasure. "You know what a fantasy this is?"

She rolled her head back and forth against his chest. "No."

"After this, I'll never hate repairing windmills again," he murmured. His thumb roved over the knot of nerve endings and she gasped.

"Trust me, sweetheart." His fingers dipped. "Let yourself go. For me."

And she did.

Eventually, they made it to the small cemetery he'd mentioned earlier, where the Thompsons were buried. The grassy patch was surrounded by a white picket fence that looked in pristine condition. It made a few of the headstones that it surrounded look even more ancient by comparison.

For the first time in a long while, she wished she had her cell phone with her so she could take pictures. She didn't need to ask who was responsible for maintaining the fence around the family plot. Because she understood that the ones buried there were considered Jayden's family.

She put her hand on the gate. "May I?"

"Sure."

She undid the latch and stepped through. The oldest of the headstones were the farthest away from the gate, situated among the roots of the enormous tree standing guard over the cemetery. She knelt down, barely noticing the way her calves and thighs protested, and read the inscriptions on the simple stone markers. "Eighteen ninety-five. Nineteen-oh-two."

"Earl's grandparents." Jayden flicked a leaf away from the deeply weathered granite. "They were some of Paseo's first settlers. Came from Boston originally." He gestured toward the three markers next to them. "They had four children. Earl's dad was the only one who lived past fifteen." He moved around to the next row where the headstones were noticeably brighter, the edges less worn. "Kees Thompson. Earl's father."

She read the marker. Jayden had pronounced the name like *Case*. "I like that name. Very different."

"His wife, Mary." He pointed at the accompanying headstone. "Nothing unusual about her name. Not until you get to Mary Junior." He stopped in front of a third headstone. "Earl's sister. Only woman I've ever known that actually used Junior in her name."

She brushed her fingertips over the engraved surname. "Thompson. Mary Junior never married?"

He shook his head. "Died when we were little."

She moved around to look at the last and most recent row of headstones. Earl. Cynthia. Caroline and child.

"So sad. Every generation lost a child before they should have."

He leaned over to brush away the leaves accumulated at the base of Caroline's square headstone. When he straightened, he was holding a large silver ring. "That's a new kind of leaf," he drawled.

She smiled and reached out to take it. Only to frown as she studied it more closely. "It's part of a loose-leaf binder." A big one. She worked the ring apart. "See?"

He was still brushing away debris and held up a piece of bright pink plastic. "Belonged to this, I expect."

Her stomach tightened as she took the jagged remnant.

"You had a notebook like this in your car, didn't you?"

Her mouth suddenly ran dry. She nodded.

"Wonder if anything else from your car landed around here. We should take a look. In case."

She wasn't sure how she'd managed to forget the inconvenience facing her when it came to replacing her driver's license and everything else that had been in her wallet. "It doesn't matter." She couldn't seem to tear her attention away from the piece of plastic binder.

Jayden noticed. "You okay?"

There was a knot inside her chest. "I kept all my research and notes in this."

"For the magazine."

She started to nod. But then she looked at him and couldn't make herself do it. She couldn't tell him an outright lie. Not anymore. Not when she'd already crossed every single line she'd sworn she'd never cross.

The self-imposed oath had been simple.

Until now. Now that she knew she was in love with him.

"For my book," she said huskily.

His eyebrows rose. "A book? That's great. You never said you were working on—" He broke off. His eyes narrowed. "What kind of book?"

"A biography." She had to forcibly swallow down the knot when it moved from her chest into her throat. "An unauthorized biography."

His lips tightened. He folded his arms across his wide chest. Arms that only minutes earlier had surrounded her with such thrilling tenderness. "Let me guess. About Gerald Robinson?"

"Jerome Fortune."

His lips twisted. "They're one and the same."

How could she make him understand? "And everyone knows everything about Gerald! At least everything he's let everyone know. But nobody seems to know anything about Jerome. Not once he supposedly died thirty-some years ago."

"What were you hoping, Ariana?"

Her nerves tightened. Because he never addressed her directly by name. And it felt so, so much worse than it should have.

"Were you hoping you'd be here long enough to grill my mother when she returns?"

"No!"

"To dig into her past just because you think writing some damn *unauthorized* book gives you the right?"

"I would never do that." Her eyes stung. "Not now."

"Why should I believe you?" He advanced on her, looking furious. He plucked the pink plastic out of her numb fingers and held it up between them. "Because you've been so honest and up-front about everything so far?"

"Because I fell in love with you!"

A muscle worked in his tight jaw as his gaze drilled into hers.

She pulled in a breath that seemed to burn. "I fell in love with you," she repeated huskily. "Whatever ends up in the book, it won't involve you."

It seemed impossible for his expression to sharpen even more, but it did. "Because you believe he's not our father."

She chewed the inside of her lip. But she'd already determined she couldn't lie. And what did it matter now, when he was looking at her with such anger? Such distrust?

"No. I do believe he is your father."

A barrier seemed to slam down behind his eyes.

"But no matter what I believe, I'm not going to write about it," she insisted even though her head told her it was useless. "Not about you. Not about your brothers or your mother."

"Then what *are* you going to fill the pages with? Details about some other slob you pick up off the street and sleep with for a story?"

She felt the blood drain from her face. Even though it took every speck of strength inside her, she managed to lift her chin. She wasn't a tramp and she wasn't going to apologize. "I never came here trying to prove you were Jerome Fortune's son. You know that. You *have* to know that by now."

"The only thing I know is that you could've mentioned the book from the get-go. And you didn't. That's as good as a lie to me."

"If I'd been trying to prove that you weren't his son, would you still feel the same?"

His expression remained cold.

But no colder than the yawning hole that had opened up inside her.

She set the metal ring on the edge of poor Caroline's headstone, then turned and walked away.

She knew he followed after her. Not because she could hear his footsteps in the clover and grass. They were just as silent as hers. But because she could feel the drilling of his eyes through the space between her shoulder blades.

She was out of breath by the time she made it all the way around the pond again, and she pulled off his shirt, turning to hand it to him.

His gaze dropped for the briefest millisecond, but she was damned if she'd cover her bare breasts now. Instead, she snatched up her cami from the rock where she'd spread it to dry and tugged it over her head. Then the rough cotton T-shirt and her jeans that were still more wet than not. She ignored the clamminess and pulled on her socks and his mother's too-large boots.

"Ariana."

It was practically a command and she hesitated.

"Don't rush around the horses. I don't want you spooking them."

Not that he didn't want her getting kicked. Just that he didn't want her scaring his horses.

He'd pulled the plaid shirt on, but the buttons weren't fastened and it flapped around his lean hips after he'd pulled on his own boots and headed toward the horses. They'd never strayed far from where they'd left them, and even though it felt like they'd whiled away an entire day beside the pond, it could only have been a couple of hours.

A couple of hours for her to taste heaven.

A couple of hours for her to lose it just as surely.

She looked away from him, blinking hard at the stinging in her eyes.

Then she lifted her head and threw her hair behind her back. She walked over to where he stood with Daisy and put one hand on the horse's withers, the other on the cantle, and mounted.

Focusing on the top of Jayden's tousled head, she pulled on the leather gloves then held out her hands for the reins.

He silently handed them to her, then mounted Jobuck and led the way back to the ranch.

No swaying, gentle walk this time. No exercise in trying to sit the trot. He didn't even make a soft clucking sound. Jobuck just moved smoothly into a steady lope and Daisy kept pace.

He couldn't have made it any clearer that he wanted to get away from her.

All too quickly, they were back at the ranch and Daisy aimed straight for the wash rack at the back of the barn.

Ariana wasn't showing off any particular skill she'd learned that afternoon. That was all Daisy.

"I'll put her up," Jayden said when Ariana dismounted. His expression was still closed. She knew there was no point in arguing. Not about helping to unsaddle the horse and groom her like she knew he always did after bringing one of his horses in. Nor about convincing him that the book she was writing didn't matter.

Because if it truly hadn't mattered, why had she really kept from mentioning it?

She silently handed him the reins and walked through

the barn. She didn't even notice the little red vehicle sitting near the house until she practically walked right into it.

"Hey there, Miss Lamonte." Charlie came down from where he'd been sitting on one of the porch chairs. "Was just beginning to think I wasn't goin' t' find you." His skinny face had a happy smile. "Got that part today after all." He waved at her car. "She's spit-shined and ready t' go."

Her eyes burned. "I see that, Charlie." Because she was badly afraid she was going to lose it and cry, she walked around the vehicle, working hard to study it. She couldn't see a single scratch. No dents. No damage.

It was as if the tornado had never crossed the car's path at all.

She bent over and looked blindly through the window. "It looks perfect, Charlie." She surreptitiously swiped her eyes and straightened.

"Runs perfect, too," he assured her. He pulled a sheaf of folded papers from the back pocket of his overalls. "Just gotta get your signature." He spread the papers out on the hood of the car and fumbled in his pocket again to produce a pen. "Insurance companies always want things good 'n' official."

She took the pen and signed her name.

"Gotcha a full tank of gas as well."

"If you tell me how much I owe you, I'll have to send you the money." Her insurance wasn't going to cover gas.

"Nah. Jayden took care of it a few days ago when he told me to make sure your tank was full."

Naturally. Even before he ever knew there was a

book at all, he'd wanted to make sure she had no reason to hang around. Not even at the gas station in Paseo.

"Thank you," she said huskily. "I never expected you to deliver the car to me like this."

"No trouble. Wanted to give it a good test-drive anyway." He refolded the papers and pocketed them again. "Figure Jayden won't mind giving me a hitch back to my place." He handed her the key fob.

"No doubt." She gestured toward the barn. Her eyes were still burning, and if she didn't get away soon, she was going to make a fool of herself in front of the mechanic. "He's taking care of the horses if you want to go talk to him. I'm going to have to excuse myself." She plucked at her jeans. "Managed to get myself all wet—"

"Sure. Sure." He tipped his grease-stained ball cap and took a step toward the barn. "See y' later, now."

She couldn't even manage a garbled response. Her throat was too raw with unshed tears and she just went straight into the house.

Sugar hopped up from her bed in the kitchen and followed close on Ariana's heels as she walked to the borrowed bedroom where she changed out of her wet things and back into Deborah Fortune's denim dress. Then, moving fast and trying not to trip over the poor dog, Ariana stripped the bed and remade it with the fresh sheets kept in the hallway linen closet. She silently apologized for breaking her mother's rules when it came to comingling laundry and shoved the sheets and the towels she'd used into the same washing-machine load and started it running.

She fed Sugar a treat and gave her a kiss on her silky head.

Then she went back into the bedroom and grabbed up the rest of her belongings and went outside to the car.

She did not look at the barn.

Did not look at the storm-cellar door.

She just tossed everything in the passenger seat.

And she drove away.

"Jayden, what's this?"

Jayden looked up from the ledger he was supposed to be updating to see his mom standing in the kitchen doorway. She'd been back a week now. It meant an improvement in the coffee situation again, though it also meant having to endure her speculative looks when she thought he wasn't aware. "What's what?"

She set a small shipping box on top of his ledger book. She'd already opened it. "Came in the mail today."

Disinterested, he glanced inside the box, then felt his nerves pinch at the sight of the glossy magazine sitting inside.

"Ariana sent it. Obviously." His mother knew they'd had a "guest" while she'd been gone. He pushed the box aside and picked up his pencil again. But the row of numbers he was staring at were gibberish.

"Not the magazine." Deborah lifted out the latest copy of *Weird Life* and set it on the table. "This." She plucked out a bank check and waved it in front of his face.

He sat back, hiding his annoyance. It wasn't his mother's fault that he'd felt more like an angry bull than a human being since she'd been back.

Actually, he'd been that way since Ariana had driven away without so much as a "thanks for nothing."

He took the check and tossed it on top of the magazine. "She's just paying me back for expenses." She'd been keeping a list, she'd said. He remembered how she'd smiled at him that day she'd picked out those ugly tie-dyed shirts. That day, he'd thought her smile could light the county.

He stared harder at the gibberish.

"A thousand dollars in expenses?"

His mother's voice penetrated. "What?" He looked at the bank check. Ariana's scrawl was distinctively messy but the amount was plain. His fingers curled, crumpling the check like the garbage that it was.

"She included a note." Deborah pulled the next item out.

Despite the fact that his mother had left the contents inside the box for him to see, she'd clearly been through it at least once.

He pushed his chair back on two legs and folded his arms. "Why don't you just tell me what you want to say? You've obviously read it already and drawn your own conclusions." She'd been trying to pump him all week about Ariana. About his mood. About every damn little thing on the entire damn little planet.

His mother's lips thinned. "Watch your tone with me, Jayden Fortune. You're not too old for me to box your ears."

God help him. "And I'm too damn old for this bull—"

She raised her eyebrows.

"—hockey," he amended through his teeth. Which was ironic as all hell, because his mother could swear a trucker into blushing if she so chose. He thumped his chair back onto its four legs and he took the small, folded sheet of paper from her and flipped it open between his fingers.

"'For lodging and incidentals,'" he read. He shook his head, actually seeing through a haze of red. "Incidentals!" He shoved away from the table, ripping the note into shreds. "Incidentals?" He tossed the paper up like confetti.

His mother had leaned casually back against the table. Her long hair was still more brown than gray and hung in a long thick braid over her shoulder, and she toyed with the ends of it, like it was the most fascinating thing on the planet. "Quite a reaction for a girl you say was *just* an unintended houseguest."

His jaw was clenched. He was not going to discuss Ariana with his mother. Because if he did, he'd end up telling her what his beef was.

And that was *not* going to happen. He was not going to question the decisions Deborah not-really-Fortune had made a long time ago.

No way.

No how.

Deborah let go of her braid and sighed. "Honey, *please*." She gestured. "If I weren't already suspicious about what went on between you and this Ariana Lamonte—" she picked up the magazine and flipped it open to a page with a small photo of Ariana in the corner "—I would be now, just because of your behavior. I wouldn't even have needed Nathan to tell me there was something personal going on between you. Clearly, she left an impression. You've been like a dog with a sore paw since I got back." She set the opened magazine down, and the small photo of Ariana—looking unfamiliarly sleek and sophisticated with a brilliant smile—stared up at him.

"She was only here for a couple weeks," he gritted out. "Nothing important happened."

"And I am the Queen of England." She straightened and brushed her hands together as if she were dusting away the entire matter. "Fine. I know you too well. If you don't want to talk, you won't talk. Who am I but just an old woman who wants to see her sons in happy relationships?"

He snorted. "Right."

She raised her eyebrows again. "You think that's so strange, Jayden? That I'd like nothing better than to see you and your brothers settled down with nice girls? Maybe give me a grandbaby or two I can bounce on my knee before I'm too old to bounce anything?"

"Don't act like you've got one foot in the grave. There's plenty of time for…for stuff like that." He'd never seen a more active woman than his mother. She had to be to keep up with Grayson's tours. And when she wasn't doing that, she was keeping up with the ranch. Considering neither Jayden nor Nathan had been around a lot once they'd joined the military, that was saying something. "And since when have you ever wanted babies around, anyway?"

The very subject of babies was like an annoying itch between his shoulder blades. Because he knew damn well that he and Ariana hadn't used any sort of protection when they'd made love. And what kind of man was he to not even think to ask if she'd been on the pill? Damn. He used to lecture the kids coming up in the army about safe sex, and he turns out to be no better?

"Why wouldn't I want a grandbaby around? It's a normal enough desire. Traditional—"

He snorted again. "Traditional? You, traditional?"

Her lips tightened. "And what is that supposed to mean?"

"Come on, Mom. You chose to have Nate and Grayson and me when you weren't even married. I know it's common enough now, but back then? You were totally on your own. If it weren't for Earl and Cynthia—" He broke off and shook his head. He couldn't let his thinking go down that road, because it kept leading to the very thing he refused to question.

What if Ariana had been right?

He braked hard on the untenable thought.

"Oh, Jayden." Deborah pulled out a chair and sat in it. Her brows pulled together as she smoothed her tanned, lined hand over Ariana's article about the Ybarras. "Of course I chose to have you. I loved all three of you before I even *knew* there were three of you. But I never wanted to do it on my own. Circumstances just turned out that way."

"It's none of my business what the circumstances were."

Her steady gaze softened. "When you were little, you used to badger me all the time for details about your father."

His jaw tightened even more. He'd badgered. Until he'd made her cry.

"And then one day you stopped." She tilted her head slightly. "I always figured that eventually you and your brothers would be old enough for the truth. But none of you ever brought it up again." And this time when she focused on the end of her braid, there was sadness in her face. "And so neither did I." Her slender shoulders rose and fell. Then she let go of the braid again and lifted her chin slightly.

It reminded him way too eerily of the way Ariana had tended to do the same thing.

Like she was facing something she couldn't change.

Deborah looked at the magazine again. "She's a beautiful girl," she murmured. "I don't know if she's a nice girl as well or not. But she certainly wrote a wonderful article about Hector and Paloma. And she has certainly left an impression on you, good or bad." She nudged the magazine closer to the edge of the table and stood. She touched his shoulder. "It doesn't matter if it was only two weeks, son. I fell in love with your father after just two days. We met in New Orleans during what ought to have been the worst times of our lives. We'd both left behind unhappy family situations but once we met—" She broke off and lifted her hands. "Everything bad that had gone before just didn't seem so important anymore. If Ariana matters to you, then do something about it." She smiled slightly and started to leave the kitchen.

Sugar got up from her bed, sending Jayden a reproachful look before following.

He pinched the bridge of his nose, trying to quell the ache there.

"Mom."

She hesitated in the doorway.

He lowered his hand, meeting her eyes and wondering what the hell he was doing. "Where did the name Fortune really come from?"

She didn't look away. "From your father. It was the only thing of his I could give you. That I could keep."

The knot that had been in his stomach for too long now tightened even more. "So, you were married to him."

She shook her head. "In my heart? Yes. But not legally. I could have been. But I wasn't."

"Why not?"

"I was afraid."

"Of what?"

"It doesn't even matter anymore. It all happened so fast. He proposed. When I hesitated, he believed it was because I didn't love him enough." She lifted her shoulder. "By the time I realized I was pregnant with you, it was too late. He was already gone. And even though I tried to find him—" She shook her head. "It was too late."

"Why?" The question came from somewhere deep and sore inside him.

"Because he died." She looked sad. "He was the only man I ever really loved and I realized it too late. Don't be like me, Jayden. Whatever your issue is with that young writer, don't let pride—or fear—keep you from having more than just this ranch in your life."

"His name was Jerome." It wasn't a question.

Something flickered in her gaze. And even though he hadn't asked for confirmation, she still nodded. "Yes. It was. Jerome Fortune."

Chapter 11

He should have called her first.

Why hadn't he called her first?

Jayden stared at the apartment building across the street and tried to shut off the thoughts inside his head.

The only reason he had the address of Ariana's apartment at all was because of that damn check she'd sent him.

Incidentals.

Even though he knew now just how right she'd been about Jerome Fortune, that comment of hers still pissed him off.

He'd thought maybe he'd have cooled down a little about that fact during the long drive from Paseo to Austin.

But he hadn't.

And now he was looking at the apartment building where she lived and second-guessing himself even more.

Which also pissed him off.

He didn't like second-guessing himself. And it was her fault that he was doing so.

He looked at the passenger seat next to him. He'd have brought Sugar with him, but he hadn't wanted to subject her to a trip somewhere unfamiliar. Instead, the seat held only a yellowed, faded newspaper.

The newspaper that had been in the storm cellar all along, if Jayden had ever bothered to actually look at it. The newspaper that his mother had collected herself, after he and his brothers had been born. The newspaper confirming, once and for all, that Jerome Fortune—heir apparent to some financial empire in New York who'd disappeared years earlier as a young man after a questionable suicide—had been declared officially dead.

He was a lot less interested in the story of Jerome Fortune or Gerald Robinson or whatever the hell the man wanted to call himself. Despite finally knowing the truth, Jayden still thought of him as nothing more than a sperm donor. Everything Jayden was—everything his brothers were—they owed to one person.

Their mother.

He blew out a breath and studied the high-rise apartment building. Landscape lights were starting to come on in the lush, well-maintained grounds that surrounded it.

You could've just called her.

Except he'd never particularly thought of himself as a coward. If anything, he tended to rise to challenges too quickly, rush to judgment too quickly.

He gritted his teeth and let out an impatient sound. Then he pushed open the door and got out. He waited for traffic to clear and jogged across the street. Even though it was closer to evening than afternoon, it was still hotter 'n hell, and he was sweating when he strode through the sleek, modern entrance to the building.

Which only reminded him of their last afternoon together out by the pond, at the windmill.

Before she'd run off.

What kind of woman ran off during a fight? Particularly after just claiming that she supposedly loved you?

He jabbed the elevator button and rode up to the sixth floor. When he found apartment number 629, he jabbed the doorbell even harder than he'd hit the elevator button.

First thing he was going to do was tell her that the next time they argued about something, she needed to damn well stick around and keep up her side of the argument.

None of this cut-and-run crap.

Only she didn't answer the door.

Not when he jabbed the doorbell the first time. Nor the second. Nor when he kept his finger pressed on it for an entire minute the third time.

He knew it was working. He could hear the strident buzz through the door.

So could the dog living in the apartment next door. The thing had started barking at the second buzz and was still barking when Jayden finally turned and stomped back to the elevator.

He should have called her first.

He rode the elevator back down to the ground floor again and returned to his truck. It was Friday. Three weeks ago, he'd been convincing Ariana to come in out of the storm with him.

How could so much have happened in such a short time?

His mind was buzzing in so many directions he

wanted to kick something. But of course he couldn't. He was supposed to be a reasonable man. Maybe not the most patient, but still reasonable.

The street was congested with rush-hour traffic and he stood at the crosswalk. She'd told him when they first met that she loved the city. Considering the location of her apartment in what he was assuming was the downtown area, she obviously got plenty of *city.*

Frankly, after two years of peace and quiet back in Paseo following his stint with army life, the busyness was enough to make him break out in a rash.

He added that to his saddlebag of complaints.

How could any sane woman ever prefer this to Paseo?

He looked up at the sky. He'd bet once it was dark, there'd still be too much city light to see the stars.

"Jayden?"

He turned around and there she was.

Walking toward him wearing one of the shortest skirts he'd ever seen with one of the ugliest shirts he'd ever seen.

He dragged his attention up from those beautiful long legs, skimmed over the *Paseo Is Paradise* T-shirt and met her eyes as she stopped a couple of yards away.

She'd pulled her hair back in a sleek ponytail. Her face was made up and her dark eyes looked even darker and more mysterious.

And wary. Definitely wary.

Once he got over the physical shock of seeing her, he realized everything about her—from the way she clutched her soft, oversized purse to the way she seemed poised on the balls of her flat-heeled sandals—looked like she was ready to run.

"What are you doing here?" she asked him.

"Looking for you." Obvious, yeah. "What other reason would bring me to Austin? *Incidentals*, Ariana? That's how you categorized what went on between us?"

Her lashes—they were twice as long as he'd remembered—swept down. But not before he'd seen a spark of temper.

At least that was something familiar.

As was the tie-dyed T-shirt. Strangely enough, it looked pretty good with the short black skirt that showed off her legs.

And it made him hope that maybe he hadn't entirely blown things with her.

"I guess I don't have to ask if you received the package I mailed." She hitched the strap of her purse higher on her shoulder.

"It came today."

That surprised her. Her gaze flicked up to his, then away. "I see."

She couldn't possibly. "Can we go up to your apartment and talk?"

Her chin lifted slightly. "I don't think so."

His jaw tightened. "So we're going to do this right here on the sidewalk with people walking by us every ten seconds?" He smiled tightly at the bicyclist who wove around them.

"Do what, Jayden?"

"Are you going to cut and run every time we have a disagreement?"

Her lips rounded. "I— What? Cut and run?" She glared. "Should I have stayed and let you accuse me of being a…a slut for the third time?"

"I didn't accuse you of being a slut."

"What would you call it, then? As if I'd sleep with—"

"I'm sorry."

Her lips slowly closed.

"If you wanted to turn the knife, the note with the check did the job. Four words is all it took. 'For lodging and incidentals.'"

"I told you I was better on paper," she muttered.

She was good on paper. Really good with words. She knew just how to use them to make her point. "The article about the Ybarras was amazing. Before I left Paseo, I stopped by their place to drop off the magazine for them."

She opened her mouth again. "I mailed—"

"I know. They already had the copies you mailed to them. Paloma said to tell you *gracias*. She was already planning to frame one copy and figuring out where to hang it in the new house."

The corners of her lips curved faintly. "How is their house coming?"

"Framing is already done."

"Even in Paseo, things can get done quickly." She sidestepped so another bicyclist could pass and looked toward her building. "I'm glad for them."

The sun behind him shone over her profile.

"You were right," he said abruptly.

Her lashes lowered again. He could see the slow breath she took. Then she looked at him. There was no need to elaborate. She knew that he was talking about Jerome Fortune. "I'm sorry."

"It means you've got at least *one* meaty chapter for your book."

She chewed off some of the pink lip gloss on her soft lips. "No."

"You can't write a book about the man's secrets and not include my mother."

"I'm not writing a book about Jerome Fortune. Not anymore." She shifted. Her hands were wrapped so tightly around her purse strap, her knuckles were white. "I returned the advance yesterday. I, uh, also resigned from the magazine."

If she'd announced she had married the Pope, he couldn't have been more confused. "Why?"

"Because I can't write any more stories about the Fortunes. I'm too involved—" She chewed off a little more pink shine. "I'm not objective enough. I'm too biased now. So you'd better cash the check fast if you don't want it to bounce."

He ignored that. "You love writing."

"Yeah, well." She shrugged one shoulder. "Maybe I'll try fiction this time." She gestured toward the apartment building. "I need to turn in my notice on my place before the manager's office closes or I'm going to be on the hook for another month of rent that I can't really afford anymore. So—"

"Did you mean what you said?"

"Uh. Yeah. As it is, I'm probably going to have to sleep in my car if I don't tuck my tail and go home to Mommy and Daddy. Mom changed my childhood bedroom into a gift-wrapping room—" she air-quoted it "—but she'll be okay. She'll content herself by telling me 'I told you so' about the way I handle money."

He shook his head, as if to clear away her answer. "No, I was asking if you meant what you said about *me*." From the look in her eyes, she knew good and well what he'd meant.

"Jayden—"

"Do you love me or not?"

Her lips firmed. "God knows why, considering you're such a patient soul, but yes."

It all oozed out. The anger he'd harbored since she'd bolted from the ranch.

The worry that he'd damaged things beyond repair.

"I love you, too."

She huffed. "No, you don't."

He took a step toward her. The fact that she didn't take one away from him he took as a good sign. "I do. You make great coffee."

Her lips compressed.

"What you do for an ugly tie-dyed shirt is amazing."

She rolled her eyes, flushed a little and crossed her arms.

"The things that you make me feel are nothing short of a miracle."

Her eyes flickered. She looked away.

"I don't know what else to do here, Ariana." He took another step closer. "This isn't exactly familiar territory."

"You haven't been to Austin before?"

"I haven't been in love like this before."

Her jaw shifted. "Tess—"

"Was a pale comparison. If I had a ring, I'd pull it out right now and go on bended knee." He hadn't even considered where they'd go if he could get her to forgive him. But the second his words were out, he knew they were right.

Her eyes widened and focused on him. "So what's stopping you?"

"I drove straight here from Paseo. Do not pass go. Do not stop at jewelry stores."

She lifted her chin. "You still have a knee, don't you?"

"Okay. Fine. You want me to grovel a bit. I can live with that." He grabbed her arm before she could avoid him and pulled her off the sidewalk. At least the main part of it where bicyclists and pedestrians were constantly passing them. Then he dropped to one knee.

"Jayden, I wasn't serious—"

"But I am." He closed his hands over hers. "Ariana, I don't know what to offer you that you can't already do for yourself. You're nearly ten years younger than me. When I'm sixty, you'll—"

"—still be in love with you," she said huskily. She pulled on his hands. "Get up, former Sergeant Fortune. I can't handle you being all sweet and tender like this. It makes me nervous."

"I'm trying to propose here, sweetheart. Don't ruin the moment."

"Yeah, honey," said a heavyset woman with gray hair who passed them on her way into the building. "Don't ruin his moment."

Ariana flushed. She pulled harder on his hands, but he still resisted and she huffed. "Fine. But you don't have to propose just because you think—" She broke off.

"Because I think what?"

"I don't know! I don't know what you think. I don't know what *to* think. You come here after everything and—" She shook her head. "Dammit!"

He stood up and stepped closer until his chest touched the words on her T-shirt. "Do you want me to get you some paper so you can write it down?"

Her eyes flashed at him. But the glint of tears in them nearly undid him.

He slid his hands along her jaw and tipped her face up to his. "I love you," he murmured. "That's what I think. That's what I feel. I'm going to keep loving you no matter what you say here on this sidewalk. I'm gonna love you when I'm sixty and you're a hottie fifty-year-old grandma."

"Grandma!" The word escaped on a gurgle of choked laughter and tears. "I'm twenty-seven. If I'm going to be a grandma at fifty, you're planning on some fast work. Not to mention putting some big expectations on that grandchild's parent."

"That grandchild's parent would be *our* child."

"I know that."

"Okay, so maybe you'll be a hottie grandma at sixty. And I'll be a doddering old rancher at seventy."

"You'll never be doddering." She swiped her cheek, then made a face when her fingers came away black. "And you're making my mascara run."

"Sweetheart, I've seen you in pond scum. You're always beautiful to me."

She laughed and sniffed. "What am I going to do with you?"

"Take me upstairs? It might've escaped your notice, but it's hot as hell out here."

She took his hand and led the way into the apartment building.

It hadn't escaped his attention that she hadn't yet said yes.

But he'd take what he could get.

For now.

The elevator they rode up in was crowded. Too

crowded to do anything other than stand close behind her as they rode up to the sixth floor.

When they walked down the hallway to her door, he could still hear that same dog yapping. "He ever quiet down?"

"Rufio?" She tapped her keys on the neighbor's door as they passed it and the dog yelped and went silent. "He just wants to know someone's out here." She unlocked her own door and gave him a diffident look before going inside. "Don't expect much," she warned.

He hadn't expected anything. All he'd thought about was her.

But the apartment was nearly bare. She had a patterned sofa that looked straight out of the eighties and a folding card table that was piled high with books and papers. A single floor lamp stood next to the table.

"Minimalist decorating style, I see."

She dropped her purse on the granite kitchen bar as she crossed the open room to the wall of windows on the other side. "Furniture detracts from the view," she said blithely.

The view of her in front of the Austin skyline was pretty perfect.

She spread her arms. "So this is the living area and the kitchen."

"Good. A tour. I was hoping."

She toed off her sandals and walked through the open doorway to the right. He followed. "Here we have the master suite. Another balcony, of course, because that's really what the ridiculous rent is for. The view—"

He pulled her to him and kissed her.

Her hands closed over his shoulders. Slid beneath

the collar of his shirt. She pulled back an inch. "Don't you want to see the view?"

He rubbed his thumb along her cheek. "I'm looking at the best view there is right now."

Her eyes went dewy. "Jayden."

"Ariana," he returned softly.

She smiled a little and stepped back. Just enough to pull her *Paseo Is Paradise* shirt off. Then she took his hand and pulled him over to the bed.

And showed him real paradise.

When Ariana woke several hours later, Austin's city lights were shining through the bedroom windows.

And the mattress beside her was empty.

She had a moment's misgiving, before she realized that the light from the living room had been turned on. Which meant that Jayden hadn't left her.

She still couldn't believe he'd come to Austin.

Not even now, when her entire body still seemed to hum from their lovemaking.

She climbed out of bed, nearly tripping when her foot got caught in his shirt. She picked it up and pulled it over her head and went out to the living room.

He was sitting at her card table, reading an old issue of *Weird Life Magazine*.

Despite all the interviews she'd done with various members of Gerald Robinson's family, she couldn't imagine how Jayden felt now, knowing the truth. "Keaton Fortune Whitfield," she said. "British. Thirty-three. The newest great thing in architecture to hit Austin." She stopped behind Jayden and put her hands on his shoulders. They were tense. "He's quite a charmer. Recently engaged, I hear, to a waitress named Francesca."

"How'd he like finding out? You know. About—"

"Gerald?" She kneaded his shoulders and wondered if she'd ever get tired of the feel of his flesh beneath her hands. Probably not. "It threw him for a loop. You've all got that in common, Jayden."

He flipped the magazine closed and sighed.

She pressed her lips to the top of his head. "If you want to meet any of them, I'm sure I could arrange it."

"And say what? 'Hey, guys and gals. Meet your big brother Jayden'?" He looked up at her. His eyes were dark, pained. "These people—" He gestured at the stack of magazines. "They're all doing so much with their lives. And who is this Kate lady?" He picked up another issue of the magazine. "She looks a little older than Gerald's usual conquest."

"She's not one of his conquests." Ariana opened the magazine to the full spread on the petite business magnate. "Kate Fortune. She founded Fortune Cosmetics. Big, big company. Lots of money. Recently moved her headquarters from Minnesota to Austin and appointed Graham—one of Gerald's sons with his wife—as the new CEO. Big believer in all things family, even the ones she didn't know existed until recently." She looked at Jayden. "And who says you haven't done a lot with your life?"

"An army grunt?"

"Sergeant First Class Fortune," she corrected him. "I did some research. The rank isn't exactly a grunt. And your ranch isn't exactly a two-cow holding pen." She slid around him and sat on his lap, looping her arms over his shoulders. "Keaton was raised by a single mom. And Chloe Fortune Elliott was, too. You and your brothers have more in common with them than you think. You all have similar experiences."

"Yeah. Moms who've been dumped by Jerome Fortune."

"Actually, they all knew him as Gerald by then. Your mother is the only one who seemed to know the real Jerome." She chewed the inside of her lip. "I think he really loved her." She expected him to dismiss the notion. But he didn't. "What did your mother say about their relationship?"

"It was brief. Intense. He proposed but she didn't immediately accept, so he booked." He grimaced. "Then she tried to find him to tell him she was pregnant with us, but he was dead." His long fingers spread over her back. "I don't want to talk about him anymore."

She brushed her lips over his and felt such a thrill inside that she hoped it never ended. "Just one more thing."

He gave a noisy sigh.

"Okay, maybe two. But then no more talk of Gerald or Jerome. I promise."

He gave her a wry look. "All right. But make it snappy." His fingers drifted beneath the shirt. "I've got a powerful distraction here."

She wriggled, not even remotely able to keep from smiling. "This is serious." She tugged at his hand. "I can't think when you do that."

"Good." He nipped at her shoulder and returned his hand right where he wanted it. "Oh, yeah. Definitely makes two of us."

"Gerald is a very, *very* wealthy man."

He swore succinctly. "That's what I think about his money. Seems to me misery follows in his wake.

Which—" he picked up the article about Keaton then tossed it down again "—evidently circles the globe. The guy has gotten around. No question."

"Okay. But here's the second thing." She caught her breath when his hand reached her breast. "I'm not so sure Gerald is totally the bad guy."

He snorted. "Right."

"Seriously." She turned to look at her work spread across the table. But of course the real guts of her research had been lost in the tornado. "Darn it, I wish I had—" She shook her head. "It doesn't matter. What matters is that I think Charlotte—she's Gerald's wife—knows more about things than she lets on. Well, maybe not about everyone. But she certainly knew about Paseo. Which tells me that she knew about your mom at least. Maybe even about you and your brothers."

"And you say you're not going to write any more articles? Not a book?"

"I'm not." She looked him in the eye. "I'm not, Jayden. I can't. Not anymore. I haven't written a single decent word since I left Paseo."

"I'm not so sure about that," he muttered. "But go on."

"You've heard your mother's side of things now. If you ever want to know the rest, you're going to have to get that from Gerald." Her thoughts were running a mile a minute through her head. "Or Charlotte, but trust me. *That* is not likely to happen. The only time I've ever seen her lose a speck of composure was when she let slip the name Paseo. You'd have better luck with Gerald. From all accounts, he's a hard-ass, too."

He slid his hand over her mouth. But his eyes weren't angry. Just vaguely amused. And maybe, maybe a little accepting. “Enough,” he said. He shoved the card table away with his foot and resettled her meaningfully on his lap. “Aside from the whole windmill thing,” he murmured as he started to unbutton the shirt, “I’ve got a real appreciation for the way you wear my shirts.”

So did she. Her skin felt like a million butterflies were dancing on her. “Take me to bed?”

“Every night from here on out, sweetheart. Every single night.”

She tightened her arms around his neck and had a hard time not just purring when he lifted her right off the chair. She reached out and turned off the light.

And he carried her to bed.

“You’re still sure about this?” Ariana pocketed her sunglasses as they stepped up to the massive front door of the Robinson mansion two days later. “Maybe meeting all of them this soon is too much.”

“You’re the one who suggested it.”

“I know, but—”

He hit the door a few times with the heavy knocker, ending the discussion. “Sooner we do this, the sooner we can get back to Paseo. I do have a ranch to run, remember?”

She nodded. Even though she’d been at the Robinson estate several times, she still felt a knot of nervousness inside her stomach. Thank God she’d returned her book advance. She couldn’t even imagine being able to write the biography anymore. She turned to him suddenly. “Just because I’m not going to tell Jerome’s story doesn’t mean someone else won’t try.”

His brows pulled together. “What?”

“The publisher,” she muttered. “They’ll find another

person to write it. I'm completely replaceable on that score."

The door opened and Ben Fortune Robinson stood there, looking as composed and polished as he always did. He was a handsome man, no doubt about it. Gerald made good-looking children.

She tucked her hand through Jayden's arm and was glad it wasn't as tense as she'd feared. "Hi, Ben. I appreciate you doing this."

"Ariana." The other man tilted his dark head. His intense gaze was focused on Jayden, though, as he stuck out his hand. "Ben Robinson."

"Not Fortune?" Jayden's words were a little terse, but he shook Ben's hand politely enough.

"Fortune Robinson. Sometimes." Ben's lips twisted in an eerily similar manner to Jayden's. "Depends on how pissed off with the old man I'm feeling," he admitted honestly. He backed away. "Come in. Everyone's waiting in the library. Don't worry, though. My mother and our…father are both gone for the day. We won't be interrupted." He pushed the heavy door closed after they entered and led the way through the lavishly elegant house.

"How's your wife, Ben?" Ariana asked him.

The man's expression lightened measurably. "Ella's beautiful."

"And the baby? Lacey, right?"

He nodded. "Almost six months old and just as beautiful as her mama." They'd reached a closed door and he pushed it open. "Here we are."

Even though she would have preferred to hang back, the hand Jayden held against the small of her back prevented it and she walked into the library ahead of him.

When she'd called Ben to ask for the meeting, she'd told him everything she'd learned. Only because Jayden had wanted it that way. And as she studied the faces of Ben's seven brothers and sisters, she could tell that he'd also prepped them as well.

"Good Lord." Sophie, the youngest of Ben's siblings, was the first one to speak. "He looks like you, Kieran."

"No. The eyes are different." Zoe, the second youngest, stood up and came over to the doorway. "I think he looks more like Graham." She extended her slender hand toward Jayden. "I'm Zoe."

Even though he was looking increasingly uncomfortable, Jayden shook her hand. "Nice to meet you."

Thankfully, Ben took charge again as he drew them farther into the library. "Let me introduce you to everyone."

Ariana hovered in the rear of the somewhat crowded room where Olivia, the third youngest of the eight siblings, was leaning against one of the tall bookcases that surrounded the room. "He does look familiar," she murmured, more to herself, it seemed, than Ariana. "But not like Graham." Her brow knit together while across the room, Ben was inviting Jayden to sit at one of the chairs near the couch.

He sent Ariana a look and she gave him an encouraging nod. "They know about your mother, Jayden. Just ask whatever you want."

"Right," Ben said calmly. He'd been the first one to decide on tracking down however many half brothers and half sisters they had. It had been a unilateral decision that hadn't always been welcomed among the lot.

"I don't know what to ask," Jayden admitted, a stiff, crooked smile on his lips.

"Well, tell us about yourself, then," Ben amended easily. "Ariana said you were in the army for quite a while?"

"Yeah." Jayden's gaze traveled around the room. He took in the collection of priceless books. The original artwork. The statues. "My, uh, my brother Nate—Nathan—was a navy SEAL. Grayson rides rodeo."

"Three boys. That was a lot for your mother to handle on her own." Rachel—the eldest of the girls—gave him a sympathetic smile. Ariana was glad that she'd made the trip to Austin from Horseback Hollow, where she lived with her husband, Matteo. Of all the children Gerald had had with Charlotte, Rachel was one of Ariana's favorites. She was just so normal.

"At once, yeah." Jayden was nodding. He glanced at Ben and Wes. "You guys are twins. You know what it's like. Only there're three of us."

"Triplets." Olivia suddenly pushed away from the wall and crossed the room to grab the rolling ladder. She was muttering to herself as she climbed up to one of the top shelves and quickly started pawing through the books there.

"Olivia." Zoe was looking up at her sister. "What on earth—"

"It's here," she said. "It's got to still be here." She reached out and shoved the ladder over another foot without even bothering to climb off it first. "Ah." She snatched an album off the shelf. "I *knew* it." She tossed the book down to Zoe and quickly came down the tall ladder.

"Knew what?"

"Look." Olivia took the book—Ariana realized it was a small photo album—and flipped it open. She stabbed at the very first picture with a shaking finger as she practically shoved it in Jayden's face. "Is that you? You and your brothers?"

His brows pulled together. Ariana could see his temper building and she quickly went over, putting her hand on his shoulder as she looked at the old photograph. It was taken from a distance but the boys were clearly Jayden and his brothers.

"How'd you get this?" A muscle was working in his jaw, but his tone was at least shy of accusation.

Olivia sank down on the couch between Rachel and Kieran as if her legs wouldn't hold her up anymore. Her eyes were glazed with tears. "I found the book in Mother's study. I was—" She pressed her lips together for a moment, clearly struggling for composure. "I don't know. Maybe six years old? Mother was furious. She said the pictures were foster kids she and Dad were paying to support. She snatched it away and put it up there." She pointed to the shelf.

Even Ben looked shocked. "What? Why haven't you mentioned this before?"

"I didn't even remember it until now," Olivia said. She dropped her hand and stared at Jayden.

Kieran sat forward. "Mother *knew*?" He grabbed the photo album and flipped another page. To another photo. And another. "They're all here," he muttered, flipping faster. "Keaton. Chloe. And—" He squinted at their mother's handwriting beneath a grainy photo. "Who the hell is Amersen?"

"The au pair's son. He lives in France. Amersen Beaudin," Graham provided, looking weary. "Remember Suzette?"

Wes took the album from his brother and paged

through it. "That guy, Nash Tremont, that you have a lead on." He shook his head when he turned a few more pages. "These ones don't even have names. What the hell was she doing keeping this all a secret?"

The question seemed to spur comments from every single one of his siblings.

Jayden swore under his breath and grabbed Ariana's hand. "Let's go."

Ben tried to stop him. "Jayden. You don't have to go."

"I do." He gestured. "I'm sorry. I'll get used to all of you. In time. But whatever deal you've got going right now is about your mother. Not mine." He suddenly clasped Ben's shoulder. "I don't belong here right now. You understand?"

Ben nodded after a moment. "Yeah. Maybe I do."

Jayden nodded. He tightened his grip on Ariana's hand and he pulled her out of the room.

He didn't stop until they'd left the house entirely.

Only when they were out in the fresh air did he seem to draw in a deep, cleansing breath. "Wacko."

Ariana opened her mouth to protest.

"Not *them*. Charlotte."

"Oh. Well, yes. Maybe so." The woman clearly had more secrets than even Ariana had imagined.

He wrapped his arms around her and pulled her close. "What a freaking crazy family. No wonder you won't say you'll marry me."

"I never said I wouldn't marry you."

"You haven't said you will."

She pressed her mouth against the distinct cleft in his chin. Her heart was pounding so hard she could hear it inside her head. "If we end up having a son one day, you suppose he'll inherit your chin?"

His head reared back. His eyes searched hers. "I don't know. I sure like the idea of finding out."

Her eyes filled. "So do I."

"You're going to marry me, then?"

"I'm a little traditional about that sort of thing," she whispered.

"Dammit, Ariana. Is that a yes or no? Do I have to get a piece of paper for you to write it down on or what?"

She smiled. "Yes."

He looked positively frazzled. "Yes, *what*?"

She stretched up and brushed her lips over his. "Yes, I'll marry you. If you think that family is crazy, though, wait until you meet mine. My mother'll be sizing you up for a tuxedo before we get through the front door. And don't be alarmed when she calls you a handsome cuss. That's just a thing of hers. And Dad will want to show you his old Mustang. So if you can't describe what's under the hood of a car, we'd better get a book so you can brush up on it first."

He gave a bark of laughter. "I can handle a car. A tux, though? I'm not so sure about that." He closed his arm around her shoulders and directed her toward his pickup truck parked in the long, curving driveway.

"I don't care what you wear when we get married," she assured him. "Except for one thing."

He lifted an eyebrow. "What's that?"

"A ring," she said adamantly. "No way am I not going to advertise to the entire world that *you* are off the market."

"Sounding a little possessive there, sweetheart."

She raised her own eyebrow. "Have a problem with that?"

His smile was slow. "No, ma'am," he assured her. "No problem at all."

"Good. Now let's go home."

"Yeah. You never got around to turning in your notice at the apartment."

She twined her fingers with his, looking up into the face that she knew with every fiber of her being she wanted to look into for at least another sixty years. "I meant Paseo. Let's go home to Paseo."

And they did.

Epilogue

The party was in full swing when Gerald slipped in through a rear door.

He shouldn't be there.

But knowing what he shouldn't do and actually *not* doing what he shouldn't do were two very different things.

Story of his life.

"Welcome to the grand opening of Austin Commons!" A pretty young woman dressed in red stuck a brochure in his hand before he had a chance to wave her off. "Do you know Mr. Whitfield? He's the architect of all this." She waved her graceful arm, meant to encompass the state-of-the-art office complex around them.

A part of Gerald's mind stayed focused on the attractive female. He'd spent a lot of years burying himself in the distraction of women. Stopping cold now, just because his whole family seemed to think they knew everything about him, wasn't all that easily accomplished. The other part of his mind was impressed with the building.

He honestly wished he could say he'd had a hand in developing Keaton's skill. Gerald had a healthy ego but not even he could claim credit on that score.

He took the brochure from the woman and strode through the building. Robinson Tech needed some additional space. He wondered if Keaton would be interested—

"Jerome?"

He stopped in his tracks, looking at Kate Fortune. She was the self-proclaimed matriarch of all things Fortune. All things that Gerald Robinson had pushed away a lifetime ago. "I told you before, Kate. I prefer Gerald."

The silver-haired woman dipped her head. She was ninety-one but looked younger than his own wife. "I know you did." She tucked her hand through his arm as if they were old, dear friends.

Maybe she thought apologizing last year on behalf of the world of Fortunes made them friends. Who the hell knew? Not Gerald, that was for sure.

He realized she was drawing him into the spacious atrium where at least a hundred people were gathered. He recognized a good portion of them. Many worked for Robinson Tech. Just as many were related to him.

He swallowed an oath when Zoe spotted him. So much for keeping a low profile. His daughter looked shocked at first, then delighted as she separated herself from her husband, Joaquin Mendoza, and headed his way. Gerald didn't mind Joaquin too much. He was smart and he doted on Zoe. She'd always been his favorite, so he was inclined to like the man for that reason alone.

"Daddy." She reached up and kissed his cheek. "I didn't know you were coming." Her lashes hid her expression. "Is Mother with you?"

He almost laughed. He and Charlotte presented a united front only when they had to. And if she knew he was at one of his "other" son's events? That assuredly didn't qualify. "She's got one of her charity things," he answered vaguely. "Who are all the men over there with Joaquin and Alejandro?" Alejandro Mendoza had been more of an acquired taste. Gerald still was getting used to the fact that his daughter Olivia—sensible and pragmatic like him—was engaged to marry the entrepreneur. At least Alejandro hadn't stolen Olivia away to Miami, though. He wasn't sure how he would have stopped it, but he would have tried.

"Alejandro's cousins," Zoe was telling him. "They're the ones going into business with him. I told you about them last week at dinner. Mark, Rodrigo, Chaz, Carlo and Stefan. Don't tell me you weren't listening. They're from Miami, remember? They're going to be renting space in this very complex."

"Of course I remember." He squeezed her shoulder. He didn't. But she didn't need to know that.

A flash of long dark hair caught his eye.

Deborah had had hair like that. Even after all these years, he could remember the feel of it in his hands. The scent of it. Of her.

But the girl with the hair was young. As young as his own daughters. She was that reporter, he realized. The one who'd written all the articles that had so annoyed Charlotte.

He'd gotten a kick out of them.

Which, naturally, had annoyed his wife even more.

But then, what was life without the small pleasures?

He looked down at Zoe. "Are you having fun tonight?"

"Of course." She smiled. Zoe always found something to smile about. It was one of the reasons why it was so easy to love her. She was the antithesis of her mother.

Zoe's hand on his arm tightened. "Be nice," she warned.

"What?" He followed her gaze.

The reporter and a tall, steely-eyed cowboy were headed his way.

Gerald actually felt a knot in his throat. "That's him?"

"Jayden," Zoe whispered. "Yes."

The couple stopped shy of them a few feet. Zoe stepped into the void, giving Ariana a hug and reaching up to kiss Jayden's cheek. Her brother's cheek.

"Congratulations," she was saying. "I just received your wedding announcement in the mail this afternoon." She laughed musically. "You sure didn't let any grass grow under your feet." She held out her hand to Gerald. "Daddy, I know you know her name, but I'm not sure you ever met Ariana. Ariana Lamonte— Oh, it's Fortune now, isn't it? This is my father, Gerald Robinson."

Jayden's arm slid around Ariana's shoulders. "Yes, it's Fortune," he said evenly. His eyes stayed on Gerald's face.

"It was a small wedding," Ariana said.

"From what I understand, everything in Paseo is on

the small side." Zoe's smile showed in her voice. "Your parents were there?"

Ariana nodded. "Of course. And Jayden's brothers and his mother."

Gerald tuned in more closely. For more than half his life, he'd been trying to forget Deborah. And he'd failed in every respect.

"I've read your articles," he said abruptly.

Ariana looked discomfited. "As it happens, I've left the magazine."

"That's a shame. Your pieces were one of the few that weren't drivel."

She smiled faintly, as if she didn't quite believe him. "Thank you."

He couldn't stop looking at Jayden.

"You have your mother's eyes."

And those eyes narrowed as if he didn't exactly appreciate the observation.

Though why would he, when it came from Gerald?

He looked at Zoe. "Sweetheart, would you and Ariana excuse us for a minute?"

His daughter immediately nodded. "Of course."

But Jayden shook his head. His arm didn't budge from Ariana's shoulders. "There's nothing for you to say that my wife can't hear."

Gerald hesitated. Not really because he was waiting for Zoe to move out of earshot, but because it took him that long to get the words past the tightness in his chest.

Maybe he was having a heart attack. It wasn't a novel idea. He'd just always figured when he went, it'd be in the bed of yet another woman who wasn't his wife.

Because all of those women, including his wife, had never filled the spot left by Deborah.

"I never knew about you and your brothers, Jayden. If I had—" He broke off. If he had known, then what? He hadn't fought hard enough for Deborah when they'd had their chance. "If I had, maybe things would've been different. For a lot of us."

From the corner of his eye, he saw Zoe's bright red dress—a flash of vibrancy among the traditional sea of little black dresses—as she returned to Joaquin's side. If things had been *too* different, he wouldn't have ever had Zoe. Or Ben and Wes. Not Sophie or Olivia. Kieran. Rachel. Graham. Because if things had been too different, he never would have married Charlotte. He was a miserable husband. And he'd never win awards for father of the year. But he did love his children.

Making them believe it had never been his strong suit, though.

Jayden was still watching him with that unsettling dark gaze.

"How is your mother?" He finally let the question loose. "Is she well?" *Did she ever marry someone else? Did she forget me as easily as I wanted to be able to forget her?*

"She's well." Jayden's voice was clipped. "A little surprised that you're not dead and buried somewhere."

The message came through loud and clear. One of his three eldest sons wished he was dead and buried. Chances were the other two felt the same.

Some things went beyond forgiveness. Gerald read that sentiment in Jayden's eyes.

"Don't tell her," Gerald told him, "but I've thought of her often." Every day.

Jayden's lips twisted. "I don't think so. Keeping secrets might be a biological trait you inherited from your father, but it's not a trait I intend to adopt."

"*My* father." Gerald grimaced. No matter what he did, how well or how fast he did it, nothing had ever been good enough for his old man. Which didn't alleviate the guilt he still felt about the way his father had died. "My father never kept any secrets from anyone. Particularly the fact that he hated the ground I walked on."

Jayden eyed the man. His father. It was still hard to accept. And right then, he wasn't sure that he didn't hate the ground Gerald walked on, too.

Ariana tugged on Jayden's fingertips. "It's late. Maybe we should be going."

Jayden curled his hand over hers, feeling something inside him calm again. "Soon, sweetheart." Gerald was his father by blood but not by anything else. But if he'd felt a smidgen for his mother what Jayden felt for Ariana, he'd had to have lived ever since knowing what he'd lost.

If for no other reason than that, he could almost feel a little sympathy for the man in front of him.

"I don't think this is the time," she murmured not entirely under her breath.

"Why not?" Jayden angled his head and focused on Gerald once more. "I didn't expect you to be here. But you are. And who knows when we'll see each other again." If Ariana reconsidered the book her publisher was still trying to get her to take on again, maybe. But in the past few weeks since they'd stood next to the windmill and said their vows, she'd been noodling with ideas for a thriller.

About an ax murderer.

He figured the ax murderer might win out. Mostly because his wife was incredibly imaginative and inventive.

And he planned to enjoy that facet of Ariana in every way possible for as long as the good Lord saw fit to keep him on earth with her.

And just that easily, he decided it didn't matter what he knew or didn't know about Gerald. Or Jerome. Or whatever name the man wanted to go by. It didn't matter that Jerome's father had been just as much a cheat as Jerome. With similar results. Jayden knew he wasn't going to be an apple off that tree, because he had Ariana by his side.

"You know what?" He looked into the older man's face. "It doesn't matter. I don't care if you know as little about your father's life as I knew about mine. I've got everything I want in this life standing by my side." He squeezed Ariana's shoulder and looked down at her face. "Are you ready to leave, Mrs. Fortune?"

She beamed at him and nodded.

And without another glance at anyone, they walked away, hand in hand.

* * * * *

SPECIAL EXCERPT FROM

HARLEQUIN

SPECIAL EDITION

Rancher Jack Hollister travels to Arizona to discover if the family on Three Rivers Ranch might possibly be a long-lost relation. He isn't looking for love—until he sees Vanessa Richardson.

Read on for a sneak peek at
The Other Hollister Man,
part of New York Times *bestselling author*
Stella Bagwell's beloved Men of the West miniseries!

"The Joshua trees and saguaros sure are pretty," Jack said reflectively. "This sort of looks like the land west of the Three Rivers Ranch house. Where you showed me the North Star, remember?"

Remember? Those moments had been burned into Vanessa's memory. Even if she never saw him again for the rest of her life, she'd always have those special moments to relive in her mind.

The thought unexpectedly caused her throat to tighten, and she wished the waitress would get back with their drinks. She didn't want Jack to think she was getting emotional. Especially because she could feel their time together winding to a close.

"I do. And I just happen to know a place not too far west of here where there's another special view of the evening star."

His eyelids lowered ever so slightly as he looked across the table at her. "After we eat, you should show me."

Did he expect her to look at him in the moonlight and not feel the urge to kiss him? Or maybe she'd get lucky, Vanessa thought, and the moon would be in a new phase and the light would be too weak to illuminate his face.

Damn it, Vanessa. Who are you fooling? You could find Jack's lips in the darkest of nights.

Thankfully, a waitress suddenly approached their table, and the distraction pushed the mocking voice from her head…but not the idea of being in Jack's arms again. She was beginning to fear she'd never rid herself of that longing.